Timothy Murphy is the author of the novel *Getting Off Clean*. He lives in New York City, where he DJs regularly and is at work on a third book.

Also by Timothy Murphy

GETTING OFF CLEAN

The Breeders Box

Timothy Murphy

ABACUS

A CIP catalogue record for this book is available from the British Library.

ISBN 0 349 11078 6

Typeset in Berkeley by M Rules
Printed and bound in Great Britain by
Creative Print and Design Wales, Ebbw Vale

Abacus
A Division of
Little, Brown and Company (UK)
Brettenham House
Lancaster Place
London WC2E 7EN

To J.H., who's there at the end of the party

Thank You

At Donadio and Ashworth, to Neil Olson and
Peter Steinberg.

At Little, Brown, to Andrew Wille, Sally Abbey and
Christina Ransom.

Also to Christina Bartolomeo, Dan Casto, Charles
Decker, Jeffrey Golick, Trajal Harrell, Tim Horn, James
Hurley, Gillian Maimon, Margaret Malina, and Maria
Striar.

And finally to Denis, Noreen and Dan Murphy, for love
and support through the best and the worst.

You never knew the teenage me,
and you wouldn't believe
the things you didn't see,
some pretty, some ugly.

And the lovely mirrorball
reflected back them all—
every triumph, every fight,
under disco light . . .

—EVERYTHING BUT THE GIRL

Prologue

The phone beside the bed rings, rousing Seb and me, launching Bella on a braying jag out in the living room, her wet snout quivering vigilantly toward our bedroom, I'm sure. It's a Saturday morning in September, lovely outside I already know from the stripes of sunlight thatching through the blinds and the cries of neighborhood children on their way to Prospect Park. Still half-asleep, I groan aloud, rolling over in bed until I'm nearly on top of Seb, who's warm and flushed with the pillow clamped over his head.

'Who the hell could that be?' he groans back, ducking under the sheets and pressing his lips against my chapped knee, just as Bella, all knobby haunches and lolling tongue, bounds into the room and up onto the bed between us in an explosion of fur and drool.

'Maybe it's the V-E-T calling to confirm her appointment this afternoon,' I say in that mock-discreet voice parents use to conceal unpleasant talk from children.

'If it is, I don't want to be here when she sniffs him out through the phone line and starts bellowing.' Seb emerges from under the sheets, his dark curly hair a bedheaded monstrosity, and fumbles for his boxer shorts on the floor.

I laugh watching him, picking sleep out of my eyes. 'Your hair looks like the bride of Frankenstein.'

'You know what that makes you,' he scowls, limping toward the bathroom. 'Aren't you going to answer the phone?' And in a moment, the bathroom door closes behind him, blunting the sudden crash of morning wizzer hitting porcelain.

I pick up the phone and salute, but I can't hear anything save the faint sound of cars in the street. *Hello*, I say again, with that irritated emphasis. Still no one responds, and I'm just about to hang up when someone speaks, low and guarded, into the phone: 'Tigger?'

Tigger. No one calls me Tigger anymore except for my Auntie Lippy and my friend Cedric and—and then the blood rushes to my head, and my legs go weak, and I absently shove Bella away from me, sending her whimpering into the next room.

'Jess?' I say into the phone, almost too shocked to say the name.

'Yeah, Tig. It's Jess. I wanted to make sure it was you that answered the phone and not Seb.'

Suddenly my mind is racing with about a million feelings— astonishment and relief, anger and concern, burning curiosity and bitter resentment. 'I can't believe this is really you,' I say, shaking, poking my head toward the bathroom to make sure Seb can't hear me, but he's already started running a shower. 'How am I supposed to know it's really you?'

'Tigger, it's really me.'

'Prove it.'

'Oh, shit, man. Uh—' there's a pause. 'Okay. Who showed you how to do the meatball in the cove up at the beach that summer? And who'd catch you when you jumped off the rocks?'

'Oh my God. Oh, holy shit.' I want to scream into the phone at him, scream and yell and cry, but I can't because Seb will hear me. So instead I hiss—a furious, temple-throbbing hiss. 'Where the fuck have you been for the past two years?'

'Listen, listen, Tig. I can't go into that right now. But listen— I'm here.'

'Here? Where? In New York?'

'Yeah.'

'You're *here*? Are you gonna turn yourself in? Jess, please tell me you're gonna turn yourself in.'

'No, man, I'm not. And you gotta promise me that you're not gonna turn me in, either. Otherwise I'm hanging up right now.'

'You fucking—'

'Otherwise, Tigger, I'm hanging up right now,' he repeats.

I'm silent for a minute, stumped. 'All right,' I finally say. 'I won't turn you in.'

'You better swear on that. 'Cause if you do, I'll never talk to you again.'

'I swear on it, okay? Now where are you?'

'In Manhattan.'

'In *Manhattan*? Aren't you afraid somebody's going to notice you?'

'No, I'm keeping out of the way. And I look pretty different now, too.'

I've been clutching the end of my pillow in one sweaty hand, and I finally pound it down hard against the headboard. 'Oh, man, Jess. This is just too weird.'

'Yeah, I know, but listen—I don't want to spend too much time on the phone. Look—can you meet me in the city? Today?'

'Why do you want to meet?' I ask, infuriated again.

He laughs nervously. 'Why do you think I want to meet? 'Cause I wanna see you.'

'You need money, don't you?'

He laughs again, galling me. 'How'd you know?'

'I just figured.'

'Can you bring me as much as you can, in cash, without attracting suspicion?'

'I guess so,' I say, increasingly anxious. 'It's your money, after all. If you turned yourself in, you could have it all. You could hire the best fucking lawyers in the city.'

'Tig, I don't wanna talk about that right now. Just—can you bring me some money? Can you meet me?'

I listen again for the shower. It's still running, but I know Seb will be out soon. If Seb, or Lippy, or anyone for that matter, knew that I knew Jess was in New York right now, they'd make me call the police. A large part of me wants to, and not even because I care about justice being served. But— but I can't betray him, at least until I've laid eyes on him to know that he's really still alive.

'Yeah,' I finally say. 'I can meet you.'

'Excellent.'

'Yeah, right.'

'Come on, Tigger. I can't wait to see you. Look, I'm right outside this little greasy spoon near Wall Street. It's just me and a bunch of bums—nobody'll know us here, okay?'

'Yeah, okay.'

'Come on, buck up. Listen, you should know I look different now. I've got a crew cut and a goatee and I'm bulkier now. I've got on a Miami Heat cap and jeans and Reeboks.'

'You're kidding!' I say, almost wanting to laugh.

'No kidding,' he says. 'They're good blend-in clothes. So, look—can you be here in an hour or so? With the money?'

'I'll see what I can do.'

'Come on, Tigger!'

'Yes, yes, I'll be there, all right?' In the bathroom, the water stops running. 'I gotta go.'

'All right.' And he gives me the location of the diner. 'Listen, Tig—not a word to anyone. Not Seb or Lippy or anyone, all right?'

'All *right*. Good-bye.'

As soon as I hang up the phone, I start shaking like a madman, my heart pounding—ugly reminders of my illness of two years ago. Bella shambles back up onto the bed, her head hanging contritely, and I reach down to scruff her neck, murmuring apologies I don't even hear.

'Thomas?' It's Seb calling from the bathroom. 'Who called?'

I take a deep breath, rise, and peek into the bathroom. He's still standing in the shower, toweling off.

'Are you all right?' he asks when he sees me. 'You're as white as a ghost.'

'I'm fine,' I say, as steadily as possible. 'I just need my coffee.'

'Did you make it yet?'

'Hm? Oh—yeah. I mean no. I mean, I'm putting it on now.'

'Okay,' he says, eyeing me skeptically. 'Who was that?'

'It was Cedric,' I lie, more lies forming rapidly in my head. 'He begged me to go to the nursing home with him today to visit his mother. You know how hard it is for him to go alone.'

'I know,' Seb responded, suddenly all sullen. 'So what did you say?'

'Well, I told him we had to take Bella to the vet this afternoon, but if he wanted to go to the nursing home this morning, I'd go with him—if it's all right with you, of course.'

He laughs ironically. 'Why wouldn't it be all right with me? You've got your own life.'

'I know. I just—'

'Don't worry about it, Thomas,' he says, conciliatory. 'When do you think you'll be back by?'

'I don't know. One? No later than two?'

He wraps the towel around his waist and steps out of the shower. 'That works out okay. I'll be right out of here to eat with you.'

He's pushed his mop of hair back wetly from his face, dark grave eyes still heavy with sleep despite his shower. He's a book editor and I'm a music teacher; we're both twenty-four and we've known each other since high school. I can fairly truly say that he saved my life, and if he can't claim anything as dramatic of me, I think he'd at least admit that he likes having someone around to cook his dinner, or polish his painstakingly collected and restored Heywood Wakefield furnishings, or play the piano when he falls into his easy chair to edit his boss's manuscripts until bedtime. Often, I think I'm fondest of him at this time, in the morning, most especially before he's risen from bed—before his ritual sullenness and hauteur kick in and he's still blinking to consciousness, absorbing everything with a childlike wonderment that doesn't really belong to either of us anymore.

'Actually,' I say, 'Ced and I decided to get a bite to eat before we go. But I'll put on the coffee first.'

'I can make my own coffee.' He's staring into the mirror over the sink now, examining his morning shadow to see if it needs shaving, deliberately not looking at me.

'No, I'll make it—it's no big deal.' I walk up behind him, swollen with guilt, and wrap my arms around his chest.

'Your hands are cold,' he says, shivering.

'Whoops. Sorry.'

In the bedroom, I dress, hastily, my mind still racing with a thousand reservations, pricks of conscience and pride. When I emerge, he's sitting at the kitchen table in his robe, the meager Saturday edition of *The New York Times* before him, fastidiously applying to his toast apricot marmalade—a gift that my Auntie Lippy, the cabaret singer, and her husband Langley, the composer and arranger, brought back to us from England, where she met his people for the first time. *Comme ci, comme ça*, she replied when I asked her how it all went. We're very close, and I can also fairly truly say that she saved my life, as well.

Seb looks forlorn to me now, like a lonely little old man, and I'm overcome by an urge to get out of the apartment as soon as possible, before I change my mind about the mission at hand.

'About two o'clock, then, okay?' I ask from the kitchen door.

He looks up, blandly agreeable. 'About two o'clock. I'll have Bella all sedated and ready to go. Give my love to Cedric.'

'I will.' And I leave him there with his newspaper and marmalade and coffee and the drooling dog. I'm off to see my brother, whom I haven't heard from in two years until today, because he is a fugitive from justice, and wanted for murder.

Outside, Seventh Avenue is already bustling with the well-scrubbed occupants of increasingly prosperous Park Slope—it's hardly the shabby, low-rent backwater it was when Seb moved here four years ago—and I feel so guilty and paranoid, walking down the street in the midst of these innocent citizens as I head off to aid and abet an unapprehended killer, that I'm convinced they must be able to read my criminality all over my face. The first thing I do is go to the bank and extract $500, the maximum allowable withdrawal from the ATM machine, then shove the booty deep into my pocket in a tight wad. I know I should go up to one of the tellers inside and take out more—thousands, say—but if he bungles this whole thing, I'll be damned if there's a paper trail to confirm my involvement. *Anyone* could withdraw a mere $500, especially on shoppers' Saturday, I tell myself as I head for the subway station. I could be going to buy a new computer monitor, or a dining room table, or a silver flask at Tiffany, or any such thing.

Now I'm on the malodorous F train, the creaking elevated part straight across the way from the old mammoth neon sign for KENTILE FLOORS, and I'm a nervous wreck. This is high Indian summer in New York, the crud-colored rooftops of warehouses quivering in paper-doll relief against an enamel-blue sky as warm as bathwater, even warmer and just slightly pinker as backdrop for the overheated skyline of Manhattan just ahead. It's so seldom I go into the city this early on a

Saturday that I should be loving this trip, loving the quiet of
the car, populated by just me and a few Russian weekend
laborers from Coney Island, and loving the view of the oncom-
ing track I get whenever the train curves, arching its brittle
rusty back just a few stories above the dividing line between
Carroll Gardens and Red Hook. But I'm not loving any of it
this morning: I'm distracted and full of tics, peevish and curious, righteous and panicked, and this cup of bad deli coffee
that I bought to clear my head just before boarding is only
serving to irritate my stomach.

I get off in Chinatown and walk the half-dozen or so barren
blocks toward Wall Street, to the designated corner. I've hardly
spent any time downtown lower than Lippy's Village apartment in the past two years, but when my life *was* centered
around the tapering bottom of Manhattan, it was in SoHo,
certainly not *here*, and these gated-up, workaday streets feel
alien and slightly spooky to me in the hush of Saturday morning. At last, heart throbbing, I come to the diner Jess
mentioned and peer through the grimy windows inside. Jess
was right—the place *is* a dive, dimly lit, and full of boozy,
disheveled old men who look as though they were never clean
and powdered babies, but instead rose fully-formed from the
grimy floors of the diner itself. Out here, I'm almost floored by
the mingling smells of cigarette smoke, griddle grease and
steam roaring through a ventilator. For my life I can't spot him
inside through the window, and now I'm wondering if he got
cold feet and copped out of the whole arrangement.

Some guy walks up to me on the sidewalk and asks me if I
know the time. I'm halfway through a distracted apology for
not wearing a watch when I look at him twice—Miami Heat
cap, Reeboks and jeans, shorn head, goatee and powerful
build.

'Jess!'

'Shhhh! Tigger, take it easy.'

'I can't believe—I didn't even know it was *you*.' That's the truth—the Jess I used to know was paler and thin, with long, unruly hair usually pulled back into a ponytail with a bit of cord, dressed in paper-thin old T-shirts and trousers splattered with paint from his studio. He had always looked wildly out of place anywhere beyond Manhattan, and now he wouldn't raise an eyebrow in any suburban mall across America.

'That's the point.'

'I guess so,' I shrug. 'You look darker. More—um—'

He laughs. 'More authentically Puerto Rican? Yeah. I could probably even pass for Dominican. But what about you?' And he startles me by giving me an awkward hug, which I return with no greater ease. 'You look good, Tigger. What are you up to?'

'Well,' I begin. Inside the diner, it seems as though two of the old bums are about to have a brawl. 'Well, I'm living in Park Slope with Seb.'

'I figured as much. You let go of the loft, I take it?'

'Yeah. A long time ago.'

There's a pause, after which he nods obliquely.

'And I'm teaching music at a girls' school uptown. And composing a little. And we have a dog now,' I add. 'And that's about it.'

He nods again, quick and tense now, as though he's ready to dart into hiding at the sound of a siren, or a voice from nowhere calling 'Halt!'

'So what about you?' I finally ask. 'What's up with you?'

'Oh, man,' he laughs again. 'Why don't we go inside and get something to eat first?'

'You sure you want to?'

He glances inside, appraising. 'Sure. I'm hungry as hell. Aren't you?'

'I think I'll just have coffee.'

Inside, the stench is even worse, and the light is murky—every naked bulb in the ceiling fixtures coated in years of grime. One of the bums barks something unintelligible at us as we make our way to a table far in the back. An old Hispanic man, grease on his apron like a map of the world, approaches us from behind the counter and asks Jess in Spanish what we'll have. He asks for eggs, toast and coffee in surprisingly better Spanish than I remember him speaking before. I request coffee and, taking my chances, toast.

'When did your Spanish get so good?' I ask once the man has stepped away.

He looks at me suspiciously. 'What do you mean? I always spoke Spanish. I took it in school for years, remember?'

'But I don't remember you speaking it that well. Even your accent sounds more real.'

He shrugs, uncomfortable. 'You pick things up as you go along.'

His answer speaks right into the void of all that he's not telling me about where he's been and what he's done for the past two years.

'So,' I broach gingerly, stirring my coffee. 'Like I said: what's up with you?'

He repeats the question, wrapping his long fingers around his cup. I remember when those fingers were constantly smeared and spattered with paint—smudges of blues, yellows and blacks caught in the seams of his knuckles or behind his fingernails. His hands are darker now, work-worn, but quite clean. 'Hey,' he snaps to. 'First off, did you bring the money?'

'Yeah, I brought you the money.'

'Uh—you think I could have it?'

'You really need it this very minute?'

'Just so we don't forget later on.'

I pull the wad out of my pocket and pass it to him just beneath the far edge of the table, where he rifles through it. 'This is all you could manage, huh?'

'That was the max from the bank machine. I didn't think it was a good idea to go up to the teller and take out thousands of dollars in cash.'

'Don't worry about it, Tig. This should help us a lot.'

'Us? Who's *us*?'

'I was gonna get to that.'

'Well, I guess you just did. Who's *us*?'

He smiles, embarrassed. 'Us is me and a girl, that's all.'

'You mean like a *girlfriend* girl?'

'I guess so.'

I laugh sharply. 'You mean you've been on the lam and you've still managed to get a girlfriend? What else did you do, earn a Ph.D. and start a company?'

'Fuck that, man. I'm a carpenter now.'

'You're kidding.'

'No, I'm not. You know I always had a knack for that.'

'I guess you did,' I say, remembering. 'So,' I continue. 'Are you still painting?'

He squirms a bit, looks relieved when the man with the apron brings him his eggs and me my toast, which seems to have been submerged in melted butter. 'Ah . . . well, not so much these days. I don't really have the time. Or the money for supplies.'

'Or the peace of mind?'

'Yeah. You could say that.'

'Well, that's a shame. You know, if you came back, even if things turned out for the worse, think of all the time you'd have to paint. You could be more productive than ever, and Grant could support your—'

'Don't even try, Tigger,' he interrupts me. 'You go be a prisoner first and tell me how you like it, okay? You could move your piano right into your little cell and keep on playing Chopin while five guys including the warden gang-rape you, and—'

'Okay, okay. Forget I said it.'

'I will,' he says, edging a bit of egg onto his toast with a fork.

I pick up the slack. 'So—who's this girl?'

He shrugs again. 'She's just a girl I met on my travels.'

'Where'd you meet her?' I ask, as casually as possible.

'I can't say.'

'Oh. Well, what's her name?'

'I can't say that, either.' He raises his triangle of toast to his mouth, but the egg falls off and back onto his plate before it gets there.

'Okay,' I persist. 'Well—what does she look like? Is she pretty?'

'Yeah. That I can answer. She's pretty. She's Cuban.'

'Oh,' I say brightly. 'That's interesting.'

'And it doesn't mean I've been in Cuba, either,' he snaps, reading my mind. 'Or Miami, for that matter.'

'I wasn't thinking that,' I say, lying.

'Yeah, right.' He smirks, and I think I can see a trace of the old jesting Jess.

So I shrug, smiling guiltily, and then we're both silent for a bit, him digging into his breakfast with an almost angry relish, me nibbling half-heartedly at my soggy toast. The bums are getting loud again; I think they're talking about the approaching Presidential elections, or the upcoming season for the Giants, but I'm not quite sure. The man behind the counter turns up the radio, partially drowning them out with salsa music.

'Look,' Jess finally says. 'Seriously. I wanted to see you.'

'All right,' I say. 'Seriously, fine. But why now, after two years?'

'Because. You know this girl I mentioned?'

'Yeah?'

'She's helping me get out of the country. So I'm going. With her. For good.'

'You mean you've been *in* the country this whole time?'

'Yeah, Tigger! How the hell could I get out?'

'Where the hell have you been?'

'I *told* you,' he says, too loud. We glance around nervously to see if anyone's noticed us, but we seem to have attracted no more attention than a brief, incurious stare from the man in the apron. 'I told you,' he says again, quiet. 'I can't say.'

'So you wanted to see me to get as much money as you could before you took off, forever. Right?'

'Not just that,' he says, infuriating me. 'I wanted to see you one more time. To find out what happened, and to see how you're doing, and know that everything's okay. And to say goodbye. I guess my money's gonna become yours eventually, huh?'

I disregard the question. 'I can't believe you're just up and leaving like that.'

'Do you really think I'm just "up and leaving"?' he snaps at me. 'Do you think I want to just leave the country forever and never come back? Why do you think I've stayed in the country the past two years, when there's a call out for me in every state? Do you think I was just lounging around next to a pool somewhere? Tigger, I've been a crazy man—hiding out every day of my life, trying to totally change my looks—'

'Well, you've certainly succeeded there.'

He dismisses my bitchiness. 'Trying to figure out what the fuck to do.'

'So I guess you've made up your mind.'

'I guess I have,' he says quietly. 'I can't live like this anymore.'

'So you're just going to become a permanent exile.'

'I prefer *expatriate*.'

'Do you even love this girl you're going with? Or are you just using her to get out of the country?'

'That's really low, Tigger.'

'Well?'

He picks up his toast, then puts it back down. 'Yeah. I love her, okay. She's been really good to me. What—did you think I'd never be able to love anyone else again?'

'Far be it from me to question your capacity for loving.'

'Come on, Tigger,' he pleads. 'Don't make this any harder than it is. Talk to me, man.'

I laugh bitterly. 'What do you want me to talk about? The hot new restaurants? I don't know anymore. I'm hardly in Manhattan, except to work and to see Lippy.'

'How's Lippy, for example? Is she still singing?'

'She's fine,' I allow sulkily. 'And yes, she's still singing. She just got back from England with Langley.'

'That's cool. What about the rest of the old gang?'

'Joey died a few months after you left.'

'Shit,' he mutters. 'That sucks.'

'Well, we all knew it was going to happen.'

'What about Cedric?'

'He's okay. He's a nurse now, and he's living up in the West Hundreds with this cool guy he met in nursing school. Anthea and Katja went to Paris and never came back, then Miko got a design job over there and followed them. And Cedric told me that Ty finally got a steady job up in the Bronx, which certainly made his wife happy. Cedric says he never sees him downtown anymore.'

'Everybody's gone,' he says.

'Yep,' I answer flatly. 'Everybody's gone. Kira's still around. Seb and I go to her and her husband's dinner parties every once in awhile.'

'Hm. What's the scene like these days? Is Sammy still spinning?'

'I think he's spinning at one of the new clubs, but I don't really know. I don't go to clubs anymore. Seb can't stand them—and I can't either, now, to tell you the truth.'

'That doesn't surprise me.'

'Yeah.'

He looks away, frowning, before he turns back to me. 'I found something that I wanted to show you, but I don't know if I should.'

'Well, you brought it up. You may as well show it to me now.'

He fishes something out of his pocket, then passes it to me

under the table. I look down: it's a book of matches, its lacquered black surface dulled and scuffed with age. On one side,
I can just make out the famous logo that Miko designed in a
burst of inspiration: two grinning tigers up on their hind legs,
either dancing or humping—nobody could ever tell which.
And then on the other side, effaced almost to illegibility, this
inscription:

The Breeders Box
New York City

I finger the matchbook, my hands shaking. 'Where did you
get this?'

He ducks his head in toward me, grave. 'This morning,
right?'

'Right?'

'I snuck over to Spring Street.'

My heart is pounding again. 'Over to—what? To the spot?'

'Yeah. Have you seen it since—'

'Just once,' I answer, hushed. 'I wanted to see if I could find
any old—you know, mementos or something. But I couldn't
deal with it. I didn't even pick around. That was over a year
ago, and I haven't been back since. I can't believe they haven't
done anything with it yet. Property is so hot in that neighborhood. But it's just—'

'Standing there in a heap,' he finishes for me.

'Yeah.'

'Tigger,' and I hear his voice breaking a little bit. 'I couldn't
believe it. It's like a graveyard. I mean, you can walk around in
the rubble and know what every room was. I mean, I even
found bits of glass from the dance floor. It's so spooky.'

'No kidding.'

'I'm just so glad that—forget it.'

'That Flip's not here to see it, were you going to say?'

'Yeah.' In a minute, I can see his eyes glassing over

underneath his Miami Heat cap, and I feel the same thing start happening to me.

'I just can't believe it,' he whispers, his voice hoarse. Out of the corner of my eye, I notice that most of the bums have left. It's just the two of us and salsa music and the man in the apron, squeegeeing the griddle with his back to us. 'It's like— what *happened*?'

I swallow back the unpleasant lump in my throat. 'Jess, listen. This isn't fair. It's not fair for you to just sweep back into my life for one shitty day after everything that happened and make me talk about this stuff. Here.' I hand the matchbook back to him, not daring to look at it again. 'I try not to think about it anymore. It's easier that way, believe me.'

'But can you really not think about it?'

I kick him under the table, biting my lip. 'Why are you pushing me like this?'

"Cause I think about it all the time. Don't you?'

'I *do*, all right? Is that what you want to hear? I do. I think about it—and I think about her—every single fucking day of my life. All right?' And now I'm crying, turning away from the man in the apron in a fit of embarrassment, and it's like all the shit that I've spent the past two years trying to lock away has crashed back over me with one little matchbook, and I'm full of sadness and anger.

'Tigger. Hey, baby,' he says, reaching across the table.

'What? What the fuck do you want, Jess?'

'I'm sorry. I'm sorry.'

He says it over and over again, like a mantra, but I can't stop the flow of bitter tears. We're sitting here in this stinking diner on the edge of nowhere, reunited, only to part again soon, two long years after it all came down.

If you went to the plot on Spring Street that my fugitive brother was talking about, you'd see that no one has bought it, no one has rebuilt it, no one has even ventured to start a community garden. It remains just what it's been for the past two years: a trash heap, fenced off by the city with two rusty strands of cheap barbed wire, filling up higher and higher with eviscerated mattresses, shopping carts, broken bottles and cigarette butts. A few lacy weeds have sprouted up majestically in the open patches, the wages of a rainy summer, and everywhere—smeared to debris, plastered on the walls of the adjoining buildings that survived, impaled against the barbed wire—are plastic bags, dozens of them, ragged and flat like the killing fields of a torrent of huge, harpooned jellyfish. When I last saw it, I couldn't even conceive that what was once there had even been there. It must have been somewhere else, I told myself, it must have been a spot I dreamed up.

But I didn't dream it up, that I know for sure. Because once, where this very lot still stands, there was a club. But a mere club by name only, because for six months—what I still and will always consider the most luridly wonderful six months of my life—it was so much more than that. Overnight, it became the king of clubs and the queen of clubs, even in a city where dark paneled rooms full of velvet banquettes and guttering candles and pounding music, their bathrooms acrid with the smell of cologne and sweat and narcotics, come and go like flickering images in a hazy after-hours dream.

It was the place where bona fide celebrities and hard-working half-celebrities, where junky artists and arty junkies, where real girls and fake girls, straight-acting gay boys and gay-acting straight boys, all converged on each other, well past midnight, in a shiny, messy, thousand-headed monster that was about the closest you could ever come to heaven on a divided and subdivided island, in a city of honeycombs, each padlocked on the inside and out. It was where, on any given Saturday night, you could see vice presidents from MTV engaged in a breakneck conversation about the spiritual implications of silicone implants with a 300-pound Colombian drag queen from the Bronx. Where some coked-up twenty-six-year-old A&R scout claiming that he was *like this* with Madonna might get tapped on the shoulder and be loudly refuted—by none other than Miss Ciccone herself. Where people on their way up, already there, and skidding furiously back down could all turn it out for at least one night and part of the next morning, on a leveled playing field bereft of either chutes or ladders.

It was the last club of its kind, and it ended, perhaps for the best, before the idea of niche-market nightlife, of consorting with your own, supplanted the riskier, trippier pleasures of throwing yourself headlong into a many-limbed roomful of people, the likes of which you'd never end up speaking with in the middle of the week, at your stupid office job, on the constipated train, in the light of day. You didn't have to be a boldface name to go there, you didn't have to be white or black or Latin or Asian or some highly photogenic combination of the above, you didn't have to be a man or a woman, or into men or into women, over twenty-one or under thirty-nine. You didn't even have to be beautiful, although everyone always looked *interesting*, to say the least, and more and more so as the night progressed. If anything at all, it helped to be a little shameless and a little modest, to have a great deal of attitude and absolutely no attitude at the same time, and, on those nights when the line behind the velvet ropes snaked well around the corner, it helped to be friends with me, or Jess, or Ty, because we all variously worked the door. And contrary to what everyone thought, it didn't help so much to be friends with Flip, because everyone was friends with Flip, and to be her friend could mean everything or nothing, depending on the evening, and her mood.

But that was all two years ago—when we used to have a show, to steal from Barry Manilow. These days, on the rare, anxious occasions when I'm in that part of town, I'll bump into an old face from those days and they'll ask me why they never see me at X, Y, or Z—and then they'll describe some new, state-of-the-art spot that sounds like it exceeds our old joint in every excess with the possible exception of style. And I'll smile politely and tell them, no, no, I haven't been, I don't get out much anymore—because that club's death was the death of a certain me, someone I buried in Manhattan below 23rd Street before I took the hearse to Brooklyn, and I don't come back often to put flowers on the grave. Why should I? There's no proper grave, as Jess just learned—only a trash heap, an eyesore, an insult to the three of us, wherever we have gone or will go to.

For so many people, the death of that club was just that—the death of a club, however ephemeral, however legendary. But for me, it was where my childhood ended, rising up and vanishing into the black sky over SoHo. It was where all my pain began, and my implacable loneliness, and this tooth-grindingly tedious, responsible, prosaic affair glibly referred to as the rest of one's life. But for a brief, vertiginous span of time, it was all my happiness, and all my world.

It was the home that Flip, my sister, built for the three of us—she, Jess, and me—when we were all in New York, meditating on each other and the colossal, restless, unmet promise of her life. It was the home she opened up to the world with her luminous, quaking open arms, and they met her there, and embraced her back. For Jess and me, it was no small preoccupation, and we worked hard for it, but it was Flip's palace, her child, and everybody knew that—no one would dare refute that it was Flip's place.

She named it The Breeders Box—to this day most people aren't quite sure why. It lasted just a half-year, but while it did, we were a family for the very last time, and we were just fucking fabulous.

Massachusetts

One

I want to tell you the story of us, but the story doesn't begin in New York City. It begins in Massachusetts, where we grew up, and although it certainly begins well before I came along, if I were to start it with me in the picture—and I don't see why I shouldn't, since I'm the one that's here to tell it—it would start on the short stretch of coast in New Hampshire, in Rye, just below Portsmouth, where we rented a cottage every summer until we had a reversal of fortune and finally bought one—not a cottage, but an actual house, an old white four-square about a block from the beach, so big and insulated you could live in it properly all year round if you wanted to.

It starts on the beach. I can't remember if it happened before or after our reversal of fortune, or even the exact year, although I guess I'd date it to the summer of 1975 or 1976, when Jess was about eleven, Flip nine, and me eight, give or take a few months. A lot of things were going on that summer—not in my head so much as Jess's and Flip's—but what I most remember is this particular late afternoon. It was five o'clock, maybe closer to six, and the three of us were supposed to head back up to the house where our mother was making dinner and awaiting our return. But the morning had been rainy; we had only come to the beach at about three and hadn't had our daily dose of waterlogging, so, when the sun started arcing down toward the horizon, we took the half-mile walk to the bouldered-off cove that filled up with still salt water during high tide, Flip stalking ahead in her Wonder Woman one-piece bathing suit, the flats of her feet leaving hard, defiant little indentations in the soft sand of the waterline, Jess lagging somewhat sullenly behind her, smashing out her footprints with his own, and me, short of breath, struggling to catch up to him, stepping into his footprints for guidance and wondering if my own feet would ever possibly be as big as his.

Flip got to the bouldered wall a good twenty yards before we did, climbed confidently up the side, tightened her ponytail in its rubber band, and readied herself to dive into the cove. She didn't idle waiting for us to catch up and she didn't look back for our approval, a deliberate oversight that was the very pith of Flip, even at nine.

Jess stopped for me to attain him and rested his hand on the top of my head. 'She knows she's not supposed to dive in. Ma told her,' he said to me gravely, his voice already deep for eleven, but he didn't hurry to stop her, just resumed his trudge and called ahead in the most indifferent voice possible: 'You're not supposed to dive in, Felipika!'

I laughed guiltily. Flip hated her real name, forbade us to use it, and routinely smacked us when we did.

She abandoned her diving posture for just a second to turn back and shout, 'Then come and stop me, *Jeeeee-zus!* If you're really *Jeeee-zus*, then you can!' (That was the other thing we all knew: Jess hated *his* real name as much as Flip hated hers. I was the only one who didn't especially hate my real name, Thomas. But since I had been two, everyone called me Tigger, or Tig, apparently because I had a habit of bouncing in my crib, or high chair, like the bouncing tiger from Winnie the Pooh. I didn't mind the nickname, I just resented the source, since I had seen the original Tigger on TV and, frankly, he frightened me.)

Flip dived in. The last thing we saw was the bottoms of her feet flailing wildly in the air until they disappeared with the rest of her behind the bouldered wall. 'You're gonna get it!' Jess called, sprinting ahead, leaving me behind, scaling the wall in a half-second, a brief, frantic tangle of long, skinny limbs, two bright arms in prayer overhead, a spring uncoiled from the bent knees, just a sheath of him in the air for a second, and then gone.

I ran ahead and scaled the wall as fast as I could, although I still had trouble with the tricky footings that Flip and Jess had mastered like jazzy dance steps. When I reached the flattened top, I saw them both, laughing their heads off and thrashing each other around in the water, oiled silver on the surface from the reflection of the falling sun.

'Jeeee-zus!'

'Feeee-*lip*-eee-kaaa!'

When they saw me perched there, tentative and shivering, they laughed harder. 'Dive in, Tigga!'

It was funny to see their heads below me on the surface of the water like two jettisoned beach balls, bobbing toward each other and then away again, slightly crumpled with the loss of air.

'I can't,' I called, shaking my head. 'I'm scared 'a you guys.'

That made them laugh harder. 'He's scared 'a us!' Jess screamed.

'We're scared 'a *you*!' Flip yelled up to me. 'You look like a little ittle bug up there. Like a little *hoss-fly* with no wings!'

'I'm not a fly!' I shouted back down, offended.

'Tigga man, we're just kiddin' you,' Jess called up, softening. 'Come on, amigo, dive in. Me and Flip are gonna catch you.'

'Are you really?'

'No!' Flip screamed, breaking out in a new round of hysterics.

'Shut up, Flippy!' Jess said, shoving her in the water. 'We are so, Tig. Come on. Get over here, Flip.'

Flip paddled in toward Jess, nearer me, forming a crescent of open arms below me. 'I'm just kiddin', Tigga honey. We're gonna catch ya.' She had that hard, businessy look on her face now that she (and she alone) picked up from our father; now I knew I could trust her.

'Come on, Tig, arch your back,' Jess called, and I did. 'Okay, now. One for the money! Two for the show!' (Flip joined in now, an octave above Jess, effectively drowning him out.) 'Threeta get ready—'

I didn't hear the last line; I dived too early, falling on them in a crash of knuckles and flesh, sorting out direction below the surface, my nose and eyes filled with astringent water. When I came up, they each had me by an underarm, steadying me, laughing.

'You landed on my face, Tigga!' Jess protested.

'Here,' Flip said, still businessy, pinching my nose. 'Now close your mouth and blow.'

I did, and instantly felt better. Now the three of us were in the cove, and everything but the color of the sun in the water was on the other side of those boulders.

'Do we still scare ya?' Flip blared, so loudly that she echoed against the boulders. She was only nine, no boobs or butt yet, no serious intimation of delinquency, but already so loud and obnoxious, so prone to speaking too loud, or out of turn, that even then our mother would look at her, cross herself, and wonder aloud what would become of someone so like her father—but a girl, help us Lord, a girl.

She made a gruesome face, went 'Boo!', and hugged me roughly, her hair sticking to her head in long, ridiculous pieces.

'Not so much now,' I said, lying a little, but happy.

'See, that's why you're Tigga,' Jess said, pushing my hair out of my eyes for me. ''Cause when you jumped in, you bounced before you went under. You bounced, man!'

'I did not!' I said. 'I'm a boy, not an animal.' But I laughed and held his hand for a second before throwing it back down into the water. It could be hard sometimes when Flip made fun of me, she had a tendency not to stop, even when she knew it bugged you; that, in fact, was when she tended to redouble her efforts. But getting kidded by Jess was different. He'd only do it once, and when you protested, he'd do something like brush the hair out of your eyes to show that he didn't mean it, that he was only doing it because he liked you.

'Let's do the meatball,' Flip said.

'We gotta go back pretty soon,' Jess said, half-grave again, treading water. 'Ma's makin' baklava tonight for dessert.'

'Let's just do a few meatballs first!' Flip insisted.

So we did. The meatball was wrapping yourself up into a ball, ducking underwater, then blowing out air, hard, so you sank to the bottom like a boulder. Down there, rolling around on the sandy floor of the cove, you could unwrap one hand from your knee just long enough to wave to the others, or, in Flip's case, to give the finger, whereupon she'd come exploding back up to the top, laughing at her own silent swear word. So we all did the meatball for a while, down and then back up, just long enough to collect enough air to go down again. While we sank and rose, the sun rolled down lower to the horizon of the water, the faraway line that, if you approached it by fishing boat, kept receding ahead of you until the silhouette of a whale's back under the sky revealed itself as the Isle of Shoals, and beyond, the currents that led out to the rest of the world.

It was Flip that saw them first, staring out at us from the top of the bouldered wall on the other side of the cove.

'Hey, look at them,' she said when we had both emerged, her throat gargly with waterlog.

They were two kids, about Jess's age, maybe slightly older, watching us keenly, shading their eyes with their hands. We all turned in the water to face them.

'Who are they?' I asked.

'Just some faggots,' Flip said, and exploded laughing.

Jess shaded his eyes and smiled. We didn't have any friends in Rye except for each other, and Jess, being the oldest, wanted new friends.

'Hey!' he called. 'Come dive in! There's no undertow!'

One of the two kids leaned down, retrieved something, stood up again. Then he called out, quite clearly: 'What you doin' polluting the water?'

'What?' Jess called back.

'You heard me. You fuckin' spic, you're polluting the water!'

'Who are they talkin' about?' Jess asked, low, but we all knew. Flip knew, and even I knew at the age of eight, and certainly Jess knew. Jess didn't say anything then, just stared back, dazed. It was Flip that called back.

'Fuck you, faggots! You're still suckin' your mother's tits!'

They raised their arms in the air, and something came whizzing toward us, fast—little rocks, pebbles from the beach.

'Duck down!' Jess yelled, and he and I did, but Flip was already swimming toward them, and she took the missile. Jess and I heard her scream underwater—a banshee's scream, we'd heard it before, full of rage and murder. When we came hurtling up for air, the two kids were already out of sight and Flip was writhing around in the water, both hands on top of her head, screaming her lungs out.

'Fuck you, you fuckin' assholes! You dirty assholes! You better run! I'm gonna come get you and cut off your dicks!' But she wasn't just screaming now; she was crying, too. We thrashed our way over to her; in the dark tangle of her hair, there was blood collecting, one thin trickle running down her forehead and dissolving in the wet pool between her eye and nose.

'Let's get you out of the water,' Jess said, terrifyingly calm and efficient now, putting one arm around her and leading her toward the shallow egress that gave way to a tiny swath of beach. I doggie-paddled around them and joined her on the other side.

'I'm gonna *kill* those fucking queerbaits!' Flip sobbed, her face bloody and possessed-looking. 'I'm gonna stick a *bomb* up their faggot assholes!'

'You can't do anything about them now,' Jess said. 'But you gotta get fixed up.' He sat her down on the sand, took her hands away, and inspected the gash coolly, unalarmed. It was always like this, everytime it happened, although this was perhaps one of the more extreme occasions, having involved an actual assault—Flip ready to kill a man, like *she'd* been the source of hate, Jess so humiliated and angry that he packed it all away and became the very model of philosophical good reason, and me so horrified by the whole thing that I usually just started to bawl, which I did now.

'Tigga baby, it's okay,' Jess said, looking up at me. 'Some people are real bad, but God's gonna punish 'em someday. Now you gotta run back to the house and tell Ma to come down here in the car with some first aid. But don't make a big thing about it, okay? Don't tell her about those kids. Just say Flip got a little cut on her head.'

'What if they come back?' I said, trying to collect myself.

'I hope they do!' Flip burst out. 'I wanna cut off their little pee-pees!'

'They're not gonna come back,' Jess said, dismissing Flip. 'They're cowards. Now go get Ma, Tig.'

I started running back toward the house, but then I stumped myself with complications. How was I going to say Flip cut her head? Diving? But wouldn't that be a lie? And what if Flip bled to death before we got back? Shouldn't we just put some sand on her head and carry her back? I turned and ran back in the other direction to consult with Jess.

But I stopped before I got to them. Flip was lying on the ground now, still crying and cursing a mile a minute, but Jess had her head in his lap, propped up on his leg, and he was parting her hair away from the gash, gently, methodically, seemingly strand by strand. He wasn't talking back, just working, and occasionally he'd look up and out into the still water of the cove, as though he wished keenly to be back inside it, underwater, well below the firing line of sticks, stones, hateful names or any of the other things he had to duck, living in this world, ours, excepting, of course, us—Flip and Tig, his sister and brother, as thick as blood, maybe thicker. I mean to say, that's how Flip and I always saw it.

'Shhhh!' I saw him motion to her, his finger over her lips, and he performed the brief miracle of silencing Flip. I didn't run to them. I ran all the way back to the house and roused our mother from the kitchen.

For the start of the story of us, I guess that's as good a place as any.

Two

But to be honest, the story doesn't really start with me. It starts right here, in this maternity ward at the hospital in Lowell, Massachusetts, close to midnight, in the middle of December 1964, a good three years before I come along. There's a woman, a nurse, olive-skinned and handsome in a sturdy, no-frills sort of way, jet-black hair in a flip under her white starched cap like an antiseptic tiara, walking briskly but with the slightest limp from a bout of polio when she was young and growing up a grocer's daughter in this mainly working-class, very Greek-American old mill town. She is married now and solidly middle-class, but no more, just over twenty-five and reluctantly childless, capable of great amounts of hard labor and of good thoughts, not greedy in any complicated or far-reaching way, except—well, she works in another wing, but every chance she gets, she comes over to see her friend Bunny who she knows from nursing school, who now works in maternity. Whenever she can, she spends her break with Bunny, smoking cigarettes, sipping coffee and peering through the glass panes that separate them from the newborns. All the time, she is thinking about babies, babies, babies. That's her; that's my mother.

'They're all so beautiful tonight,' she whispers to Bunny, blowing smoke up against her own reflection in the pane.

'You think so, Nikki?' says Bunny, who's a little tougher than my mother, happily single with several sharp-looking boyfriends and her own new Mustang convertible with a cassette player. 'I was just thinking they were a little on the small side tonight.'

'Babies *are* small,' my mother says, reverently, and Bunny thinks twice before snapping something back. 'That's why they're babies.' She scans the cribs from left to right, back again down the next row, until she's seen virtually all: a gallery of faces, tiny soft pink fruits, their eyes and mouths squinting inward in need, their tiny fists clutched together like the shells of blossoms waiting to be pried open and kissed.

She puts out her cigarette. 'All their mothers must be so happy,' she says, her right arm wrapped crossly around her waist, and she doesn't look up from the pedestal ashtray when Bunny thinks she should.

'Come in here,' Bunny says, putting out her cigarette and looking furtively up and down the corridor for the head nurse or stray obstetricians. 'There's one you didn't see.'

'I can't go in there, Bunny!' my mother protests, her face ablaze with anticipation.

'Barbara's sleeping in the lounge. No one's gonna see,' Bunny says, and she leads my mother into the nursery, a hysterical chorus of cries and screams, a pink and blue grid of squirming new life, twitching under flickering fluorescent panels of light.

'Look at this one,' Bunny says, leading my mother to the far left crib in the last row. My mother gasps; there's a baby boy in there: not standard-issue pink, but light brown, a placid, sleeping face the color and creaminess of caramel. Already, there's a thatch of black hair sticking straight up on his head, and my mother's first thought is that he looks like an old, wise, kindly man returned to a state of infancy and solace.

'He's an angel!' my mother exclaims in a whisper to Bunny. What she wants more than anything is to hold him—at least to let him grab her finger with his wise little hand—but she doesn't dare. She just stares down and smiles.

'He's a cute little thing, isn't he?' Bunny concedes. 'And guess what?'

'What?' my mother says, distracted, still glowing down into the crib.

'His mother hasn't seen him and she never will. She doesn't want him. He's an accident.'

My mother looks up from the crib with a little 'Oh!', puts her hands over her mouth, then looks down anxiously again as though she's sure he's heard what Bunny just said. 'Are you serious?' she whispers.

'Uh hunh,' Bunny whispers back, crossing her arms. 'The girl's only sixteen, and there doesn't seem to be any father in the picture.'

'Bunny, stop! You're kidding.'

'I'm not, Nikki! What do you expect from these Puerto Ricans, running around all over Lowell now with their little screw-me polka dot dresses on?'

'Bunny, stop it!'

'It's true, Nikki! I'm assisting on the pregnancies of unmarried sixteen-year-old girls every week now, and it's all *them*,' Bunny says, thumbing back at the boy's crib.

'Hmph,' my mother says, biting her lower lip, always easily silenced by even the suggestion of factual authority. Then she looks back into the crib. 'What's his name?'

Bunny peers around to the card at the foot of the crib, then laughs. 'Oh God, Nikki, you're not gonna believe it! Two weeks before Christmas, too!'

'What's his name?' my mother giggles in anticipation.

'Jesus! Jesus Ramirez!' Bunny announces, oblivious of the Spanish pronunciation. 'Oh, the poor kid! How can these people name their kids something like *Jesus*?'

But my mother doesn't laugh. 'Don't you think that's kind of special, though? I mean, especially so close to Christmastime?'

'Nikki, please! What are people gonna call him? Jeezie? J.R.?' Bunny keeps on laughing, and my mother, still harboring the funny feeling that the baby understands everything they're saying, bends down into the crib again to protect his feelings.

'Hi, sweetie! Hi, buddy! Hi, Jesus!' She smiles a little at the oddness, the portentousness, of the name, in spite of herself. 'He's adorable Bunny, isn't he?'

'Oh, definitely,' Bunny says. 'He's awfully dark, though.'

'Bunny, look at me!' my mother exclaims, holding out her arms. 'I'm dark!'

'You know what I mean, Nikki.'

'I guess so,' my mother says, even though she doesn't know what Bunny means at all. She looks back into the crib now, and the boy is staring back at her, blank, unyielding. She smiles and coos, conciliatory, but drops it when he doesn't respond, just keeps staring, and so does she. *I can't take my eyes off this baby*, she's thinking, and she wraps her arm around her waist again with a pang of something she can't place.

'Is anyone trying to adopt him?' she asks Bunny.

'Not yet, as far as I know. He's been here three days now. The state's handling it. You know how they are. Slow, slow, slow.'

'The poor little thing,' my mother says, low. 'How could a mother not want her baby?'

'She didn't even want to see him,' Bunny offers. 'She said if she did, she'd just cry and cry.'

'Look at him,' my mother says.

They both hear steps coming down the hallway outside. 'Oh, shit!' Bunny whispers. 'That's Barbara. Duck down!'

Bunny grabs my mother by the arm and they both crouch down between cribs until the footsteps advance, stop briefly, and retreat. At first my mother is as scared as Bunny. Then she puts her head and hand against the boy's crib, closes her eyes, and forgets herself.

'I think the coast is clear now,' Bunny says.

'Hm?' from my mother, eyes still closed.

'Nikki! I said I think the coast is clear. We better get back on duty.'

'Oh. All right.' My mother stands up, smooths her uniform, looks back into the crib. The boy's eyes are closed now. 'Bye bye, sweetie. I'll come see you again, okay?' Tentatively, my mother leans in, pauses, then, barely touching, strokes the boy's cheek with her knuckles. One tiny hand reaches up and grabs her index finger.

'Look, Bunny! He just grabbed it!'

Bunny arches her eyebrows at her friend—the high school honor student who became a nurse because her Old World father wouldn't let her go on to anything but nursing school or Katie Gibbs; the one who didn't rebel like her sister Felipika, crazy Lippy, who had run off shortly after high school graduation to New York to pursue her own course as, of all things, a singer; the one who refused to take the answers to nursing finals even when they were circulating around the entire class; the one who married Tommy Mitchell, the handsome Irish rogue playboy of Lowell, not for his good looks or ambition but because when he smiled she said she could see his 'good heart,' whatever that meant. Also, the one who tried harder and harder every year to get pregnant, with increasing frustration and always to no avail, the one who put her arm around her waist, like a gesture of prayer or shame, every time she looked through the glass pane at that night's new crop of infants.

'He likes you,' Bunny says.

'Who could just walk away from their baby?' my mother says again, gently prying the boy's fist away from her finger, then kissing it, guiltily, with the skipped beat of a heart, before she lays it back down.

'Good-night, Jesus,' Bunny calls as they walk away from the crib.

'Good-night, Jesus,' my mother calls. 'Good-night, Jess.'

'Jess! That's a name a kid could live with,' Bunny says, offering my mother a stick of Doublemint when they've closed the door behind them.

'I guess he could live with that,' my mother says, smiling, mildly proud. She and Bunny squeeze hands briefly, then hurry away in opposite directions down the empty fluorescent corridor.

That was the beginning of that. From that moment, my mother didn't stop thinking of Jesús Ramirez. She thought of him all through her shift until her break, when she could sneak away to the maternity ward, slip inside the nursery, check on his progress—to her, he seemed to be getting bigger and needier every day—and spend an illicit five or ten minutes in conversation with him while Bunny stood guard outside. Of course, he couldn't talk back to my mother's questions: *How are you today, Jess? Did they feed you good today? You're getting bigger, huh? You're gonna be a handsome little man one day, Jess. Don't you worry, someone's gonna come for you real soon.* He just looked up at her out of his big serene eyes and held fast to her finger with his tough, tiny fist. Then she thought of him for the rest of her shift, thought of their stolen seconds together—she embarrassed herself, thinking indignantly of the two of them as mother and child in forced separation— and then maybe she was just slightly less than meticulous changing somebody's sheets or dispensing medicine, because she was wrestling with a thousand clashing thoughts.

She thought of him after work, preparing dinner for herself and my father in their apartment on the slightly sagging second floor of an old triple-decker, and she thought of him when my father returned home from the liquor distributing company where he was a rising young salesman, gobbling up new accounts and putting more and more miles on his car every week. She thought of him while she dully reheated dinner, because in the past year my father never got home earlier than eight o'clock, especially around the holiday season, even though he usually made a point of calling around six and saying he wasn't more than fifteen minutes from home, he just had one more quick call to make. Often, at the invitation of the local restaurateurs who were his clients, he'd take his dinner on those final calls, sitting at their bar, talking new lines of whiskey over a Manhattan or two and a plate of surf and turf the likes of which my mother seldom had the time or the money to make at home. Later, sitting at their fold-out Scandinavian-style modern table in the living room, heavy with work, steak and cocktails, he'd pick desultorily at the moussaka and feta salad my mother had made, keeping his previous dinner to himself. He didn't like 'foreign' food; he didn't know why my mother couldn't just cook up a hamburger or a sloppy joe, or an occasional boiled dinner, like anybody else's wife.

'Why aren't you eating, Tommy? You think you got a bug or something?' my mother would ask anxiously from across the table, although she herself had little appetite for her own food. It never tasted the way her mother had made it.

'Nah,' my father would answer, trying to sound blithe. 'I'm just too busy to be hungry these days, Nikki.'

'I know,' she'd sigh. 'I feel the same way. The holidays are hard.'

'Yuh,' my father would say, and they'd resume their picking. Afterwards, he'd snap on the TV while she did the dishes. Usually, when she finished and came to join him, he would be snoring on the sofa. He was most tender to her in the two minutes of half-sleep during which she woke him, pulled off his Florsheim wing tips, and put him to bed.

They had been married now for nearly three years, and the truth was they had grown apart. When they first married, he was embarrassed that she made more money than he did; the happy plan had been that she would keep working just until he could pick up some speed at the distribution company and then she would stop, obviously to have the Mitchell children they both wanted. They started trying after a year, after he was promoted from the book-keeper's office to a sales route of his own, and it was such fun to try. He felt as light as air in the morning, ready to meet the liquor-buying needs of the entire state of Massachusetts with nothing more than sheer energy, nerve and charm. My mother went to work convinced that she felt heavier than usual, even though she knew that wasn't how it worked, ministering to her patients with a kind of heavenly forbearance and kindness that inspired reverence, all the while humming to herself, *Is there someone inside me? Is there someone inside me?*

But there wasn't—not after weeks, months, a full year, and God, how they had tried. It's probably nothing, the doctor said, it's probably just bad timing, but if you really want to know, you'd both have to be willing to submit to tests—

'I don't think we really gotta go that far yet, do you, Nikki?' my father said immediately when my mother mentioned the visit.

'Well, no, but—it's the only way to know for sure. Don't you want to know for sure?'

'Let's just keep on trying.' My father grinned at her across the table. 'It's pretty fun trying, isn't it, Nik?'

'Yeah.' My mother blushed. 'I guess that's the thing to do.'

'For now,' my father said.

'Right. For now.'

They never had that conversation again, even though for most of the following two years they kept on trying, to no end. They became secretly suspicious of each other, then resentful; it was someone's fault, his or hers, but the prospect of taking 'the tests' had frozen into a taboo. Their friends were starting to have children of their own; they hardly saw them now for dinner or for card-playing, and when they did, their constant talk of sleeping patterns and diaper-changing was intolerable, especially to my mother. When they started to sense they were becoming isolated in their childlessness is when they started to grow apart. He started working harder and talking faster than ever before, and was duly rewarded with a promotion to sales manager. She stayed on, listlessly, at the hospital; when they asked her to work late-night shifts for time-and-a-half, she accepted, and my father was too preoccupied with his own work to complain. They hardly ever 'tried' anymore, except occasionally in a kind of drugged, imprecise, mutual half-sleep in the morning before my father stumbled into the shower, leaving my mother behind, instantly to sleep again, in their modern Scandinavian-style marriage bed.

And then, at the end of 1965, all my mother was thinking about was the orphan, Jesús Ramirez.

It exploded on Christmas Eve of that year, as they desultorily opened each other's presents under a fake white tabletop tree. (They had forsaken a real one this year, for the first time since they married.) They had both worked that afternoon, they were both exhausted from a long season of overtime, and they were already running late for dinner at my mother's mother's home. They had agreed, this year, that instead of buying each other a laboriously chosen profusion of small items, each would give the other one exquisite gift. My father unwrapped his: an expensively tooled leather briefcase with his initials in gold on the flank.

'Aw, this is sharp, Nikki! Thank you, baby,' my father said, leaning over to kiss her cheek.

'I figured if you're gonna be sales manager now, you better look the part,' my mother said as she set aside wrapping paper and lifted the cover off a large box from Jordan Marsh.

'You better scream when you see this, honey,' my father said.

He had given her a fur coat. Not rabbit or fox, but mink; not a stole or a jacket, but a full-length coat of rich black pelts that glistened silver under the blinking lights like a live thing.

'Oh my God,' my mother said, taking it up in her arms.

'You love it?' my father asked.

'Oh my God,' my mother said again, and in a moment she was holding the pelts up to her face, kneeling on the sagging floor of their living room and sobbing.

'You love it, hunh?' my father bellowed. 'I bet it's not many nurses at Lowell General that can come in—'

'No!' my mother sobbed, and my father stopped dead. 'Tommy, Tommy. This isn't what I want at all!'

'Sorry?'

'I don't want a mink coat! I don't *need* a mink coat! Tommy, I want a baby!'

My father looked at my mother, sobbing over the coat he had paid for with his holiday bonus, his first ever, and something gave way in his stomach. He knew what it was, they both did, even if they never discussed it anymore. It was the hole in a marriage that was dying before their eyes, it was the hole that was widening, going deeper, and driving them apart.

'Nikki, honey,' he said, low. 'We're *trying*.'

'We're not trying anymore, and there's no use in trying! You know that,' my mother wept. 'And anyway, I know the baby I want. He's already alive.'

'What?'

'He's a baby at the hospital. He's a—his mother doesn't want him. I go to visit him every day. He's so beautiful. His name is Jee—' and my mother caught herself. 'His name's Jess. He's so beautiful, and he's got no mother. Tommy, I love him. He's what I want.'

Even in this state, there's a lot my mother didn't tell my father. Like that she thought it was God's plan for her to have this baby. Why else couldn't she have a child of her own? Why would he have ended up in *her* hospital? Why would Bunny have even pointed him out to her in the first place? And she knew it was corny, coincidence, but she couldn't get over his name, and the time of year. Jess was alone tonight of all nights, while she got a mink coat! But she didn't tell any of this to my father, and she certainly didn't describe Jess in any physical detail. She just kept on crying, softer now, staring down at the stiff lacquered cover of the Jordan Marsh box, feeling like a fool, but finally unburdened of her deepest Christmas wish.

'Honey, I need a drink,' my father said, and he stepped out of the living room into the kitchen. For what felt like an eternity, my mother knelt there on the floor, staring at the reflection of the tree lights twinkling on the Jordan Marsh box, wondering what damage she had done. Her first real thought of the coat, of what it had to cost, and the picture of my father consulting minutely with an envious salesgirl at the big Jordan Marsh in Boston, made her wince with guilt. *But I couldn't help it*, she then thought defiantly. *I can't go on like this, I cannot.* Somewhere between that maternity ward and this sagging old apartment that lacked nothing but the beating heart of a young life, she thought, her life was closing in on her.

My father came back into the living room, a Manhattan for himself in one hand and a glass of ginger ale—all my mother would drink—in the other. He handed the glass to her (she accepted it with a sheepish murmur), sat down on the couch and stared at the stiff white tabletop tree. He looked more tired than he had ever before in his life. In two weeks, he would be thirty.

'What did you say this kid's name is?' he finally asked her.

'It's Jesus,' she said, and blushed when he raised an eyebrow. 'Can you believe it? But I—Bunny and me, we call him Jess. That's better, isn't it?'

He smiled, feebly, and when he spoke his voice cracked. 'Nik baby, you really just wanna give up?'

'Oh, Tommy,' she said, putting her head in his lap and embracing him around the waist. 'It's not giving up. It isn't. It's—it's the start of something. Maybe.'

'Baby, I'm so sorry. I never pictured it this way.'

'It's nobody's fault, Tommy. It's God's plan, right? There's gotta be a reason, right?'

My father sipped his drink and played absently with the shiny ends of her flip. A man like him wasn't supposed to stay a salesman all his life, he thought, and wasn't supposed to not be able to father his own children. But if, despite your hard work, things didn't flush out a certain way, what did you do? he thought. You swallowed what you had to swallow, and as for the rest, you just worked harder. *Right?* he asked himself.

'Maybe after the new year, you could sneak me in to see this kid,' he finally said, concentrating again on the tree.

'Oh, Tommy,' my mother said, rising up to his face. 'Thank you. Thank you for the beautiful coat. For everything. Tommy, don't cry. It's Christmas Eve, Tommy!'

Three

That was how Jess became my older brother. Of course, my mother was keeping something about him from my father, knowing it wasn't right, but figuring that he would find out for himself when he saw him, but that it wouldn't matter when my father saw just what a beautiful baby he was. And so late one night, a week after the New Year, my father drove over to Lowell General, met my mother on her break, and slipped with her, guarded again by Bunny, into the nursery.

'He's *brown*,' were his first words.

'I know,' my mother said, her heart pounding. 'Isn't he an angel?'

'What *is* he?'

'He's—his mother's Puerto Rican. His father, too, I guess. But what does it matter? His mother said she didn't even want to see him, poor thing, 'cause it would break her heart.'

'Every stranger on the street is gonna know he's not yours. And they're definitely gonna know he's not *mine*. Have you even thought about that?'

'I've thought about that!' my mother snapped, defensive. All the while Jess was holding on to her finger—still my mother hadn't dared to pick him up and hold him—watching them impassively. 'I don't see why it really matters.'

'I think you're being a little naive.'

'I don't think so.'

'If we're gonna do this, couldn't we adopt a white baby? A little white baby boy?'

'How can you say that?' my mother hissed in a whisper, terrified that Jess might have heard. 'I don't see what that has to do with anything, anyway. *This* is the baby I love. And no one's trying to claim him yet. I've been checking.'

My father looked down into the crib, met eyes with Jess, and looked away. 'A spic baby,' he said under his breath.

'God heard that.'

'Good!'

'Tommy, please, look at him! Look at those big hands. Don't they look like ball player's hands? You could teach him how to play ball.'

My father stared back down into the crib. 'Hey, amigo,' he finally said, holding one finger in front of Jess's fist. Jess grabbed it, squeezed hard, and my mother was convinced she saw him smile fiendishly. 'Hey!' my father exclaimed, startled. 'What a grip, for God's sakes.'

'I told you.' My mother laughed. 'See? He's gonna be a ball player.'

'We'll see about that,' my father muttered.

Adopting him wasn't as hard as my mother expected. They never met Jess's real mother, didn't want to—*how could a mother just abandon her child?* my mother still thought, secretly grateful now—and even as the papers and the various legal machinations were going through, they knew very little about his origins except that he was born healthy and on schedule, an easy birth. A nurse in the maternity ward mentioned to my mother that she thought she remembered a relative of Jess's real mother mentioning that they were eventually planning to move back to Puerto Rico, which my mother was eager to accept as certainty, and anyway, the adoption clause stipulated that contact between biological parents and children couldn't be made until after the child was of age, and then only by mutual interest, brokered through the adoption agency. My parents had no idea who Jess's biological father was, or where Jess's kin hailed from in Puerto Rico (they presumed that Puerto Rico was an island somewhat like Bermuda, where they had honeymooned for a week). Neither of them even spoke a word of Spanish, but they didn't dwell on any of these thoughts much. What was the point? Jess was theirs now, and he'd grow up in a house with English, just like any other American kid. His name wasn't Jesús Ramirez anymore, either. It was Mitchell, and for all but legal purposes, *Jess* Mitchell.

They would bring him home in two weeks, and my mother told the world their happy news, wanting the world to be happy for her. Mostly, it was happy, but some people's stray remarks didn't escape her.

From the other nurses at Lowell General (excluding the ever-faithful Bunny, of course): 'Don't you want to adopt a white baby?'

From old Mrs. Kouros in the apartment upstairs: 'He's *what*? Oh. They smell, you know, those people.'

From her own mother, superstitious and weeping: 'He'll bring you nothing but heartache, Nikki, listen to your mother!'

And from my mother, always, the murmured responses: *You love a baby, not a color. That's a stereotype, Mrs. Kouros.* And, *Mama, I've* had *nothing but heartache—I'm through with it!* My mother was learning to talk back, to trust her own authority, something she hadn't learned in high school or her nursing program.

It was only her sister, Felipika, whom everyone called Lippy, living in near-poverty in some part of New York City called Greenwich Village, singing nights in the piano bar where she worked as a cocktail waitress, who seemed to share my mother's happiness fully.

'You just love that boy with all your heart, darling, and tell the rest of the world to fuck off, you hear me?' Lippy would say to my mother over the phone.

'Lippy, honestly!'

'Well, it's true, Nikki! There's too little love in the world as it is for something stupid like the color of a baby's skin to get in the way.'

'You sound like you're turning into a hippie.'

'I may as well. There's nothing more I could do to piss off Mama anymore, anyway. Do you know the last time I called her, she told me that Daddy had his stroke and died because of *me*, because I had broken his heart? Can you believe she had the nerve to say that to me?'

'Oh God, Lip,' my mother said, distressed. She was caught in the crossfire of the estrangement between Lippy and her mother, between Lippy and all the relations she had gladly left behind, and she hated it.

'Don't worry, darling,' Lippy said, and my mother could hear her lighting a cigarette (she *hoped* it was only a cigarette) on the other end of the line. 'I just said "Good-night, Mama, God bless you," very gently, and I put the phone down and went to work. That was three months ago. We haven't spoken since.'

'Oh God.'

'*Anyway*,' Lippy said, blowing out smoke. 'Little Jess sounds adorable. Just tell all those provincial bigots to fuck off. A little bit of disapproval in your life will be good for you, Nikki. It makes you stronger.'

'I suppose,' said my mother, not quite knowing how to take that.

'What about Tommy? Is he excited?'

'Oh, I guess so!' my mother said, trying to sound breezy. 'He's hardly around, though, he works so hard. But he's very excited—of course.'

'Hmmm,' Lippy said, in the skeptical tone she used when she referred to my father. (Relations between them had been

chilly at best since she found out, during my parents' engagement, that he thought she was, in his words, a freak.) 'That
man of yours is going to be quite a success someday.'

'He hopes so,' my mother said, surprising herself, and they
both laughed. 'Are you seeing any men, Lip?'

Lippy laughed. 'Nikki, I see a *lot* of men. Every night at
work. And I usually end up refereeing their lovers' quarrels.'

'Oh,' said my mother, who had no idea what crazy Lippy
was talking about. 'Are you ever coming home, Lip?'

'Of course I'm coming home—to see my new nephew, the
baby Jesus! And when he gets older, you're bringing him here,
to see his insane runaway godmother sing on Broadway.'

'I love you,' my mother said to Lippy in Greek.

'I love you too, darling. But no Greek. I'm so sick of the
Nana Mouskouri jokes from all these queens.'

They brought Jess home on a Saturday in April, my mother
bouncing him on her lap in the passenger seat and talking a
mile a minute, either to Jess—*hey, buddy, you're finally coming
home with your new mommy and daddy, isn't that fun, hunh, isn't
that fun?*—or to my father, or just out loud to no one in particular: Did I get the right diapers? I think I should have
bought more formula. I really don't think we've got enough.
What if he hates his room? Oh God, what if he misses the hospital? Oh no, what was I thinking?

'Nikki, everything's gonna be just fine,' my father said,
glancing uneasily at Jess (who stared back at him with cool,
impassive brown eyes), then looking away and fiddling with
the radio dials to perfect the reception of the ball game.

In the apartment, my mother jogged Jess from room to
room, giving him the breathless tour. 'This is the kitchen, Jess,
and here's the den. And what's that funny box with a window?
Ooh—that's a television! And oh boy, what's this? What's this
room for a big boy? It's Jess's room! See, there's his name on
the wall: J-E-S-S. Jess!' Jess, in tiny train conductor's overalls,

took all this in through his still, brown eyes, laughing once, out of nowhere, at the sight of my father's high school graduation picture on my mother's dresser.

'Who's that?' my mother said to Jess. 'Who's that, hunh? That's Daddy! Tommy, come here! He knew it was you in the picture!'

'Hunh?' my father called from the other room, where he was rummaging through his briefcase.

'He noticed you in the picture, and he laughed! He knows who you are!'

'Smart kid,' my father said, stepping over to pat Jess on the head, but Jess squirmed away with a scowl. My father retreated a few steps; the apartment had felt wholly different to him, hijacked, no longer his own, from the moment my mother carried Jess over the threshold. 'Nikki, honey,' he said now, 'I gotta go into the office, just for a few hours, okay and—'

'What?' my mother interrupted.

'I said I gotta go into the office for a few hours.'

My mother's lower lip trembled. 'Do you know who we just brought home?' she said, low.

'Yeah,' my father said.

'Well?'

'Well—well, he's gonna be here when I get back, isn't he?' he said, trying a joke.

'Tommy,' my mother pleaded, but my father stepped forward again and kissed her on the cheek. 'I'll be back in two hours. Three at the most. Maybe we'll go get some ice cream later, all right, Slugger?' he said, patting Jess on the head again. Jess didn't move. Neither did my mother. They all just remained there for a second. Then, as fast as he could, my father scooped up his hand-tooled, monogrammed briefcase and was out the door.

My mother kept standing there. She was about to cry, then she looked at the baby in her arms, and, convinced that he looked about to cry too, she stopped herself and smiled wide, hitching him up on her hip.

'Hey, buddy, what are we gonna do? Are we gonna go see your new room, hunh? Are we gonna go look at your new toys? You wanna see a tiger? You wanna see an airplane?'

Jess gurgled something, deadpan, and swatted the side of my mother's nose.

Six months later, the three of them had moved out of the apartment in Lowell and into a house just outside the city— not the ranch house my mother had envisioned, but a little white cape with a tiny shaded backyard and a bulkhead, which my mother thought was even better. She spent all her time with Jess and my father spent all his at work. They hardly saw each other, but the dark ache had gone away. They both had what they wanted now, my father his ambition unfettered and my mother her child delivered, and what they couldn't or wouldn't bother changing—the fact that they had grown per- manently apart, that each was no longer the other's foremost concern—they accepted with an extraordinary degree of good humor. In some pocket of time at the very end of the day, they made room for each other's stories, a not-really-so-awful little obligation before bedtime, and in this fashion they kept a home intact. They still made love, occasionally, but they didn't even call it 'trying' anymore. It was an afterthought; they didn't call it anything. A year passed much like this.

Then the surprise came. My mother, who had privately declared herself barren years ago, got pregnant. The news elated and jarred her, and my father seemed wholly in love with her again for the first time in years.

'We're finally gonna have a kid!' he whooped, when she flatly told him the news.

'Tommy, we *have* a kid. We have a two-year-old son.'

'Of course we do!' my father whooped again, undaunted. 'But you know what I mean, baby!'

The delivery was a nightmare; my mother was in excruciating labor for sixteen hours. Pregnant for the first time in her
life, she thought that all deliveries were this bad, and wondered how some women could endure this again and again.
Only later Bunny told her it was the most ornery delivery she
had seen in a year.

My mother had a shriveled, tortured-looking baby girl who
screamed when the doctor slapped her backside—and
screamed and screamed and screamed.

'She's so beautiful! Isn't she beautiful, Nik?' my father
gushed, cradling her by my mother's hospital bed, as though a
husk had fallen away from his person.

'I can see your face in hers,' my mother said, overjoyed by
this, her first daughter, but somewhat cowed by the infant's
wails. 'My God, she can yell.'

'She's got strong lungs, then!'

'Jess has a new friend,' my mother said. 'I hope he adjusts
okay. You never know how he's gonna react to anything. He's
a little mystery that way.'

'Why don't you concentrate on your new baby for a
second?' my father said.

'She's beautiful,' my mother said, yawning back post-
delivery exhaustion.

My mother had promised Auntie Lippy long ago that if she
ever had a baby girl she would name her Felipika. My father
hated the name, but the promise had been made, and my
mother insisted they stand by it. Besides, try as she might, my
mother just couldn't come up with anything else. She'd look at
her new daughter's screwed-up, combat-ready little face and
draw an absolute blank.

'She's gonna kill us someday when she realizes what we
named her,' my father said. 'Someone's gonna say to her
"*What's* your name? Felipika?" And she's gonna flip, Nikki,
she's gonna flip.' He paused a second, cocking his head. 'Hey.
Did you just hear that, Nik?'

'Hear what?'

'What I said. Felipika. *Ful*-lip-ika. *Flip*-ika. Flip! We can call her Flip. She looks like a Flip, doesn't she?'

'Why would you want to call a girl Flip?' my mother asked. 'It sounds like a pet's name.'

'It does not!' my father said, offended. 'Besides, she's not gonna be your average girl. She's too tough for that. You can tell already. Isn't that right, Flip?' he cooed, taking her up in his shirtsleeves. 'Isn't that right, baby?'

My mother's face darkened at my father's remark. What was wrong with an average girl? After a delivery that had been the most nightmarish experience of her life, my mother thought that having an average girl would do just fine.

They brought Flip home, and Jess, just two, wouldn't stop crying. He cried the minute he saw her (she howled back), and he wouldn't stop crying until, despite their best efforts at conciliation, my parents took Flip away. This went on for a month. Nursing Flip, my mother would ask her privately, *Why do you wanna make your brother cry, little girl? Why can't you make it nice for him?* Then one day, something happened: In her unflagging goodwill campaign, my mother brought Flip in to Jess one morning. He looked her straight in the face and started bawling. Flip let out the most tremendous caterwaul of her four-week-old life, and Jess suddenly stopped dead and stared at her as though for the first time. Then, from nowhere, he laughed. He reached out, swatted her on the nose, and laughed again. Flip burbled approvingly, and Jess never cried at the sight of Flip again.

Time went on, and somewhere in there, my parents tried-didn't-try again, successfully, because shortly after the passage of a year, I arrived: Thomas, named for my father, shortly thereafter dubbed Tigger by a visiting Auntie Lippy, because I bounced up and down in my crib whenever she put Dionne Warwick on the hi-fi.

I was an easy delivery, and that's how my parents took me—

easily. They hadn't necessarily planned me, but by this point they were used to babies and in a decent enough disposition for one more, although after me they took steps for the first time for it not to happen again.

'He's a sweet baby, isn't he?' my mother said after the delivery, just happy enough not to have been utterly demolished like she was after Flip's.

'He's a good-looking kid,' my father said, stroking my head, and, unlike Jess, I didn't wiggle away. They tell me I sort of purred, instead.

'You finally got your Mitchell boy,' my mother said.

'So did you,' my father said, glancing at her sideways.

'I thank God for all my children.'

They brought me home, and they tell me I fell in love instantly with Jess and Flip, my favorite sleeping position having been curling up in a ball with each of them pressing in on either side of me, serene Jess and rumbling Flip, and when I had finally fallen asleep, they would scooch toward each other until they were brow to brow, just above my own, and fall asleep themselves.

Now just one more thing: shortly afterward, my father, who had been buying stocks in it for years, bought the liquor distributing company to which he had devoted much of the past ten years, and we became more or less rich. We moved out of the little cape and into a cavernous old thirteen-room house with pillars in front, set back from the road in the rural, horsey town of Topsfield, a deal my father made through some connection in the booze business, a connection that also allowed us to buy the summer house in Rye. My father drove a black Mercedes, and my mother kept her five-year-old station wagon, despite my father's protestations.

That was us now, a red-faced mick, his olive-skinned Greek-American wife, and their three babies, one noticeably, mysteriously darker than the other two, trucking around an archaic Massachusetts country town still populated by the

sallow-faced descendants of the Mayflower, all of us on our
way back to old Lowell on Sunday morning for Greek
Orthodox services. All except for our father, that is, a negli-
gent Catholic, who on Sundays was either at the office or out
on the road, setting up displays in some overchilled package
store on Route 1 or 28 or 114, making possible some gentri-
fied family wardrobe that probably didn't look like it fitted any
of us quite right at all.

That was that. That was us, the Mitchells. From there,
everything was poised for us to proceed in the regular fashion
of families.

Four

If you had seen the five of us at the local lobster house on a Saturday night, crammed inside one of the enormous Naugahyde booths, if you had seen us fighting over fried scallops and lobster claws, if you had heard our father's booming laugh over one of Flip's smart-assed remarks, or my mother's semi-shrill exclamations that Jess or I was choking on the neck of a steamed clam (not Flip, though, who virtually swallowed her food whole), certainly if you saw the easy, loud dogfights between me and my older brother and sister, you would have thought we were the happiest, most prosperous family in the world.

Which we were, in many, many ways. Our parents were still young and handsome, and the three of us were becoming much the same, Jess's deepening shades of dark contrasting with mine and Flip's strange blend of fairness and shadows. (This meant virtually black hair that acquired shocking blond streaks in the summer.) In our first years in Topsfield, of course we got strange stares because of Jess, and of course when our parents enrolled Jess in elementary school, he was called certain things—never with much specificity or malice, because Topsfield was too far away from Lawrence or Lowell for the clueless Mayflower people who lived there to know anything *about* Puerto Ricans. But when he was called those things, he never lashed back, and he never cried. He blushed, actually, and turned (or walked) away, bewildered, because he didn't really know what they were talking about. In a matter of years, too, he was taking on height and heft—he then became a rather admired athlete, and a popular boy, courteous and diffident, and other kids wanted to be his friends more than his tormentors.

And so it came shortly to be in very Waspy, very Protestant Topsfield, that we, the motley Mitchells, were understood to be a family—and it was understood that Jess Mitchell was a sweet, handsome boy with a big, capable frame, a sensitive, artistic bent, and some sad story from his infancy, before he became a Mitchell. It was also understood, in a brief span of time, that Felipika Mitchell, his younger sister with the bizarre given name and the more appropriately blunt nickname, was quite apparently not of the same blood as Jess. She was understood to be a nightmare, rather, some ghastly hybrid of her garrulous, probably alcoholic father and her faintly exotic, socially oblique mother, who filled her carriage with odd things in the supermarket behind an invisible veil of prickly, old world aloofness.

Jess Mitchell labored dutifully through his classes, admirably overcoming whatever literacy deficit was the result of his presumable Caribbean infancy; Felipika Mitchell had a boundless talent for speaking—no, shouting—out of turn in her reading group, but, apparently due to her alternate spells of hyperactivity and listlessness (depending on the period of the schoolday), showed no great early skills for composition, reading comprehension, or the arts, although she might have been good in math if she had ever bothered to check her unfathomably messy work. She had no real girlfriends except for a timid gaggle of younger girls whom she mercilessly bossed around at recess, although she seemed quite popular with the boys—especially the cruder, low-class ones—with whom she could either be found wrestling or showing off her underpants.

Jess Mitchell was demonstrating great promise in his art classes, and his work—construction-paper montages of what he thought Puerto Rico might look like (all jewel-blue ocean and lemon-lime-colored palm trees)—was proudly hung in the lobby of the school for the spring fair. Felipika Mitchell played tuba (poorly, even for a sixth-grade novice) in the school band before she had a tantrum one day in rehearsal and threw the leased instrument down on the floor, permanently gashing its broad, gleaming mouth. Jess Mitchell broke his teachers' hearts with his enormous, sad brown eyes and single-minded determination to conquer the SRA box. Felipika Mitchell terrorized her teachers by burping in their faces and announcing before the entire class that they had a booger hanging out their nose or food stuck in their teeth—to the point where the teachers would sit around in the lounge, smoking and plotting the various things they could do to Miss Felipika Mitchell if they ever met her outside of class, in a dark alley.

And it was also understood, vaguely, that adorable Jess Mitchell and odious Felipika Mitchell had a younger brother coming up quietly through the grades. He was neither adopted nor dark and stocky like Jess, but somewhat fragile, with translucent white skin underneath which you could see the murmuring blue veins on his forehead, and a shock of almost-black hair. Neither a slow charmer like his brother nor a hellion like his sister, he wasn't an all-A's student, but he far from bordered on academic delinquency. He did okay in math and science, and liked to read immensely, even though his oral and written expression lacked force. He took piano lessons, and so far hadn't vented any prepubescent rage on the piano itself.

His teachers called him Tommy, but they knew that his brother and sister called him Tigger, for one reason or another. They also knew that he worshipped his brother and sister in an almost mute, awestruck fashion, and that they in turn were fiercely, stoically protective of him—this much was apparent

from the way the three of them sat together in an imper-
meable, whispering huddle at lunch, the one period of the
day when they bridged their vast social and temperamental
differences and effaced their own individual personalities, like
humbled siblings gathered together to console each other over
the long illness or sudden death of a parent.

He was the last of the Mitchells, this Thomas, the baby of
the family—of course, he was I.

To this day, I remember my father as a basically decent man.
Yes—he drank, he was often loud and exuberantly profane,
and some of his business dealings might have been a little
crooked, but he never hit or harrassed any of us, nor our
mother, nor anyone. He wanted to be jovial and generous, to
see to it that the rest of the world had a good time, because it
was the only thing he knew how to do with any aggressive certitude, and when presented with anyone who wasn't a
like-minded soul—someone inward, someone prone to melancholy or cynicism, someone from whom he sensed the faintest
disapproval—he tended to withdraw in blustering, exasperated confusion.

I remember an evening when my father came home late
from work and stuck his head into Jess's bedroom, where Jess
lay cobbling out his math homework long after Flip had flung
her own disastrous half-attempt aside. 'How you doin',
Bandito?' he'd say. For some reason, he had stumbled upon
Bandito as a nickname for his eldest son. He seemed to choke
on 'Jess' as much as Jess choked on 'Dad', and of course no one
actually called Jess by his given name.

Jess looked up briefly before turning back to his math, his
face the very image of affectless indifference. 'Okay, thanks.'

'You workin' hard, Bandito? What's that, math?'

'Yeah. Would you not call me that, please?'

'Call you what?'

'Bandito. It's not my name.'

My father laughed a dry, impatient laugh. 'Well, that's just a nickname. Whaddya want me to call you?'

'How about my name? Jess. That's what Ma calls me.'

'You want me to call you Jessie?' my father said, all professional, affable laissez-faire, as he might have spoken to a new stockboy at his company.

'No. Just Jess is fine,' Jess said, without looking up.

'But your Ma calls you Jessie,' my father said after a pause.

'But I wish you'd call me just Jess.'

Another long pause from my father, not necessarily of anger, because Jess never really incited anger—he seemed always to go about his life well above the realm of discipline and reproach. From my father, it was the usual response to Jess—an empty bafflement, a blank illiteracy. He fingered the knot of his tie. Jess still didn't look up, but his pencil was motionless, waiting.

'All right, Ban—all right. Jess. Whatever suits your fancy.'

'Thank you.' Finally Jess looked up, repeated himself in exactly the same voice that betrayed nothing beneath its calm surface. 'Thank you.' And he turned back to his work.

Then my father poked his head into my room, where I had been lost in a child's version of *Twenty Thousand Leagues Under the Sea* until I heard the low, defensive tones coming from next door.

'Hey, Tigger, my little man. You workin' hard?'

I looked up. I'd never be especially close to this bluff former salesman who overwhelmed me with his big liquory voice and his strong liquory breath, but I didn't hate him either. Jess, on the other hand, I adored. What, then, was the right tone to strike?

'I'm reading this book!' I exclaimed, stiffly overeager. 'It's so good, Daddy. It's so exciting. I'm gonna write my book report on it.'

'What is it?' I held it out for him to see the cover. 'Oh, yeah,' he said, feigning slow recognition. 'Oh, yeah. That's a good one.' He was lying, of course. He'd hardly read a book in his life.

'I'm on the part where they think an octopus is gonna wreck the submarine,' I continued desperately. 'Daddy, it's *scary*.'

'Don't be scared of anything, Tigger,' he said, knee-jerk, and then, as if someone had cued her to come stand in for the very image of fearlessness, Flip bounded through her bedroom door and into the room, where she flung herself around our father's waist.

'Daddy, Daddy, you're such a fatty!'

'Whoa, baby. Whoa, Flipper! Don't call your daddy a fatty,' he boomed, kneeling down and swallowing her up in his arms. He came to life, then. It was typical—when he came home, he seemed to forget who he was, how he was supposed to be, until he saw Flip, whereupon he gladly reclaimed himself. The two of them exploded into yards of raucous, vulgar laughter. I recoiled on my neat little bed. Next door, I heard Jess close his door—no histrionic slam, just a firm, chilly *ka-boom*.

'Daddy, in school today—' Flip could hardly pull herself together. I looked at her, hair streaming down in her face, corduroyed legs dancing in place. She was a mess.

'Take it easy, Flipper,' my father said, brushing hair out of her eyes. 'In school today. Tell me. What is it?'

'In school today,' Flip began again breathlessly, full of self-congratulation. 'You know Mrs. Cardoni?'

'Sure, sure,' my father egged her on. It didn't matter that he didn't know who Mrs. Cardoni was. He never quibbled with the truth on little things like this; it was part of his business plan.

'Daddy, she's such a bitch!'

'Hey,' my father laughed, 'don't use language like that. Your mother doesn't like it.'

'Hmph,' went Flip, rolling her eyes. 'Anyway, I drew an ugly picture of her in art class, like, with slime coming out of her eyes and ears, and the art teacher said he loved it! Then he hung it up with all the others, even though I wrote Mrs. Cardoni's name on the bottom of it. And Mrs. Cardoni *saw it!*' Flip's voice went through the roof; she was nearly foaming at the mouth.

'Oh, honey,' my father said with a burlesque groan, taking Flip up in another hug. 'Oh, honey, you can't be doin' stuff like that all the time, or you're not gonna have any allies in this world. What're you gonna do without any allies, huh?'

Flip laughed—a low, oddly seductive burble and played with the knot of my father's tie. '*You're* my ally,' she said, plopping herself down on his knee. 'You are.'

'I'm always your ally, baby.'

'And Jess's my ally. And Tiggah too. Right, Tiggah?'

What did she expect me to say? Of course I was her ally—I didn't have any choice—but I hated it when she virtually made love to our father right before our very eyes, knowing full well that when she was in the room, he saw Jess and me as no more than her own mute bookends.

'What, Flip?' I said, not looking up, feigning absorption in my book.

'You're my ally, right?'

I kept my eyes on the pages of my book, as though it were a question too passing, too trivial, to cobble out an answer.

'*Right?*'

'Hunh?'

'Tig, your sister's askin' you a question,' my father said dutifully, not even looking at me.

'*What?*' I burst out, with much more force than I had expected.

Now Flip looked like she was ready to explode. '*Are . . . you . . . my . . . ally?*' she said through gritted teeth.

'Yes, Flip, I'm your ally, whatever that means,' I said, trying to roll my eyes as she did.

Then, in her usual fashion, she transformed. The teeth

unclenched and her face unfolded into a smile so radiant it
threatened to seduce all the world. Gently, she unlaced herself
from my father and walked over to my bed. 'Thank you,
Tiggah,' she said, putting her arms around me and scratching
my back for a moment. 'You're my favorite little brutha. You
know that, right?'

'Uh hunh,' I sighed, trying to sound weary, but the truth
was that I craved attention from Flip. Everybody did, in fact.
She exerted this force, which somehow meant that if you
could withstand the tremendous rigors of giving Flip what
she wanted, you would also come to know the pleasures of
doing so as well. At this time, she was ten years old.

Her sentimental moment was over. 'Now I gotta call
Frances,' she said. (Frances was her only friend at school, a
cross-eyed, pear-shaped clarinet player who had developed a
weirdly nonverbal fixation with Flip. Their friendship con-
sisted mainly of Flip discoursing for hours on end about her
problems with various people at school, as Frances nodded or
grunted along in reverent silence. Jess secretly called Frances
Igor to Flip's Dr. Frankenstein, which seemed like an appropriate analogy to me.)

'Are we still playin' baseball on Saturday, Daddy?' Flip
asked, kissing him on the forehead and leapfrogging over the
place in my bedroom doorway where he still crouched—
unbuckled and rumpled, home for the night to the big house
that was rightfully his, rough-housing with his best girl.

'You bet we are, honey.' He rose to his feet with a slow
expulsion of *Oh, Jeez, Daddy's gettin' old.* 'Don't ever stop
readin', Tig,' he said, exiting, Flip just behind him. 'It keeps
the mind sharp.'

In a moment, I heard the soft sound of the door closing on
my parents' bedroom. Inside, he would make himself a scotch
from the bottle of cheap stuff he kept on his dresser, pouring it
into the dirty glass my mother for some reason refused to take
down to the kitchen. Slowly, he'd strip out of his coat and tie,

with vague plans to pad downstairs and finish his scotch in the company of my mother, who might have been awaiting his arrival over the treacly likes of *Eight Is Enough* or *Little House on the Prairie*. Sometimes he made it downstairs, only to fall asleep in the armchair, leaving my mother to dislodge the scotch glass from his hand before it spilled. Most nights, though, he didn't—one of us would find him snoring, out cold on top of the sheets in nothing but his boxers, his gold watch and one sock, the scotch glass either sitting upright on the floor, barely touched, or atop his chest, empty and on its side.

I felt peculiarly alone moments after they had both left me, so I padded next door to Jess's room and knocked on the door.

'Uh hunh?' from inside, low and toneless.

'Jess, it's Tig. Can I come in?'

It was a few seconds before the doorknob turned. There was Jess, so utterly dependable and mournfully handsome at the age of twelve, his enormous brown eyes slightly dazed from an hour of algebra. He exerted this power over me— glimpsing him down the hallway at school, or across the playing field, or even now, in our own house after several hours of his absence, he could still move me to wonderment as though I had never seen him before, as though he weren't even my own brother.

'What's wrong, Tig?' he asked, his eyes narrowing slightly.

'Daddy came home and gave Flip a big hug, but he didn't give one to me.'

Jess laughed softly. 'He didn't give one to me, either.' Then he pulled me inside, closed the door, and drew me close. 'Aw, Tigger,' he crooned, running his hands through my hair. I could hear his heart beating, steadily and surely, through his soccer jersey. 'You don't get enough attention, do you?'

'I don't care,' I said stoically, although the utterance of what happened to be such a plain fact in our house almost pushed me to the brink of tears. I pulled him closer and pressed my head into his stomach, glancing around his room of posters:

Celtics posters, Red Sox posters, Patriots posters—and a copy of the flag of the Commonwealth of Puerto Rico that Auntie Lippy had sent him last year.

'What are you working on?' I finally asked him.

'Algebra. You want me to show you how you do it?'

I nodded—I hadn't the least interest in algebra but I seized the chance to curl up with him on the floor and doze under his soft, donnish voice. We had hardly begun when the door flew open.

'Tigger, what are you doing in here bothering your brother when he's supposed to be doing his homework?' We both stopped short and looked up. It was our mother, haggard, our father's empty scotch glass in her hand.

'I'm showing him how to do algebra, Ma,' Jess answered on my behalf.

'Jess, honey,' our mother said, sitting down on his bed (she smoothed it out first) and taking his face in her hand (he winced visibly), 'Tigger doesn't need to know how to do algebra yet. He's only in the fourth grade. But you *do*. Now, did you finish all your homework?'

He rolled his eyes. 'Yeah, Ma.'

'Are you hungry? You want some cereal before you go to bed?'

'No, I'm not hungry. Why don't you ask *Tig* if he's hungry, too?'

Our mother looked surprised for a moment, then looked at me, wide-eyed. 'Well, Tigger, are *you* hungry?'

I didn't answer. I wanted her to put her hand to my cheek, or atop my head, or *something*—I wanted her to earn my response. So I just looked up at her tired face and tried to look inscrutable.

She stared back at me for what seemed like ages before she finally opened her mouth as if to speak, then didn't, then finally did. 'Your piano sounded nice today, Tigger. Was that for your lesson on Wednesday?'

'Uh hunh,' I managed.

'You're gonna be the next Beethoven, man,' Jess said.

'See, honey?' my mother said. 'All your hard work is paying off.'

'I guess so.'

'Do you wanna bowl of cereal before bed?'

'That's all right.'

'All right,' she sighed, bending down to kiss me, then Jess, on the cheek. 'Get to bed soon, then, okay? Jess, honey, make sure Tigger doesn't stay up much more. He's gotta get up earlier than you two for school.'

'All right, Ma.'

'Good-night, guys,' she said, before turning to leave.

'Is Daddy still up?' I asked her, startling myself.

'No, Tig. He's asleep already. So keep hushy, okay?'

'All right.'

She was gone then, clicking the door back into place behind her. When she left, something slightly sour hung in the air between Jess and me. I couldn't look him straight in the face because of it, so instead I stared deep into the binding of the math book.

'She's *loca*,' Jess whispered to me, trying out one of his Spanish class words.

'What's that?' I asked, not looking up.

'Crazy,' he whispered. I laughed soundlessly into the book, then curled up on the floor, appeased. He scratched my back for me, and I would have fallen contentedly asleep right there if Flip hadn't burst in, sobbing, her face contorted with fear.

'Jess, Jess!' She fell to her knees and took Jess's hands in hers. 'Daddy's dead! I know it! I went in to say good-night to him and he wouldn't wake up, even though I kept sticking my finger in his stomach. We gotta do something! We gotta call an ambulance!'

'Flip, settle down,' he said, taking her in his arms, where she collapsed, utterly and wholeheartedly distraught. 'Daddy's not dead. He's just drunk and he passed out, like he does every night.'

'Oh, no, Jess, this time I know it!'

'I'll bet you not,' Jess said, laughing.

'Daddy can't die! He *can't* die! What would I do without him?'

'I don't know. We're not gonna put up with you.'

'Fuck *you*!' Flip sobbed, pounding his back as he laughed.

But Flip was undeterred. 'Jess, Tigger, why does Daddy drink so much? He's gonna die, I know it, then we'll be all alone. Who's gonna pay the bills?'

'We'll all get jobs at Dairy Queen and chip in,' Jess said reasonably. 'It'll be fun.' We smiled at each other over Flip's shoulder, but Flip kept on sobbing. 'I'm just kidding, Felipika—'

'Don't *call* me that,' Flip snorted.

'I'm just kidding. Daddy's not gonna die. Everything's gonna be fine.'

Flip composed and withdrew herself and stared Jess in the face. She ran a hand through his black hair. Then, with a tremendous sigh, she heaved herself onto his bed, where she lay prostrate. 'Jess?' she called, staring up at the ceiling.

'Yes?' he called back comically in the same intonation, looking at me with a raised eyebrow. I glanced back at him warily.

'Aren't you gonna come lie down with me a little before bed?' Flip had pulled this before, but it hadn't been in quite some time. We thought she was getting a little too old for it.

'It's late, Felipika,' Jess called back softly, but I couldn't help noticing the tone in his voice had changed.

'Just for a few minutes, Jesus?' Flip's tone never strayed from its steady, prepubescent pitch.

Jess looked down awkwardly at his book, then at me, then at his book. 'All right,' he finally said with a huge manufactured sigh, heaving himself up. 'Just for a few minutes.' He went over to the bed and laid down on his side with his back

to Flip. She purred in satisfaction and put her arms under his
and around his chest. Their legs were locked together at right
angles. This was the position they always made; they called it
Making the Chair.

I just sat there on the floor, abandoned, too paralyzed with
humiliation even to get up and leave. Finally, Jess looked up
from the bed and over at me. 'Get over here, Tigger.'

Flip looked up, too. 'Yeah,' she said, grinning my way. 'Get
over here, Tigger.'

Without a word, I did, slipping onto the bed in front of Jess,
twisting my butt into a comfortable position against his lap
while he slipped his arms under my own and around my chest
until I could hear his steady breathing right behind my ear like
the roar of the ocean up at Rye. Flip reached over and ran a
hand through my hair.

'I love you guys,' she said. 'You're my two favorite guys.'

'What about Daddy?' Jess laughed.

'Daddy's a man,' Flip said sensibly. 'I mean guys. You know.
Boys.'

'I'm not a boy anymore,' Jess protested.

'Oh yes, you are,' Flip said in her know-it-all voice. 'Oh
yes, you are. And so are you, Tigger. You're both little boys.'

'What are you, then?' I couldn't help myself from asking.

There was a pause before Flip answered, primly, 'A young
lady.'

Jess and I erupted laughing. 'Shut up! Shut the fuck up!'
Flip nearly screamed, but she was laughing, too. You could
feel all three of our bodies rocking and shuddering together.
We subsided; we started to fall asleep even though we knew
we'd be awakened in a matter of minutes by our mother, who
always put us into our separate beds without ever comment-
ing on our sleeping arrangements.

Anyway, this is how it always worked out: the three of us
abed, arms linked, Jess in the middle.

Five

Flip was prescient: Two years later, our father died of an aneurysm, helping a customer carry cases of scotch into his air-conditioned package store on a sweltering day in July. He had been out late the night before, at a foray to a Red Sox game that he had organized for his thirteen salesmen and one saleswoman, and they all later recalled how he had complained (good-naturedly) of a headache that night, writing it off on the Fenway Franks and the bad beer. We were all at the house in Rye when the package store owner, a beery, cheery man named Jerry Mullane, called us from the hospital to tell us the news. It was a Friday afternoon and we were waiting for our father to put his week's business aside, drive up the coast and take his usual six o'clock swim with us before we showered for dinner. We were playing Monopoly on the front porch when the phone rang. Our mother, who had been reading *Redbook*, said, mischievously, 'Betcha that's Daddy!' and headed into the house, the screen door slamming behind her. In a minute, we heard her screams and her sobbing. We all ran inside.

She was bent over the kitchen table, the phone still in her hand, the grape leaves that she had picked off the road the day before soaking in a huge silver bowl in front of her. 'Daddy's dead!' she cried. 'Your daddy's dead!'

Flip cried back as though someone had just shot her in the chest. She ran to our mother and the two of them clutched each other, screaming in the big kitchen filled with afternoon coastal light. Jess looked like he was going to throw up; soundlessly, he stalked over to our mother and Flip and put his arms around both of them, squeezing them tight.

I didn't know what to do; I wanted to join them, but they scared me, too. I ran out of the house barefoot—suddenly I was bawling in a terrifying frenzy of shock—across the street, mindless of cars, down the asphalt, through the hot, soft sand and halfway out into the low tide, where I stood, staring at the horizon of sky and water, crying and crying. I didn't even know what my father had died from, or how, but suddenly he seemed as vast and unattainable as the point where the sky met the water. He wouldn't be coming back tonight; he belonged to that endless horizon of all you'll never reach, twenty thousand leagues under the sea now. He had intimidated me and entertained me, failed to understand me and brushed me aside, and instantly I couldn't imagine life in either of our houses without him.

I can't even remember how long I stood there crying in the low tide before I turned around, dizzy, and walked back up to the house—from across the street it suddenly seemed much too large and frail, too wide open for just our mother and the three of us. They were still in the kitchen, my mother and Flip clutching each other's arms, stricken, Jess sitting alone on the other side of the table, his face an absolute blank. He nodded for me to come over, and when I did, he stood up and took me in his arms. We heard game shows on the TV, dimly, in the other room. No one uttered a word.

'We have to go to the hospital,' my mother finally said in a hollowed-out voice. Jess nodded. The old station wagon was waiting in the broad driveway in front of the house. But none of us moved to go to the hospital for at least another hour.

*

At the request of my father's people, the funeral was a Roman Catholic one, with services held at the old church in the part of Lowell where my father had grown up, and a wake at the very same funeral home where my father's father had been buried some twelve years ago. The wake was exactly as he would have liked it to be: a testament to his far-ranging popularity, crowded with all the Irish of Lowell and all the liquor-trafficking of Eastern Massachusetts, a sea of thickly gregarious, red-faced men in suits and ties whose occupations or affiliations to my father escaped us entirely. The noise in the room crested and fell all day long: the first cursory efforts at respectful murmurs, just until an impromptu reunion of five or six old buddies and their walnut-faced Irish wives found its momentum, then the loud exclamations of a bar at happy hour hitting full swing. Until they remembered that it was a *wake*, after all, and they quieted their tones—but only out of respect to the widow, because when you thought of Tommy Mitchell, you didn't want to bow your head dolefully or have to suppress the grimace of mixed emotions—no, you wanted to smile, to laugh out loud, to get an anecdote off your chest.

The widow, of course, was my mother, Tommy's shy Greek wife, shell-shocked and stoic in a black dress, standing ramrod straight for hours on end in the receiving line, clutching a tear-streaked Flip with one hand and me with the other (my whole face itched from the sympathetic pinches and kisses of women I had never seen before), while Jess shuffled awkwardly on my right in a coat and tie, even more out of place than my mother in this heaving room full of the custard of Irish Lowell. I couldn't help noticing that, even in her grief, transactions were taking place: longtime colleagues of my father would approach her, take her hands, kiss her on the cheek, then hand her a business card and utter a few short words that obviously had to do with something other than condolences. Our parents' lawyer, Mr. Kittredge, was there, too, with his dry Yankee kisses for our mother and Flip, and stiff and not unkind handshakes for Jess and me. He was old Topsfield, with an office in Boston, and he was also to be our trust fund officer over the coming years.

'Thank you, you're so kind, I'll be in touch very soon,' my mother would murmur to each and every one of them, slipping the business cards into her sad little black purse, the silent center of a congregation of mostly strangers.

The wake passed painfully but uneventfully until near its very end, when Flip—who had been ominously silent all day save a steady stream of private tears—slipped away from the evaporating receiving line and walked toward the open casket, step by tiny step. She did it so quietly that no one really noticed her but me, and Jess, who spoke out as she passed.

'Flip, don't,' he said. 'Wait until we all go up together to say a prayer.'

But Flip didn't listen to him. In a moment, she was standing over the face of our lost father, and in a moment the room cracked in half with her screams.

'Daddy! Daddy! Don't leave me!'

The entire room fell silent. Flip fell to her knees in front of the casket, clutching the railing.

'Don't leave me, Daddy!'

'Felipika, you stop it this instant, young lady,' our mother called, tense, from the line.

'C'mon, Flip,' Jess said, low.

'Yeah, Flip,' I seconded.

She spun around, her eyes wild. 'No, I won't stop it this instant, you fucking bitch!' she screamed back at our mother, and the gasps flew up in the room to the ceiling. 'Daddy was the only one that loved me. *You* never did, you only loved Jess, who's not even your real son—'

'Flip, *shut up*,' Jess shouted, harsher now.

'Yeah, Flip, shut up,' I seconded, shocked and indignant.

'And now you've still got Jess, *but I've got no one!*' Flip looked around the whole room wildly, taking in a sea of horrified faces, then bounded up from the kneeler and streaked from the room, dodging between the legs of callers. In a minute we heard the front door of the funeral parlor slam shut.

'Just ignore that,' Jess said after an agonizing moment of silence. 'I'll deal with it,' and in a second he was out the door as well.

Hastily, people approached my mother to bid goodbye. She stared past them into the middle distance, even while accepting their parting kisses, their apologies, their assurances. When the room was empty save the murmuring presence of my father's aunt and her two daughters conferring in the back, my mother collapsed into a chair and began to cry, the tears cutting ghastly streaks into her make-up. I stood before her, too wary to take her in my arms. She surprised me, though, by taking me in hers, hugging me longer and harder than she ever had before.

'Tigger, honey?'

'Yeah, Ma?'

'It's not true what Flip said. You know that, don't you? I love all of you equally. You're all my children, it doesn't matter if you're adopted or not, and you're all special to me. You know that, right?'

'Uh hunh,' I said dutifully.

'Have you gone all these years thinking I loved Jess more than you?'

'No,' I said, glad that I was staring over her shoulder.

She squeezed me closer. 'Good, because it's not so. I love you so much, you couldn't even know. You're my baby, Tigger.'

'I know. I love you, too.'

'We're going to get by okay. I'm going to take over Daddy's business.'

'We'll help you.'

'Let's just take it one day at a time. God's gonna help us, too, you know.'

I wondered when she was going to release me. At length, she said, 'Do you want to go over to Daddy and pray with me now?'

'No,' I said, and I was surprised at how easily the truth slipped out. 'I want to go find Jess and Flip.'

'Okay,' she said, letting me go. Her face was ravaged by tears and make-up, and what I felt for her in that moment was something more akin to Christian pity than filial devotion. 'Go find them and bring them back here, okay? It's been a long day.'

'Okay, Ma.'

'Tell that Flip that I love her, please?' she called back to me with a feeble laugh.

'I will, Ma.'

I stepped outside into the sweltering afternoon, set on finding Flip and Jess. But when I was about to turn the corner of the funeral home, I heard them in the alley, and thought better of joining them. Instead I crouched down and listened.

Flip was still sobbing, and Jess was protesting over her tears: 'Fucking bitch? Fucking bitch? *You're* the fucking bitch, Flip! You just humiliated Ma in front of a whole room full of people. God's gonna punish that, Flip. I know it.'

'What do you care?' Flip choked back. '*You're* not gonna get in trouble, and in a few weeks you're gonna go away to school anyway, and leave me an' Tigger all alone with—with *her*— an' we're never gonna see you, an'—'

'What are you talking about?' Jess interrupted. 'St. Peter's is, like, an hour away. I'm coming home on weekends and holidays all the time.'

'It doesn't matter,' Flip cried. 'It still doesn't matter.'

'What's *wrong* with you?' A pause. Then again, softer: 'What's wrong, Felipika?'

Soft, now, from Flip: 'I can't live here without you, Jess.'

Jess laughed uncomfortably. 'Come on, Flip. It's only for two years, then you're probably coming to St. Peter's, too.

Then Tigger after you. We'll all be there together for a year, right? And in the meantime you've got Tigger here.' He paused. 'And Ma.'

'That bitch,' Flip scoffed.

'Hey, watch it!'

'And as for Tigger—'

'Yeah?' Jess asked. 'What about Tigger?' My heart was pounding in my chest.

'He can't live without you either, Jess. You know we're both crazy about you.'

Jess laughed again, more uncomfortably. 'I love you guys, too, Flip. You know I do. But I gotta learn to be by myself, you know, because—'

'Jess, I'm so crazy about you.' Flip had that old, calm, insistent tone in her little twelve-year-old voice again.

'Because—' Jess spluttered.

'Will you just give me one of your big hugs?'

'Flip, come on, baby!'

'Just one?'

'Jesus Christ,' I heard Jess say, exasperated—and then there was silence. I could have peered around the corner of the funeral home, but I didn't. For some reason, I didn't. I just sat tight and listened. Did I hear rustlings or murmurs? I couldn't tell.

Suddenly, Jess spoke, aggrieved: 'Oh my God. Oh my God.'

Flip shushed him. 'Don't worry about it, Jess. It's all right.'

'Oh, *God*.'

'Jess, it's all right!' An awkward pause. 'Jess?'

'*What*, Flip? *What?*'

'Thank you. Thank you.' Flip laughed a little, and so did Jess, reluctantly. They were silent again. I just crouched there, behind the hedges in front of the funeral home, wanting to know what it had felt like for Flip right then to be in Jess's arms, and suddenly feeling distinctly alone.

S i x

Our mother's crazy sister Lippy couldn't make the funeral because she was in the closing weekend of a supper show in New York, but she arrived at the house in Rye two days later to take a vacation and spend the rest of the summer with us. We hadn't seen her in about six years, but I remembered her as this theatrical creature from another planet, which is why—when she appeared on our front porch in gladiator sandals and a flowing white dress, her mounds of salt-and-pepper hair hidden behind a huge straw hat and her braceleted hands clutching what looked like an old-fashioned cargo bag—I was surprised to realize for the first time, behind her blood red lipstick and painted eyes, just how much she looked like our mother.

'This *isn't* a happy family,' she said, releasing my teary mother from a long embrace and staring at the three of us. 'I haven't seen *you* in centuries,' she said, bending down to plant a lipstick kiss on Jess's cheek (he scowled and wiped it off as soon as she turned her back), 'or *you*,' she said, embracing Flip, her namesake, who hugged her back limply and peered suspiciously at her shoes, 'or *you*,' she said, stooping down and putting both her cool, powdery hands on either side of my face before kissing me full on the forehead. She smelled like something exotic, some mixture of perfume and tea, a smell that within a few days I realized I actually didn't mind.

'This is the one that used to do the shimmy in the crib, remember, Nikki?' Lippy said, her hands still on my face. 'Remember, when I'd put on the stereo?'

'I remember that,' my mother said thinly, as though the memory of anything from that age of marriage and toddling children filled her with pain. 'He's a musician now, Lippy.'

'I knew that,' Lippy glowed, turning back to me. 'You're the piano maestro, right?'

'I don't play so good,' I said.

'We'll see about that. There's got to be a piano in this beautiful old house, right?'

I nodded. A year ago, at a flea market in Northampton, somebody had been selling an old upright for one hundred dollars, and I begged my parents to buy it for the summer house, which they did, even though my mother was convinced it wouldn't fit through the front door, which it had—easily.

'You're going to play for me,' Lippy said.

'I don't know.'

'Oh, yes you are,' she laughed. 'But in the meantime'—she opened up her cargo bag, and fished around inside—'I brought gifts from New York for all of you.'

'You didn't have to do that, Lippy,' my mother said.

'It's obvious I did! Look at all of you!' Lippy laughed, and no one laughed back. She looked at us all sternly, then shook her head. 'I'm not having this complete and utter *gravity*,' she intoned dramatically. 'You know what?'

Everyone was silent. 'What?' Jess finally said.

Lippy doffed her hat and took the pins out of her hair. 'In New York, in the industry, you wouldn't believe how many young people I know—a few girls, but mostly boys, talented boys, all wonderful musicians and singers and actors—who left their little towns all across the country and don't even *talk* to their families back home. Their mothers and fathers don't know *anything* about them—when they're sick, or broke,

or terribly unhappy—and sometimes I think they don't want
to know, because they can only picture the worst, and people
would rather pretend that the things they fear don't even
exist.'

'Lippy, that's horrible,' my mother gasped.

'It is! Sometimes I feel like they've got nobody except each
other, the blind leading the blind—and *me*, for God's sake.
And I can't be *everyone's* mother! But look around'—and she
took us all in with one sweeping gesture, bracelets ringing—
'Look at all of you!'

Which we did, awkwardly, a round-robin of dumb glances.

'You've all got each *other*. You—we—are *family*.'

None of us spoke. None of us knew what to say. Finally,
Flip, her throat catching, said absurdly, 'We are?'

'You *are*! And everything is going'—and she kissed my
mother on the forehead—'to'—then Flip and Jess, whose grimace twisted into a reluctant smile—'be'—she swept down on
me, more scent of perfume and tea—'*just fine*.' She engulfed
me in her arms. That was that—for some reason, some odd
collision of misery and relief, I started bawling. So did Flip and
Ma.

'Get a grip, you guys!' Jess exploded before he started bawling, too.

When we had collected ourselves, Lippy reached down into
her valise. 'Look what I have here,' she said, pulling out three
gleaming strands of shell and rock, passing one each to my
mother and to Flip. 'I bought these when I was singing this
winter at a resort in San Juan.'

'In Puerto Rico?' Jess asked, skeptical.

'The very one,' Lippy said, handing him the final strand.
'This one's for you, because it's a man's piece. You can tell
because it's shorter than the others, and the shells are smaller.
See, you wear it like this.' Lippy opened the front of Jess's
shirt and clipped the chain back. 'Look at those against that
tan! Savage!'

'It's really from Puerto Rico?' Jess asked again.

'Last I checked.'

'Jess is Puerto Rican,' Flip offered helpfully.

'I know *that*, thank you,' then to Jess, 'Don't worry, honey, you'll get there some day.' Lippy spread Jess's collar a notch wider. He looked away, blushing deeply underneath his tan. Flip rolled her eyes, fingering her chain ambivalently.

'Didn't you get Tigger anything?' Flip blurted, effectively expressing just what I was uneasily thinking.

'What do you think, Tigger?' Lippy asked, hands on hips. 'Do you think I got something for my maestro?'

'I don't know,' I said, but of course I did. I really did.

Out of her valise she pulled a large box, squatted at my feet on the porch, opened it, and unfastened several layers of wrapping until she held in her palm a triangular instrument, lacquered white and black, fitted with chevrons of old chrome. I didn't have one, but I knew what it was.

'You know what it is?' she asked.

I nodded. 'It's a metrophone.'

She laughed. 'It's a metro*nome*, but close enough, darling. You won't need it forever, but you'll always want to keep it. It's an antique—*Deco*. You know how much it's worth, Tigger?'

I shook my head. It was a good-looking thing, I had to concede. It reminded me of some old black-and-white dancing movie I had once watched late at night with Flip and Jess: elegant.

Lippy flipped its switch, the steady, alto tick-tock of the mallet commanding everyone's attention, including hers. 'I don't know either, exactly, but it's worth a lot. A lot.' She concentrated on the mallet, as did I, as did we all. 'It was Tony's. He was my best accompanist at Julia's Room, for five years, until his cancer set in. Of course he didn't use it. Didn't have to, because, *God*, he could swing a song.' She laughed a little, low.

'Doesn't he still want it?' I asked.

'Can't you tell he's *dead*, Tigger, you idiot?' Flip broke in. 'He's *dead*, like Daddy!'

'Felipika!' my mother said.

Lippy just laughed again—already I loved her laugh. 'It's all right, Nikki. He *is* dead. It happened just two weeks before Tommy. They were about the same age, in fact, and it's almost as though Tony were my husband like your daddy was your mom's, even though we never actually got *married*.' For the first time, I heard a strange catch in Lippy's voice, before she caught herself—'but look what's *mine*!' she sang, holding the metronome aloft. 'Look what's *yours*,' she said, flipping off the switch and handing the piece into both my careful palms.

'Thank you,' I said in the sudden silence.

She kissed me on both cheeks, brushed hair out of my eyes. 'You're welcome, my darling.'

There was a clatter on the far end of the porch. The black-spotted crab we had captured that morning had toppled its watery pail. Now it side-scuttled across the wet floor boards and flung itself over the edge of the porch, into the lilac bushes below.

'Ugh!' Lippy shrieked theatrically. 'Nature!'

'There goes Pedro,' Jess shrugged.

'Nikki, I've *got* it!' Lippy ran over to my preoccupied mother and grabbed her shoulder. 'Let's all pile in the station wagon and go to Marky's and have lots and lots of *lobster*. I haven't had New England lobster in ages.'

'It's so expensive, Lip,' my mother frowned. It had never quite set in with her that we were pretty rich.

'It's *my* treat. Nikki, I'm dying for lobster.' She whirled around to Jess, Flip and me. 'Aren't you people dying for lobster?'

Of course we all screamed yes—it seemed like the obvious thing to do, and besides, we had hardly left the TV set, and our mother her too-big, king-sized bed, since the funeral.

'You're all ganging up on me,' my mother sulked. And then,

for the first time since our father died, our mother, as though it killed her, smiled.

This time it was Lippy who was right—if there was ever a miserable family, it was us, and if we had ever needed her, we needed her then. Not only was our father gone, but it was to be our very last summer together in one place for several years: a fact that might have caused incalculable grief and hysteria if we hadn't had Lippy there to distract us from it—and, in a sense, from each other.

No one could distract like Lippy, whose appetite for inspired craziness seemed as steadfast as our own mother's distaste for it. Before Lippy, we woke in the morning to funereal domestic silence pierced only by the gulls swooping around the front porch—after, to the smell of strong coffee and eggs Benedict in the kitchen, where Lippy 'played house' until her itchy alto showtunes eventually summoned us from bed and to the table, where she prodded us with sleepyhead cracks until first Flip, then Jess and me, started cracking back. Before Lippy, our mother walked around in the black hole of the present—after, when she came back with Lippy from picking grape leaves or shopping the flea markets, we saw traces of a girl, dark, spirited and big-hearted, that had existed long before she ever met Tommy Mitchell. Before Lippy, Flip cried a lot, Jess brooded, and I wanted to be invisible—after, when Lippy insisted that we all go kite-flying on the beach each night before dinner, or when she popped out of her black bathing suit one afternoon in the high tide when we were all trying to knock her off the rubber raft—well, after, we changed. She burst into our suspicious, insular threesome and demanded that we make room for one more, demanded that we accept her, like it or not.

Eventually we did. Jess was wariest of her, this song-belting, eye-rolling woman who seemed to live for attention, then, suddenly, focused all her attention on you and seemed to know exactly what you were thinking. For years now, Jess had been painting, landscape watercolors mostly, and good ones for his age his teachers at Montserrat's after-school classes told him, but, except for our mother's drooling 'My Jess is so artistic,' no one had ever really paid them much attention, or bothered to compliment him on them—it was simply what Jess did. Now, suddenly, there was this woman who asked to see his entire collection, who inquired after how he achieved a particular shade of green, who told him how crazy he'd be for the Gauguins at the Museum of Modern Art, where she would take him when we all came to visit her in New York at Christmastime, who sat quietly behind him, smoking, while he painted a view over the dunes, then, eventually, before him.

'Are you waiting for me to paint you?' he asked her one day, point blank, as she sat behind his easel, humming while he mixed colors on a scrap of cardboard.

Lippy laughed. 'What makes you ask that?'

Jess laughed back. 'Why are you wearing that crazy hat today?' he asked, pointing to it, a ridiculous outsize straw number bordered with silk gardenias.

'This old thing?' she asked, touching it, all mock-innocence. 'Because . . . because of the sun!'

'Auntie Lippy, the sun's going down. That's why I'm out here painting.'

'You're damn right it's going down!' she protested. 'That's when the rays are worst. You can't feel them, but take it from me'—and she drew the brim of the hat down tighter over her head, shoving her enormous black sunglasses up higher on her nose's prominent bridge—'this is when they'll getcha.'

'You want me to paint you.'

Lippy shrugged. 'If you need me, use me. It's all in the interest of your education.'

So Jess did—a not-bad, boldly colored image, hat included, that played on all Lippy's best features, arched brows, huge nose, wide red mouth, in a way that made her look ten times as exotic, and as crazy, as she actually was. Of course, Lippy loved it.

'That's me!' she said to our mother. 'That's the essence of me! I'm telling Ira'—Ira was her publicist, to whom she constantly referred—'to use this in my press kit. Look at that gorgeous neck on me. Nik, your son is the next Modigliani.'

'He's so artistic,' our mother nodded. Jess scowled, but Lippy knew—we knew—that he loved the response. After that, he started painting all of us.

As for Flip, Lippy might have been the first female friend she ever had—at last, here was a member of her own sex whom she couldn't disgust, shock or bully. Not to say she didn't try.

'I can see your titties through that bathing suit,' she said to Lippy the first morning we all headed down to the beach.

'That's nice,' Lippy said, biting into an apple, unfazed. 'Maybe in a few years, you'll be able to see your own.' Of course, Jess and I burst into laughter.

'Fuck you guys,' Flip said, furious, under her breath. But Lippy heard her.

'You're much more attractive, Flip, when you talk like a lady,' she said. 'Take it from me. I've learned the hard way.' And with that, she sashayed out the screen door toward the beach, leaving the three of us, stunned and silent, in her wake.

Three days passed, and Flip could hardly talk to Lippy, let alone look her in the face, even though Lippy treated her as though the exchange had never happened, going so far as to ask Flip if she wanted to try on her jewelry or make-up, invitations that Flip refused with a shake of her head. Still, Lippy kept on chatting away about nonsense to Flip as though nothing had passed. It came to a head one night while preparing dinner, when Lippy, in the throes of song, took Flip into her arms to waltz around the kitchen.

'*Shut up!*' Flip screamed, wrenching herself away. 'Shut the fuck up!' She slapped Lippy on the arm, then stood there, shaking.

'Ouch!'

'I'm so sick of you!' Flip continued. 'You come in our house pretending like nothing has happened, like life is one big play. You're so loud and weird. My daddy was right. You're a nut!'

'Thank you, Flip,' Lippy whispered, calm as ice.

'You're a freak!'

The word rang out in the kitchen, caught on the edge of Lippy's chin, which trembled. For ages, none of us said a word.

Finally, Lippy spoke, dagger-cool. 'Jess and Tigger, would you mind stepping outside for a moment while I have a talk with your sister?'

'I'm not talking to you,' Flip said.

'Oh, girlfriend, yes you are. You and I are *talking*, sweetie. We are going to *talk*,' and Lippy's voice rose so monstrously on that last word that Flip stepped back, into a chair, silenced.

'Gentlemen?' Lippy said, not taking her eyes off Flip.

'Come on.' Jess kicked me under the table. We scrambled out of the kitchen and onto the front porch.

'What's she gonna do, Jess? What's she gonna do to Flip?' I was crazy with excitement and anxiety.

'Let's just sit right here'—Jess planted me in one of the old metal beach chairs, sat down in the one beside me—'and wait.' To me, he seemed oddly at peace.

From the house, we heard first nothing, then Flip's raised voice, then Lippy's, then both. Then Flip crying, then Lippy. Then nothing. Then Lippy laughing, then both. Then, again, nothing. After what must have been an hour—of curious silence, on the part of both Jess and me—Lippy stepped out, a dish towel in her hand.

'You gents can come in now,' she said casually, which we did, bursting with curiosity. Flip was setting the table wordlessly. She looked up, her face scrubbed, hair pulled back into a tighter ponytail than before. The four of us sat down to dinner, moussaka, which Lippy claimed she hadn't made since she was a teenager. (Our mother was away that night, at a meeting about our father's business.) We ate silently until Flip turned to Jess and me.

'How do you think I'll look with new wave earrings, like Debbie Harry?' she asked, pulling at her earlobes.

'You don't even have pierced ears,' Jess said.

'I will tomorrow. Lippy's taking me to Hampton to have them done.'

'She is?'

'Uh hunh,' Flip said calmly. 'And you guys can't come.'

'I'm sure you two will find something to do,' Lippy said, passing the casserole dish. 'Your sister and I are going to have a girls' day.'

'Who said we wanted to come anyway?' Jess said, startled. 'Right, Tig?'

'Right,' I said, even though I did want to go. I wanted to pick out new Nikes with the birthday money I had saved from April.

'All the better, then,' Lippy said, before smiling slyly at Flip, who smiled down into her plate. 'Now,' Lippy continued, 'who's playing Scrabble with me tonight?'

What passed between Lippy and Flip, Jess and I never did discover. But the next day the two of them came back from Hampton with bags of things, chatting, Flip with gold starter studs in her ears, claiming that the procedure hadn't hurt one bit. After that, there were lots of giggly, whispered conversations between Flip and Lippy, and if our own mother had ever felt as though she didn't know the whole story of her only daughter, Jess and I now felt that way about our only sister, occasionally, as well.

The day after Flip and Lippy's shopping trip, scoured by the sun, I left the group on the beach earlier than usual and treaded back up to the house to practice piano. Before we had left for the summer, my teacher in Topsfield had given me a Gershwin piece, 'They Can't Take That Away From Me', full of fat, trickily flatted chords and long, jazzy sequences that were meant to sound improvised; it was the toughest piece I had ever attempted and I was grimly determined to perfect it by the end of the summer. I stood under the cold outdoor shower behind the house, dried off, changed into dry shorts and sat down at the used console in the hallway. Two lines in, I was stumped. Why did my pinky keep flubbing over the B flat? Stubbornly, I kept at the line, plinking regular A each time instead.

The front door slammed behind me. Lippy slipped in, ridiculous tent-striped muu-muu over her bathing suit. 'You've got to go half a step up, darling,' she said, sitting down beside me and landing on the B flat with her painted fingernail.

'I know,' I said, embarrassed. 'My pinky keeps missing. My fingers aren't wide enough.'

She took my hand in her own, warm from the outdoors. 'They look wide enough to me,' she said. 'Just turn the note— the "that," you know—into a tight little chord, and it won't feel so funny. Like this.' Her fingers wandered over six or so keys until she settled in on four. 'See,' she said, and she struck the chord, which sounded funky and blue, too cool for my dumbed-down beginner's sheet music version.

'That's not how you'd sing it, though,' I said.

'You're right. If I were singing it, I'd probably go like this— play the line for me.' Which I did. '*Of all, of all, of all, all tha-a-ey-a-AT!*'

We both laughed. 'That's wicked cool,' I said.

'That's called melisma, breaking up a syllable like that. But if you were accompanying me, you wouldn't play the melody line under me. You'd just strike a few low-key chords, then you'd follow up my line with a counterline of your own. Like this.' Gently, she bumped me over until she sat at the center of the bench, then resang the line, sketching out her own simple, jazzy accompaniment along with it.

'I didn't know you could play the piano.'

'Honey, your mother and I *both* played when we were little. Didn't she ever tell you that?' I shook my head no. 'We did. She was pretty good, too. Strictly classical unlike me; I liked standards. But she tapered off in high school, then once she met your daddy—well—boom boom boom,' Lippy trailed off.

'What?'

She laughed, coming back to earth. 'Well, she didn't have time for anything anymore. And she was a working woman, too, mind you. And I had already left for New York, so there wasn't anyone there to egg her on. She could do some fancy fingerwork, though.'

I didn't say anything. I was wondering why my mother had never told me that she had played the piano too; it seemed odd. I looked up and caught Lippy's stare, which seemed faintly guilty, until she reclaimed her smile. 'Maybe someday you can come to New York and accompany me at Julia's Room.'

'I don't think so.'

'Tig, honey, it's not that hard. Like this song, see,' she said, pulling out her reading glasses and pointing to the sheet music. 'You've got one bar of filler after the phrase ends, after the *that*, right?' I nodded. 'So if I sing it, how would you respond with a line of your own? It's in E flat, right, so just stick mostly to black keys and you'll be okay. Ready?'

I arched my fingers over the keys. Lippy sang and I stupidly diddled out some eighth notes.

'That's it!' Lippy cried, scruffing my head. 'See that? You parroted me, but you developed it a little, too. You answered me back and you didn't even have to think about it. You've completely got the instinct.'

'You think so?'

'I know so! All you need is practice, then you can get gigs as a jazz accompanist at any joint in New York someday.'

'Are you serious?'

'Of course I'm serious! Do you know what a girl will pay for a good accompanist? He can make or break her show. God!' she burst out. 'I wish you could've met Tony. He could've shown you a whole bag of tricks. Wouldn't that have been a great bill: Song stylists Lippy Pappas and Anthony Cerretano, with a special guest appearance by Lippy's prodigal nephew, Thomas Mitchell, Junior. Oh, God! Did I say prodigal, honey? I meant prodigy. Prodigy!' She was laughing hysterically, mostly to herself.

'You liked Tony a lot, hunh?' I asked, partly to calm her down.

'Hmm? Liked Tony a lot?' She was calm now, suddenly still. 'Yes, Tigger, in answer to your question, I did.'

'Were you guys in love?' I persisted, knowing that Lippy always gave an honest answer to questions that my mother would have called rude or impertinent.

'Were we in love?' she repeated, pursing her lips. 'Yes, I guess you could say that. We were in love, in our fashion.'

'Why didn't you get married, then?'

'That's what I always wanted to know!' and she burst out laughing again before she settled down. 'I guess—,' and she looked at me keenly, 'because I guess there are some kinds of being in love where getting married isn't necessarily the best thing to do. Or the right thing to do. You know what I mean?'

'I guess so.' I had no idea what Lippy meant.

'You got a girlfriend at school?' she asked, still staring me down. I shook my head no.

'Why not? You're good-looking. You're smart. You're talented. I'd think all the girls would be all over you.'

'Some are,' I conceded.

'Why haven't you picked one to be your special girl, then?'

'I don't know,' I shrugged, feeling faintly uncomfortable.

Lippy didn't say anything, just kept on looking at me with an odd smile on her face. Self-consciously, I squinted at the sheet music.

'Don't mind me, Tig,' Lippy finally said, putting her arm around me. 'I'm just being a nosy biddy. But listen,' she paused. 'When you do like someone, you're going to know it. Boom, like that. And when you do, you just remember that it's your life to live, and no one can live it for you, okay?'

'Okay,' I said, bewildered.

'And listen. You're going to go off to prep school in a few years, like Jess and Flip, right?' I shrugged yes. 'When you do, I just want you to remember your Auntie Lippy in New York. Because you can call her anytime—for any reason—and you can even come down on the train to see her, and she'll show you the town, as long as you don't mind that all of her friends are crazy. Okay?'

'Okay,' I said, then, for lack of anything else, 'thank you.'

'You don't have to thank me, darling. I'm your goddamned aunt, for God's sakes.'

'I know.'

'Do you miss your daddy?'

I nodded. What else could I do or say?

She peered over her glasses at the piano keys, picked some out. 'He was a decent man,' she mused, more to herself than to me. 'People leave, Tigger,' she looked back at me, nodding gravely. I nodded back. 'People leave. And you know what's worse?'

What? I raised my eyebrows.

'They leave people behind.'

I nodded again.

'And you know what?'

What?

'We'—and her sweeping gesture encompassed the two of us, sitting on the piano bench in the afternoon light—'have to keep them with us here,' and she placed her hand over her heart, then mine. 'And that's how you keep them from really leaving.'

Her hand was still on my heart, but she suddenly seemed

very far away. I didn't know what to say, so I stared at the old metronome on top of the piano, then smiled at her; it seemed to do no good. I reached up and put both my arms around her, and we stayed that way until she unlaced us and said, ceremoniously, 'Now I'm going to show you some tricks when you're playing Gershwin. You start with thirty-two bars, almost every time, and from there—'

A crash and a girl's scream from the front porch below interrupted us. Lippy and I ran out the door and down the steps, where Jess and Flip were emerging from underneath the porch, in their bathing suits, tanned and covered with dirt.

'He did it!' Flip screamed, pointing to Jess, laughing hysterically, hair in her face. 'He knocked out the pole!'

'We were looking for Pedro,' Jess said, flustered, looking away. 'We wanted to bury him.'

'He knocked out the pole!' Flip screamed, laughing. She couldn't control herself.

'Honestly, Flip,' Lippy said, scowling.

Jess couldn't look at any of us. He turned almost fully away, craned up at the sky. 'We were looking for Pedro.'

Lippy stared off, bemused and inscrutable, then turned to me. 'Tigger, darling, your siblings are bonkers.'

'I know,' I mumbled. Flip was making me sick with her hyena squeal. *So where was Pedro?* was all I wanted to ask, but didn't. *If I were Lippy*, I thought to myself, I'd ask, '*So where's the goddamned crab?*'

It was Labor Day, it was Lippy's return to New York to put together a new cabaret show—'and you're all comped at the holidays, and you damn well *better* be there with those kids, Nikki!'—it was us going back to Topsfield, then it was the morning my mother drove Jess to St. Peter's in central Massachusetts for freshman orientation. It was me mute, it was Flip boiling over with rage, it was my mother holding back tears, and it was Jess, stiff in khakis and loafers, nervous, excited and visibly guilty for his excitement. It was Jess, Flip and me, all having slept in the same bed the night before, Making the Chair, and not talking about it today.

'Daddy would be proud of you,' my mother said to Jess, smoothing back his hair.

Jess flinched. 'I guess.'

'Don't go to St. Peter's,' Flip implored through clenched teeth in front of the station wagon. 'Go to the high school.'

'I'm all enrolled, Flip,' Jess said, squirming.

'Don't make this any harder than it is, Felipika,' our mother said.

'How am I gonna get to Columbus Day without you?' Flip continued, ignoring our mother.

'Work hard in school, and the time'll go by like that,' Jess said.

'You asshole.' Flip stalked away, biting her lip.

'Just ignore her,' Jess said, taking me in his arms and raising me up off the ground. 'She'll be fine. You gonna be all right?' I nodded yes, blue in the face. 'Do good in school, okay? And keep up the piano. I'll see you in a few weeks, *mi hermano*. Okay?' Again, I nodded yes, wriggled down to the ground. 'I love you, buddy.'

'I love you, too, Jess.'

'You ready, Ma?'

'I'm ready, honey.' My mother walked around the car, stooped down to peck me on the cheek. 'I'll be back in time for dinner, Tigger. Be good for Sherry, okay?' I nodded yes. Sherry, a flinty, unflappable Yankee divorcée from nearby Rowley, was our new all-day housekeeper now that our mother would be busy overseeing the liquor company.

They were both inside the station wagon, my mother turning over the engine. I stared at the back of Jess's head—when had his hair gotten so curly?—then hurried around to his side of the car.

'Jess.'

'What's up, Tig?'

'Are you gonna keep up art at St. Peter's?'

'You know I am. I'm gonna take classes and stuff. Are you gonna keep up piano?'

I nodded.

'Good. Us artists of the family gotta stick together. Right, Ma?'

'Your brother's right, Tig,' my mother said. 'I'll see you tonight, honey.'

But I wouldn't leave the side of the car. 'Jess. Jess.'

'Tig, man, what's wrong?'

I didn't know what to say. I didn't know what was wrong. But something was wrong, in the pit of my stomach, all wrong. I wanted to bawl, wanted to drag Jess out of the car, back up into the house and under the bed with me, where I'd never let him out. But I didn't bawl; instead, I just stood there, rocking on my heels, blue in the face.

'Tig!' Jess laughed. 'It's gonna be okay. I'm just going a few hours away. I'll call you tonight, okay? And I'll see you in a few weeks. All right?'

I stared down at the gravel.

'All right?'

'All right.'

'That's it.' He reached his hand out the car window, drew me in, kissed me softly on the cheek. 'Be real big for me, Tigger.'

We said good-bye again, then the station wagon was down the driveway. I stared down, counting pieces of gravel under my foot, until I finally trudged back into the house.

Sherry was vacuuming in the hallway. 'Your sister was carrying on,' she called to me as I went up the stairs.

I stood blankly in the doorway of Flip's room. She was at her little white desk, scribbling furiously.

'Hi, Flip,' I rasped.

She didn't turn around, just stopped scribbling for a minute, then started up again. 'I'm writing Jess a hate letter.'

'Why?'

'Because I hate him.' She kept on scrawling, then stopped abruptly, wheeled around in her chair. She had been crying; her face was blotchy and her eyes looked scorched. 'How could he do this to us, Tigger? How could he just leave me here?'

'He had to go to school, Flip. You'll be there too next year.'

'I hate him,' she hissed, ripping the letter into shreds, before breaking out into fresh tears. 'I hate him, I hate him, *I hate him!*'

The vacuum stopped below, and Flip's cry, pitched as it had been to compete with its electric wheeze, rang out with uncommonly sharp bile through the house.

Seven

St. Peter's is a previously Episcopalian, now ecumenical, almost A-list prep school that was retrofitted in 1925 out of an old farm outside of Worcester. It's not Andover and it's not St. Paul's, but when we were younger, my father had had a client, an upwardly mobile restaurant owner, who sent his two sons to St. Peter's and was forever singing its praises to my father. Somehow, my father got it in his head that *his* three kids would go to St. Peter's, too; it fit in with his general Kennedy-like vision of what he wanted his family to look like, our less-than-Celtic complexions notwithstanding. After our father died, my mother didn't want the three of us going away to school—and though she didn't say, I'm sure she didn't like it that Jess was the first to go—but Jess had been accepted back in the winter, when my father was alive, moving my father to one of his rare demonstrations of undiluted pride in Jess ('That's the way to go, buddy!' he had exclaimed, startling Jess with a rough hug), and my mother wasn't going to anger his ghost by undoing the plans.

Flip wouldn't talk to either of us for about a week after Jess left—in fact, she would only talk to poor Sherry, snippily, to tell her how she liked her room cleaned and her clothes pressed for school (and, to her credit, Sherry would snip right back). Eventually she returned to some semblance of her old solipsistic, gabby self. She was also a seventh-grader now, and the gaggle of scared girls that had been her subjects in elementary school were now the popular girls, with Flip, perilously, at the center. It was the year she started wearing low heels, Calvin Kleins, new wave eyeshadow like her idol Debbie Harry, fat colored combs in her back pocket and stretchy gold-threaded tops that set off her recently filled-out chest. (She sent Lippy a Polaroid of herself with an attached note: 'See, Auntie Lippy, you were right. xxoo Felipika'.)

Apparently it was also the year that she stopped fighting with boys and started 'dating' them; at least Flip would have had you think as much by the way she dumped out her Bermuda bag on the kitchen table to show you the profusion of phone numbers and love notes she had received that day. And now that Jess wasn't around to bridge the two of us when we Made the Chair, I became more invisible to Flip than ever before. It didn't bother me; I had expected it. In fact, with no Jess around to notice me, I almost got used to being invisible in my own home, grew to like it, as though I was the household spirit who made sounds come from the piano but whom nobody ever really saw.

At last, Jess came home for Columbus Day weekend—whereupon, in the midst of our hyperactive excitement, he seemed oddly quiet—then again for Thanksgiving, by which time he had let his hair grow out into long corkscrew curls, wore only shirts, jeans and sneakers splattered with paint, and refused, to the dismay of our mother, to do anything about it. If he was quiet upon his last visit, he seemed downright surly this time, as though he was watching us all through some new, highly unflattering lens.

'Look at that hair!' Flip screamed, running her hands through it. 'You almost look like a girl.'

'So do you,' Jess snapped back, stepping away.

'Fuck you!'

Jess elaborately pushed his hair out of his face. 'Honestly, Flip, grow up.'

Later that night, after a dinner in which Jess managed to brush off or cut short most of our questions about prep school life, I stepped outside to put out the garbage, only to find him hunched down by the garage door, smoking a cigarette.

'Jess!'

He looked up. 'Oh shit,' he said, exhaling. 'Keep your mouth shut to Ma, okay?'

'I didn't know you smoked.'

'You have to at that place,' he said wearily. 'Everybody does.'

'What's everybody like at that place?' I asked him. Of course I was curious; I was supposed to go there myself in three years.

'Rich.'

'It's not like we're poor,' I answered, feeling wise.

'It's a different kind of rich,' he said. 'Everybody's, like, *blond*. I mean everybody. I'm the darkest one there except for this Chinese girl.'

'Are they mean there?'

'Not like they are in Topsfield. They all just talk about you behind your back.'

'Do you have any friends there?'

'Not really,' he said, then, after a pause, 'well, there is this one guy I've sort of become friends with, basically because we're both outcasts.'

'Who?'

'This other freshman, Amos Goolsbee.'

'Amos *Goolsbee*?' I laughed.

'Yeah, that's his name. He's from this pretty rich family in Connecticut. Anyway, I guess this past summer, he and his family were on the Cape. And he and his little sister had swum really far out on this rubber raft. And I guess they were horsing around, and somehow the sister, like, fell off the raft, and Goolsbee couldn't save her, and—well, I guess she drowned.'

'Are you serious?' I remembered that day we learned our father had died, how I had stared out into the recesses of the sea as though it were a vessel of the dead.

'Completely,' Jess continued. 'But anyway, I guess Goolsbee spent summers on the Cape with this other guy, Scott Harrell, who also was going to St. Pete's. And as soon as Harrell got there, he went around telling everyone that Goolsbee had, like, *let* this thing happen, because he hated his sister, or something like that. Not that he drowned her directly—just that he sort of let her fall out of the raft and didn't try to save her until it was too late. So of course, from the very first week of school, everyone stays away from Goolsbee, like he's this ax murderer or something. And he'd sit alone at lunch, studying, and so would I. But one day I look up and there he is, at the table next to me, and I just feel so bad for the guy that I struck up a conversation. At first I thought he was a huge snob 'cause he has this funny, Thurston Howl way of talking, you know?'

'Yeah.'

'But then I found out he wasn't so bad. He showed me how to play tennis, and I showed him some painting techniques. And one day, out of the blue, he looks at me and says, "They don't get it. None of these people get it. I loved my sister more than anyone else in the world." And I didn't know what to say, so I just kind of nodded and said, "I believe you." And he just looks the other way and mumbles "Thanks."'

Jess paused for a minute to light another cigarette. 'So I guess we've kinda become friends, if only because nobody else talks to us.'

'So you really hate St. Pete's?' I asked.

He exhaled again, carefully, like he was still learning how to do it. 'No, I don't hate it. It's just as good as anywhere else. Except the food sucks. But I like my art teacher. She's just there for a year, though. She's a real artist. From Brazil. But I started doing some of these pictures in oil, and she thought they were really good, and thinks I should go to art school after St. Pete's.' He looked up at me abruptly, as though he were suddenly ashamed to be talking so much about himself. 'How you doin', anyway? You still playing piano?'

'Yeah. Except Flip tells me to shut up when she's blabbing on the phone, which is all the time now.'

We both laughed, which made me feel good. 'Is she driving you *loco*?' he asked.

'Whatever. She's too wrapped up in herself to notice anyone else,' I said, repeating exactly what our mother said about Flip all the time.

Jess laughed. 'That sounds like Flip,' he said. He held the cigarette up to me. 'Hey, you wanna try this?'

'Are you serious?' I asked. I didn't want to try it, but I couldn't ever let Jess know that.

'Yeah. Just don't tell Ma or I'll fuckin' kill you.' He handed me the cigarette and I held it awkwardly between my thumb and index finger. 'Now just suck it in—easy, easy!—then hold it in your chest for a minute, and exhale it.'

It was foul. Much as I suspected, I gagged on the smoke and started coughing. 'Quiet, Tig. Shhh!'

I contained myself and slumped down next to Jess against the garage door, taking in huge gulps of cold, fresh air.

'You'll get the hang of it eventually,' he said, plucking away the cigarette between his second and third fingers. 'You wanna know something though, Tig?'

'What?' I croaked, still dizzy.

'In a few years—assuming she gets in, 'cause her grades aren't even that good—Flip's gonna have a hard time at St. Pete's.'

''Cause of the work?' It was understood by Jess and me—and, I suppose, by Flip as well—that while we all had a fair amount of brains, only Jess and I had learned to apply ourselves in a manner that proved it.

'The work, yeah. But more than that. 'Cause of the people. She's not gonna like them. And I don't think they're gonna like her.'

Some of what he said didn't surprise me—it was hard to like Flip until you really got to know her, and even then, it could still be a trial—but I didn't know why she would have a particularly hard time at St. Peter's, and I didn't know how to ask. So I didn't.

Jess stubbed out his cigarette, then looked at me, again so abruptly that he made me blush in the dark. 'You just better hurry up and get there so we can *both* fight her battles, 'cause I sure don't feel like doing it alone. At least you *look* like her brother,' he laughed, roughly, before standing up and trudging inside. I stayed there, just a hazy moment, trying to sort out all of his harsh new words.

Flip didn't even want to go to St. Peter's—'I guess it's only because Jess shouldn't be there alone that I should go,' she said—but she was accepted nonetheless, not on account of her academic record, which was checkered, at best, but because St. Peter's couldn't be quite as choosy as other schools, especially among students who could fully pay their own way. Soon, it was Labor Day again, but this time it was only me staying behind with Sherry when we packed up the car for the trip to St. Peter's. Jess and Flip were both edgy—Flip struggling to find a way to fit her rabbit fur coat, twelve pairs of Calvin Kleins, fourteen pairs of shoes, a giant make-up box, and a high-tech blow dryer into two bags; Jess watching her darkly, running behind the house to inhale a cigarette, turning to me and saying, *sotto voce*, 'This isn't gonna be any picnic.'

They both looked exhausted when they came home for Thanksgiving, and my mother became infuriated when she learned that, on only her third weekend at St. Peter's, Flip had fled the campus, taken the Worcester bus to New York, and shown up unexpected Friday at midnight at Julia's Room, where Lippy was finishing her set. Apparently, the two had spent the weekend shopping, Lippy having taken her favorite niece to a salon where Flip got a spiky 'European' haircut, then dragged her to a theater party in Hell's Kitchen until two on Sunday morning.

'Honestly, Nikki,' sighed Lippy when my mother called her to chastise. 'The poor girl needed a little holiday. She was exhausted from school.'

'She was only in school for three weeks!' my mother protested feebly.

'That's a long stretch to be stuck up in the middle of nowhere,' Lippy said, exhaling smoke into the telephone.

As for Flip, it was obvious—she didn't like St. Peter's at all. 'You should see all the girls, Tig,' she said to me over Thanksgiving. 'They're such fucking prisses. They all run around in their little boat shoes and kilts and headbands and call everything "too cute to be true" and "to die for"'— here, Flip's usual rasp transmuted itself into a disdainful nasal squeal—'and they've all got queer names like Bunny and Binky and *Abby*, and they all think Jess is just so *cute* and *artistic* and *exotic-looking* with his beautiful curly long hair.'

'Shut up, Flip.' Jess blushed. 'You know that's not true.'

'It is, too! Whenever I tell one of them who I am, they're like, "Oh, you're Jess Mitchell's sister. He's so *cute* and *artistic*—I love his paintings *so much*." Then, they're like, "Um, are you guys, like *real* brother and sister?" And I always go, "Yeah, we are. Why?" And then they don't even know what to say. They're just like, "Uh, I don't know, you just—you just look so *different*, that's all." They're so fuckin' *fake*.'

'Come on, Flip,' Jess said. 'What about all the guys that have a little crush on *you*?'

'Nobody has a crush on me!' Flip exclaimed. 'They all think I'm a freak because I don't look like their little Bunnies and Binkies.'

'What about Amos Goolsbee?' Jess asked, raising an eyebrow.

'He's an asshole! He thinks he can have any girl just by,

like, looking at them, just because he's, like, the richest guy there and he wears all Brooks Brothers and stuff.'

'You told me you thought he was cute.'

'That's before he opened his mouth. *Shah, shah, shah,*' Flip said, imitating lockjaw. 'He thinks he's God's gift to St. Peter's, and he's totally got a stick up his ass. You said so yourself.'

'I thought you liked Amos Goolsbee, Jess,' I interjected.

'That's before *I* got to St. Pete's!' Flip declared, half-triumphantly.

Jess shot her an exasperated look. 'Don't give yourself so much credit.' Then, to me: 'I guess we've kind of gone our separate ways since freshman year.'

Later, when Jess snuck out of the house for a cigarette, I crept along after him. The night was cold and clear, and it was nice to lean up against the side of the garage with him, looking up at the stars while he packed his cigarettes and cupped the match flame against the wind.

'I hope you're comin' in a few years, Tig,' he said.

'I do too.' I was; I couldn't wait for the three of us to be together again as we had been in grade school and summers in Rye.

'"Cause you know why, partially?'

'Hm?'

'"Cause I really need help with Flip. I gotta be with her all the time, 'cause she hates everyone so much. It's like, I can't even really hang out with people, or with girls, without her, 'cause she gets all jealous and mad. She says it's my responsibility to help her along 'cause I've been there longer than she has, but she doesn't make any effort to be friends with anyone. I've always gotta have lunch with her—just the two of us, sitting way off in the corner—and she calls my dorm every night to say goodnight when I'm in the middle of a paper or something. And—'

'And what?'

'It's just hard, Tig, because I'm always hearing people call her things when she walks by, and they don't think I hear.'

'What things?'

'Things. You know.' He exhaled. 'Like a freak. And a slut, and stuff. But that's bullshit, you know, it's not true. It's just because she's more, like, stylish than the other girls there. 'Cause of Lippy. You know, her make-up and her Calvins, and things.'

'She loves her Calvins,' I said.

'Yeah,' Jess said, rolling his eyes. 'She does. She does. Anyway, they probably call me stuff, too. Behind my back. But at least I'm *sociable*, you know?'

'Yeah. So what happened with you and this Goolsbee guy?'

He shot me a glance, smoke straying out of his nostrils. 'Why do you ask?' he asked sharply.

'I don't know. 'Cause you used to tell me that the two of you were good friends, I guess.'

'What did Flip tell you about him?' he asked, as though certain she had said something.

'Nothing, okay? Why are you all freaking out, Jess?'

'I'm not freaking out,' he enunciated, looking studiously away and exhaling. '*He's* the one that freaked out. He started doing weird shit, and I didn't want to hang out with him. So I started getting to know some other people, that's all.'

'What kind of weird shit?'

'Just— weird shit.' He shook his head, vague. 'Nothing to get kicked out for, but, like— you know, he started showing me some really sick magazines he kept under his bed. Not your typical *Playboy*, but really extreme stuff, you know?'

I nodded gravely, but of course I didn't know. Jess had snuck a *Playboy* home from junior high school once and let me peek at it before he hid it away, but aside from that, I hadn't ever ventured upon anything 'extreme,' and had no particular desire to do so.

'And other stuff,' Jess continued. 'Like, we were walking through the woods one day after having a cigarette, and suddenly there's, like, this crippled rabbit limping around in a circle. And Goolsbee starts throwing rocks at it, laughing his head off.'

'That *is* sick.'

'No kidding. I told him to cut it out and dragged him away before he could really hit the thing dead on. But he sure thought it was funny. He said that as the superior species, it was our duty to put the thing out of its misery. Weird stuff like that.'

'And Flip *likes* this guy?'

'She knows he's an asshole, but she thinks he's cute. And she likes the attention she gets from him. She doesn't really get the other side of him, even though I've tried to tell her. But you know Flip—she does what she wants to do.'

'No kidding,' I nodded, and for a moment the two of us just sat there in silence.

'So, anyway, Tig, my man'—he smiled ruefully and put his arm around me—'I'm just glad you're coming, because—'

'I know, Jess,' I said, suddenly feeling very needed and very adult.

'—because I've gotta protect Flip, and I've gotta do it all myself, you know?' He inhaled long on his cigarette, then sighed it out. 'I've gotta do it all myself.'

I didn't know how screwed up things at St. Peter's really were until I went there myself—after I had been accepted the following spring—for an orientation weekend for next year's freshmen. Our mother was busy with work and Sherry was dispatched to drive me there; she left me with my duffel bag in front of the admissions building, a little white clapboard house surrounded by dozens more little white clapboard houses, all of it settled amidst acres and acres of soccer fields and forest. I took stock of the students passing by—Flip and Jess were right: they were preppy, cartoonishly so, almost uniformly Aryan-looking—and I suddenly understood what both my older brother and sister had meant the past two years about not quite fitting in. There were other prefrosh lounging about in front of admissions, all looking as though they had already mastered the St. Peter's dress code, and I suddenly felt extraordinarily self-conscious in my public-school Levi corduroys and dirty leather Nikes—not to mention the fact that my hair fell most unorthodoxically over my ears. I crossed my legs uncomfortably and waited for Jess and Flip.

A girl stepped out of the admissions building, catching my eye because she stuck out even more than I did. She wasn't blond; instead, she had an enormous pile of black curly hair that sprung out of her head in all directions, little round glasses, and a long, baggy black dress that fell all the way to her feet, which were shod in tall, pointy black boots. She looked weird and witchy, and when she saw me, she stared at me keenly, peering over her glasses, until she approached.

'Are you Thomas?' She hitched her lumpy army surplus bag up higher on her shoulder. 'Are you Tigger?'

'Yeah.' I was startled. 'How did you know?'

She smiled, and didn't look half as sepulchral as she had a moment before. 'I'm Kira. I'm a friend of Jess and Flip. They asked me if I'd look for you 'cause they both don't get out of class for another five or so minutes. God—' She looked at me closer and laughed.

'What?' I blushed.

'You *do* look like Flip—except your hair's a little longer, I guess. I like it. It's very mod.'

'Thanks, I guess. I like yours. It's curly.' It was all I could think to say.

She pulled it back for a moment, set it free. 'I know. My brother calls it a Jewfro.'

I didn't quite know what to say—we didn't know a lot of Jews in Topsfield. 'Does your brother go here, too?'

'No. He graduated last year, before I came. He's back in Boston, going to Berklee Music. I'm a freshman now.' She rolled her eyes.

'Do you like it?'

'I don't really like the people, except for a few, like Jess and Flip. We're considered freaks, but Jess is still pretty popular, especially with girls. Some of the faculty is cool, especially the English department and the arts. But, I mean, I went to public school in *Cam*bridge, you know?'

'Not really.'

'I mean, I'm used to seeing a few *black* people, or Hispanics or something, you know? It's, like, Hitler Youth here or something.'

'Why'd you come?'

She pulled red lipstick out of her army bag and applied it in a compact mirror. 'Because my brother did. And 'cause I got scholarship money. You know something?' She looked up. 'Flip gave me this lipstick. She brought it from New York, when she went to see your Auntie Lippy. She almost got kicked out for that, you know, 'cause she didn't come back until late Sunday night.' She finished application and recapped. 'It's a cool shade, though, don't you think?'

'It's very Flip,' I said. 'But it looks good on you, too.'

'Thank you, darling,' she said throatily, smacking her lips. We both laughed. 'Are you freaked out that I know so much about your family?'

'Like what else?'

'Everything. Flip tells me 'cause we're each other's only friends, except for Jess, I guess. Like, I know that Jess was adopted 'cause your parents didn't think they could have kids, but then they did—they had Flip, then you. I know your nickname is Tigger. I know you're supposed to be an excellent pianist.'

'Not really,' I said.

'Flip said you were. So did Jess.'

'Are you serious?' I asked. I was a little incredulous, and flattered.

'Uh hunh. You gotta play for me sometimes. I love Chopin. Can you play any Chopin?'

'One little piece.'

She nodded slowly. 'That's cool. You know, Flip and Jess are kind of famous here. Or infamous, or something.'

I laughed. 'Are you serious?'

'Sort of. Everyone's afraid of Flip, 'cause she's more, like, new wave and glamorous than the other girls—I mean, we wear make-up, which none of these preppy girls do here. And the guys don't really get Jess 'cause he's so, like, brooding and artistic—he doesn't play any sports and he's always in the studio when he doesn't have class—but all the girls are totally hot for him, except they're kind of afraid of him 'cause he's, like, dark and tortured-looking—not that I think so; I think he's a total sweetheart, and a totally brilliant painter. So, usually, Jess and Flip just hang out with each other. And me. But sometimes I get a vibe from them to leave them alone. So I do.' She smacked her lips. 'And that's it.'

I blinked, rather overwhelmed.

'So where do you fit into this whole scenario?' she asked me.

'I don't, I guess. I don't even go here yet.'

'But you will, though. Soon enough. Aren't you psyched?' She rolled her eyes again.

I didn't have time to answer. 'Ola, Tigger!' I heard, turning to see Flip running across the lawn in her high-heeled boots, Jess loping, disheveled, behind her.

'It's my baby brother!' Flip screamed, dropping her shoulder bag, throwing her arms around me, kissing me on both cheeks and spinning me around. 'Look, Kira, it's my baby brother Tigger. Now we're all here! Tigger, you're getting so tall!'

'Hi, baby,' I asphyxiated, kissing her back.

'Did Sherry drive you here? Did you have to listen to country music the whole way?'

'Yeah, and no. We listened to classic rock.'

'Score!' Jess had approached. 'Look at him, Jess! Can you believe he's finally here!'

'I'm glad, man,' Jess smiled wide, embracing me clumsily. 'Welcome to the wild, wild world of St. Pedro's.'

'I've already told him how suffocating it is,' Kira said.

'Umph!' went Flip. 'It *is*, Tig!'

'Come on, Flip, it's not that bad,' Jess said.

She ignored him. 'But it doesn't matter, now that we're all here. And Kira,' gushed Flip, throwing her arm around the beaming Kira, 'is the best! She's the only girl here I can tolerate. You have to know, Tigger,' Flip went on, taking my arm, 'that Kira knows *everything* about all of us. It's because she's so bored with everyone else here.'

'It's true,' Kira said.

'She even knows how you got your nickname.' Flip burst out laughing; Jess smiled at me sympathetically.

'Oh no,' I said. 'How?'

''Cause you bounced around in your crib like Tigger from Winnie the Pooh when you heard Roberta Flack.'

'Dionne Warwick,' I corrected.

'*Sorry!*' Kira said, shaking out her big hair, and we laughed. If Jess and Flip liked her, I had no choice but to like her as well; thankfully, I did. She wasn't like any of the silly little girls I knew in Topsfield.

'Tig, you're gonna *die!*' Flip gushed again. 'There's this cheesy dance tonight that the prefrosh are invited to, and Jess is the DJ!'

'You are?' I asked him. He nodded ruefully.

'I'm making him play *tons* of B-52s.'

'And Talking Heads—' Kira said.

'We're gonna freak out all these Deadheads,' Jess said.

'And The Go-Go's, and—' Kira stopped, looked beyond us. 'Oh God, you guys, look. Coming over. It's Amos.'

'Oh, puke,' Flip said, turning away.

'That's the guy you used to be friends with, right Jess?' I asked. Jess looked stony-faced. 'No comment.'

Amos approached—deeply tanned, darkly blond, icily blue-eyed, wearing an oxford shirt with a bow tie, baggy pants embroidered with whales, and Topsiders without socks. He was smiling, and as he neared us, his smile seemed to get manically wider and wider until his eyes were just gruesome little squinting slits. He slowed down as he passed us, from some feet away.

'Is that the youngest Mitchell?' he called. Jess was right—he *did* talk like Thurston Howl.

'Sexy bow tie,' Flip called back, hands on hips.

'Sexy legs,' he called back. Flip scowled and pulled down her miniskirt. 'You Mitchells psyched for the dance tonight? What are you gonna play, Jess? *We are family. I got all my sisters and me*—' he sang at us, Hustling a bit.

Jess smiled back, tightly. 'You're crazy, man. You're totally crazy.'

'We all are, Jess. Hey, Felipika, save a dance for me tonight, okay? Name your price.'

'All I really want is your bow tie, Amos, honey,' Flip called back.

'Oh, come on. You deserve more than that.' He smiled again—the same scary, squinting smile—bowed deeply, and walked on.

'He's such an evil fuck,' Kira hissed, not quite out of his earshot.

Goolsbee whirled around. 'How would *you* know, Kira, when you've probably never been fucked at all?'

'You're an asshole,' Kira called back.

He grinned broadly. 'I do my best. *Adieu*, kids. *Adieu*, Felipika.' And with that, he walked on, someone's old Harvard gym bag swinging behind on his shoulder.

'Kira,' Flip said, 'I promise, if I ever *do* get him naked, I'll castrate him and we'll roast it for dinner.'

'But you have to get him naked first,' Kira said.

'You're right,' Flip conceded. 'I guess I'll just have to fantasize about it.'

'About getting him naked?' Jess asked.

Flip socked him in the arm. 'No, you idiot! About roasting it for dinner.'

Jess just raised one eyebrow, then put his arm around me. 'Not in front of the kid.'

'I think it's too late,' Kira said. I blushed. She was right.

'Ow!'

'Hold on!'

'It hurts!'

Kira had snuck us into the dressing room of the St. Peter's theater, where she insisted on 'remaking' me for the dance. First, she trimmed my hair; now, she was taking the huge thatch on top and making it stand on end with an industrial supply of gel and hairspray. She had popped a tape into the old cassette player in the dressing room, spiking my hair to a fuzzy radio recording of 'Whip It'.

'That looks ridiculous,' I said.

'It looks cool. Now come here.' She uncapped something.

'What's that?'

'It's just a tiny little bit of black eyeliner.'

'No way!'

'You'll look bitchin'. Like David Bowie.'

'I can't believe I'm letting you do this. I'm afraid to go out in public.' To be truthful, I *was* a little intrigued by my image in the mirror—I certainly didn't look like I was from Topsfield.

'Well, darling, you've *got* to get over that. Let the public deal with it. There, check that out.' She pulled away. I looked spooky and cool in the mirror. 'Now, stand up,' she demanded. I did; she fastened the top button of one of my father's old white dress shirts and fastened around the collar a thin black satin tie. She had taken my corduroys and sneakers away and fitted me in tight black pants and pointy black shoes from the costume department. 'Check you out!' she said now. 'You look totally Goth!'

'So do you, I guess.' She had sprayed out her hair, hollowed out her cheeks, darkened her eyes and lips, and stepped into a black antique lace dress from the back room that fell in scallops at her ankles.

'Happy Hallowe'en,' she said, and laughed, then, 'oh God, I almost forgot. It's Passover next week. I've gotta go home for seder.'

'What?'

She looked at me, frowned for a minute. 'It's like Jewish Easter,' she said.

'Oh.' We stared at ourselves in the mirror, playing with our hair.

'Pssst!' from outside the door. We both started. 'It's only me,' we heard, then Flip slipped in, hair slicked back, eyes heavy with shadow, body poured into a tight pink- and black-striped jersey minidress.

'Look at you!' she screamed at me.

'Look at *you*,' I screamed back. 'When did you get this new look?'

'I got all this in New York. Kira, you've turned my baby brother into a total glamboy!'

Kira beamed. 'Doesn't he look fabulous?'

Flip stepped back, appraised me. 'You actually get away with it, Tig. You're lucky you're so skinny.'

'And he's got such big, sexy lips,' Kira added. They both laughed; I blushed in my stomach, feeling an odd mix of embarrassment and titillation.

Flip stepped in to touch up my hair. 'Jess is gonna die when he sees you. Oh, hey,' she said to Kira. 'Look what I brought.' She reached down into her boot and pulled out a tiny flask. 'It's whiskey. I snuck it from home at Christmastime. Want some?'

'Definitely,' Kira said.

Flip took a long draw herself, held her breath, swallowed, grimaced, and handed the flask to Kira, who did the same, passing it to me as she recovered.

'I don't want Jess to smell it,' I said.

'Jess has his own flask, Tig,' Flip said. 'Just take a little. You won't feel like such a kook walking into the dance.'

I took the flask and sniffed at it. It smelled noxious.

'Just remember,' Kira said. 'Swallow it down in one big gulp. Otherwise, you'll choke on it.'

Of course, I failed at the big gulp, and, of course, I choked. I sat down, feeling dizzy and nauseous.

'You'll get the hang of it,' Flip said. They each swigged again. The second time it came to me, I managed it more smoothly. After my third draw, I felt pleasantly warm inside, and suddenly giddy.

'You guys look like'—I burped—'punk rockers.'

'Oh God,' Flip groaned, pulling cigarettes out of her other boot. 'My baby brother's already tipsy.' She lit a cigarette, inhaled, passed it to Kira.

Kira dragged on it dramatically, passed it to me. 'He's cute when he's tipsy,' she said to Flip.

'Uh oh,' Flip groaned again, and they both started laughing. I laughed, too. Flip came over and suffocated me in a hug. 'Oh, Tigger,' she said. 'Oh, my Tigger.'

'Oh, Flip,' I mimicked and we all started laughing again.

'Come on,' Kira said, taking my hand. 'Let's go hear Jess.'

'Wait a minute,' Flip said. She pulled out Binaca and gave us each two squirts before we fled.

I had never felt so good walking across a lawn, under the stars, toward rising music, as I did that night, Kira and my sister's hand in either of mine. Jess was playing J. Geils when we walked into the field house; everyone in their chinos and rep ties, espadrilles and Laura Ashley dresses, turned to gawk as we cut across the floor toward Jess's turntables. Flip squeezed my hand as we passed. 'I love freaking out these boring twits,' she said to me over the music. I laughed, supremely amused by everything.

Jess screamed when he saw us. 'You're all freaks! Tig, what happened to you?'

'Kira gave me a makeover,' I preened, cracking myself up.

Jess narrowed his eyes at me, then at Flip. 'Flip, did you get him fucked up?'

Flip cracked a crooked smile. 'Just a little.'

'Y'all better be careful,' he said. He looked at me again, broke a smile. 'Tig, man, you're too much. Now go dance and let me spin.'

'Play the B-52s!' Kira screamed.

'In a little bit,' Jess said, sorting through albums. 'I have to play all the preppy party music first.' Two of the Laura Ashley girls, one a little blonder than the other, ran up to Jess's table and stopped short, breathless.

'Hi, Jess,' one of them yelled.

'Hey, Amber. Hey, Allegra. What's up?'

'You look really good tonight,' the one called Amber said, eyes bright.

'Thanks. So do you. So what's up?'

'Can you play "American Pie" for us?' the one called Allegra asked, eyes brighter.

'I'll save it for the end of the night, to slow things down,' Jess said.

Amber: 'Maybe you can come dance with us.'

Allegra: 'After you get it going.'

'Maybe,' Jess said. 'It's hard to leave the turntables alone.'

Amber and Allegra both smiled. 'Whatever,' Amber chirped. 'Well. Thanks, Jess. See ya.'

'See ya.'

Allegra: 'You're doing a really good job, Jess.'

'Thanks. See ya later.'

The two girls smiled at each other and ran away. Jess looked at us, smiled and shrugged.

Flip turned to Kira and me. 'I'm gagging,' she said.

'Me too,' Kira said.

'You're so *popular*, Jess,' Flip sing-songed.

Jess shrugged again. 'I can't help it. Now go dance, you guys. This one's for the three of you.'

He cued up 'Bad Girls'—he had a guilty love of disco from the past five years of hearing it on AM radio in our mother's station wagon—and Flip and Kira screamed as we headed onto the dance floor. On the way, we passed an awkward, immobile gaggle of kids who looked as young as I did. I knew they were the other prefrosh, and that I was supposed to be getting to know them, but I didn't feel like it; I wanted to spend all my time with Flip and Kira. They looked at us, laughed, and started talking amongst themselves. One of them, an especially tall, gawky boy with dark, curly hair, stared after us blankly as we started to dance—Flip, Jess and I had been dancing together ever since we were in elementary school—but I didn't think twice about any of it. I was drunk for the first time, reunited with my sister, who was shocking the room, and my brother, who was the DJ, and we were with this new, fun, crazy girl from Cambridge, I would be fourteen in five days, and I was having the time of my life.

We danced hard, pulling out all our old living room disco moves from a few years back as everyone else bobbed miserably in place around us, until Flip said, 'I'll be right back,' and headed off toward the bathroom. Kira took my hands and made me spin her.

'You can really move for such a geek,' she said.

'Thanks a lot!'

'I'm just kidding. Your eyeliner's smearing a little.'

'Oh shit!' I surprised myself by swearing; I seldom did.

'Don't worry about it. It just adds to the look.'

I saw Flip stalking back from the bathrooms, just perceptibly weaving her way across the room, and when she rejoined us, I smelled whiskey on her breath, heavier than before. 'It's so *hot* in here,' she moaned, finding her groove again as Jess wove Donna Summer into 'Rock With You.'

'You're insane, Flip,' Kira yelled.

'So are you, girl,' Flip yelled back, taking Kira's hand and twirling her around a bit, reclaiming everyone's attention.

'Oh, God, look,' Kira pointed, and we looked. Amos Goolsbee was swaggering toward us in a tweed coat and yet another bow tie, the same squinty smile plastered on his face. Flip saw him, grimaced, then turned to us.

'I'm gonna mess him up,' she said.

He approached, put a hand on her waist. 'Nice dress,' he said.

She put her hand over his. 'Nice elbow patches.'

'Mind if I dance with you? Or am I too square for your scene?'

Flip laughed—a little unhinged, I thought. 'Of *course* you can dance with us, Amos. If you can keep up. Can you?'

'Mm—'

'*Can* you?' Flip took him by the waist, put one booted leg between his. Amos looked startled and delighted. In a moment, Flip was up against him, head back, eyes closed, bumping and grinding up against his Oxford cloth chest with theatrical abandon. Of course, everyone was watching. Kira rolled her eyes at me. I glanced across the room at Jess; he, too, was watching, stony-faced.

Goolsbee's face was shiny with sweat now. 'You're a wild girl,' he said to my sister.

She laughed that crazy laugh again. 'You knew that, Amos, honey.'

'Do I really know that?'

'Do you want to find out?'

'What does that mean?' He looked the slightest bit uncomfortable.

Flip didn't flinch. 'Do you want to find out?'

Goolsbee smiled, making my stomach turn. 'Find out what?'

'What do you think? *And when the groove is dead and gone*—' Flip mouthed along with Michael Jackson.

Squintier smile. 'How should I know?'

'You wanna get some air, Goolsbee? *You know that love sur-vives—*'

Goolsbee stared at her, stared around the room—they had everyone's attention—then stared back. 'Okay,' he said, not smiling now. 'Okay. Great.'

'*Great,*' Flip said back, more pointed. She turned around toward us and winked before she took his hand and dragged him off the dance floor, toward the door. I looked toward the turntables; Jess was staring after them, as grimly as before.

Kira watched them go, unsmiling, then she took me by both hands and picked up the rhythm. 'Your sister *is* insane, you know.'

'I know,' I said.

'She hates his guts, you know.'

'I had a feeling.'

'She just wants to make him feel like a fool.'

'Flip can be like that.'

'That's why I love her.' Kira came in a little closer, put a finger in one of the loops of my belt. 'She doesn't take shit from anyone. She just gives a lot.'

'That's why I love her, too,' I said, placing my right hand on Kira's waist, so lightly that it wasn't really there at all. 'I mean, most of the time.'

'I know what you mean.' She smiled, kissed her own finger, then traced it on my lips. I looked down, flushed. When I looked up, she was still smiling. I looked away briefly. That gawky prefrosh with the curly hair had seen it all. So, I noticed, had Jess. He was watching me, smiling obliquely, shaking his head.

The dance lasted until eleven o'clock, throughout which Jess played all the songs that Flip had requested, even though Flip never came back. Kira and I danced through most of it, stopping for a few minutes, sweaty and tired, to get a glass of lemonade and take some air outside. The drunkenness had passed; we were less goofy than before, faintly businesslike.

'I wonder what happened to Flip,' I said.

'Don't worry about her,' Kira said. 'She probably got him all hot, then told him to fuck off. She's probably back in her room, reading *Vogue* and smoking on the sly.'

'She's even crazier than she was before she came here.'

'If you have an interesting bone in your body, this place'll do that to you. You have to keep yourself amused.'

'I guess so.'

'What do you want to do after high school?' she asked me.

'I don't know. Maybe go to music school, like your brother.' I had been bouncing the idea around in my head ever since the first summer that Lippy came and told me that I could be a real pianist.

Kira nodded slowly. 'That's cool. I think I wanna go to college in New York City—maybe NYU or something—and take Russian and study Russian literature. Then I actually wanna go to Moscow for a year or two. Then come back to New York and get my Ph.D. and eventually become an academic.'

'Wow. You're ambitious.'

She shrugged. 'I have to be. Both my parents are academics, and my brother's, like, this saxophone prodigy. It's pressure, you know.'

'I guess so,' I said. 'My father owned a liquor company before he died.'

'I know. Jess calls him The Bootlegger. Come here,' she said abruptly, and before I knew what was happening, she had pulled me close and kissed me. It was my first real kiss: it was wet, and I had felt her tongue in there. It was intoxicating, and startling, and faintly disconcerting at the same time.

'Thanks,' I said, my lips itching.

She smiled. 'Don't worry about it. Oh, listen—' The music had stopped. 'I guess it's over. Let's go see about Jess.' She popped up and headed inside; slightly disoriented, I followed.

Jess was breaking equipment down. 'You sounded great, Jess,' Kira said.

He looked up at us, taut and expressionless. 'Thanks,' he said, before turning away.

'Can you believe Flip just took off with that asshole Amos Goolsbee? She's crazy!' Kira persisted.

'Flip can do whatever the fuck she wants!' Jess exploded. 'I'm not her fucking chaperone!'

Kira and I exchanged glances. She nudged me. 'Let's go wait outside. We'll be outside, Jess.'

He didn't look up. 'Good for you.'

So we did, neither of us saying much. Finally, Jess came out and joined us, wordlessly, lighting up a cigarette.

'Someone might catch you with that, Jess,' I said.

'So what if they do? At least I'm not a drunk.'

More silence, until Kira finally said she was turning in, that she'd see the three of us at breakfast tomorrow morning. We were even more mute after she left.

'You've gotta sleep in the freshman lounge with the other prefrosh, you know,' Jess said.

'I know.' Tick. Tick. Tick.

'So what did you think of that Allegra, hunh?'

'She seemed nice,' I said. I couldn't tell if he was being sarcastic or not.

'She's always coming up to me like that.'

'Oh, yeah?'

'Yeah.' Tick. Tick. Tick.

'You know what I am, Tig?'

I turned toward him, raised my eyebrow in response.

'I'm a fuckin' spic.'

'Jess, cut it out.' I think it was the first time I had ever heard him say the word.

'I am. I'm a spic, all right? Look at this'—and he pulled at a clump of his curly hair—'I'm a fuckin' dirty, raggedy spic. That's what I am. No problem.'

'Jess, you're my brother.'

'In a way. In a way. I wonder who else's brother I am.'

'Jess, come on!' I pleaded, starting to feel queasy.

He sighed, flicking the remains of his cigarette into the walkway. 'All right, Tig. All right. Forget I said it. We'd better turn in.'

'Yeah,' I said, but neither of us moved, or spoke, for another five minutes.

We heard fast heel-steps coming around the path. It was Flip, breathing hard, make-up smeared and dress soiled. She stopped short, looked at the two of us like a stunned animal. 'Oh my God,' she said. Then she started bawling hysterically and ran into Jess's arms.

We were stupefied. 'Flip, what the fuck?' Jess demanded. 'What happened?'

She tried to speak, but kept choking on her tears, which came in violent waves, one after the other. She clung to Jess, shaking. 'Oh, Jess,' she managed. 'Oh, Jess.'

'Flip, did that fucking asshole do something to you?' Flip just broke out into a new round of racking sounds.

'What the fuck did he do?' Flip couldn't answer. 'All right,' Jess said, trying to unlace her. 'That's it. I'm gonna find him and beat the shit out of him.'

'No!' Flip suddenly yelled, pushing Jess back down. 'It's okay. It's okay. Just—hold me for a little bit, okay?'

'I want to know what the fuck happened. Why are you all dirty? Are you hurt?'

'I'm fine, I'm fine. I'll tell you later. Just—let's all just stay here for a minute, okay?' She regained her breath, wiped her eyes with the back of her hand, smearing make-up everywhere. 'Um, Jess, do you have a cigarette?'

'Sure, sure.' He pulled one out, lit it for her. It trembled precariously in her hand.

'We missed you at the dance. Jess played all your songs,' I said. I didn't know what else to say.

'Oh, Tig,' she sniffled, taking my hand. 'You were so cute tonight. I'm sorry. I'm so sorry.'

'For what?'

'I'm just—I'm just—forget it,' she laughed, putting an arm around each of us, drawing us close. 'You two,' she said, 'you two are my two main guys. You're the best, you know that? You're my guys. Right?'

'Sure we are, Flip,' I said.

'Right?' she repeated, staring straight ahead. We all knew who it was directed to. Jess sighed long, lit another cigarette, pulled a long tendril of hair down over one eye.

'Right,' he said, his voice as good as dead.

Eight

Jess and I never did find out exactly what happened to Flip that night, but the following September when I joined them at St. Peter's, something had changed. Flip no longer consorted with Amos Goolsbee (who seemed to have receded back behind his freshman-year armor of smug solitude, a flickering, uneasy presence around campus), and Jess had abandoned his half-baked attempts to 'get with' popular girls. My brother and sister had drawn curiously into one another, associating with only a few other people (including Kira, my only real nonfamilial friend that first year, who confided in me that even she felt 'excluded'). Of course, I felt obliged to join them; I studied hard that year and kept up with piano, but when I wasn't working, I was with them. It was like elementary school all over again: the three of us huddled together at morning assembly, in the refectory, at various events—and, better than that, the three of us escaping St. Pete's as many weekends as possible to crash with Lippy in New York, who introduced us all to a world of singers and actors, artists and freaks, so fascinating that we all couldn't wait to leave St. Pete's and join our crazy aunt permanently in a city that made Boston look like some dowdy backwater.

Eventually, Jess *did* leave, immediately after the summer in Rye following that school year, to live with friends of Lippy's in a huge loft in SoHo while he attended the School of Visual Arts for painting (SVA, he said they called it). Come September, Flip withdrew into herself even more back at St. Pete's; the two of us would walk the trails in the woods together at dusk before dinner and she would point out to me all the secret spots where she and Jess would smoke cigarettes, get stoned, tear everyone on campus to shreds in their first year together at the lonely school. Flip had a life of her own now; I watched her in private, cold conversations with various preppy boys, many of them two years her junior, before she walked on ahead of them into the woods—before they counted breathlessly to ten, then followed, before she exited, buttoned up and tight-jawed, throwing the stub of a cigarette behind her, and before the boys re-emerged, shirts clumsily retucked, five minutes later. I had more work that year than the last—I was also playing piano in a jazz group—and was less able to accompany her to New York on free weekends. She set off anyway, always return-ing with a new haircut, new vintage clothes, new shoes, new albums, erecting around herself a fortress of style that clearly told the rest of the apple-cheeked campus to stay clear.

She stayed with Jess when she went, and at Christmastime he told me how it was typical for Flip to leave the loft, lac-quered to the nines, around midnight, returning late the next afternoon only to grunt something elliptical about her where-abouts and crash on his futon until the clock neared midnight again. He said he was always putting a sleep-deprived zombie on the bus back to Worcester on Sunday afternoon, a girl who'd cry at the thought of returning to St. Pete's, a girl who begged him on several occasions to let her stay the week—they'd have so much fun, she'd implore: she could accompany him to art classes, then they could go get sushi in the East Village—and that when he firmly declined, she'd cry some more, threatening to run away from Port Authority and back to Lippy, who'd gladly put her up. But she never did, Jess said, she never did.

And besides, Jess told me, he had a *real life* for the first
time. His art was getting better, weirder, stronger, and people
appreciated it. SVA held a student show at the end of the year,
and a handful of rising dealers inquired after the work of this
young Jess Mitchell, so full of tropical colors, of trees, fruit,
animals and people distorted and inflated into surreally sug-
gestive shapes and poses. He had made a handful of close
friends at school, especially this Bahamian sculptor guy named
Wendell, with whom he went out searching for girls—babes,
they called them, *mamis*—and these mamis didn't sound like
the blue-eyed bitches that had teased him and withheld at St.
Peter's.

Another summer passed—our mother cried and cried over
us in Rye, but she knew as well as we did that a certain era
revolving around beach summers had come to an end. Besides,
she was more involved with the company than she ever
thought she would be, and to no one's surprise as much as her
own, she found herself 'seeing' one of the salesmen—a middle-
aged, sleepy-eyed Armenian widower named Mr. Gulezian
who had been one of our father's best friends since back in the
days when they both had their own booze routes.

Eventually it was Flip's turn to move to New York, and her
excuse was Barnard; she hadn't done great at St. Pete's—hadn't
bothered, and frankly didn't care if she went to college at all.
But our father would have insisted, and she knew in her typical shrewd, corner-cutting fashion that she was an easy in, if
not at Columbia, then at its less exclusive women's counter-
part. She lived miserably in the dorms for half a semester,
then, armed with a school nurse's diagnosis of 'generalized
anxiety disorder,' received a special waiver to go off-campus—
which meant, of course, straight downtown, into the very loft
where Jess lived, because one of his roommates had moved
out . . . and, of course, how could he say no to his own sister?
How could anyone, for that matter, say no to Flip?

Suddenly, I was alone at St. Pete's. I had a few music friends, was close with a handful of faculty misfits, and of course there was Kira (also a senior like me because she had taken a year off to live in Tel Aviv with her father), my surrogate sister who accompanied me on nearly all my trips to New York to see Jess and Flip (Lippy, as we suspected, had taken Kira under her wing as well). But beyond that, I realized for the first time how St. Pete's, like Topsfield, like the rest of my life, had been defined by my older brother and sister, and how now, without them, I felt eerily unmoored, the faceless boy with a trendy military haircut half-obscured by the raised lid of a grand piano. Did anyone here even know who I was?

Inevitably, Kira and I started fooling around. It started as it had promised to start three years before, drunk outside a Friday night dance, when, our lipstick smudging together, I had my very first kiss with tongue. I liked her lips—meaty and spiked with peppermint schnapps.

'Remember when we almost did that when you first came to St. Pete's?' she asked, unbuttoning my shirt and slipping a hand over my right nipple.

'Yeah,' I drawled. I was terrified of doing the same thing to her, but did it anyway; I always thought boobs would be firmer, but hers were curiously, startlingly, pliable.

She laughed, put her other hand between my legs. 'Do you know all the guys in Israel had big dicks?'

I laughed back, scandalized and dizzy. 'How would you know?'

'How do you think I'd know?'

'You're not a virgin, are you?' I asked, blushing like a rube.

She grimaced. 'But you are, right?'

'Oh, please.' It felt good to be horny and drunk. 'I guess you're gonna make a man out of me, right?'

Being with her made the final year at St. Pete's more bearable, if not marked by a sort of melancholy that felt oddly predestined. There seemed to be some curious logic to it; Jess and Flip had expected it all along, or so they told us when we visited them in New York the following weekend. Kira had, too, she later revealed—she just wondered when it would happen—and I guess that, in some sort of docile, unremarkable fashion, I had as well.

Back at school after the holiday break, a frigid January night, we had just done it in the locked dressing room of the theater when Kira sat up and pivoted my chin toward her. 'When you were growing up, did you ever feel a little squished in between Jess and Flip?'

'I guess so,' I said. Then I suddenly seemed to have a moment of colossal clarity, more liberating than bitter. 'Of course I did,' I said. 'Always.'

'Hm.' She seemed to meditate on this for a moment. 'Do you think Flip is sexy? I do. She's the sexiest girl I've ever known.'

'I guess so. I mean, she's my sister. Why do you ask?'

'I dunno. You think Jess is sexy?'

I laughed. 'I dunno!'

'You do, don't you? It's easy to tell.'

'Kira, he's my brother!'

'But you're not really related. I wonder how he feels about that.'

'About *what*?'

She paused, lit a cigarette, offered some to me. 'Nothing. You're sexy, you know, Tig. Even if you don't think so.'

'Thanks,' I said, thrown. 'I guess you are, too.'

'You don't have to think I'm sexy,' she said agreeably. 'I mean, you're here with me, right? That's fine. I mean, for as long as it lasts, that's good enough. Until you—'

'Until I *what*?'

She exhaled, smiled. 'Nothing. Come here, Tigger. Come here.'

I was forced to take a world literature class that final semester, in which I sat invisibly in the back row next to Sebastian Hurwitz, the dark-haired kid who had looked at Flip and me funny when we hit the floor back at that dance the spring before I started at St. Pete's. I didn't know much about him except that he was from New York City, the editor of the literary magazine and center of a small, grumpy, and self-styled 'intellectual' subset at St. Pete's, and, according to Kira, one of about four Jews, including herself, on a campus of five hundred students. (*Sebastian*, according to Kira, was 'a ridiculous name for a Jew.') In four years he hadn't stopped giving me dirty looks, something I attributed, as usual, to my association with Jess and Flip, who had always said that it didn't matter how fucking intellectual the literary clique thought they were so long as they looked like such geeks. Naturally, I felt awkward sitting next to him, especially when he raised his hand frequently to offer grave and elaborate insights into *Gilgamesh* and The Upanishads while I sat there, glassy-eyed, dying for a cigarette break before jazz block.

In two weeks, he didn't say a word to me, until finally, one afternoon, he tapped me on the elbow with his pencil.

'You've got some sort of debris in your hair,' he announced in a whisper.

'Hunh?'

'You've got something in your hair.'

'This stuff?' I whispered back, fingering the white streaks that Flip had worked into my spikes the weekend prior in New York.

'Yes.'

'That's streaks. They're supposed to be there.'

'Oh,' he said. 'Sorry.'

I turned away, rolling my eyes inside my head. In four years, I had learned what Flip meant when she said that I was going to find St. Pete's intolerable. Now I simply couldn't wait to move to New York, where I could dye my whole head platinum blond and nobody would look twice.

A moment later, he tapped me again. I turned.

'What compelled you to do it?'

'*What?*'

'Why did you do it.'

'I don't know. I was in New York last weekend, and I felt like it.'

'Who did it for you?'

'My sister.'

'Flip?'

'Yeah.' I smiled in spite of myself. If Flip hadn't been exactly popular at St. Pete's, she had certainly been well-known.

'She had a very striking aesthetic.'

'I guess so.' I shrugged, wondering if that was a compliment or an insult—and why, after four years, Sebastian Hurwitz was finally talking to me.

'I'm from New York,' he offered.

'Oh yeah?' I said, even though I knew damn well he was from New York. 'That's cool. Where?'

'Upper East Side.'

'Cool,' I said, though I knew it wasn't. Lippy called it the Upper East Snide. 'I can't wait to get out of here and move to New York next year.'

'Are you going to go to Mannes for music?'

'Probably,' I marveled. 'How did you know?'

'I know you're a musician. My cousin goes to Mannes. It's a good school.'

I nodded assent.

'How's your brother? Does he like SVA?'

'Pretty much,' I answered, all the while thinking, *How does Sebastian Hurwitz know so much about my family?*

'He's probably a lot happier in New York than he was here, don't you think?'

'I think so. So will I be, too.'

He finally smiled, his black eyes crinkling into twin slits. 'So will I.'

'—about the Sibyl the other day, Mr. Hurwitz.' It was the instructor Mr. Forbes' voice from the front of the class.

Sebastian's head snapped front. 'I'm sorry?'

'Your comment about the Sibyl the other day, Mr. Hurwitz. You said she—'

He cleared his throat. 'I said she—'

'Double jeopardy?' Mr. Forbes prompted.

'I said she's in a, um, a metaphorical double jeopardy because not only does she know her own plight, but— but she can't articulate it to anyone.'

'Thank you, Mr. Hurwitz. So now, if the Greeks believed in a concept of consciousness predicated on—'

Forbes droned on. 'Nicely done,' I whispered to Sebastian. He smiled, looked down, wrote intently in his notebook. I peered over: it was doodle, nonsense.

Kira, Sebastian and I became friends, an uncanny alliance. It turned out that Sebastian—or Seb, as we were finally allowed to call him—wasn't a literary snot, just an egghead lost in a world of rugby players, that he didn't think Kira and I were freaks, but agreeably urbane for two kids from New England ('Cambridge isn't exactly Appalachia,' Kira sneered). Kira's heart went out to him; she thought he was a self-loathing Jew, all the more confused for having had to spend four years in the company of Aryans; she knew there was a 'sybarite' locked inside him and she was determined to let it out.

We taught him how to get stoned, which, to our great amusement, made him uncharacteristically goofy. In April, when Kira went home for Passover, Seb and I stayed behind (his family didn't observe), snuck into the woods, smoked a fat joint, then returned to watch *Airplane* on the VCR in the common room, laughing hysterically. Everyone was at an organ concert in the chapel, and we finally agreed, buzzing with marijuana, to head over and join them.

'You've got a Jewfro,' I said as we wove our way across the dark lawn toward the strains of the organ. 'That's what Kira's brother calls it.'

'Fuck you!'

'You do! That's what you've got—a Jewfro.'

'Fuck you, Tigger. I'm not really Jewish. My mother wasn't Jewish.'

'Wasn't?'

'She died two years ago.'

'I'm sorry—'

'It's all right.'

'But you still got a Jewfro.'

'Fuck you, Tigger!'

'That's what it is!'

'Fuck you . . . *Thomas*.'

'Nobody even ever calls me that ever.'

'But that's your name.'

'So fuck you, Jewfro!'

'So fuck *you*, Thomas.'

The organ roared. Suddenly, I had my hands in his Jewfro and we were kissing on the lawn, sidestepping our way behind the statue of St. Peter. In the woods, a moment later, we were unzipping each other's pants.

'I *am* sorry about your mother,' I said.

'That's okay. She was really sick.'

'Still, you know. My father died, too.'

'This is life.'

'Uh hunh.' The twigs on the ground poked into my bare knees. I thought about what Kira had said about Israeli guys. Then it occurred to me that I didn't want to think about Kira, not just now.

'So come here, Tigger. Stand up.'

I did. It was cool outside, and I could still hear the organ coming from the chapel. I put both my hands on top of his head, ran them through his heavy curls. It's what Jess used to let me do—*asked* me to do, I thought, when we used to Make the Chair.

He looked up, all eager and worried. 'You like that?'

'I guess so.' I sighed, caught my balance again on his head. The night air felt curious against my bare thighs. 'I guess so.'

We didn't talk about it. Kira came back, complaining about her father's tedious seder rhetoric. That whole week, when the three of us were together, it was unbearable.

'Seb,' Kira asked, 'are you gonna be the godfather of Tig's and my first kid? We're gonna need a mensch around.' Seb and I squirmed miserably. 'You guys smoked too much dope when I was away,' Kira said.

Thursday night, fooling around with Kira on the old mattress in the costume room, I had a terrifying vision of something I couldn't even describe. 'Oh shit.' I rolled away, my head in my arms, disgusted with us both, and with the filthy mattress.

'What is it?' she asked.

'What's what?' I mumbled.

'What's *this*?'

'I don't know.'

Silence. I wouldn't look up. I heard her light a cigarette in the dark, exhale. 'I got into Columbia,' she said matter-of-factly. 'So did Seb.'

'I know.'

'I guess that means we're all gonna be in New York next year.'

'I guess so.'

More silence. 'I guess you finally did it, hunh?'

I felt sick. 'Did what?'

'I guess you unlocked the sybarite before I could, hunh? Didn't you, Tig? When I was away for the holiday, right?'

'Should I even bother to lie?' Stubbornly, I wouldn't look up.

'No. You shouldn't.' I heard her stub out her cigarette on the floor, gather her backpack. 'I'm going back to my dorm. I think I want to be with some girls.'

'All right.' I didn't sit up until minutes after she had left. When I did, I sat there in the dark, cross-legged. There was a horrible silver lamé feather boa strung over one of the clothes racks, winking at me in the dark, and I stared at it, stricken, as though it were a real serpent, just waiting to strike.

The next afternoon I said not a word to Kira or Seb, save to leave a note on Seb's door telling them I was going to New York for the weekend. From Port Authority I went straight to Julia's Room, where Lippy was finishing a set to a crowded room. I took a seat in the back; she spotted me in the middle of a song and blew me a happy, puzzled kiss. I ordered a scotch and soda, downed it, then, halfway drunk, ordered another, then one more. A group of guys pushing fifty, all sweatered and coiffed, were crowded around the table next to me, mooning over Lippy.

'She's in sublime form tonight,' one of them declared.

'She gets better with age,' said another, to which a third responded, 'Not unlike yourself, honey.' They all crowed and crowed; I smiled crookedly, proud of Lippy, and ordered another drink.

By the time Lippy had finished her set and was wending her way through the room to me, collecting kisses and accolades like so many roses, I was thoroughly bombed.

'Auntie Lippy—' I said thickly, standing up to greet her and nearly falling

'Tigger, are you drunk?'

'You were *sublime*.' I planted a wet kiss on her cheek.

'Oh, God help us. Jack, would you bring me a martini? And black coffee for my nephew? Sit down, Tigger.' I did, clumsily, resisting the urge to rest my head on the table. 'Now what the hell are you doing here on a Friday night? Alone? *Bombed?*'

'I wanted to see your show,' I slurred.

'You just saw the show last month, with Kira. Where's Kira?'

'At school.'

'Why didn't you come down with her?'

''Cause she hates me.' I laughed, too loud. Then the gravitas of what I just said actually hit me. Suddenly, my head was on the table; I was crying, boozily, grimly fascinated by my own melodrama. Frederick, her new accompanist, was playing 'I Can't Get Started'. I didn't like the arrangement—too many arpeggios, too little swing. I felt Lippy's warm hand on the back of my neck.

'Tigger. Do you want to tell me what's going on?'

'You remember you said I could come to you someday? Remember you said that, after Daddy died?'

'I do. That first summer in Rye.'

'Well. So here I am. Here I am.'

'Tigger,' she said sternly. 'Look up.' I did, sloppily. 'Here,' she said, handing me a napkin. 'Wipe your face. Now look around. Look around at all these men. Is *this* what this is all about?'

It was such a Lippy way to address a problem, so theatrical, that I had to laugh a little, which I did. 'Sort of.'

She smiled, bemused. 'Did something happen with a boy?'

I blushed. 'Sort of.'

'Does Kira know about it?'

'Sort of.'

'Sort of,' she repeated, amused, pushing a cup of black coffee in front of me, then picking up her own martini, pausing for a moment to blow a kiss to a waving fan across the room. 'In other words, yes, right?'

I nodded.

'Have you told Jess or Flip? We'll just skirt the question of your mother for a minute.'

I shook my head. 'It just happened. I just got here. This is the first place I came.'

'Well, I'm glad you did, because I always thought you might bump up against this someday. Did you hear some of my set?'

'A little.'

'I did "Bewitched". I wish you'd been here for it.'

'Why'd you always think?'

'Tigger, you spend almost every night of your life in this

room for the past twenty years, you get a sense of these things. Now, this boy—do you like him?'

'I don't know,' I mumbled, embarrassed. 'I guess so.'

'Look at me. Look at me. Do you know what to do, and what absolutely not to do? Sexually, I mean. Because I'd go crazy, Tigger. And so would your mother.'

'Yeah, more or less.'

'You better find out just what. I'll get someone to tell you. Now, look. Do you like Kira?'

'I love her, kind of.'

'But sexually?'

'I guess—I guess I could take it or leave it.'

'Well, look, honey. You're seventeen years old.'

'Eighteen now.'

'Eighteen. Which reminds me I owe you a birthday present. Hi, sweetie! Congratulations on *Sweeney Todd!*' Lippy suddenly shouted across the room before turning back to me. 'Okay, eighteen. And you're coming to New York next year. And you're going to have a world of new experiences, new people and things, on your front doorstep. So Tigger, darling? Just cut yourself some slack right now. Everything's going to fall into place. You go back and have a good talk with Kira. Don't lose that love, okay?'

'Okay.'

'And one more thing. Look around this room.' I did. 'Do these guys look so miserable to you?'

I shook my head. I actually wished they'd clam it a bit.

'That's 'cause they're not—at least not on Friday nights. It's a marvelous city, Tigger. And they've got each other. And they've got *me*.'

I laughed. 'Jesus, Lippy. You're so vain.'

'And so do you,' she said. 'You're staying with me tonight. We'll get Jess and Flip up to the Village for brunch tomorrow. Now, come on,' she said, wiping my eyes and dragging me out of my seat.

'Lippy, what's up?'

'Come *on*!' She dragged me up to the now untended piano, and the room fell silent. 'Ladies and gentlemen,' she began dramatically, hands together. 'I have a treat. All the way from St. Peter's School in God-knows-where, Massachusetts, this is the very promising, very talented keyboard stylist, Thomas Mitchell. Who also happens to be my nephew.'

A round of applause and kitschy, good-natured *Awwwws!* from the room. Mortified, amused and resigned, I sat down at the luxurious baby Steinway.

'You start in, Tig, in A. I'll pick you up. Can I give you a swing?'

I smiled, nodded. 'One, two,' Lippy breathed, snapping her long, painted fingers, 'one, two, three *and*—'

I found a fabulous, swinging vamp, off-center and spare. Lippy let me play it out, picked it up, turned to the room with the pursed lips and arched eyebrow that kicked off her every number, then stepped in throatily:

> *The way you wear your—HAT—*
> *The way you sip your—TEA—*
> *The memory of all —THAT—*
> *No, no, they can't—take—that away from me.*

And we swung that room for an hour until we found ourselves walking home, arm in arm, through the winding streets of Greenwich Village at two o'clock in the morning.

Things worked out in a funny way back at school. I stopped sleeping with Kira, but I didn't sleep with Seb again either. Our friendship didn't explode; it was a sweet spring, we were graduating in weeks, we were all moving to New York, and perhaps for that reason, our uncanny alliance stayed intact, however fragile. We'd still get stoned in the woods, but then we'd all go our separate ways back to the dorms, to crawl humming, alone, into bed before the lights check. We didn't really talk about what had happened, or why. We would sometime down the road; that May, though, none of us knew just what to say, except that we were all glad we'd be together again come September.

Suddenly it was commencement; Jess and Flip were there, and so were Lippy and Ma and Sherry, who had become my mother's best friend in the past few years.

'Tigger, you're free!' cried Flip, who was just barely hanging in at Barnard but having such a good time in New York, and looking so chic while having it, that she hardly cared.

'And baby, guess what?' Jess said, hugging me. 'Chloe's moving out for the fall, so you can have her space in the loft until you get your own.' I couldn't get over Jess—Flip told me he was the star of his year at SVA, that one of his instructors told him, only half-joking, that he'd better watch it or he'd be the next Basquiat. Flip had even dressed him in a stark, loosely fitting black suit to *look* like an artist for my graduation; neither my brother or sister had ever looked so good as they did now, and I knew my classmates were thinking the very same as they passed.

Some healthy years of distance had taken the edge off my mother's preoccupation with Jess and her tension with Flip; now she cried in an agreeably conventional fashion. 'If only your father were here to see how fine all of his kids are turning out. He'd be so proud.'

'And he'd have you to thank, Nikki,' Lippy said, embracing my mother indulgently. 'You did it all yourself.'

'No, no, that's not true,' my mother sniffled. 'Sherry's kept a beautiful house for us. And she's always there for me, too.'

'For God's sake, Nikki.' Sherry laughed, embarrassed.

'Sherry, you're *fabulous*,' Flip gushed, kissing Sherry extravagantly on both cheeks.

'Not more than you, honey,' Sherry deadpanned. Jess and I exchanged a droll glance. We both knew that if there was one person on earth whom Flip would never succeed in charming, it was Sherry.

We were piling into the station wagon after the ceremony to have dinner at a nearby inn when I decided it was wise to hit the john in the dorm before we left. I short-cut to the first floor bathroom; standing at the urinal, my eyes floated upward to some graffiti I had never noticed before:

Jess Mitchell is a fucking spic.
Flip Mitchell sucks cock for 99 cents.
Tigger Mitchell sucks it for even less.

I stared at this odd, three-line piece of verse for some time. Then I bolted up to my room in the stuffy old dorm, found a black marker, bolted back down to the john, and wrote in the space just below: *Too bad you can't afford either one of us, racist asshole.*

I slipped the marker in my pocket and headed back out toward the station wagon. There was my family, mingling with the families of Kira Stern and Sebastian Hurwitz, who were joining us for dinner. There were my brother and sister, Jess and Flip Mitchell, with whom I'd be reunited in just a few weeks. Here were the velvety green hills of St. Peter's School, which after today I'd never have to countenance again. And over those hills, glitzy and high-pitched, sat New York—like Auntie Lippy said, even like she swung it, Manhattan, a marvelous, marvelous city, that dear old dirty town.

Manhattan

Nine

'You like me, you *really* like me,' I slurred at Seb, drunk on three very stiff martinis, as we walked, propped up on each other, back from Tribeca toward the loft, nearing midnight on a Friday in April of 1989.

He burped indecorously. 'What makes you say that?' We had met straight from my last class of the week at Mannes, straight from work for him, and his tie was loosened around his neck, a satchel full of bad manuscripts swinging low on his hip.

'Because!' I began, catching my step. 'Because you're a fucking editorial assistant, 'cause you make—you make, like, maybe two hundred dollars a week, and you take me to Odeon for my birthday. See?' I said, resuming my Sally Field drawl. 'You really like me.'

'I like steak frites. And you only have to pay twenty-five dollars a month on Visa.'

'At that rate, you'll only owe eight thousand dollars by the end of the year.'

'Nine, more like.'

We reached the old industrial doors of the loft on Broome Street. 'Let's not go up yet,' I pleaded, pulling at his tie. 'Let's go dance at the World.'

'Thomas, I'm tired. And you told me you had all that out of your system.'

'It's my *birthday*.'

He huffed. 'All right, maybe. Just come up and let me give you your birthday present.'

'All right,' I grumbled, key in the lock. Three years in New York, and Seb and I had worked out in a strange way. At first, we were friends who fooled around together because we didn't know anybody else. Then, he got more serious—he wanted to be a book editor, although I had no idea why since the whole industry seemed so constipated and poverty-stricken—and I got wilder, maybe because of Flip, maybe because that's what the city does to certain people. At any rate, I couldn't stop going out, couldn't stop missing classes, couldn't stop hooking up with guys I never saw again. Then, on a random Saturday morning in January, I ran into Seb at a diner in the Village. He was alone, reading manuscripts, and I was alone, too, coming from a stranger's apartment a few blocks away, hungover and miserable.

'You're fucking it up, Thomas,' he said, setting aright the coffee cup that had fallen out of my hand.

'I know.' My head felt the size of a watermelon. 'I know.'

'You wanna come over my place and sleep while I work? I'll make you a proper dinner tonight.'

That was that—he wanted to domesticate me, and I let him. I was twenty-one as of tonight and virtually married. Jess, similarly involved with someone, was glad to see it happen. Flip, committed only to the entirety of downtown Manhattan, called us both bores. And still the three of us lived together in this dark, cavernous loft that Lippy had secured for us at a ridiculously low rate, stayed together because the rent was low, because it made Lippy and our mother happy to know that they could reach us all in one place, and because of something worse than inertia—more like a ghastly unspoken fear of going our separate ways.

The loft was dark, empty, aglow with candles when we stepped in.

'What the fuck?' I exclaimed. Seb laughed triumphantly just before the stereo blasted the Beatles' birthday song and they all came bounding out from around the corner, led by Flip in a silver lamé miniskirt and white go-go boots, flanked by Urethra Franklin and Barbara Ghanoosh, Flip's two drag queen best friends, who carried the cake, spiked with twenty-one sparklers. (By day, they were Cedric Williams, an itinerant construction worker, and Joey Saab, who managed his Lebanese father's imported carpet showroom on Madison in the Thirties.)

'She's a woman tonight!' brayed Urethra, who planted an imprint of fluorescent white lipstick on my cheek. Barbara pecked the other one. '*Habibi*, take a sparkler, 'cause you're sparkling right now!'

'You do sparkle, honey,' Flip shrieked, smothering me in her arms. 'You're all grown up.'

I extracted a sparkler from the cake, held it aloft, a little weepy. 'This is amazing,' I said. 'Look at the candles. Look at all of you.'

'Guess who art directed it?' Flip bragged.

Urethra turned to her, huge arms crossed over her beaded bustier. 'Girl, stop there! You had *assistance.*'

'I did, I did,' she conceded.

Barbara wagged a painted finger at her. 'You *did*, habibi. Give credit where it's due.'

Everyone was there, gathering around me: Kira and Jeffrey, her bright, sweetnatured and colossally dull boyfriend from Columbia; Jess, two years out of SVA, along with Damienne, his D.A. girlfriend whom Flip secretly called 'the Haitian Sade'; Lippy, glowing alongside Langley, her middle-aged musical director beau of the past year ('He's not gay,' she assured us, 'just British'); and Anthea, the wraithlike amateur alcoholic and dotty failed actress from London who owned the lamp-shade boutique downstairs, presently sharing a fat black cigar with her latest girlfriend, a stunning, endlessly beaming

Slovenian model named Katja, who spoke hardly a word of English. Grant Fekkai, the hotshot, fortysomething art dealer who had taken Jess under his wing while he was still at SVA, was there, too, with some ennui-ridden art babe *du jour* on his arm. And hanging back with characteristic feral quiet on the periphery of the crowd was Ty, a hulking bouncer on the downtown club circuit and Flip's part-time lover—a guilty one, too, because after each torrid 4 a.m. melee he still had to put his clothes back on and board the 6 train back uptown to his shrieking common-law wife Shereen and their two kids in Harlem.

The outer circle was there, too: some of my friends from Mannes, Jess's art buddies and Damienne's activist rainbow coalition, some of Lippy's cabaret set—and, of course, ubiquitously, Flip's nocturnal coterie, the most random confederation of anorexic party girls, junkie dudes, fashion fags, drag queens, music industry types, indie filmmakers, aspiring actresses who practiced 'massage therapy' on the side; drop-dead humpy bartenders all waiting to be discovered by Calvin Klein; fair-skinned midwesterners who had transformed themselves into urban vampires; legitimate prodigies, premature has-beens, and plain old never-weres.

Flip had collected all of them in the past three years of relentless nightclubbing, ever since, with a huge sigh of relief, she dropped out of Barnard (needless to say, she and our mother hardly spoke these days) and began supporting herself by shooting the occasional avant-garde music video, promoting the occasional party, styling the occasional shoot, waiting the occasional chic table—and blowing through her lump-sum trust at a rate that stupefied Jess and me, who didn't even like to dip into ours to pay the rent. (Jess taught intermediate painting at the New School and I gave private piano lessons to rich Upper East Side kids when I wasn't in class.)

Just how our sister had managed to assemble this particular mini-mob of Flipitistas Jess and I weren't sure, but over time this unlikely coalition had become her entourage, phoning the loft all day and leaving baroque messages on the machine, converging at the loft almost nightly to 'attend' Flip, cocaine and sushi in tow, while she put her 'look' together for the evening from a personal costume department girded with endless racks of platform shoes, Day-Glo minidresses and bouffanted wigs, much of which was usually on 'permanent loan' to the drag queens. Almost every weekend and most weeknights, at very least a half-dozen of these creatures would crash on our floor, rousing us near dawn with their coked-up shrieking, then leaving us to high-step gingerly around their passed-out, splayed-about bodies until dinnertime the next day.

Oddly, Jess and I turned out to like most of them more than we thought we would, particularly Urethra and Barbara, early supplicants of Flip, both so agreeable and low-key out of drag that Jess and I couldn't help calling them plain old Cedric and Joey, even when they came reeling into the loft on a Saturday night in matching platinum *ancien regime* wigs fitted with birds' nests and tiny cottages. They were the core of a rotating cast of supplicants who finally took the pressure off the two of us to give Flip constant attention—and what's more, they made the loft an interesting place, a constant sideshow, a happy shrine to the charismatic power of my voracious older sister. If other folks, like Damienne and Seb, didn't feel quite the same way—well, that was another story.

Someone put the terrific new De La Soul CD on the stereo, and already the loft was so loud I couldn't even hear what Seb was saying into my ear. Eventually, Lippy's raspy voice emerged from the din; she had one hand in Langley's, the other wrapped around a glass of champagne, many bottles of which were circulating care of one of Flip's crafty bartenders.

'It isn't right—' she began, then lost her train of thought.

'But it isn't *wrong*,' Urethra called back, provoking Barbara to snort champagne out her nose. Seb nudged me; we traded glances, then I glanced at Jess, who was smiling indulgently, and at the braided, jeans-clad Damienne, whose smile seemed a little more forced. They had met at a party six months ago, where Damienne had told him how she and her parents, pro-democracy intellectuals who had spoken out against the Duvalier regime, had fled Port-au-Prince for New York, when she was only thirteen, after tontons macoutes machine-gunned bullets through their windows in the dead of night. Here in New York, she said, her parents had worked like dogs in order to send her to parochial schools, which propelled her on to a full scholarship at Brown, which propelled her on to Harvard Law School. And then she said to Jess, *So what about you? Were you born in the islands or here in the States?*

'I'm definitely not an islander.' Jess laughed, a little bitterly.

'But you're definitely a person of color,' Damienne countered. 'It's obvious you've got some sort of Latino roots.'

Jess said that he could hardly think of himself as a person of color when he didn't even know who his real parents were, hadn't ever been to Puerto Rico, grew up in a white family in a white town in Massachusetts, and could only speak functional Spanish.

'It doesn't matter,' Damienne said with her usual cool certitude. ('That must be how they teach you to talk at Harvard Law,' Flip observed of Damienne soon after.) 'Believe me, to cabbies late at night, you're definitely not white. Haven't you found that?'

Jess shrugged, stymied. He *had* found that, he mentioned once, and always attributed it to something else. 'I don't know,' he said to her. 'Maybe it's just my long hair.'

'It's not just your long hair. But it *is* beautiful,' Damienne allowed in the same measured, appraising voice she used to talk about her indigent clients.

'Thanks. So is yours.' And he played briefly, awkwardly with the ends of a few of her infinite braids.

Damienne cracked the faintest smile. 'Thank you.'

And that was the start of that—after three years of go-nowhere flirtations and one-night stands, Jess had his first real squeeze. The day after Damienne's first overnighter at the loft, when she and Jess had stepped out for breakfast, Flip climbed up into my bunk and woke me.

'What do you think of her?' she hissed from the top of the ladder.

'Hunh?' I mumbled, sweeping back sleepiness.

'Her! The girl. Dam-*yen*,' she said, overpronouncing the Frenchness.

I shrugged. 'She seems really cool. Smart.'

Flip's eyes narrowed. 'Don't you think she's kind of militant? I mean, about race and gender and everything? I knew girls like that at Barnard. I couldn't stand them. Why do you think I left?'

'I just thought you didn't like school.'

'It wasn't just that!' Flip said dramatically. 'It was those *girls*! All they could talk about was *oppressed, oppressed, oppressed*. And then, you know, this whole *person of color* thing she's laying on Jess. Well, I can be a person of color, too. All I have to do is put on red lipstick and blue eyeshadow.'

'Honestly, Flip.'

'But as though Jess doesn't *know* he's Puerto Rican? He got called a spic all the time growing up. And who, may I ask, was always there to defend him? How quickly he forgets.'

'Flip, I can't believe Damienne is causing you all this fuss.'

'I didn't say that!'

'Why don't you just *try* to like her? For Jess.'

Flip looked offended. 'Of *course* I'll try to like her. That's the kind of person I am.' She seemed a notch more contented. 'Do you want a mimosa?' she asked me brightly.

'It's Monday morning!'

'So? Anyway, it's just Jess's best interests I'm looking after.'

In her fashion, Flip *did* try to get on with Damienne. In

Flip's world, the highest compliment you could pay someone was about their hair, and the highest service you could offer was suggestions for hair improvement. 'I really love your braids, Dam-*yen*—' Flip said to her one afternoon when we were all lounging about, somewhat uneasily, in the loft.

'Thank you, Flip.'

'—but, you know, have you ever thought of getting one of those really *amazing* black hairdos? Like a basket or something?'

'They take a lot of work, Flip.'

'But, I mean, they're so *amazing*. For this benefit last week, Cedric showed up with this great Patti Labelle wig—I mean, it was out to *here*—and he just looked so fabulous.'

'But Flip,' Damienne said, infinitely patient, 'Cedric is a drag queen.'

'So? He's got a better sense of style than most real women I know.'

'I just don't think I'd be taken very seriously in court with a look like that.'

'It's your attitude that counts,' Flip persisted.

Damienne sat there, open-mouthed, stumped. 'I like your braids,' Jess said, filling the gap.

'So do I,' I said, being honest.

'Thanks, guys,' Damienne said, a little sourly. 'But Flip, I'll keep the idea in mind for the next big event.'

Flip shrugged. 'Whatever.' She rose and stood with her empty glass in the center of the room. 'Does anyone want another vodka tonic?' We three politely declined. 'Very well,' Flip sighed, lighting a cigarette before shuffling into the kitchen, where we heard her slamming dirty pans around in the sink.

'It isn't *right*—' Lippy continued over the din, 'to celebrate— people, people, *please*!' Lippy gestured to Jess, who turned down the music, and the room subsided to a dull roar.

Lippy smiled, regally satisfied, and obviously a little tipsy.

With the exception of Langley and Grant, she was the only person over thirty in the room. In two years, as our own mother grew increasingly perplexed over the shape of our lives (she didn't have a particular fondness for New York, and visited infrequently), it was Lippy who had slowly but firmly established herself as our mother's surrogate, summoning us regularly to her tiny Village apartment for dinner (Greek take-out, usually), setting us up with various jobs or connections (there were times, walking down Bleecker Street with her, when you got the sense that Lippy knew everyone below 23rd Street who had lived in the city longer than ten years), crowing to everyone who'd listen about the enormous talents of her two nephews—and, more and more often, scowling over the sketchily channeled talents of Flip.

Our sister had been closest to Lippy in our early years in the city; it was usually Lippy whom Flip would flee to when she simply couldn't tolerate 'constipated' Barnard, and Lippy would usually let her hide out afternoons in her apartment while she was at rehearsals, cutting class so that she could 'catch up on her reading.' (In truth, she watched talk shows until two, then left Lippy with a sinkful of dirty dishes and an unmade sofabed while she gave her credit card a workout in SoHo for the rest of the day.) But Lippy had strongly disapproved of Flip's dropping out of school, and once Flip did so, only to embark on a full-time tour of Manhattan by night, their relations became strained.

'Where's Flip?' Lippy would ask grimly when Seb and I, Jess and Damienne, met her and Langley for Sunday brunch.

Jess and I would eye each other warily. 'We don't know,' Jess would say. 'She probably stayed over a friend's last night in Chelsea.'

Lippy would raise an eyebrow. 'She knew we were all having brunch today, right?'

'I think so,' I would say, embarrassed for Flip. 'We talked about it yesterday.'

'I'm not happy with that girl.' Lippy would frown and gather her black satchel. 'Come on, Langley. I'm not happy with her at all.'

Langley shrugged extravagantly at us while Lippy huffed out the door. Seb, Jess and I exchanged bemused glances. We had our suspicions about Langley's orientation, so to speak, but we certainly weren't broaching them to Lippy, truly happy again for the first time since the years before the death of her dear, unattainable accompanist Anthony Cerretano.

This night, though, as befitted the general mood, Lippy was getting on fine with Flip, as well as all her friends, who bestowed upon Lippy the highest honor a real woman could receive in clubland: 'She's just like a drag queen.' So Lippy played it up, to everyone's delight, including Langley's. He stood near Seb and me, champagne glass in hand, and declared again and again, 'She's a marvel. Isn't she a marvel?' Of course, Seb and I nodded politely in agreement.

'Thank you so much,' Lippy chimed now. 'Now, it's not right to celebrate my nephew's birthday without a proper serenade. So Urethra and Barbara and I have arranged something. Ladies?'

The room buzzed. 'It was her idea,' Cedric deadpanned as he and Joey followed Lippy to my old upright in the far corner of the loft. Lippy sat at the bench while Cedric and Joey draped themselves over opposite corners. (They looked resplendent tonight in chiffon; it was spring, after all.)

Lippy started a vamp, then sang, in a gravelly striptease voice, '*I wanna be loved by Tig*—'

'*Just Tig*—' Urethra exhaled, blowing me a kiss, Marilyn Monroe style.

'*And nobody else but Tig*—' Barbara followed, cartooning a belly dance.

'*I wanna be loved by Tig alone*,' they all sang, then—in stunning slow harmony that Lippy must have taught them (they were always pushing Lippy to get them cabaret gigs)—'*boop boop be doo.*'

'Oh no!' I groaned, embarrassed and delighted, happier than I had been in months. Seb slipped his hand into the back of my pocket.

Cedric pointed at me. 'She's blushing.' Everyone laughed. I was blushing, and I continued to, until they had finished the song, to lush applause, and we plunged into the cake and champagne.

By three in the morning, it wasn't really my party anymore, it was Flip's, but I hardly cared, I was so high. Lippy and Langley had left over an hour ago, as had Seb, as had Damienne and Kira—in fact, as had most of the people that weren't a part of Flip's travelling circus, the members of which were now dancing to pounding music in various stages of undress, committing various acts of sodomy in various dark corners of the loft (including, I was sure, my own bed), slumped about in various states of unconsciousness, or gathered around the glass-topped coffee table, which had become, not for the first time, a perfect surface for snorting various lines of powder. I had visited it a few times, I must concede, and now I couldn't seem to stop dancing in place to the music or wondering if I'd ever feel like going to bed. I knew I was backsliding, having one of those nights I'd later regret, but for the moment, I was standing in the middle of a throbbing house party, the first night of my formally adult life, temporarily freed of my boyfriend in a room crawling with cute boys, knowing all along that I wasn't really alone, that I was safe, because my brother and sister were somewhere in the crowd, carrying on.

Moving toward the dancing throng, I bumped into Grant, slouching against a wall, savoring a joint as though it were the rarest of delicacies.

'Tigger the Tiger,' he said when he saw me, throwing an avuncular arm around my shoulder. 'You getting your freak

on, baby? Here, have a sip of this tea.' He passed me his joint
like a chalice.

'Thanks.' I took a drag and passed it back to him with equal
reverence. Grant had this habit of speaking in a sort of retro-
beatnik patois, which made sense of sorts, since everything
about him had about it the faintest air of datedness. He had
gotten his start as a dealer about seven years ago—when the
everyone-who-was-anyone crowd, trailing after Warhol as
though he were the Pied Piper, shifted its attention from the
withering Studio 54 to the burgeoning SoHo art scene—and,
either because of nostalgia, ignorance or mere indifference,
most of his tastes—excepting, lucratively, those in art—
seemed semi-preserved in the amber of 1979—the
considerable amount of chrome and mirror that filled his loft,
the Brie and white wine he put out for every party or opening,
even his outfit tonight: a too-tight, spread-collar Pierre Cardin
shirt, trousers that one could decidedly call 'slacks,' brown
stack-heeled boots that zipped up the sides, and a thick silver
bracelet—all of it swathed in the scent of something that had
probably sat in a bottle on his dresser since the Bicentennial
year.

'Where's that girl you were with?' I asked him, the pot settling in around me and mixing curiously with the cocaine.

'You mean Janine?'

'I guess so.'

'She's a smart girl,' he offered. 'Just got her Doctorate in art
history from Yale. She's gonna be teaching at Oxford next fall.'

'Wow. Impressive. So where is she?'

He shrugged, took another hit off the joint. 'She's around
here somewhere. She's looking for this friend of hers, this
chick Sasha.'

'Why? Are they leaving? It's so early, though.'

'Tigger baby, we're *all* leaving.'

'Oh, you mean you're gonna drive them home?'

He turned to me, smiling slyly through a haze of blue

smoke. 'Maybe in the morning I will. After a little continental breakfast.'

'Oh.' I suddenly felt very stupid and naive. 'Oh God, Grant. You amaze me.'

He shrugged again, modestly. 'What can I do? I'm crazy about this Janine, but she said she couldn't leave her friend behind. And I don't want to break up a beautiful friendship. So we'll see how it goes.'

That was this other thing about Grant—his enduring bachelor's luck even in the face of age and cultural obsolescence. I liked Grant immensely—we all did, including Lippy, who had known him for years and had introduced him to Jess—but I couldn't understand the attraction he continued to exert over even the most beautiful and aloof young things. Jess held him in a kind of awe and envy (something he wisely concealed from Damienne), and even Flip conceded that she found him wildly sexy. When I asked her why, she responded, 'Because you can tell just from talking to him that he knows what to do with a woman,' as though this should have been completely obvious to me all along.

'So happy birthday, baby,' he finally said to me, grinning with general contentment into the middle distance of the party. 'How's your music coming along?'

'Pretty good. I'm taking this twelve-tone class I really like right now.'

'Very cool, very, cool.' He nodded slowly. 'So listen,' and he turned to me again with renewed keenness. 'Have you seen any of the stuff your brother's been bringing in to show me?'

'Just a few things. It's pretty good, huh?'

'Yep. It's pretty damn good. I think in a few months he'll be able to have a pretty damn good show. And I think we'll both be able to make some pretty damn good money. I've already got a bunch of ladies-who-lunch who have seen his slides, and they're all lined up to wallpaper their brownstones with Jess Mitchell.'

The lovely Janine stepped up then, hand in hand with a thoroughly plain-looking, somewhat amorphous girl who seemed to hang back in abject fear, scuffing her right foot on the floor like a nervous mare.

'Grant,' the lovely Janine said throatily, 'this is Sasha, one of my best friends from Yale. Cambridge is publishing her dissertation on the Primitivists next year.'

'You like the Primitivists?' Grant asked, offering his hand to Sasha, stroking her hand gently with his thumb as they shook an introduction.

Sasha flushed purple, and she and Janine erupted in nervous laughter. 'Well—um, you'd probably have to like them a little to write a three-hundred-page dissertation on them.'

'This is true,' Grant nodded, smiling agreeably. 'This is true. You know, Sasha, I've got this friend at the Modern who wants to put together a Primitivist show for 1991. Want me to see if she needs some help from another expert?'

Sasha gasped. 'Oh my God—no—I mean, of *course*! Of course! I'd love that—oh my God, thank you, uh—Mr. Fekkai—'

'Grant,' interrupted Grant.

'Grant! Okay, Grant. Um—thank you so much! Wow— uh—*wow*.' Now Sasha was scuffing her right foot with wild abandon.

'Don't worry about it,' Grant said, carefully extinguishing his joint and redepositing it into a little pewter box he pulled from his pocket. Then, as naturally as possible, with perfect synchronicity, he reached out to latch back a stray tendril of Sasha's hair, grazing her ear with his fingertips as he did it. Sasha made a little contented noise and stopped scuffing her foot—and *presto*, everything had fallen into place.

'Go get your coats in Tigger's room,' he said to them both. 'I'll be right here.'

They turned to go. 'I *told* you everything would be cool,' I heard Janine say to the shellshocked Sasha as they walked away.

I turned to Grant. 'You blow my mind.'

He shrugged again—there was no visible trace of vanity to his machinations, ever. 'She looks like a nice kid. Primitive,' he said, and I was laughing, shaking my head, as we embraced good-bye like two white hipsters drunkenly parting ways in front of the Cedar Tavern, circa 1958.

Ten

The hour had slipped around to four, and, at once stoned and speedy, I shouldered my way into the crowd to dance, warming to the crush of flushed bodies. Cedric and Joey, shirtless and stripped down almost to their workaday selves, had some eighteen-year-old cutie sandwiched between them and were feeling him up from either side.

'Birthday girl, come join!' Joey yelled, high as a kite, dragging me into their threesome.

I was chest to chest with the eighteen-year-old. 'I know you from Palladium,' I said.

He smiled, put his hand over my chest. 'I know you, too. Where's your husband?'

I smiled back. 'Home in bed.'

'Alone?'

'What?' Someone had turned up the music.

'*Alone?*'

'I hope so.'

He shrugged. 'I don't.'

'That's shady of you,' I laughed.

'Awww,' he mock-pouted. 'I'm sorry.'

'I'm sure you are.' Suddenly I had my hands on his waist and we were kissing, both of us swallowing back the chemical tang in our throat.

Next thing I knew, the kid was sliding his hands down the back of my pants. 'Do you want to get out of here?'

'Where do you live?' I asked him, gulping back my throat's guilty lump.

'Here in SoHo.'

I ran my hands up under his shirt. 'Oh yeah?'

'Yeah,' he said back in his obnoxious Valley voice. 'Do you have any more blow?'

I kissed him again. 'I can get us some.'

'From where?'

'From my sister.' Then I stepped back from what I had just said, shamed. But I knew it was true; it was a long time since Flip had supplied me, but it wouldn't be the first time.

'Your sister is so fabulous,' he gushed.

'She's the best. Hold on a second, okay?' Joey said something to me in Arabic as I broke away.

'What did you just say, Barbara?'

He smirked smartly. 'The Arabic version of see no evil, hear no evil—'

'Nothing's going on, feta mouth, so you better shut up.'

'Hmph, the birthday bitch!' He kissed me on both cheeks. 'Just be safe, habibi.'

I scowled and walked off. By the open door, someone woefully out of place in a pinstripe suit was lighting a cigarette, head bent into the flame. I gasped when he looked up, an amused half-smile squinting keenly around the room. It was Amos Goolsbee, the asshole from St. Peter's. He had gone to Princeton after high school, then moved to New York and become an investment banker. I remembered Flip paling about a year ago when someone had casually mentioned that Goolsbee was in the city, working in midtown and living in a co-op on the Upper West Side. Then she smirked. 'It doesn't seem very likely that our paths will cross.'

But they did cross, occasionally. It seemed Goolsbee hadn't forgotten Flip, waking her at three in the morning with drunk phone calls her first semester at Barnard (she'd tell him to fuck off, then hang up), and, in the past year, roughly figuring out her nocturnal schedule so that he and his suit buddies, once in a blue moon, could somehow gain entry into the dens she frequented, where he tried to ply her with drinks and coke while his friends made facetious passes at the gayboys and drag queens, until Flip finally had had enough and enlisted Ty or one of the other bouncers to escort them out. Flip confided in me about these visits; she wouldn't tell Jess, who surely would have gone after Goolsbee if he had known that he was nearly stalking our sister.

She worried me. 'Aren't you freaked out?' I'd ask. 'Don't you feel like you should get a restraining order on him or something?'

She'd shrug. 'He's not gonna do anything. Cedric alone could take care of him, even in heels. He's just a lonely, pathetic Wall Street loser. I almost kind of feel sorry for him, especially when he shows up places with his *brief*case.'

I'd raise my eyebrow. 'If you say so.'

'Honestly.' To this day, Jess and I didn't know exactly what had happened between Flip and Goolsbee that night at St. Pete's; Flip had never mentioned it again after the night she wigged out, and I think maybe Jess felt freed from the duty of avenging her as long as he didn't have the whole story. 'Maybe they just had a verbal fight,' he had said to me shortly after the event, uneasily. 'You know how Flip loves melodrama.'

Now, I cut away before Goolsbee could see me, picking my way through the crowd until I found Jess, slouched on the couch sharing a joint with some cute Latino queen from FIT (the Fashion Institute of Technology, in Chelsea, otherwise, and only half-affectionately, known as Fags In Training), their legs curiously laced together.

'Jess,' I shouted down, a trifle indignant.

He looked up, sleepy-eyed and stoned. 'Hey, baby. How you doin'? You a'ight?'

'I'm okay. Have you seen Flip?'

'Baby, I don't know *where* she's at. Probably off doin' the lambada with her man Ty.'

The FIT queen ran his hands through Jess's hair. 'You got curls like Gloria Estefan, honey.'

Jess laughed, brushing his hand back. 'Fuck you, man!' He took another long drag at the joint, then passed it to the queen, who held it archly, like some old movie queen with a cigarette in a long holder.

'Guess who's here?' I shouted to Jess, more indignant.

'Who, baby?' He passed me the joint; I paused, then took a modest hit.

'Fuckin' Goolsbee. He just walked in.'

'Are you fuckin' serious? Who's he with?'

'Alone, I think.'

Jess laughed, his head slumped against the happy queen's shoulder. 'You think we're gonna have to fuck him up, Tigger?'

'I don't know.'

'He's good to go as long as he doesn't work up Flip, you know?' Now Jess was nuzzling his face sleepily into the queen's shoulder. The queen put his arm around Jess, looked up at me and smiled smugly.

'Jess,' I finally yelled, exasperated. 'What the fuck are you doing?'

'What?' he laughed. 'I'm just loungin', Tigger. I'm loungin' on the lounge.'

'He's tired, poor baby,' the queen purred. 'It's hard bein' a *artiste*.'

Whoever was spinning put on a hard remix of 'Love to Love You, Baby', which made me think of the boy from Palladium. I scowled reprovingly at Jess, who smiled goofily, and at the queen, who blew me a kiss, then squeezed my way back onto the dance floor.

Palladium Boy grabbed my hand. 'Are we leaving?' he asked, his hands all over me again.

'Yeah. Yeah. In a second. I just gotta find my sister.'

'Hurry up, okay?'

'Okay.' Cedric and Joey were making out—they always did when they were horny and high, even though they insisted that they were 'just best girlfriends.' Then I bumped into Anthea and Katja, snogging up against the refrigerator.

'Anthea.'

She looked up, lipstick smeared. 'Hello, Tigger, love. Happy birthday, darling.'

'Happy happy, darling,' Katja said brightly in broken English.

'Thanks.'

'Are you looking for your sis, darling?' Anthea asked.

'How'd you know?'

'Everyone's always looking for Flip. Why should you be any different? She's in her room with the nasty lad. Goolsbee.'

'Honest?'

'To goodness.'

'*Why?*'

'I dunno. She probably wants to have herself some, just like the rest of us. And he's the only real man here, with the exception of your brother.'

'Don't be shady, Anthea. And don't be so sure about Jess tonight, either.'

Anthea's eyes lit up. '*Reeelly?* I'm speechless. I certainly hope not.'

'Don't worry. I think he's just high. And why do you care? You've got yours.'

'I'm tired of fish and chips. This is America—I want red meat!'

'Anthea!' I nodded toward Katja, minutely absorbed in a coupon for twenty-nine cents off Marlboro Lights that Flip had magneted to the refrigerator.

'She doesn't understand, Tigger. Isn't that right, darling?' Anthea bellowed into Katja's ear.

Katja looked up, smiling brightly. 'Right and happy, darling.'

'See?' Anthea shrugged.

'You're wicked, Anthea.'

Anthea shrugged again. 'So be it.'

From the dance floor, Palladium Boy threw me a look that said *Well*? I signaled one minute, then headed for Flip's room, where Ty, all six-and-a-half muscled feet of him, stood sulking just outside.

'What's wrong, Ty?' I asked.

'Nothing,' he murmured, and I had to strain to hear over the music. Ty spoke low, almost to the point of inaudibility, and it was something of an acquired talent to string together the occasional words or phrases enough to carry on a conversation. Chats with him never lasted long anyway—at length, he'd trail off, looking obliquely beyond you, leaving you to wonder about the inner life of this grown-up homeboy who had such discretionary control over the glittering world of downtown, and seemingly so little control of his own tiny household 150 blocks above us. Word on Ty was that he also carried a pistol in his pants while on the job—'packin' a gat,' Cedric called it, swooningly, for he was crazy for Ty. 'Now that's a *fine* piece of brotherhood,' he liked to say of him, and thrilled to even the most half-hearted crumb of attention from him.

So, 'Nothing,' Ty mumbled again now, "cept your sister just stepped on into her room with some mofo in a suit and tie. I seen his face around before, at the clubs.'

'That's just Amos Goolsbee, this asshole we know from high school. Flip's probably just dicking around with him, then she'll kick him out of here. She can't stand him, Ty, honestly.'

Ty shrugged skeptically. 'Maybe I should be gettin' on home now, seein' she's got company.'

'What did you tell Shereen tonight?' I asked. We all knew about Ty's family uptown—when he first started working the clubs, perhaps to assure himself that he hadn't been kidnapped to some strange and alien planet, he'd pull their pictures out of his wallet and show them to anyone who would look. Then his flirtation with Flip began—playfully on her part, clumsily and curiously on his—and by the time it became public knowledge downtown that they were occasional bedmates, Ty stopped pulling out the pictures, drawing an unmistakable line between his two worlds once and for all.

'Same old same old,' he answered me now. 'That I had to work a late night. I told her I'd be back up there by noon to take the kids to the park. She's going shopping with her mother and sister.'

'You can crash in my room if you want.'

He pulled out a Newport and lit it. 'Thanks Tigger, but that's a'ight. Makes most sense for me to go on home, prolly, be a good father.'

Something about the wistful way he talked about 'going home' broke my heart. I imagined his life uptown—trapped in a two- or three-room apartment with a screaming wife and two little kids—and I wondered how it was that even someone as utterly indifferent to fabulousness as Ty had ended up in Flip's orbit, searching for something he couldn't even quite define.

'Well,' I said, all tough love, 'you know it's never any guarantee waiting around for Flip.'

He laughed, low and ironic. 'Believe me, Tigger, I got no false notions about your sister. You get what you get with Flip, and don't expect no more or less.'

I smiled. 'So what are you still doing here, standing outside her bedroom door?'

'A man's gotta try.' He smiled back philosophically. 'Ain't that right, Tigger?'

'You deserve better than Flip,' I said. It seemed to be one of the few times when a blunt assessment of Flip's character was called for. 'At least Shereen's there for you all the time.'

'I know!' He laughed, a sudden burst of animation. 'That's just the goddam problem!'

Now we both laughed, and he gave me his complicated handshake. 'A'ight Tiggerman, I'll be seein' you soon. An' you tell your sister that her loverman Ty say adios for now.'

'I will, Ty. Take care.'

'Peace.' And in a minute, he was weaving his way toward the door, head and shoulders above the crowd, studiously oblivious to the rapt stares he commanded from men and women alike.

I was just about to knock at Flip's slightly ajar bedroom door when I heard her agitated voice from inside—'so *pointless*,' she said in harsh tones—and froze just outside.

'Not necessarily,' someone answered back calmly. It was Goolsbee.

'—pointless to come,' Flip continued, 'especially dressed like that. You know you hate these people, Goolsbee—a bunch of drag queens and fags—'

'Like your little brother?'

'Yes, like my little brother, whose birthday party this happens to be, and who has more human beingness in his little finger than you have in your whole disgusting body. You hate them. And you know they hate you. So why aren't you at some party on the Upper West Side?'

'Because.'

'Because *why*?'

'Because maybe I wanted a change of scene.'

'But you weren't *invited*.'

'Maybe I wanted to see you.'

'Maybe I want you to fuck off and die.'

'Maybe I brought you some really good blow.'

Flip laughed bitterly. 'Maybe I can get that anywhere.'

'Maybe I want to fuck you silly.'

'*FUCK YOU!*' I heard the crack of palm hitting face.

Silence, then, lower, from Goolsbee. 'Mmm, mmm, good.'

'You're asking for it, Goolsbee.' Through her defiance, Flip sounded as though she were going to cry. Finally, I stepped in the room. Flip's back was to me, and Goolsbee saw me first.

'Hi, Tigger!' he beamed, eyes squinting. 'Your sister just *slapped* me.'

Flip whirled around, humiliated. 'Tigger, get the fuck out!'

'What the fuck's going on?' I asked, thinking how ridiculous I sounded when I tried to be threatening.

'How's your boyfriend, Tig?' Goolsbee asked. He was clearly drunk, in a decorous sort of way. 'Now, does *he* give it to *you* up the ass, or do *you* give it to *him*? Or, um, have you figured out how to give it to each other at the same time?'

'At the same time,' I shot back with blessed speed. 'You and your Dobermann showed us at St. Pete's, remember?'

Flip burst out laughing. Goolsbee smiled calmly. 'All the Mitchells are so funny,' he said, sing-song.

'Tigger, get out,' Flip cut him off. 'I'm fine. He's not staying.'

'Jess knows he's here,' I warned. 'So do Cedric and Ty.'

'How's *Jess*?' Goolsbee clapped his hands together. 'I hear he's got a fine negress now. How does that make you feel, Flip?'

'You are so profoundly sad,' Flip said evenly.

'They really know how to make a Latin man happy, Flip. More than a white girl from Massachusetts ever could.'

Flip took a breath and turned to me. 'Tigger darling, what did you want in the first place?'

'I don't know if I should go.'

'Did you want this?' she said, holding out a small vial of coke. I stood, speechless. 'If you want it, take it.' And she walked over to me, slapped it into my hand. 'Now would you please leave the two of us in peace so we can finish our little conversation?'

'Why are you even *talking* to him?' I hissed at her under my breath.

She was just about to hiss something back when Goolsbee interrupted cheerily. 'Where you gonna put that blow, Tigger?'

I moved to retort—what? what?—but Flip stopped me, hand on my shoulder. 'I'll see you later, Tigger.'

'Flip—'

'I'll—see—you—later.'

'Bye, Tiggy,' Goolsbee said, wiggling his fingers at me.

Half-furious, I stormed out of her bedroom and back over to the couch. Jess's head lay, eyes closed, in the FIT queen's lap while the queen stroked his hair.

'He's sleeping, baby,' the queen said to me.

'Too bad. Jess.' I shook him on the shoulder.

He looked up, disoriented, smiled. 'Hunh?'

'Flip is in her room with Goolsbee.'

'Goolsbee's a motherfucker,' he yawned dreamily.

'It's getting kind of nasty.'

Jess laughed. '*Who's that thinking nasty thoughts?*'

The queen cackled. 'You like Janet, honey?'

'Um. Yeah.'

'*Jess.*' I was beginning to lose my patience.

'Tiggah,' he croaked, mocking our late father. 'Do you really think Goolsbee came over uninvited? Flip wants some booty.'

'*Jess!*'

'She's a horny chick, Tig. She wants some booty.'

'It's what the world wants,' the queen philosophized.

'That's right,' Jess said. 'You know Flip, Tig. She goes where the booty is.'

The queen nodded sagely. 'She's a love pirate.'

An enormous crashing noise from Flip's room overwhelmed the music. For a moment, the din in the room subsided— Donna Summer moaned—before people resumed dancing.

'See, Jess?' I warned.

He laughed. 'Sounds like she's getting some.'

'Why are you being such a dick?'

'Tig, it isn't *my* dick that's out of my pants.'

'She *didn't!*' gasped the queen.

Suddenly, I couldn't give a shit about my sister *or* my

brother. 'I'm getting out of here. To hell with all of you,' I said, but Jess had already dozed off again. 'Buenos noches, baby,' the queen smiled.

'Yeah, honey,' I scoffed before turning. 'Good *luck*.'

I stalked back onto the dance floor and grabbed Palladium Boy out from between Cedric and Joey. 'I got it. Let's go.'

Cedric sucked his teeth at Joey. 'Impatience will get her *every*where.'

'I'm not doing anything wrong!' I suddenly exploded, feeling very crummy.

'Nobody's judging you, Tigger,' Joey said absurdly.

'I don't care if they are!' I snapped, yanking at Palladium Boy.

'I gotta get my shirt!' he yelled, tugging away from me. 'I took off my shirt and I don't know where I put it.'

'It's warm outside,' I said. 'You'll be fine. Come on. I wanna get out of here.' I led him out of the crowd toward the door. Last thing before I stepped out, I turned to Flip's room—the door was closed—then to the couch, where the FIT queen was trying to make out with my barely conscious brother.

'That's the first Latina *he's* ever been with,' I said to Palladium Boy as I flew down the stairwell ahead of him.

'What?'

'Never mind,' I said, stopping on the landing, grabbing him by his belt loops and pressing my tongue between his teeth. 'What's your name, anyway?' I said on a caught breath.

'Parker.'

'I'm—'

'Tigger.'

'How did you know?'

'Your sister talks about you all the time. She tried to set us up before you got together with that guy. I think you thought I was kind of an idiot.'

I stepped back a moment, and looked at him. He was skinny—his jeans sagging down two inches below his boxers,

in the new hip-hop style—all ribcage, pale chest, watery blue
eyes, baby's mouth, and Nazi-cropped straw-blond hair, a dead
ringer for about a thousand other high school drop-outs from
the Midwest who moved here every spring and got lost inside
the thousand reflections of themselves in some nightclub's
giant mirrorball. He made me feel, at twenty-one, very old
and very randy.

'What do you do, again?' I asked, catching his nipples
between the insides of my fingers.

'Mmmm.' He sounded like a five-year-old taking ice cream.
'I work for Anthea two days a week. But I'm really here to be
a—'

'An actor?'

'No. Mmmm.'

'A model?'

'Yeah.'

'You get any gigs yet?' I slipped my hand inside the back of
his boxers, and it occurred to me how thrilling it felt to be
shallow and predatory, so bluntly insistent with a stranger,
after so many months of tedious good conduct for Seb's sake.

'Yeah. Um. Yeah. I got a shoot with Esprit next Tuesday. Do
you wanna get out of here?'

'Uh hunh. Come on.'

It was quiet out on Broome Street, cooler than I thought,
and it felt good after the steam and noise of the loft.

'Jesus, it's freezing!' Parker shuddered, wrapping his arms
around himself, his jeans slipping lower on his shorts.

'Come here,' I said. I took off my shirt—it was a big, gauzy
WilliWear that Flip had gotten me for Christmas a few years
ago—and slipped it on him. 'We don't want you getting pneumonia before your big shoot on Tuesday.'

'Thanks.' He shuddered again, putting his arm around me,
and for a moment I felt, with an unexpected little shiver of
comfort, like somebody's older brother.

He didn't live quite in SoHo, which really didn't surprise

me, but in a fifth-floor studio the size of Flip's whole closet in a grim building far west on Canal Street, tucked in near the entrance to the Holland Tunnel.

'Hold on,' he said at the door, hurrying into the room to light candles and slip a Roxy Music cassette into his miniature boom box. It was a familiar kind of space to me—clothes and records stored in milk crates, Bruce Weber images tacked up on the wall, scattered copies of *GQ* and *International Male*, a twin-sized futon covered in faded old Snoopy sheets, a squat half-fridge (empty, probably, except for orange juice, peanut butter, and some cheap vodka), burnt-out sticks of incense, and, as I suspected, the framed pictures by the bed—dad's face as flat and plain as Kansas, mom's framed by big, sensible, ugly glasses, sister with freckles, bad make-up and a stiff halo of moussed hair. (The kind of sister, I always thought grate-fully, I had been spared.)

Parker stepped unfussily out of his jeans and threw them on a milk crate alongside his black Chuck Taylors. He sat down near me on the edge of the futon, nervously fingering the Snoopy sheets, and I ran my hand over his brush cut. He seemed anxious to say something, but couldn't get it out. I raised an eyebrow encouragingly.

'Do you like having a boyfriend?' he finally asked.

I laughed, but he just stared blankly, so I sobered up. 'I guess so.'

'Do you guys have a— a—'

'An open relationship?'

'Yeah.'

'Um.' I squirmed a little. 'No. Not really. I mean, we haven't really said, one way or the other, but—'

'Unh?'

'I mean, I don't think he'd be too happy if he knew I were here.'

'So why are you?'

'Because you're cute.' If it wasn't quite the only answer, it certainly was the appropriate one. He grimaced and turned away to finish his water.

'Have you had a boyfriend in New York?' I asked him.

'Not really. Well, sort of one, when I first got here. We went out for three weeks. He helped me find this place.'

'So what happened?'

'Well. You know. He was pretty successful. I think he was a lawyer or something. But, you know, he was thirty-nine years old.'

'You could have had it easy,' I said.

'I know, but— I wanted to pursue my own career and every-thing. You know?'

'Yeah, I do.' I leaned in to kiss him, and he pulled back, startling me.

'Did you bring that blow you said you'd bring?'

'Yeah. Why? You want some?'

'Maybe later. I think I wanna just chill a minute, okay?'

I shrugged. 'Okay.'

He lay down on his back, hands behind his head, and stared up vacantly at the ceiling.

'You like Bryan Ferry?' I asked, lying back, propping my cheek on my fist.

'Hm?' he asked dreamily. 'Oh. Yeah.'

I ran my fingers over his stomach—his ribs stuck out like a little kid's—then into his boxers, where I pulled out his crum-pled dick. I didn't really do anything to it, just held it and waited to see it unfurl—which it didn't, curiously. I looked up at him. He had fallen asleep, mouth open and eyes closed. I took off my shirt and shoes, lay down, turned him on his side and wrapped my arms around him.

He chuckled in his sleep. 'Scotty,' he said.

I squeezed him tighter, grimly amused. 'That's right,' I mut-tered back. 'Everything's okay. Scotty's here— Scotty's—' And I slid into sleep.

*

Horns honking outside near the Holland Tunnel woke me at nine the next morning, a monstrous headache rising up out of the fog of my half-consciousness. 'How can you ever sleep in with this?' I rasped to Parker, who just drew up tighter in a fetal position and barely managed a mumble.

'I'm just gonna let myself out. I'll stop into Anthea's shop sometime, okay?' More mumbling. I pulled the sheet up over him and rose from the futon, holding my head like a bruised and leaking cantaloupe, then pissed, washed my face and smeared toothpaste on my teeth in his coffin of a bathroom, threw on pants and shoes, and clattered down the five flights, out the door.

Outside, it was mercifully warm and cursedly bright. I bought three-dollar fake Ray-Bans, an enormous Coke and a pack of Camels at the nearest deli, put them all to immediate use, and started home, surprised to find that I felt peculiarly high-spirited despite my headache and drug-ravaged bones. Here it was, one of the first spring days that suggested summer, the city looked dazzling (thankfully, through smoked lenses), and I had managed to have a one-night stand without really cheating on Seb—technically, at any rate. I'd decided to go home and surprise Jess and Flip by starting to clean the loft before they even woke up.

But I was wrong. I was *really* wrong. Stepping inside the loft, peering across a long, dark expanse of debris, I saw Jess sitting on the couch, wearing nothing but his boxers, head in hands, smoking a cigarette and staring into space.

'Hey,' I called.

He looked up, startled. 'What are you doing home?' he snapped.

'Um . . . I live here? Have you gone to bed yet?'

Before he could answer, Flip bounded out of Jess's bedroom, breathless—and naked. She spotted me and stopped dead in her tracks.

'Oh! Hello, Tig,' she said with a horrible brightness,

wheeling around and darting back into her room, slamming the door behind her. In a moment, I heard her sobbing.

I felt something unseemly, confusion and a rising nausea. 'Jess?' I whispered across the loft.

He stubbed out his cigarette, fast and clumsy. 'Just wait a minute, Tigger.'

'Jess?'

'Just wait a minute.' He was stumbling toward me, my own brother, piquing and terrifying me all at once. But before he could reach me, I was back out the door, down the stairs and in the middle of the street. Now the confusion was really swelling in my head—I couldn't go back upstairs and couldn't go back to Parker's, but intensely didn't want to go to Lippy's or Seb's. So I walked west, faster and faster, over the West End Highway and onto one of the Hudson River piers, right out to the very edge, where I sat, blinking and smoking, all morning long.

Eleven

We didn't talk about it. None of us. Not right away, anyway.

When I finally gathered my wits about me late that afternoon, I took the subway out to Seb's apartment in Park Slope—*no way in hell am I going back to the loft tonight*, I thought to myself—picking up dinner and a conciliatory bottle of wine on the way. I knew dully that he was angry about the night before, that, as per my old bad habits, I hadn't dutifully followed suit when he pronounced grimly at three in the morning that he was heading home, but had chosen instead to carry on into the night. And it didn't surprise me when, after ringing up and announcing myself, he took longer than usual to buzz me in.

'Why are you still in your clothes from last night?' he asked sullenly as I sidled my way into the apartment, which looked prim and civil as always, and, today, more of a welcome change from the cavernous loft than he could ever know. Ravel played on the stereo, manuscripts littered the coffee table, and water was boiling on the stove top for his usual afternoon tea.

'I just fell asleep in them,' I shrugged itchily. Wasn't it more or less the truth?

His eyes narrowed. 'Late night, huh?' He closed the door,

turned his back to me and busied himself with teabags. 'You want a cup?'

'Yes, please,' I whispered, grateful. 'I guess it was a late night.' I lowered myself into a chair, reminded upon sitting that my hangover hadn't yet completely dissipated. 'I guess they still happen every once in a while,' I said, faintly defensive.

'I *guess* so,' he said, his back still to me.

He brought the teapot and cups to the kitchen table and we both sat, blowing on our steaming cups. The Ravel had played itself out and we sat in complete silence now. 'I brought some dinner,' I finally ventured.

'I already bought something.'

'Oh.' The fluorescent light hummed over our heads. I felt a peculiar wave of misery swell up in my stomach; between the revelation of that morning and the freeze-out I was getting now, I thought I would surely disintegrate right there in my very chair. 'Look, Seb, I'm sorry about last night,' I finally burst out. 'I'm sorry. I got carried away. I'll go if you want me to.'

He looked up at me, irritated. 'What would that solve?'

'Well, I just—I mean, I'm *sorry*, okay? What do you want me to do?'

'Do you *really* know what I want you to do? What I wish *you* wanted to do?'

'What?'

'Break away from your fucking siblings a little more, that's what.' He put his cup down, white-faced. 'There. I said it.'

I stared at him, rather incredulous. Even after what had happened that morning, I was so startled by Seb's remark that all I could think to say was: 'Why?'

'Because! Because they totally run your life, especially Flip. I mean, I think it's great and all that you three are so close, and who am I to talk being an only child? But Thomas—don't you think it's just a little *odd* how much time you guys spend together? I mean, you *live* together, that's one thing. But some-times—no, actually, *most* of the time—I think you guys wouldn't care if you ever saw another person again except each other, and maybe Lippy. Thomas,' he said, softer. 'You're twenty-one. Don't you think it's just a little unnatural?'

That last word in particular made me wince. I hadn't ever really thought much about how close the three of us were—as children, none of us had really had any best friends save each other, and even at St. Peter's, where we did have a few other friends, like Kira, they existed inevitably as satellites to our essential orbit of three. It was much the same now; of course, I couldn't really speak for Jess, but I knew that Flip would turn her back on the whole of lower Manhattan if she had to choose between them and us, and certainly I—and I banished that thought with a guilty pang, sitting there with Seb, who had virtually saved me from myself a few months ago. But the thought remained, impervious to guilt and good intentions: he was a footnote in my life compared to my brother and sister.

Unnatural. Maybe, but I had to be perfectly, bluntly honest with myself: if what had happened last night between Jess and Flip was unnatural—and it probably had happened, after all—it ultimately didn't strike me as that surprising. After all, hadn't it been obvious, at least on Flip's part, for years? And even if he hadn't necessarily encouraged Flip, Jess certainly had never resisted. And then, the hardest truth to swallow, *me*: because if my first reaction in that awful, frozen moment this past morning had been shock, then my immediate second one had been a bruised, enraged jealousy of Flip. She had it on me—in some smug, perennially adolescent recess of her mind, she knew that Jess wasn't completely invulnerable to her gifts.

A big bang was coming, it suddenly occurred to me—I could sense the early tremors as soundly as earth shifts under-foot—and if I wasn't the first to clear the area, I would be the one to get hurt.

'Thomas?'

'Hm?'

'Did you hear my question?'

I turned to him, with a gravity that surprised him. 'Yeah. I did. And you're right. It is a little fucked up. A lot fucked up.'

He blinked, taken aback. 'You really think so?'

'More or less,' I said coolly.

'You're not just saying that to appease me?'

'No,' I said, and I meant it more than he could have known.

'So? What do you want to do?'

'Do you mind if I hang out here for a while? Until I figure out what to do about a living situation?'

He picked up his teacup. 'You're always welcome here. You know that.'

'Thank you, baby.' I got up, leaned over, kissed him. 'Want me to start dinner?'

He nodded, slightly bewildered but pleased nonetheless, I could see. *This is it,* I thought to myself as I took the groceries out of the bag. *This is the beginning of the end of us.*

I passed an unprecedentedly quiet week with him, cooking meals in the evening, biking in Prospect Park, renting videos, listening to music and reading. No Manhattan, no Grand Central Station of an apartment, no all-night parties. Seb seldom said so, but I knew he was happy. So was I, I guess, and when I found myself wondering about Jess and Flip and what they might be up to—as I did, about a hundred times a day—I simply banished the thought from my head, and turned back to Seb, or *The New Yorker*, or the pot of risotto I was experimenting with.

During the day, when I wasn't in classes, I spent all my time in the practice rooms at Mannes—just me, a well-tuned console and sheafs of notation paper before me, sealed inside sound-proofed walls. I flew through my assigned exercises and spent the rest of my time sketching out the first draft of the piece I wanted to present at the year-end recital—a long, complicated effort that took the most well-known phrases from 'I Got Rhythm' and reiterated them in constantly changing mode—Aeolian, Lydian, and so on. It was the first time since my initial weeks at Mannes that I threw myself so wholly into my music, and it recalled for me that solitary year at St. Pete's after both Jess and Flip had left, before Kira and I hooked up, when I spent almost all of my time alone with a piano in the arts center, working on studies to send to Mannes for admission. What I remembered was the unfamiliar satisfaction of having something all my own, unconnected to Jess or Flip, and now that old feeling came back to me with a queer, almost exotic pleasure. Jess had said something much the same once about his first year at SVA—had said it was the first time he had ever felt 'all real' without anyone else around to confirm it for him.

During my second week in Brooklyn, Lippy caught up with me by phone at Seb's.

'Tigger,' she exclaimed, and it occurred to me that I hadn't heard my old family nickname in days (Seb thought it was foolish and refused to call me anything except a proper Thomas). 'Have you been at Seb's all this time?'

'Uh hunh.' I knew I was in for a come-uppance of sorts; it was impossible for Lippy not to concern herself with our lives, or, as she saw it, our welfare.

'Have you been home at *all*?'

'Just once, to get some stuff.'

There was an awkward pause. 'Tigger,' Lippy went on, more sternly, 'exactly *what is* going on?'

'What do you mean?' I answered, as innocently as possible.

'Flip spent the night here last night—she was a nervous wreck. She said that she hadn't seen either you or Jess in days. She was sullen and preoccupied, and when I asked her what had happened, all she kept saying was "They hate me, they both do, and they're trying to punish me." Did something happen at your party?'

'No, not particularly,' I lied. Suddenly I felt distinctly awful for having abandoned Flip; I could picture her in that big, gloomy loft all alone, and only God knew what she was doing with herself. Jess and I would be all right; we had Damienne and Seb, after all. But, excepting her monstrous crowd of hangers-on and the occasional illicit visit from Ty, Flip really had nobody. 'I just wanted to spend some time in Brooklyn with Seb,' I said to Lippy.

'Well,' and she sounded suspicious. 'Have you talked to Jess recently?'

'Not since the party.'

'Well, Tigger, I suggest you give him a call at that girl-friend's of his and arrange for the two of you to check in on your sister. She doesn't seem herself at all, and I worry about her alone at home with only those characters to keep her company. Tigger,' and Lippy's voice dropped. 'Maybe I'm being paranoid, but I'm afraid she's going to get involved with drugs.'

I laughed ruefully to myself. Poor, sweet Lippy, so naive despite her *chanteuse* drag—she probably thought a night of stiff martinis was the height of vice. 'I don't think so,' I lied reassuringly. 'Flip is smarter than that.'

'Well,' she hesitated. 'Would you *please* give Jess a call and see about this? I hate it when you three aren't in touch. How am I supposed to keep track of all of you when no one knows what's going on with the other?'

'All right, Lippy. Love to you.'

'Love to you, Tigger. How's your classes and lessons?'

'Pretty good.'

'All right, then. Love again. Love to Seb. And *call your brother*.'

I hung up, stared hard at the phone. Perhaps it was time to give Jess a call after all. We couldn't go on not speaking to each other forever. I dialed his studio, and someone at the front desk paged him to one of the phones in the corridor.

'Hello?'

'Jess? It's Tigger.'

Silence, as I predicted. 'Oh. Hi. How you doin'?' he finally managed.

'Okay. I've been staying with Seb.'

'Yeah. Yeah, I figured. I haven't been at the loft much, either.'

'Yeah. Listen, Jess. We have to talk. Lippy called me here, and she's worried about Flip. She said Flip stayed over last night, all upset, and that she wouldn't say anything except that we had, like, deserted her, and that she thought we hated her.'

A long pause from Jess, then, finally, 'Listen, Tig, about Saturday morning—'

'Jess, I don't care about it,' I cut him off. I absolutely didn't want to hear a word from him about it, truth or no truth. 'But I think we should talk.'

'Yeah, so do I. In fact, I was gonna call you today to say the same thing. I have to talk to you.'

'You wanna meet at the loft tonight?' I asked him.

'No,' he said hastily. 'Not the loft. Actually—actually, why don't I come out to Brooklyn?'

'Brooklyn?'

'Yeah. Can you meet me at Moony's at, like, five o'clock?'

'I guess so,' I said. Moony's was an old pub on the border of Park Slope and Flatbush that attracted crusty old Brooklynites as well as the new wave of young hipsters. Seb and I liked it, and on the rare occasions when Jess or Flip came out to Brooklyn, inevitably we wound up there, Flip marveling drunkenly at how 'unpretentious' everyone in Brooklyn seemed.

'Okay. Done deal. Five o'clock.'

He wasn't there at five, as I had predicted; anyone who didn't live in Brooklyn always underestimated the wait for the trains.

I sat at the quiet bar, listening to Steely Dan, nursing a beer and a cigarette I had scammed from the bartender. I wondered exactly what Jess was going to say; surely, he'd agree with me that we had to end this cold war. Surely there was a way we could all remain close without necessarily forfeiting our own lives. Surely he'd agree that we simply couldn't abandon Flip. And maybe my idea of moving out of the loft had been too rash; there must be some way of making it work out, and after all, it was too fabulous a piece of real estate to abandon just like that.

At twenty past five, he arrived, looking harried, his paint-splattered working rags underneath his leather jacket. 'I can only stay 'til six,' he announced, sitting at the bar. 'I gotta go back to Damienne's and change and meet her at this amnesty benefit thing at seven.'

'You're the one who's late,' I bristled.

'Yeah, I know, I know. I'm sorry. The fucking trains.'

'Whatever.'

He took a cigarette from his pocket, lit it. Funny, I thought. I hadn't seen him in something like nine days. I couldn't remember us being apart for a span of time that long since my last year alone at St. Pete's.

'How you getting along?' he asked me briskly, exhaling. I shrugged.

'How's Seb? Happy to have you?'

'He's okay. How's Damienne?'

'She's all right. Busy these days. Case overload and that kind of stuff.'

That's what happens when you're out to single-handedly save the world, I thought nastily to myself, but I managed a polite 'Hmph.'

'Look, first of all, Tig,' and he sounded oddly businesslike, as though he were determined to make this most touchy of meetings as neat and clean as possible. 'I'm sorry about Saturday morning.'

'Jess, I said I didn't want to hear about it, okay?'

'I know, but still, it was stupid of us. Even though nothing was going on, it was a bad scene for you to walk into.'

I said nothing. Did he really expect me to believe that nothing had been going on? And if it hadn't, why did he think it was such a bad scene for me to walk into? It wasn't the first time I had seen him hungover in his boxer shorts, and it wasn't the first time I had seen Flip naked—she had always been rather casual about that, almost perversely so.

'You do believe that, right?' he asked me.

'Of course,' I scowled, lying.

'Good.' He took a final drag, stubbed out his cigarette. He wasn't even ordering a drink, I noticed. 'And the other thing is,' he continued, 'I'm moving out of the loft and in with Damienne, permanently, just as soon as I can. Maybe it's not such a bad idea for you to consider doing the same thing with Seb. We can't all live together forever, right?'

I paused, a bit stunned. Just when I had begun to think the idea of dispersal was rash—and certainly not very supportive of Flip—here was Jess, proposing just that.

'Have you thought of doing that?' he asked me when I failed to respond.

'Well, yeah, but—what about Flip? She can't afford that big loft all alone.'

'She won't have to live there alone. I can think of a million people that would want to live in that place with her. I heard Cedric saying he wants to move.'

'But if it's not Cedric, do you think it's such a good idea for Flip to live with one of those random club people? Who's gonna put her to bed when she passes out on the couch?'

Jess latched a loose strand of hair back behind his ears. 'Tig, man, that's just the point. Flip has gotta learn to take care of herself. We can't go on being her babysitters forever. She's gotta get a real job—and some kind of real life.'

'You never talked that way about her before. It seemed you always liked her that way.'

'Yeah, well—' and I knew who, in part, was speaking for him.

'Damienne wants you to move out, doesn't she?'

'She wants me to do what I think is right.'

'How generous of her,' I said sarcastically. 'You know she hates Flip, don't you?'

'Tigger, that's not true. But Flip treats her like such shit, I wouldn't blame Damienne if she did. She's condescending to her. She's condescending to everyone. It's like we're all part of her little zoo of curiosities. Her menagerie, or something. Oh, here's my exotic Puerto Rican adopted brother with his exotic, righteous Haitian girlfriend. Oh, here are my fierce black and Arab drag queen friends. Oh, here's my cute little gay pianist brother. Aren't you tired of being part of her circus?'

'A lot of those people in her circus are my friends,' I said. 'And yours, too. And you know she's gotten me gigs through them. And she's hooked you up with art people, too. Why do you think she does that? Because you're a *curiosity* to her? No. She does it because she loves you, 'cause she looks out for you.'

He looked at me rather coldly. 'You don't get it, do you?' he asked.

I stared, uncomprehending.

'No,' he said dully. 'I guess you don't. You couldn't.'

'Jess,' I pleaded, frustrated and wounded. 'I know how you feel about Flip. She's a lot to handle.' He grimaced, turning briefly away. 'But we can't just abandon her. She'd fall apart. And Lippy would kill us.'

'Tig, just because you move out on someone doesn't mean you're abandoning them. We'll see each other all the time.'

'No, we won't,' I sulked. I was sure Damienne would see to that.

He tapped his fingers impatiently on the bartop. 'Come on, Tigger. Don't make this harder than it is. You can't tell me you haven't been thinking about it, too. Can you?'

I stared off pointedly away from him, not answering. 'It'd be nice to live with Seb, wouldn't it?' he went on. 'He's a great guy. Brooklyn's great—it's so fucking *sane*. And he told me that if you ever moved in, he'd help you bring in a piano.'

I still wouldn't answer. He was trying to pleasantly surprise me, but Seb had mentioned the piano thing to me about a hundred times. He knew I hated the beat-up old upright we had in the loft, and how hard it was for me to play there with the constant stream of visitors and the relentless pounding of dance music from the stereo system.

'When are you thinking of officially moving out?' I finally broached.

'In a month or so, as soon as we can line up roommates for Flip.'

'Have you told her yet?'

He shook his head sheepishly.

'Have you even seen her since the party?'

'Just once, when I went over to get some things. She was sitting around watching talk shows. We didn't have a lot to say to each other.' *I'm glad I wasn't a fly on the wall* that *morning*, I thought to myself. 'I'll tell her soon enough. Maybe we can tell her together.'

Coward, I thought, saying nothing.

'Anyway,' he finally said, sliding off the barstool. 'I should get going. Let's be in touch soon, okay? You know you can always reach me at the studio, or at Damienne's.'

I shrugged, not really able to meet his eyes.

'Come on, Tig. It's not gonna be so bad. It's not like we're moving to separate *cities* or anything. You know we're all stuck with each other.' And he gave me a clumsy little hug and a peck on the cheek. 'You wanna walk me back to the train?'

'I think I'm gonna stay and have one more drink,' I said coldly. I didn't really want another, but I certainly didn't feel like seeing him back off to his officious homewrecker girlfriend.

'All right, amigo. Talk soon.' He clutched the back of my neck briefly, then was gone. I stared blankly after him as he trudged on down Flatbush, hands in pockets. I ordered another drink and sat there, staring into the sudsy dregs of my beer, wondering when and how it would all come down.

Another week passed, and I still couldn't bring myself to go to the loft. Flip was on my mind all the time, and spectrally present in my dreams, but something kept me from going. Instead, I plunged deeper into my music, and in the evenings, Seb and I maintained our domestic rituals—dinner, video rentals of all of Douglas Sirk's films (with which he had a particular semiotic fascination), books (or, in his case, manuscripts), then bedtime, marked occasionally by a kind of studious, rote sex which I had long ago accepted as about as comforting as chamomile tea on a rainy Sunday afternoon, and about as exhilarating, too. Seb cleaved to this evening schedule with an almost monastic devotion, and if I originally found it reassuring in this rather topsy-turvy time—New York spring edging restively into New York summer—it now began to have a sedative effect on me.

Seb hated bars and clubs—he often said that he'd rather stay home on a Saturday night and teach himself ancient Greek than pay ten dollars to go deaf in a roomful of drunk, prowling homosexuals—and it was such that one lonely evening, when he was having dinner on the Upper East Side with his father and stepmother, that I stole into Manhattan to check out a flashy new joint that had opened in Chelsea. It wasn't that I wanted to horse around—I truly didn't—but after my first six months with Seb, I had discovered a certain odd thrill in sneaking alone into bars and standing about sullenly with a beer and a cigarette, posing as though I did, then half-reluctantly changing locales just as conversation loomed.

It was in just such an attitude that Cedric happened upon me—not Urethra, but Cedric, butch and workaday in his steel-toed boots and flannel shirt, a Budweiser in one hand and a Kool in the other.

He started in mock-reproval when he saw me. 'I thought you were all happily shacked up in Crooklyn.'

I hadn't seen anyone in Flip's set since the night of the party, and I was glad to see him despite, or perhaps partially because of, his familiar old bitchiness. 'I am, I guess,' I responded, leaning in dutifully to accept his salutatory peck on the cheek. 'Seb's with his family tonight, and I thought I'd get out for a little while.'

He sucked his teeth. 'Maybe the next time you have a night free from your husband, you could go pay a visit to your long-lost sister. Maybe that way Ms. Ghanoosh and me wouldn't always have to be keeping her company.'

'Why?' I asked, guilty. 'Isn't she all right?'

He shrugged elaborately. 'I guess that depends on what you call all right. You call sitting in the apartment watching *Dynasty* reruns and living on Doritos and old, scraped-up lines of blow all right? If you do, I guess you'd say she's just fine.' He leaned back from me and gave me that judging look that said *Mmhmmmm?*

'You mean she's not going out at all?'

'No, girl. These days, if you wanna see Miss Flip, you gotta go to her.'

'Is anyone else visiting her except for you two?'

'Anthea, I suppose.' He swigged sloppily at his beer and chased it with a long drag on his cigarette. 'Oh, an' Ty told me last night he stopped by to visit. You wanna know what he told me?'

'What?' I asked, bracing myself.

'He said he stopped on by, asking her if she wanted some dinner or groceries or something. An' she said no, all she wanted was some booty. So they get started, and just as they get down to the act, your sister starts bawling and runs into the bathroom and stays there for, like, a half-hour. An' when she finally comes out, Ty gotta rock her to sleep on the couch and he ends up being an hour late for work.'

He held his stare, one eyebrow raised in anticipation of my response. 'What about Flip?' I finally asked. 'Is she working at all? Waiting tables or anything?'

'They fired her at Bubalu last week. She slept through her shift.'

'Are you serious?'

'Yes, Tigger, I'm serious. Now may I ask you one question?'

'What?' I asked, grimacing.

'Why, exactly, are you and that brother of yours facing your own sister, who loves you both so much?'

I blinked. They were all so catty with each other that it was easy to forget just how gravely devoted Cedric and Joey were to Flip, and I supposed, vice versa. Now, I felt even more chastened than I had felt when Lippy had called. 'I'm not dissing her, Cedric. I'm just trying to sort some things out, and I need some space. You know that Flip can be so suffocating.'

'That's what you gotta expect sometimes from a warm blanket. All difficult divas can be suffocating. But we still love them, *n'est-ce pas*?'

I laughed. 'What would your construction coworkers think if they heard you saying the word *n'est-ce pas*?'

He seemed quite miffed. 'Honey, they *do* hear me sayin' *n'est-ce pas* and any other motherfuckin' queeny French I want to use around them. And believe me, they better not lay a motherfuckin' hand on me.'

I laughed. 'You are fierce, Miss Franklin. You wanna finish this beer for me?'

'Why would I wanna finish your beer? I don't need charity.'

'Because I'm going over to see Flip.'

He threw his hands up in mock ceremony. 'The great maestro decides to make her rounds,' he said thickly.

'Good-night, Cedric. Say hello to Joey for me. I'll see you both soon.'

'Don't I get a kiss good-night?'

I bussed his cheek ostentatiously. 'Thank you,' he murmured, before turning from me and staring pointedly in the other direction.

Even before I turned the key in the door, I could hear the shouts of *Family Feud* on the TV within. When I stepped inside the gloomy chamber, across a vast expanse of debris—old pizza boxes, half-empty bottles of liquor, mangled copies of *Mademoiselle* and *Vogue*, a random collection of shoes, stockings and bras—I saw her sitting up on the couch, paranoid and unkempt in her bathrobe and mules, staring at me, stricken, through the half-light. Cedric had been right: there was a small mirror and razor on the coffee table, dusted faintly with the remains of white powder. She looked ghastly, and I nearly quailed in dismay and self-recrimination before I caught myself and stepped forward.

By now she had crumpled back onto the couch and resumed watching the TV.

'Hi,' I said tentatively.

Just a fraction of a pause, then, from her, dead-sounding: 'Hi.'

'How have you been?' It sounded like a profoundly stupid question.

'Fine.' She had her arms wrapped tightly around her chest, her legs drawn up almost into a fetal position, her right foot tapping manically, her jaw grinding away at a clump of lank hair in her mouth. 'Ma called for you about four days ago. About your tuition.'

'Oh. Thanks.' *Family Feud* shrilled on. 'I just ran into Cedric, out having a drink.'

Finally, she laughed, bitterly. 'Did he tell you I was home, all strung out? He's such a fucking drama queen.'

'Well,' I answered carefully. 'He said you hadn't been out much. And he told me about Bubalu.'

'He and Joey are such goddamned gossips. Bubalu wasn't my fault. They got the schedule all fucked up.'

'Whatever,' I said. 'Restaurant jobs are a dime a dozen.'

She turned, annoyed. A chalky pallor hung about her face and the circles under her eyes were enormous. 'How would *you* know? You've never had one in your life.'

'Flip, I'm in school. You could have stayed in school, too, if you'd wanted to.'

'So sue me for not being Jane Austen,' she said, rather inexplicably.

I sat down in the butterfly chair opposite the couch. 'So,' I said, rather weakly. 'I just came by to see how you were doing.'

'Tigger,' she answered with infinite weariness, 'don't bother. Just go in your room and get whatever it is you came for and go back to Seb. I don't care. I like having the place to myself, without a bunch of pig boys to pick up after.'

This remark, and the current state of the loft, made me want to laugh out loud. The idea of Flip casting herself in the role of patient handmaid to her two careless brothers was just too absurd, especially since it had always been Jess and I who picked up after *her*, usually while she slept in until one o'clock in the afternoon.

But I didn't laugh. 'Flip, I didn't come for anything. I came over to see you.'

She turned to me, glaring. 'Why, Tigger? *Why?* Because Lippy and Cedric and Kira told you that I wasn't my usual bubbly self and I was sitting here putting leftover garbage up my nose and watching soap operas? So what? I'm sick of being everyone's cruise director. I'm taking a little vacation, I deserve it. And I don't need your condescending sympathy, or Jess's either. In fact, I don't know who pisses me off more—you for trying to give it to me, or Jess for not even bothering.' She stopped short and flushed; it had been the first time she invoked Jess in front of me since that ghastly Saturday morning. I flushed too, looked away.

'And look,' she finally continued. 'If you're planning on moving in with Seb, all I ask is that you let me know enough in advance to get a roommate. And you can tell Jess that I know he's moving in with *her*, and I don't fucking care, but would he at least please be man enough to let me know so l can replace him, too? I can think of a million people who would give an arm and a leg to live here,' she concluded, eerily echoing Jess's remark.

'I can't speak for Jess,' I said, 'but I don't have any immediate plans of leaving,' even though the very fact that she had put the possibility out in the open now suddenly made the thought of doing just that easier to swallow. 'I'm taking a little break, that's all.'

'How lovely for you. Are you gonna start an herb garden and adopt two little Korean babies like all the other yuppie queers in Park Slope?'

I didn't know if I should laugh or tell her to fuck off. So I did neither, holding my breath and counting until I felt sufficiently calm. She saw my effort and snorted with disdain.

'Lippy wants us all to have brunch soon. She says there's some new English place on Hudson Street that Langley wants to go to.'

'I don't wanna go,' she snapped. 'I can't stand seeing Lippy with that British fag that uses her for a beard.'

'Flip, that's not true! Langley cares about Lippy a lot!' I protested, even though Flip, in characteristic fashion, had just voiced exactly what we all more or less thought.

'Well, whatever. It's Lippy's life, not mine. But I still don't want to go. And besides, I haven't been feeling so good. I've been puking and weak for the past three days.'

'Maybe you should modify your diet a little,' I said, gesturing at the empty bags of junk food, the liquor bottles, the cocaine paraphernalia.

I thought she'd snap something at me about not being so self-righteous when I had scammed blow off her only the very last time I saw her. But she didn't. 'Why stop now?' she said airily, turning back to the TV.

'Do you need anything?' I asked, increasingly desperate. 'Any groceries? Or cough syrup or something like that? Or TP?'

'No, thank you,' she said peaceably, picking up the remote control. 'Just peace and quiet.'

'All right,' I murmured, at a complete loss, rising from my seat. I wanted to kiss her good-bye, but I thought the brush-off might be too deadly to handle. 'Call me at Seb's if you need anything, all right?'

'Yep.' She didn't turn away from the television. 'Oh, look! Here's an old *Sanford and Son.*'

'You promise you'll call?'

'Yep.' Her right foot started tapping wildly again. She sniffled, her wide, haunted eyes glued to the inane goings-on of the sitcom.

'All right. All right, Flip. Bye. Take care of yourself, okay?'

'Yep. Ciao.'

There was no more use in trying to talk to her; she was freezing me out. I actually did want a few things from my room, but I'd be damned if I was going to fetch them now and confirm her suspicions of why I'd come.

On the creaky, underpopulated F train back to Brooklyn, I was grim and preoccupied. Should I have stayed, cleaned up the apartment, forced her out for some fresh air and a real meal? Should I move back in, monitor her drug and alcohol use, perhaps make her seek help? Or was this merely an intercession, breathing space, that she needed as badly as Jess and I?

I didn't know what to think. Elevated now, the train passed the big pink neon sign for KENTILE FLOORS. Tonight, half the K and the last E were blown out, omissions that strongly suggested the inscription 'LENTIL FLOORS'. It was just like Seb, I thought irritably—frumpy, antiquated Seb—to live without regret in so shabby a borough that a sign for a floor company burnt out to the point of advertising lentils.

As soon as I got to Seb's that night, I left a message for Jess on Damienne's machine; I wanted to tell him what I had seen that night at the loft and ask what he thought we should do. Days passed, then a full week, and, first to my puzzlement then to my indignation, he didn't call me back. I wondered if I should stop in on Flip again, but then Lippy rang to tell me that Flip had called her and they had lunched at Elephant and Castle the day before. Flip seemed in better spirits, Lippy reported—apparently, she had mentioned something about getting some work at Kira's boyfriend's law firm, and perhaps going to Miami for a week with Cedric and Joey—and, apart from a nasty stomach bug that she was trying to shake (the only flaw on an otherwise serene lunch, Lippy reported, was that Flip had hastened rather abruptly to the bathroom to throw up her omelette)—she seemed considerably improved since her last visit to Lippy's. That calmed me, and I decided to let the matter rest for a few more days before I bothered Jess again, or stopped by the loft.

But, two days later, Jess finally called me back—at two thirty in the morning, stirring Seb and me from deep sleep.

'It's your brother,' Seb mumbled, handing me the receiver before rolling over and falling back to sleep.

He sounded considerably shaken. 'Can you get to the emergency room at St. Vincent's right away? Maybe call a car service?'

'Yeah,' I managed, coming to. 'Why?'

'It's Flip. She called me in the middle of the night, hysterical. She said something was wrong with her and she didn't know what. So I rushed over, and she was bleeding all over the place. I dressed her and we got in a cab and came right here. The doctor just took her inside.'

'Of course I'll be there,' I said, fumbling for my clothes, my heart pounding. 'What do you think it is?'

'I don't know, I don't know. I'm scared it's some kind of drug overdose, or alcohol poisoning.'

'I'll be right there.'

I finished dressing, hastily explained the situation to Seb.

'What's wrong with her?' He sat up.

'I'm not sure.'

'You want me to come?'

'No, I'll be okay. Go back to sleep.'

'You sure, Thomas?'

'Yes!' I snapped, fumbling with a sock, before leaning over and kissing him. 'I'm sorry. You're sweet to offer. But I'll be okay.' He nodded, seemingly mollified, which is why I was startled and just the tiniest bit irritated to find him still sitting up staring intently into the gloom, as I closed the bedroom door behind me.

I called for a car, which hurried me over the Manhattan Bridge to the emergency entrance of St. Vincent's. I joined Jess in the chaotic waiting room—he, too, was here alone—and we waited, almost wordlessly, for over an hour until a doctor emerged and plodded over to us.

'You two are with Ms. Mitchell?' he asked.

'That's right,' I answered. 'I'm her brother.'

He looked at Jess. 'You her husband? Boyfriend?'

Jess and I laughed weakly. 'No, sir. I'm her brother, too.'

He glanced up from his chart. 'You are?'

'Yes, sir.'

The doctor eyed us for a moment longer, then shrugged it off. 'Well, your sister's okay. She's got pretty high levels of alcohol in her system, though, some traces of cocaine, too, and she's pretty dehydrated. I think you'd better seriously talk to her about getting into some kind of drug treatment program.'

'I knew it was some kind of drug poisoning,' Jess said to me. 'That stupid girl.'

'No, it's not drug poisoning per se,' the doctor said, 'even though she's going down that path if she doesn't do something about it.'

'So what is it?' Jess asked. 'What was all that bleeding?'

The doctor shrugged. 'She was six weeks pregnant. She was treating her body like hell, and she miscarried. She cried when we told her what happened. I hate to say it, but it doesn't surprise me at all.'

It certainly surprised Jess and me, though. We stared blankly at the doctor's blunt, impassive face, and neither of us had a thing to say.

Twelve

They kept Flip in the hospital for two days, during which Jess and I took turns staying by her side, then we took her home. She groaned, weak and demoralized, when she saw the state of the loft, and after Jess and I put her to bed, we set to cleaning, removing the liquor bottles, the drug paraphernalia, all the agents that had led to the ruin of this unborn, unattributed child. She swore she hadn't even known she was pregnant— she thought she had had some kind of stomach flu—and we didn't dare ask her where she thought it might have come from. Jess told me in secret that he didn't know what had happened that night between her and Goolsbee—he had passed out on the couch with the FIT queen, and awakened after dawn, long after everyone had left—although he added that Cedric and Joey had said Flip and Goolsbee had been in her bedroom, the door locked, for quite a long time before Goolsbee slipped out unceremoniously and Flip returned, dazed and silent, to the party.

Then there was the question of other possibilities: Ty, of course, although Flip had laughed once that he insisted on 'two-ply' protection, so frightened had he become of unplanned paternity. Or Flip's occasional nights out—as recently, we knew, as the past few weeks—when she found her way home with one of the bouncers, bartenders, petty drug dealers, aspiring models or other subgenres of the more-or-less heterosexual men who populated her various haunts, all of whom she knew at least casually.

But there was also the possibility that none of us talked about, even though it hung so heavy in the air between the three of us that sometimes I thought I would scream it out loud unless someone else brought it up. Jess never mentioned the pregnancy without somehow implying, however cryptically, that it belonged to some other guy, and Flip appeared equally frozen to the possibility with the exception of one chilling remark she made to me once when we were alone in each other's company.

'I bet it would have been such a beautiful baby,' she mused absently, sipping at her mineral water.

'What makes you say that?' I ventured, full of trepidation.

'It's just a feeling I have,' she answered, and said no more.

I hated seeing her in such a wretched state—weak and groggy, in beastly, blessed withdrawal from alcohol and drugs—but in truth, I was also colossally relieved that what had happened had happened naturally (of sorts), especially if the possibility which dared not speak its name had been a verity. As for Lippy, who knew by now of the 'accident,' our gravest speculation was, of course, thankfully lost on her. She seemed largely relieved of worry when Flip confided, under Lippy's pressure, that, yes, the hospital had given her an HIV test, and, yes, the results had finally come back—negative. If we all lived in understandable trepidation of the virus, Lippy was terrified of it, having witnessed its darkest early years, devoting the better part of the last decade to nursing friends and performing in as many benefits as she possibly could, only to stand by helplessly as dozens of friends and colleagues faded out of her life.

And finally, where our mother was concerned, we all agreed—perhaps, most vociferously, Lippy, who lived in fear of our mother's accusations that she had led us all down the road to ruin—that it was best to tell her that Flip had had a nasty case of bronchitis, but was now doing fine, just fine, and that she needn't worry at all.

It was summer now, and Jess and I relinquished any immediate plans of abandoning the loft and moved back in to look after Flip as she recovered. In the instance of her illness, much of the unspoken rancor that had divided us that spring was hastily forgotten, and we quickly settled back into our old confederation of three, shutting out most of the world except for regular visits from Lippy, Kira, Cedric and Joey. Needless to say, Seb and Damienne were not pleased. They tried to be understanding, but we later heard through Kira that they had bumped into each other on the street and had had a long, indignant conversation about 'exactly what it was they thought they were holding out for,' or something of that huffy nature. Jess and I slipped off to see our respective intendeds on odd evenings—stolen visits that felt more like obligations of appeasement rather than romantic reprieves, and usually we were both grateful to escape their poorly concealed resentment and return to the loft.

Given the circumstances, it turned out to be an oddly happy summer. School was out for me and Jess lightened up on his work, and we found, much to our surprise, that we were more than content to hang around the dark, cool loft with Flip, whose health and spirits improved every day. As her strength increased, it became common in the evenings for the three of us to take short strolls around the neighborhood, often ending up at one of the sidewalk cafés nursing iced coffees (Flip wasn't touching drink, drugs or even cigarettes these days, apparently precluding the need for us to enroll her in some sort of rehabilitation program) and watching the twilit passersby.

'You know,' Flip said one night as the three of us sat out on Mott Street when two old Italian women passed, arm in arm, 'I never noticed how many old people there are in this city. Or little kids.'

'That's because you were usually asleep when they were going about their lives,' Jess said, 'and they were asleep when you were going about yours.'

'I guess you're right,' she considered. 'It's kind of funny, isn't it? All these people just doing their things, all so close to each other and not really noticing everybody else. I can't believe I've lived here for four years and I never really even looked around.'

'*Watch out, the world's behind you,*' Jess sang. It was 'Sunday Morning', the Velvet Underground, one of our favorite bands when we were all at St. Pete's. '*There's always someone around you who will call.*'

'That's kind of a depressing song, isn't it?' Flip mused.

'It is,' Jess answered, 'but it's true. Don't you think, Tig?'

I smiled, drowsy and serene. 'No,' I said. 'Not right now.'

I loved Flip more that summer than I had in years, since the times in Rye when she would run ahead of Jess and me and lead us into the sea-filled cove, and I don't think I'd be exaggerating to say that Jess did, too. All the qualities that had so endeared her to everyone when she first left Barnard and took downtown by storm—her sharp wit, her warmth, her bravura, her endless desire to bring people together, her willingness to shed her ample light on all the dimmer stars around her—indeed, all the qualities that seemed to have soured in the unhappy month after my birthday party returned now, lavished solely on Jess and me and the handful of people dearest in her life. No longer wired on liquor or blow, no longer subject to frantic nights and sleep-deprived mornings, and no longer at the mercy of a throng of vapid sycophants, it seemed that many of her worst qualities—her endless hunger for attention and stimulation, her withering tantrums at being ignored for even a minute, her sometimes shockingly foul mouth—seemed to recede into a general disposition of good humor and repose.

Her serenity was contagious. Freed temporarily of the pressures of school and the traditional chaos of the loft, I slept well for the first time since moving to New York, and Jess seemed to lose the brooding snappishness he had acquired about most things, especially work, in the past few years. As for Seb and Damienne, it wasn't that we were outright ignoring them—like I said, we saw them often enough, and invited them frequently to the loft for dinner (invitations they almost always declined, eventually without benefit of a reason)—but there was something marvelous that summer about our renewed intimacy of three that we didn't want to spoil, perhaps because we all silently knew that, come fall, it would probably have to end. Jess and I had promised Seb and Damienne, on the quiet, that in September we would revive our plans to move out. And anyway, Flip was talking so earnestly now about getting a real career in the fall—get into the buyer's training program at Bloomingdale's or Bergdorf's, maybe, or perhaps Lippy could get her an events-planning job with some trendy non-profit organization—and we were reasonably confident that, once she was up and running, with decent new roommates, she wouldn't fall back into the abyss just for lack of our daily presence.

One evening in mid-July the three of us were out on one of our after-dinner strolls on Spring Street when we passed Bubalu, the chic club where Flip had waitressed.

'Look there,' she said, hurrying to the broadsheet pasted to the locked black door. 'Bubalu went under! Probably because they couldn't get their fucking work schedules right,' she laughed gleefully. 'Now it's for rent. I wonder what it's gonna be next.'

'Probably some other fifteen-minute hotspot that'll have a sign just like this on its door by this time next year,' Jess groaned. 'The street's become so expensive that I don't even know if fuckin' Disney could keep up the rent on this place. They should just turn it into a Gap or something.'

'A Gap!' Flip shrieked. 'Those Gaps are popping up every-where! It can't be a Gap. It's got to be something really amazing. Somebody should do something like Nell's when it first opened, but only better.'

'What would that entail?' I asked. To the extent that I cared anymore, I couldn't imagine any spot outdoing Nell's in its early years; when I finally got in, after three failed attempts, I felt as though I had penetrated the last sanctum of glamor and chic.

'I don't know,' Flip said, considering. 'Like if you took the best things away from a really good gay club—the deep, deep house music, the great DJs, and that kind of serious black attitude—and put it in a club that was even, like, *posher* than Nell's? You know? Like the perfect mix of speakeasy and juke joint, you know?'

Jess rolled his eyes. He hated it when Flip rhapsodized over some club having 'serious black attitude' as though she had gone on safari. 'Well, time will tell,' he said indifferently, and walked on.

Flip took one more look at the inscrutable black façade before moving on. 'I just hope whoever gets it doesn't mess it up. It's too good a space to waste,' she said to me judiciously.

'Well, you'll probably be so busy with your fabulous new career you'll be too tired to check it out anyway,' I said. 'They're all the same after a while anyway, don't you think?'

'Hm? I guess so,' she mumbled. 'I guess so.' But it was clear her mind was somewhere else, and probably not in an orien-tation meeting for members of the Bloomingdale's buyer training program.

Two days later, while Jess and I were lolling about watching TV, she came bounding into the loft with shopping bags from Betsey Johnson (we knew she had fully recovered when she announced it was time to update her wardrobe), bursting with some kind of news.

'Darlings!' she exclaimed, plopping herself down on the couch into my lap. 'The sweetest thing just happened to me!'

Jess and I raised our eyebrows, me gasping for air. 'Yeah?' Jess asked.

'Well,' she began. 'You know that Japanese guy Miko, who designed some lamps for Anthea when she first opened the shop? He always came to parties here with that severe flat top and that boyfriend of his that looked like Ricardo Montalban?'

'Kind of.'

'No, not really.'

'Well, anyway,' Flip rushed on, 'I bumped into him on the street in front of Dean & Deluca. I was buying some of these'—she pulled cranberry scones out of her bag and passed them around—'and there he was on his way to show his bed-spread designs, or whatever, at Calvin Klein. And you know how he got in *there*?'

'How?'

'Well. Anthea told him that *I* was chummy with the guy—that guy, Raoul, you know, with the tattoo?—who goes out with that guy Blake who handles, like, product development or something for Calvin Klein housewares. And apparently when this Blake at CK found out that Miko was friends with *me*, he just came *alive*. He started going on, like, "Oh, I'm so crazy about the Flip girl, she's so fabulous, she's got such spirit, I always go home from parties she's been at and memory-sketch her outfits so I can give them to Calvin's sportswear people, and if she likes your lampshades, then you *must* have talent because she couldn't wear a wrong thing if she tried" . . . and so on and so on and so on. Miko said he was meaning to call and thank me.' She was flushed with triumph.

'You know all those fashion queens love you,' Jess said mildly.

'I know, but isn't that *amazing*! I got him in at *Calvin Klein*! And I hardly know that guy Raoul. I mean, I did lines with him at, like, two parties or something last year.'

'That's the foundation for a life-long friendship,' I dead-panned. Jess laughed.

'That's not the point, you little shit,' she said good-naturedly. 'The point is, *I know all these people.* And, I mean, there's got to be something better I can do with all those connections other than join a stupid department store training program or take some measly $25,000-a-year AIDS job.'

'Jesus, Flip!' I spluttered.

'Well, you know what I mean,' she said, contrite. 'I should start an AIDS group of my own, or something like that.'

'What are you gonna do?' Jess asked. 'Come in and style their hospital rooms? Wrap Mylar around their IV drip poles?'

But Flip seemed surprisingly unperturbed. 'You go ahead and laugh,' she said, retreating into her room with her bags. 'But I'm more resourceful than you think.'

She closed the door behind us. 'Did I say she wasn't resourceful?' Jess asked innocently. I just shrugged, curious, and turned back to the TV.

One evening, upon arriving home from a 'family trip' to the grocery store, we found among the accumulated mail a letter for Flip, addressed in a painfully crabbed hand.

'This is return addressed from Goolsbee!' she said, and Jess and I stopped and turned away from setting down the bags. I think it was the first time anyone had said Goolsbee's name aloud since the night of my birthday party, and it hung in the air like a malediction.

'What is it?' Jess asked darkly.

Flip tore open the envelope. 'It's a check made out to me for five thousand dollars!' she gasped, astonished.

'What?' Jess and I said at once.

'Wait, there's a note here,' Flip said, pulling out a piece of stationery. '"Dear Felipika—I hear you've had hard times recently, and I wanted to send you this as a gesture of support, and also to make up for any damage that might have been done to the

apartment the last time I saw you. I would have contacted you
sooner, but I've been in Hong Kong for most of the summer
structuring a deal. Please don't be alarmed over this sum of
money, as it represents only a small fraction of what I collected
as a bonus for my work there. I hope things are going better for
you, and I'd love to take you to dinner in SoHo some night if
you have the time. All the best, Amos Goolsbee".'

'That motherfucker,' Jess muttered.

'Wait, there's a P.S. here,' Flip said. '"I said unkind things to
both you and your younger brother at his birthday party, and
I apologize. Please send my regards to both Jess and Tigger,
and I hope their respective artistic pursuits are going well".'
Flip looked up, amazed. 'Can you believe this?'

'That slimy motherfucking piece of shit,' Jess said.

'No kidding,' I echoed. Was this Goolsbee's pathetic way of
accounting for a child he might have fathered? Or paying—
*over*paying—for a procedure Flip had never had?

'I'm just absolutely speechless,' Flip said. Oddly, she looked
as though someone from the prince's counsel had just fitted
her foot into the glass slipper.

Jess approached her. 'Give me that fucking check so I can
rip it up into a million pieces and shove it up Goolsbee's ass.'

To my great surprise, Flip jumped away, check in hand.
'No!' she cried.

Jess stopped, stunned. 'What?'

'No!' Flip said again, then, haltingly, 'I mean—I mean, why
should I throw away good money just because Goolsbee's a
stinking piece of shit?'

'Jesus Christ, Flip!' Jess looked horrified. 'He's trying to *buy*
you!'

Flip laughed defiantly. 'Well, fat fucking chance he's going
to! Why shouldn't I take his money? It's just as good as anybody else's.'

'Flip,' Jess tried to reason. 'If you cash that check, then
Goolsbee's going to think he owns you.'

'Well, then, Goolsbee will think wrong. And anyway, maybe I need the money.'

'For *what*?' Jess and I chorused again.

'Well, I haven't been able to work for months.'

'Flip,' I said. 'You have a trust fund.'

'So? What's wrong with a little supplementation?'

None of us said anything for a moment. Then Jess, shaking, said low, 'What are you, a fucking whore?'

Flip's whole body tensed, and she suddenly looked as though she'd plunge a knife through Jess's heart if she had one in her hand. 'Who are *you* to call *me* a whore?' she screamed. 'You'd let any curator in this town, woman or man, suck your dick 'til kingdom come just to get your freaky work in one of their exhibits. Shit! You'd probably let them suck it just to get a ten-word notice in the fucking *Village Voice*! Don't you dare ever call me a whore again!'

But somewhere in the middle of this diatribe, Flip's ferocity had unraveled, and now she was racked with loud, convulsive sobs. 'Don't you *dare*! Ever!'

Jess stood in place, trembling, then turned sharply to me. 'Give me the keys,' he barked.

'Where are you going?' I asked.

'*Just give me the keys!*' Frightened, I threw him the set. 'I have to get the fuck out of here.' And with that, he stalked out the door.

Flip ran to the door. 'I hate you!' she called down the stairwell, her sobs rattling down four flights of metal stairs. '*I HATE YOU!!!!*' She slammed the door, ran across the room and threw herself down on the sofa, weeping, as though an entire summer of good spirits had collapsed in a moment.

I dragged the phone into my bedroom and called Seb.

'Hey,' he said, surprised. 'I thought you were at the supermarket.'

'Yeah, I'm back. You feel like spending some time together?'

'Uh . . . uh . . . yeah. Of course I do.'

'I'll be out there in a half hour,' I said, and hung up. I was using him, I knew it, but I didn't care. *I'm not having this*, I thought to myself.

I stuffed some clothes into my backpack and stepped back outside. 'I'm going to Seb's,' I said curtly to Flip.

Her sobs stopped abruptly. 'You're what?' she said, sitting up. 'You're *what*?'

'You heard me. I'm going to Seb's. I can't take this stupidity anymore.'

She gaped at me, blotchy-faced, hysterical, enraged. 'You're *leaving* me? Now?'

'I'm sure you'll be fine. Good-bye, Flip,' I said, then hurried down the stairwell, her curses and screams chasing me all the way.

It was like that grim part of spring all over again, only worse, and miserably humid. I hid out at poor Seb's for another week, not bothering to call either of them nor hearing from them myself. Seb stonily had nothing to say on the subject; guiltily, I cleaned house while he was away at work, had a square meal and a decent bottle of wine on the table for him when he got home—in short, I threw myself into the role of complaisant housewife, as I did each time I fled Manhattan and crash-landed down upon his meticulous household—but this time it lacked the novelty of the last, serving only to beg for us both the question of when, and if, our householding would ever graduate from an occasional game to a full-time reality. But the question remained suppressed, and our cohabitation this time around had the faint air of a business agreement—he'd give me a temporary home as long as I looked after it and eliminated the need for him to stop at the pizza place on his way home from work—and this feeling lingered even at night, when the two of us lay still at opposite ends of the same bed.

Finally, at the end of the week, Flip called, one insufferably muggy night while I lay sweltering on the couch watching a men's diving competition on ESPN, and Seb busied himself at the kitchen table with a manuscript.

He walked into the room to hand me the phone. 'It's your sister,' he said, as though he were announcing the Grim Reaper himself.

'Hello?'

'Tig?' Flip's voice sounded uncharacteristically small and contrite, and I felt a little stab of hurt for her in spite of myself. 'How you doing, sweetie-pie?'

'I'm doing all right. How about you?'

'Okay, I guess.'

'Did you patch things up with Jess?'

'Um,' she wavered. 'Sort of. That's kind of why I'm calling. Do you think you could come to dinner at the loft tomorrow night? Jess is coming. Um. There's something I wanted to talk to you guys about.'

I quailed inwardly. 'Is it bad news?'

'Bad?' she said, startled. 'No, no. It's good news, actually. It's exciting.'

'Well? What is it?'

'I can't talk about it now. I've gotta go out and meet Cedric and Joey for a drink. Just—can you make dinner tomorrow night? About seven?'

'I guess so,' I said. What else could I say?

'Fabulous. And Tig, don't worry about it. It's exciting news. I'm excited.'

I brought the phone back into the kitchen. 'That was Flip.'

'Apparently,' Seb said without looking up.

'She wants me and Jess to come to dinner tomorrow night. She says she has exciting news.'

'Oh, my.'

'I wonder what it could be?'

'I'm sure we'll all know soon enough,' he said, just as bored as possible. I stood there for a minute, staring at the back of his head. I wanted to smack him, or tell him that he could really be a bit of an asshole when he wanted to, but I didn't. He'd never like Flip—not Flip, who couldn't ever be bothered to glance at the front page of *The New York Times*, who still occasionally called him 'Seth', after a guy at St. Pete's she had always confused him with, who had told him that she couldn't get past the first ten pages of *Middlemarch*, his favorite book—and he'd never understand the things about her that made it impossible just to walk away from her, no matter how difficult she could be. So instead I said nothing, padded back into the living room and resumed watching the diving competition with a certain vacant longing, wondering through my desire exactly what Flip had up her sleeve this time.

She wouldn't tell us right off the next evening, nor would we ask. Instead, we all made some pretense toward civility as we sat over her painstakingly assembled Niçoise salad, making small talk about Anthea's half-baked attempts to teach Katja English, the need to ask the landlord to fix the intercom system, and the goings-on of Cedric and Joey, who had brought some twenty-two-year-old Swede home from a party the night before and now were arguing over who could claim rights to him again before he went back to university in Stockholm. Obviously, Jess and Flip had reconciled just enough to be sitting here peaceably together; I didn't know what she had done with Goolsbee's check, and I sure as hell wasn't going to ask.

It was only later, when plates were cleared, iced coffee poured and cigarettes lit that Flip turned on some Sade and sat back down. 'So,' she began, then made an elaborate point of pausing, 'I now have a career.'

Jess and I glanced at each other. 'Did you get into the Bloomingdale's program?' I asked, preparing myself to be enormously relieved for her future—for all of our futures, in fact.

'No,' she said shortly. 'I never applied. The truth is . . . I'm starting a business.'

Drop-dead silence but for Sade. 'You're what?' Jess asked, almost inaudibly.

'I'm starting a business,' she repeated. 'You know that great space where Bubalu was, that's been for rent all summer? Well, I've rented it. I'm starting a nightclub,' she dragged on her cigarette, 'and it is going to be *the end*.'

Jess and I stared at her as though she had told us she wanted to be the first human being on Uranus. She held our stare, smiling composedly, waiting for us to respond.

Jess finally did. 'Where do you expect to get the money for this?'

'I have it already. I had a long talk on the phone a few weeks ago with Mr. Kittredge about my trust fund.'

Another dramatic pause from her. 'And?' I finally prompted.

'And—I asked him if I could take, like, an advance on the principal instead of just drawing from the interest every month, like we all do, and he said that, you know, he hoped that eventually I would put it into stocks or mutual funds, but that yes—it's my money and I'm free to do what I want to do with it.'

'Did you ask Ma?' I asked.

'Mr. Kittredge said I didn't have to. I'm of age. I wanna get the club up and running, and then I'll tell her. Lippy's gotta know, of course. I need her support. But of course she'll keep it a secret.'

Jess and I swapped glances, and he cleared his throat. 'Flip,' he began, as gently as possible. 'Do you have any idea how hard it is to keep a club open in this city for more than a month? You'd have better luck opening another Indian restaurant on Sixth Street.'

'Yeah, I know how hard it is. I've been talking to a ton of people about this for the past six weeks. But it's not gonna happen to my club.'

'Why not?'

'For a lot of reasons. First of all, don't you think I have backers going in with me?'

'Like who?'

'Like—like a lot of people. Some you know, some you don't. That's just the way it's done. And they're *not* Japanese,' she added, referring to the current wave of high-tech clubs that were opening with Japanese money. 'All those places aren't going to make it because they want to be corporations. I'm not opening a corporation, I'm opening a place people can call home,' she concluded soundly, as though to indicate she'd have no more of the subject of financing.

'Second,' she continued, 'I don't have to work up a guest list. I already have the biggest and best fucking guest list in this city, thanks to all the nights I've promoted and all the people I know. Do you think when I was working for Kristal Kleer'— one of the city's most scrofulous drug dealers/drag queens/promoters, for whom Flip had coordinated a few parties at Roxy about a year ago—'and all those people, that I wasn't copying out Rolodexes? Of course I was. And finally, I won't have to turn over huge cuts to promoters because *I'm* the main promoter, just like Nell Campbell, or just like Steve Rubell before he and Ian Schrager went to jail, and I'm sure all my friends will promote it for free, and help me organize different parties on different nights. Cedric and Joey are already talking it up, and they told me that all the black queens are in a frenzy waiting for it to open. And they're gonna help me get a weekend DJ who's going to become as legendary as Larry Levan.'

'But Flip,' I said. 'What's this club gonna be? Gay? Straight? Black? White? Hip-hop, or acid jazz, or house music, or what?'

'Tigger,' and she was suddenly very serious. 'That is just it. It's gonna be everything. I'm so sick of this "This is for gays, this is for straights, this is for uptown, this is for downtown, this is for the art crowd, this is for the Eurotrash, this is for

what*ever*" shit. My club is gonna belong to everybody—all
the glamor people that used to go to Studio, all the art freaks
that went to Area, all the black queens that went to the
Paradise Garage, all the white queens that used to go to the
Saint. That's the *whole point*.' And when she said this, her face
looked beatific.

'Flip, you know that's not gonna work,' Jess said. 'The only
white folks who like hip-hop are teenagers, who you don't
want anyways, and the only white folks who like house music
are gay guys, and you're not gonna get a real black scene if you
play cheesy Euro techno shit. And what are you gonna do
with the Latin crowd?'

'And besides, Flip,' I added, 'gay and straight haven't really
mixed in clubs since, like, the first years of Studio 54. That
was a total pre-AIDS phenomenon.'

She lit another cigarette, violently. 'That's the stupidest thing
I've ever heard. I'm the biggest het ho' on earth and *I* go to gay
clubs all the time. I *live* there!'

I laughed. 'Flip, that's 'cause you're a big fag hag!'

'No, I'm not!' she protested as she always did when somebody called her this, but we knew that secretly she wore the
term as a badge of honor. 'It's just because I love the music and
the crowds and the sexual vibe. Straight clubs need more of
that; they've got to go a little *deeper*, you know what I mean?
And gay clubs have to get swank. Why do you have to go to
some scumbox meat warehouse or garage on West Street every
Saturday night just 'cause you're gay? Why shouldn't you have
someplace fabulous and beautiful and glamorous to go?
Believe you me, no fag is getting into *my* club in those stupid
cloney boots and jeans and tank tops.' (This, I must concede,
I had to applaud.) 'No one gets in looking like that. Drag is
great, as long as it's excellent drag—I don't want any skanky
Gansevoort Street mutts walking around.'

She came to a sudden halt, as winded as Jess and I were
overwhelmed. 'Now,' she said, dragging on her cigarette with

a renewed authority. 'There's something else. I've given you guys a lot of help over the past few years, getting you gigs and work space and stuff, and now I need yours.'

Jess was as silent as a stone. 'Like what kind of help?' I asked.

'Like all kinds of things. Like, Tig, I want you to work with Cedric and Joey and just *comb* all the fierce spots downtown, and show people that the club's not just for black queens and their Lebanese friends—'

Out of the corner of my eye, I caught Jess shiver.

'—and work with me and the DJs in putting together a music program, you know, like, is acid jazz better on week-days or every other Sunday—that sort of stuff—and should we maybe find some big fat divas to do special appearances—but not *huge* house appearances singing to a music track, but more *intimate* settings, you know, kind of like bistro-style in a sep-arate room with a little band—you know, like fusiony Cassandra Wilson stuff?'

'You mean, like, have dance music in some big spaces, but then have these quiet, cabaret-like spaces?' I asked.

'Exactly.'

'Separate covers?'

She shook her head emphatically. 'No. Absolutely not. It's all one fluid, beautiful space, all full of nooks and crannies, and you can change the mood just by walking from one area to another. One minute you're carrying on to C&C Music Factory under the big lights, the next you're sipping martinis in a banquette and making somebody, you know?'

'I can see that,' I said slowly, nodding.

'Now, this is where you come in, Jess.'

Jess just stared at Flip, poker-faced, hardly raising an eye-brow.

'Okay, like, Miko and Anthea and this other guy, this guy Brennan who apprenticed with Philippe Starck, or some-thing—they're redesigning the whole place, they've already showed me the preliminary plans, and it's gonna be so fierce! And I've already talked to these contractors, so that's settled. But here's the thing—' and she paused dramatically. 'I want you to paint it. I want you to sit down with Anthea and Miko and decide what you're gonna do, then just go crazy. I want you to have free rein, and I want everyone to know the club as the place that Jess Mitchell painted, just like Francesco and Keith and Jean-Michel, poor things, did at Area in '85.' (She meant Clemente, Haring and the Basquiat, all of whom she knew or had known to various extents over her three years downtown.) 'And I'm gonna pay you, too, Jess. I'm gonna pay you both. I already budgeted for it.'

'Who helped you do a budget?' Jess finally asked.

'I just—' and she flushed curiously. 'I just got some help with a budget, that's all. You can go anywhere for that.'

'You wouldn't have to pay me,' Jess said.

'You don't have to pay me, either,' I added quickly, glad to have taken a positive cue from Jess.

'But—' Jess and Flip both said at once, and Flip laughed, radiant. 'But I will, though!'

'But I'm not doing it, Flip,' Jess said matter-of-factly.

Flip snapped her mouth shut, opened it again, snapped it shut. 'What?'

'I said I'm not doing it,' he repeated, cruelly serene. 'I'm not painting the club, and I'm not gonna have anything else to do with it, either. I have my own work to do. And I think it's a risky idea, anyway, and a waste of your trust.'

Flip gripped the end of the table, rigid. 'How can you say that?' she asked, so quietly I wondered how he could hear her from across the table.

'Jess,' I was surprised to hear myself saying. 'How *can* you?'

'I'll tell you how I can,' he said, pushing back his chair. 'I can say it because I'm twenty-four years old. Because I have a career of my own. Because I have a life of my own, and a girl-friend of my own, even though you refuse to acknowledge either one of them, Flip. And because pretty soon she and I will have a place of our own. And because, Tigger, you have an allegiance to Flip that I don't have. That I'll never have. Because the two of you are bound by *blood*'—and I couldn't believe how he shook when he said this—'and for all that the three of us grew up together in the same home, went to the same schools, live in the same apartment, I'm not bound to either one of you that way. My name—' he said slowly through clenched teeth, and I was horrified to see that he was shaking, then, and swiftly crying. 'My name is Jesús Ramirez. And I am a fucking Puerto *Rican*, not Greek or Irish. And my parents are *not* named Thomas and Nikki Mitchell. And—*and I am not your brother.*'

'Jess—' I cried out, rising from my seat, devastated.

'*Jesús! Jesús!*' he cried. '*My name is JESÚS.*'

'Jesús!' I said, and it sounded tragic and ridiculous to me. 'Don't say that! You *are* our brother.' I threw my arms around him but he cast me off.

'No, I'm not! I don't know whose brother I am. Or whose son, or anything. I don't *know*.' And the two of us collapsed back into our chairs and cried, our heads in our arms, while Flip sat there frozen, dry-eyed, saying nothing.

I don't know how long we remained like that until Jess finally raised his head, wiped his eyes—looking profoundly shamed—and sat up. 'I'm leaving now,' he said, and his voice had never sounded so hollow. 'I'm going to Damienne's.'

'Wait a minute,' Flip spoke up, rising to meet his eyes across the table. 'You can't go yet, Jess.' The grim, flat tone of her voice chilled me. 'Because you're wrong about something. You say that you and I aren't bound by blood. But we are, Jess. We are.'

He stared at her, stricken, said nothing.

'We are, Jess,' she went on, infinitely composed. 'Sometimes it hurts so bad I want the world to know.'

'Get out of here, Tig,' Jess said without taking his eyes off Flip.

'This is my house, too. I don't wanna get out!'

'Tig,' Flip said, louder, without taking her eyes off Jess. '*Get out of the fucking house.*'

I slammed my glass down on the floor, shattering it, and stormed out of the loft, more from rage than acquiescence, out into the too-warm August evening. *I'm not going back this time*, I fumed to myself as I stalked to Finelli's and asked gibberishly for a beer at the bar. Obviously something fucked had been going on between the two of them—still *was*, for all I knew— something probably more fucked than I had even imagined in my most craven dreams. But I didn't care what it was, any- more. It was *their* drama, not mine, and I had *my* own life to live, and it would be an infinitely more ordered one than theirs. *They throw their depravities around everywhere*, I thought, *heedless of everyone in their path, including innocent bystanders like me. Well*, I decided, downing beer after beer, oblivious of the gathering crowd making merry around me, *I'm not standing by anymore. It's not fair to Seb. It's not fair to me.*

And that's what I intended to announce when I returned to the loft a very drunk ninety minutes later, making a great deal of deliberate noise on the stairwell as I ascended, walking in and holding myself upright to begin my proclamation. If Jess weren't there, I'd resolved, I would inform Flip of my inten- tions immediately and tell Jess first thing tomorrow morning.

But they *were* there, both of them, still at the kitchen table, now with blueprints spread out festively before them, Flip chattering on about floor plans and lighting grids, Jess fol- lowing her, following the plans, with glassy, defeated eyes.

'Tig!' Flip cried brightly when I appeared. 'Where have you *been*? When I said leave, I meant for, like, five minutes, not two hours! God, we were starting to worry about you!'

I listed in place a bit, bewildered but still determined. 'I've got something—something to tell the both of you—' I started thickly.

'Tig, you're *wasted*!' Flip laughed.

Jess looked up at me like a dead man. 'Hold on a minute, Tig. Everything's cool. I'm on for the club, okay?'

I stared, quite mute, stunned right out of all my resolve. 'You are?'

'Yeah. You are too, right?'

'Well—' I spluttered, completely thrown.

'You are and you know it!' Flip burst out. 'I saw the look in your eyes when I was telling you about the music program. You were all over it!'

'But—'

'We don't have to talk details tonight. Let's just celebrate instead.' And Flip ran into the kitchen, throwing back a giddy little hootchy-cootchy shake at us as she departed.

I had never seen Jess look quite so vacant before. 'But—' I began again.

He shook his head, put a finger to his lips. 'Just—just forget about it, Tigger, okay?'

'Okay,' I answered weakly.

'And I'm sorry I said those things to you before. Of course we're brothers. We'll always be brothers.'

'Okay,' I said, more chilled than mollified.

'Whoo! Look what I found!' Flip bounded back in with an unopened bottle of champagne that must have been in the refrigerator since my birthday party, along with a corkscrew and three glasses from an old set of Lippy's. Hastily, she uncorked the bottle, shrieking as it exploded, then poured out three sloppy glasses, handing them all around. 'To the three of us, and to happiness,' she announced, holding her glass aloft. Jess and I extended our glasses and they met in a round of differently pitched *clinks*.

'Mmm, a cigarette,' she said, reaching for her pack.

'Spare one of those?' Jess mumbled.

'Yes, *dahling*,' Flip laughed, all sweetness and light. She extracted two from the pack, put them between her lips side by side, ignited, then, drawing languorously on her own, fitted the other between Jess's frozen lips.

'Didn't someone do that in a movie once?' Flip prattled on cheerily. 'Garbo? Or Lauren Bacall?'

'I dunno,' Jess mumbled again, and something about the cigarette propped absurdly between his unmoving lips, just a notch or two below his unseeing eyes, conferred upon him the distinct impression of a man too stunned even to enjoy his last request before resigning himself to an imminent death.

Thirteen

'*It's fabulous,*' Flip, Anthea and Miko chorused from the dining room table, huddled over blueprints and sketches beneath a cloud of cigarette smoke that hung in the air like a sunless blue heaven. Jess, Ty and I looked up from the other side of the loft, where I was typing the hundreds of addresses that Flip had collected over the years into a coherent mailing list. Jess was scratching aimlessly in his sketchbook—ideas for the club, I assumed, but couldn't be quite sure—and Ty, who had dropped by before work hoping to get some booty from Flip, found himself instantly dispatched not to the bedroom, but to Pearl Paint to buy more drafting pencils for Miko. He languished on the couch now, nursing a beer and taking in the goings-on with a kind of sullen, skeptical interest.

'What you all doin' over there that's so fabulous?' he drawled.

'You'll see,' Flip called back as Miko and Anthea giggled. 'All in good time.' The phone rang then, and she pounced on it, instantly embroiled in details with the contractor.

It was just a week after our fateful dinner, and already the loft had become Command Central, the place where phone calls were made and received (hundreds a day, although *never* before noon—such was the schedule of the nightclubbing business), papers were signed, and meetings were held—

elaborate, cacophonous meetings that often wound from midday until well into the night, during which food was ordered in, plans carpeted the old warped floors, and an endless entourage of designers, technicians, artisans and self-proclaimed 'consultants' brainstormed, cajoled, bickered, compromised and eventually converged on aesthetic consensus, as blueprints and swatches, light charts and furnishings were rejected, modified, earmarked, and finally approved amidst shrieks of self-congratulatory mirth.

Anthea and Miko, the chatty Japanese guy whom Flip had apparently 'gotten in' at Calvin Klein, were there constantly, forever running over to the defunct Bubalu to check measurements and loads, endlessly whispering secretly over cryptic sketches, promising something *absolutely fucking brilliant* and bitching extravagantly over their deadline. For our opening night was scheduled for New Year's Eve 1989, the last night of the decade—a nerve-rackingly tight time frame since it was now just past Labor Day—but Flip had insisted on it: it was only fitting, she reasoned, that what was to be the last great club of the century should open at the start of that century's final ten years—'our nineties,' Flip declared, gesturing grandly at the chaos of plans fanned out on the floor. And we took her declaration on a kind of heady faith, with no real assurance that the club would ever get off the ground, let alone survive long enough to become the defining space of a season, never mind a decade.

In those final months, Flip *insisted* on everything—and generally got what she asked for. Looking back, I must concede it was exhilarating to watch her in those fleeting weeks, when her ambitions were more focused, her judgment sharper and her spirits more stable than they had been since she was perhaps eight years old. She didn't sleep in anymore, rising at noon only to lurch toward the afternoon soaps; now she was up at nine, face and hair in place, cigarette and coffee in hand, going over the day's agenda, working her infinite contacts to wind through the maze of bureaucracy that led to city licenses for liquor, dancing, and the like, as well as insurance for the space, the price of which she merely referred to as 'un-fucking-be*liev*able!' She hardly ever had unkind words for the world now, because everyone was, at very least, a potential accessory to her grand plan, and consequently had to be treated with the utmost consideration.

If before she had been a ubiquitous creature of the night, now she stayed in, pointedly out of sight, even as Cedric and Joey and her legion of worker bees spread the carefully planned word: 'Flip Mitchell is *nowhere* to be seen because she's turning Bubalu into her *own* club . . . and it's going to be the next Studio 54, the next Area, the next Garage and the next Nell's *combined* . . . and it opens *New Year's Eve* . . . and, oh, haven't you gotten your invitation yet? . . . well, give me your number and I'll call Flip's people tomorrow and see what I can do.'

And before long, Flip got her item in *Paper*, she got her item in *Village Voice*, she got her item in *Seven Days*, and the slug was always basically the same, sensational yet necessarily skeptical in tone: Flip Mitchell, downtown promoter and party girl, has acquired the old Bubalu property on Spring Street and is currently planning the ultimate pleasure space for the '90s, a combination disco and lounge meant to cater to every crowd and style as long as they fit into the world according to Flip Mitchell. Those attached to the venture include . . .

And the list of accomplices was always breathtaking (if, at times, overreported), but nothing created a bigger stir with the *demi-monde* than the news that Flip had signed as her Saturday night DJ none other than Sammy Fingers. If you had any affiliation with downtown nightlife at the end of the 1980s, you had to have heard of Sammy Fingers—he was the quietly imperious spin master from Bushwick who had come up through all the major clubs of the past ten years and apprenticed with the fabled Larry Levan, becoming by this time a

kind of dance music *auteur* who created and popularized
remixes for all the great divas of the age, everyone from
warhorses like Aretha Franklin to newcomers like Janet
Jackson. He was *like this* with Madonna, he worked frequently
with Quincy Jones and Shep Pettibone, and he was a regular
visitor to Diana Ross's home in Greenwich . . . and all because
he had earned a reputation as a kind of musical alchemist,
someone who could keep a packed house dancing for hours
on end, as though possessed, with his soulful vinyl mix of the
deepest grooves and rhythms, one hypnotic track constantly
melting into another, rising and falling, a remarkable odyssey
that usually didn't end until the final song, a heart-wrenching
ballad lush with piano, brought everyone back to earth and
out into a Sunday midday, the sun harsh and unforgiving on
bodies still throbbing with music.

Cedric had promised Flip a DJ to end all DJs, and even
though I knew he went back a long way with Sammy
Fingers—knew, in fact, that upon being introduced to Flip
once through Cedric, Sammy had said, 'So *you're* the one who
oversold my Valentine's Day party at Mars last year'—I would
never have guessed in a century of Saturday nights that he was
negotiating with The Great One. So you can only imagine my
shock one night when Flip, bursting with her secret, buzzed
up Cedric with Fingers in tow—La Fingers himself, all burly
six feet two inches of him, smiling unassumingly in his black
leather jacket in the middle of our loft.

'Sammy, you remember my girl, the club promoter Miss
Flip Mitchell, don't you?' Cedric asked coyly as Flip stood by,
dwarfed in the overwhelming shadow of Sammy Fingers, who
nodded wordlessly and smiled.

'And Flip, just in case you forgot, this is the DJ Miss Sammy
Fingers.'

'Of *course* I didn't forget, Cedric,' Flip scowled, then, overcome: 'Sammy Fingers . . . Mr. Fingers . . . Oh, God!'

Sammy Fingers laughed, at once a much slyer and sillier

laugh than I'd ever thought he'd possess, and curiously at odds with his *basso profondo* of a speaking voice. 'I'm standing in your house, honey. You can call me Sammy.'

Cedric caught me staring, agape, in the background. 'And Sammy, this is Flip's little brother, the *very* fabulous jazz pianist Thomas Mitchell.'

I extended my hand, which he promptly swallowed up in an enormous hand of his own. 'I love your new Patti remix,' I offered. 'All my DJ friends are playing it.'

'Thank you, Thomas.' He seemed remarkably modest and polite for the Sun King of a fiefdom so drenched in attitude. 'Maybe you can lay down some piano lines on some of my new stuff. You wanna talk about that?'

I managed a small hiccup of response.

'Tigger, honey,' Flip interrupted. 'Why don't you run to the store and get Mr. Fingers—uh, get Sammy something to drink. What would you like? Beer? Wine? Something hard?'

'Actually,' and Fingers looked surprisingly sheepish, 'you got any milk? I try to drink a glass a day, and I haven't had time today.'

Flip laughed, given as much pause as I. 'Milk? Well, um— do we have any milk in our refrigerator? No, I don't think we do.' (Truth be told, we seldom had *anything* in our refrigerator, save perhaps one fossilized Chinese dumpling, lonely in a take-out box from three weeks before.) 'Tigger, why don't you go get some milk for Mr. Fingers—'

'Sammy,' he interrupted gently.

'Right, Sammy. And, um—well, I guess I'll have milk, too. Cedric?'

'Milk sounds right by me.'

'All right, then. Tigger?' And I duly took my cue, running to the deli for two quarts of milk, returning to pour it quietly all around—they had already begun negotiations ('I'd *love* to start out the night with classic disco,' Flip was gushing. 'Nobody's done *that* yet.')—then slipping into my room, trying to listen through the door. A good hour later, after I had heard them leave, hugs and kisses all around, Flip knocked at my door.

'That's that,' she said, beaming. 'We're going to meet with lawyers tomorrow to sign the papers: every Saturday night and special events for one year, contract open for renewal after that.'

'I can't believe it. You got an exclusive Saturday contract with Sammy Fingers. Nobody's ever done that before.' Then a new thought entered my head. 'Flip, how are you gonna afford him, anyway?'

'Oh, I can afford him. For a year, at least. It's all accounted for in the budget.'

Flip alluded to this 'budget' quite a bit, but she never quite told us how it broke down, nor how much was covered by what I feared were the less-than-handsome remains of her trust, nor how much was financed by backers, nor—perhaps most troubling of all—who these mysterious 'backers' were.

'Just leave the money stuff to me, Tig,' she'd snap when I so much as hinted at the subject. 'I'll make sure you get your little stipend.'

I wanted to tell her that it wasn't my 'little stipend' that I was worried about—it was the prospect of her going bankrupt and Jess and me having to support her ever after that frightened me—but, as usual, I didn't. I shut up and left the finances to her, which was the way she wanted it. Math had been her only good subject, after all, and even if she had always been constantly in credit-card debt, at least she knew by how much—and how much she was accruing on her savings, even against sky-high interest payments, by not paying off all her plastic in one fell swoop.

By the increasingly chill days of October, as plans and blueprints and various city licenses came painstakingly to life, I wish I could say that the growing tide of excitement effaced certain other nagging problems, but unfortunately I can't. On that grimly unforgettable night when first Jess, then I, had pledged our allegiance to Flip's club, we had hoped that promise might translate into something modest: a spare hour here or there in the evening or on weekends, bolstered, of course, by our warm and unflagging moral support.

Flip soon made it clear, however, that the kind of support she had been talking about was just a notch short of 24-7. Taking care of our respective principal duties—from Jess, design contributions, from me, music programming (a complicated, though not joyless, task that included ferreting out affordable but quality DJs and talent for all the nights but Saturday)—were not enough; Flip forever wanted us 'just around', to interview bouncers, bartenders, waitresses and busboys (a better-looking, or dimmer-minded, group of people I had never seen, even after three years in New York), or answer the phone, or fetch her lunch while she gabbed the afternoon away with the demi-celebs whom she was courting as subjects for her nocturnal kingdom. My work languished, and I wasn't too cowed by Flip to let her know it from time to time—but Jess, curiously, had little to say on our indentured servitude, had had very little to say at all, in fact, since the night he ultimately agreed, glassy-eyed, to do Flip's bidding. With as little visible enthusiasm as duress, he worked on his sketches for the club's interior and performed Flip's other legwork as needed—sometimes with such Zen-like quietude that he spooked me.

'If *she* asks you to go all the way to Canal Street to get her sashimi for lunch today, tell her to get off her diva's ass and go get it herself,' I said to him one afternoon while Flip haggled on the phone with Miko over wall sconces.

I thought he'd respond in kind, but much to my surprise he only looked up and said: 'Tigger, if sashimi is what Flip wants, then sashimi is what Flip will have. After all, she's restoring New York nightlife for the 1990s. The least *I* can do is get her sashimi.' And just before he turned back to his work, he gave me a smile so wickedly sweet, so phonily cherubic, I shuddered slightly in response.

Neither were Damienne and Seb happy about the situation, particularly as we had promised our respective other halves that we would move out of the loft and into their places that fall. But, not surprisingly at all, work on the club left little time for orchestrating a major move, and Jess and I found ourselves crashing at the loft after a hard day's work so often it was as though we had never planned to move in the first place. Jess studiously wouldn't discuss with us his situation with Damienne, but I knew she was furious nonetheless— she never stopped by the loft now, could hardly speak to Flip when she called looking for Jess, and God only knows the fights she and Jess must have had on the odd evenings that he spent at her house.

As for Seb, he had greeted with a kind of muted dismay the news of the club, particularly since he had earlier broached plans for the two of us to go to Paris that fall just after I moved in for good. I was too busy to see him much, and when I did, I took his reticence as a sign of stoic resolve—a major misinterpretation on my part, as I learned one free Sunday afternoon in October as we walked through Prospect Park. He had been telling me about some fledgling AIDS activist group with some ridiculous acronym—ACT OUT, or something of that nature—that he felt compelled to join; I had heard of it vaguely, but I had never followed politics too closely (people in clubland had a way of ignoring such unpleasant daytime goings-on), and these days I was so wrapped up in the club that it was all I could do to keep up with classes at Mannes. Still, I listened politely as he talked, just glad to have a few hours alone with him on a brilliant autumn day and hear him discourse in his usual wound-up fashion.

Then suddenly, out of the blue, he stopped and regarded me with a startling frankness. 'You're not hearing a word I'm saying, are you?' he asked, with a kind of epiphanic clarity.

'Of course I am,' I laughed, trying to take his hand, which he pulled away. 'What makes you think that?'

'I just—you don't ever hear a word I say, do you, Thomas? You don't really give a shit about me or my life at all, do you, as long as I'm there with a warm, quiet house for you on the nights you feel like taking a breather from your brother and sister?'

I laughed again, full of nervous guilt. 'What are you *talking* about?'

He paused, considered. 'I guess what I'm talking about is— we really shouldn't be together, should we?'

'Seb!' I cried, truly panicked now. I was suddenly hit with the full impact of just how much I had taken him for granted over the past few months. He loved me, was endlessly devoted to me, God knows why. And I loved him, or at least . . . well, didn't all love in the end come down simply to mutual comfort and dependence? At any rate, I thought hastily, I absolutely couldn't lose him.

'Seb, what are you saying? I'm crazy about you, you know it!'

He stared, cold. 'Do I?'

'Well—well, if you don't, you *should*. It's just—you know Flip's got me all caught up in this club thing for the time being, and I guess I'm distracted, and—' I suddenly felt a bit embarrassed for the force of my entreaty, as well as the loudness of my voice; some neighborhood teenagers passed, grinning, and I knew what they were thinking: *Oh, look at the two fags having a lovers' quarrel.* 'You're absolutely wrong,' I said again, softer.

He sighed, unmollified. 'Thomas, face it—our lives don't even overlap. I mean, you *love* going out 'til all hours—your whole family does; even Lippy can sing until two in the morning—and you know I hate that scene. I have a *job*; I can't be coming in every night at the crack of dawn. But I don't want to keep you from that, if that's what you really love, and once

Flip's club opens, that's it, I know it. You're going to be there all the time.'

'You're so wrong!' I protested. 'I can't wait until Flip's club is up and running so I can have my own life back. You know what I really love?'

He snorted. 'What?'

'This!' I said, trying to sound as impassioned as possible. 'I *love* this—getting away from Manhattan and being with you,' I pressed on, increasingly desperate now. 'You're my salvation. Don't you feel the same way?'

He seemed to regard me with a kind of exasperated pity. 'I'm not looking to be saved, Thomas. I'm just looking for a boyfriend.'

I opened my mouth to speak, then snapped it shut, resolving not to be offended. 'You have one,' I said, taking his hand, and this time he didn't pull it away. 'Me. I'm not going anywhere.'

'It's not you going anywhere that I'm worried about. It's whether or not *we're* going anywhere that I want to know.'

I sighed; I could only stand these 'relationship' discussions for so long—they seemed so pointless—and I had just about reached my limit on this one. I drew him in and kissed him briskly as though to bring the conversation to a close. 'Can we finish this after dinner?' I asked now, venturing forward a few steps.

He shook his head, weary and defeated, and followed. After dinner and too much wine that night, we fell asleep on the couch together listening to *Dinah Washington in the Land of Hi-Fi*, the planned finale of our conversation that afternoon neatly averted, and that was just fine with me.

Oddly enough, it was out of this abortive confrontation with Seb that came something that Flip, of all people, very much needed. For if plans for every other aspect of the club were progressing nicely, we were missing one very crucial thing—a name. We had been mulling over it for weeks and weeks now, since the moment Flip had announced plans, and although dozens of people had suggested dozens of titles, none of them seemed to stick. There were the predictable ones, stylishly curt names like 'Noir' or 'Soirée' or 'Fiesta' or 'Intoxication', but Flip felt that they all sounded like the names of cheap perfumes. Cedric, Joey and Miko had the funniest suggestions by far, including everything from 'Lady Marmalade' and 'Lucky Dance Sensation' to 'The Ho's Hell Motel' and Joey's rather mordant 'Good-bye Beirut', but Flip concluded that they all lacked a certain cryptic quality, something evocative yet absolutely untraceable. Jess ventured, all full of mock-innocence, that we should simply cut right to the chase, to the main attraction, and put up a huge neon sign that flashed in six-foot letters 'FLIP' with an equally colossal blinking arrow beneath—an idea that Flip greeted with just a nanosecond of excitement before we all broke out laughing and she registered the appropriate indignation.

But despite the endless stream of proposals no name emerged triumphant, and meanwhile, the entire project was known simply as 'The Club', in written documents, around the loft, and on the streets. Time was passing and days were getting colder; the club itself was taking shape, the guest list for opening night was nearly assembled, soon invitations and broadsides would have to be designed and printed, and still we had no name.

And so it came to pass that Monday after my row with Seb that I was working with Flip in the loft and decided to let her know, as I liked to do from time to time, just what was transpiring in the world beyond her all-consuming venture.

'Seb and I had a fight yesterday,' I announced flatly. 'He said maybe we shouldn't go out anymore because he doesn't think we have anything in common.'

'Mm?' she mouthed, half-listening.

'He said he thought I was too devoted to clubland,' I

continued, perversely. She shrugged again—to her, clubland was the only world worth devoting oneself to; it was where identities were formed, alliances forged, communities consolidated, and romance made vividly real. As far as she was concerned, anything that happened during daylight hours was largely irrelevant, a mere prelude or coda to the witching hour.

'Maybe Seb should get out more,' was all she said. I knew she had no special fondness for Seb, whom she found, as she did Damienne, profoundly self-righteous—and a tremendous geek to boot, whereas at least Damienne cut a striking profile.

'He hates going out. You know what he said about the club?' I persisted with a delicious frisson of nastiness.

She sighed. 'Whatever did Seb say about the club?'

'He said, "Thomas, if you're putting all your time into a club, couldn't it at least be a queer one in the East Village instead of this yuppie breeder's box that your sister's opening in SoHo?"'

'Did you tell him that my club is for everyone?' she snapped.

'Well, yeah, but he said—'

'Seb's just bitter because he knows he couldn't get into *any* club worth getting into, straight or gay. And God knows he wouldn't get into mine if he weren't your ball and chain. But you'd better take him shopping for something to wear opening night, because he's *not* coming in in that pathetic old herringbone jacket and beat-up earth shoes he wears everywhere. We're not adolescents at St. Pete's anymore.'

And with that, she finished off her Diet Coke and huffed into the kitchen, suitably miffed for my purposes. A moment later, though, she walked back into the room, hands on hips.

'What did you say Seb called the club?' she asked.

'Hunh?'

'You said he said that I was opening a *what*—a breeding tank?'

'Oh,' I laughed. 'A breeder's box.'

'Where did he get that?'

'I don't know. You know how he's always coining these little phrases.'

'That's really good, actually,' she said slowly.

I turned. 'What is?'

'That name. Breeder's box. The Breeders Box. I really like that. It's just so—so—'

'Procreative?'

'No, no. But it's like—we're all in this, like, *box*, and we're, like, *breeding* something. Like a new generation, or something.' She seemed rather lost to me in a Whitmanesque reverie all her own.

'I don't know, Flip. Don't you think people will think it's all straight, then? Or a gay club making fun of straight people?'

'That's what I like about it. It's just so—weird, and ambivalent.'

'Do you mean "ambiguous"?'

'Hm? Oh—yeah. I guess so.' She paused another moment, then said, 'That's it, Tigger. That's the name. I'm gonna call Miko and tell him he can finally begin designing the logo, and all the printed stuff.'

No one really liked the name until they saw Miko's logo—a kitschy, clever, faintly Asian rendering of two grinning tigers either dancing or humping—you couldn't quite tell—underneath which THE BREEDERS BOX was spelled out in slightly jumbled, cartoonishly stone-age lettering. The effect was terrific—retro-hip, admirably goofy and just a touch pornographic. Soon, the tigers became the cornerstone of an avalanche of printed material—matchbooks, cocktail napkins, invitations, and, most handsomely of all, the tiny bronze sign that would announce the club, so chicly discreet that, upon passing the austere black-façaded building, unless you squinted up close you wouldn't have any idea what it was at all. Word spread, first by mouth, then into the local mags and rags that covered such things: Flip Mitchell's much-anticipated watering hole finally had a name, albeit a rather puzzling one.

Flip liked the head-scratching that surrounded the name; to the very end, she would insist it had no special meaning, and if it did, she kept it steadfastly to herself.

And as for Seb, when I informed him that his offhand and mildly disparaging remark had become the inspiration for the name of what promised to be the hottest haunt of Manhattan's new decade, all he could do was put his head in his hands and groan. As usual, Flip had had the last laugh.

Fourteen

Mid-November brought Jess's first solo show, smack in the middle of the madness. He had managed to turn out a significant body of work in the past year, most of it completed before Flip launched plans for The Box (as we all referred to it, now that it was christened), and although he wasn't happy about having the show in the midst of such chaos, Grant smoothly insisted upon it—he had been talking it up for ages, he said, and had promised everyone a viewing before the holidays.

So it was that we all arrived at Grant's track-lighted Wooster Street gallery on a Saturday night, animated with excitement and pride—Lippy and Langley, Cedric and Joey and Anthea and Miko, Seb and I, Kira and her boyfriend Jeffrey, and of course Flip, who talked on and on about Jess's 'artistic growth' as though she had been its sole catalyst, even though she had always been as mystified by his work as I, and had constantly asked him when he was going to do some really 'fun' work like Warhol or Haring had done. ('When Warhol and Haring come back from the dead,' Jess would reply, irate.)

This particular collection, though, which I had only glimpsed in pieces over the past year, was as dazzling as it was confounding, an almost visceral explosion of colors and ideas, all in oil: slashes and blobs of the deepest, most sensual tropical tones, arranged on the canvas in ways that suggested, but never telegraphed, a secret world of intricately swollen and coiled semi-human limbs, ominously lush vegetation, and opaque green-blue waters. Further, all the pieces had titles like 'Guava Woman's Story' or 'Lychee: The Sequel' or 'My Three Equators', which only left me more mystified, and which Jess coolly refused to elaborate upon.

'It means whatever you want it to mean,' he'd smile when we probed, knowing full well that his amiable reticence only left us more exasperated.

Still, the night was a triumph, and our first real vision of Jess's growing success. There he stood, so handsome in his smart black suit—fielding compliments, sweatily clutching the same wine glass all night—and there was a dazzlingly coiffed and draped Damienne standing by, full of quiet pride, as Jess and Grant received an endless stream of admirers. From time to time, Grant led away to his back office some rich-looking old gal who wanted to write a check for one piece, or two, or more.

'You'll all excuse us,' he'd say, impossibly sexy in a belted avocado pantsuit that his old friend Halston might have designed for him ten years ago. 'Jess, sweetheart, I'm sure you can feed the sharks while I'm gone,' he'd mock-whisper, much to the titillated delight of the middle-aged patroness who hung heavily on his arm, dressed self-consciously in basic Donna Karan black for a night downtown.

Then he'd whisk her away, leaving in his wake the lovely Janine and the dramatically improved-looking Sasha, as well as a third girl, Toshiko, a luminous nineteen-year-old SVA student, fresh from Japan, who spoke less English than Katja. By now, all three of them were more or less living with Grant, and whatever the household or bedroom dynamics might have been in his loft, they seemed to have formed a friendly threesome, huddled together smoking, drinking and confabbing with an ease that suggested no technicalities of feeling or language whatsoever.

All night the gallery buzzed with art-biz types, museum people, press people—and by eleven-thirty, when all the wine and virtually all the Brie was gone and it was just our core group standing in the gallery, flushed with triumph and wine, Jess had sold nearly half that exhibit's showing at a sum total that made even the prosperous Grant reel with surprise. *ArtForum* had expressed interest in a story, someone from the Whitney had told Jess they wanted to have lunch, and he was asked by someone visiting from Boston if he might want to show his work at the ICA. Grant took all of us to Odeon in celebration of a perfect evening, marred only when we started making plans to take the party to a club and dance the night away.

'It'll probably be the last time in ages when we get to go to someone *else's* place!' Flip insisted.

Jess looked anguished with conflict; he was drunk and ecstatic, he obviously didn't want the night to end, and dead silence fell upon the noisy table when he turned to Damienne with raised eyebrows and she sighed, 'I'm so tired, Jess. I was at the office all day today.'

Flip threw her hand over Damienne's in a gesture of mock concern. 'Well, go home and get a good night's sleep, honey. Jess can tell you all about it in the morning.'

Jess looked from Damienne to Flip, then back to Damienne, who stared down blankly into her plate. 'I think I'm gonna get a good night's sleep too, Flip. I'm kind of tired out from the opening.'

A chorus of boos went up from the table. 'You just told me you felt like staying up all night!' Flip protested, while Damienne concentrated minutely on her napkin.

Jess squirmed. 'I did, but—but I just crashed.'

If Damienne couldn't see Flip's burning face, she certainly must have felt it, for she kept her head down penitently, masking any trace of triumph or relief she might have been feeling. 'Fine,' Flip finally said quietly, glowering at Jess. 'Go home and get your sleep.'

And after Grant discreetly took care of what must have been a staggering check, we filed out of the noisy bistro with considerably less happy commotion than we had entered it. Jess and Damienne parted ways with the rest of us on the sidewalk in a round of awkward and excruciatingly long good-byes; once they had rounded the corner, we poured into two cabs and headed off to Palladium. Flip was at my side, staring out the window and saying nothing.

'Damienne's such a wet rag, isn't she?' I whispered to her. 'Even Seb's coming, and he hates dancing.'

She shrugged, not turning to face me. 'I'm not gonna twist anybody's arm,' was all she said. And we weren't at the club more than fifteen minutes before I lost complete track of her for the whole night—didn't see her again, in fact, until she stumbled into the loft at four the next afternoon, haggard and wilted and disconcertingly quiet.

A few days later, en route to picking up lunch for Flip, Anthea, Miko and me, I stopped in at the Wooster Street gallery to say hello to Grant and see how Jess's exhibit was going. Grant's assistant, Maeve, an ample, frowning redhead pushing forty with a yellowing master's degree in art history from Columbia, had stepped out to get some lunch as well, and I found him alone in his office, his back to me, sneaking a joint with the window wide open, bare sun-browned feet up on the desk and stack-heeled shoes cast aside on the floor.

'You degenerate,' I laughed, standing in the doorway.

He coughed up a trachea full of smoke and swiveled around in the chair, bug-eyed, before composing himself and clearing his throat.

'Tigger! Tigger the Tiger!' In a moment, he was carefully stubbing out his joint, then fumbling around in his desk drawer for the Visine. 'Jesus, I'd usually never toke up during the day, but I had such a fucking migraine—' He trailed off, sheepish.

'It's just me, Grant, not Maeve.'

'I know, buddy. I know. She's a ballbuster, man.'

Maeve had been in Grant's employ for six years, and he still lived in a certain understandable fear of her. He had never been particularly meticulous about keeping his books or maintaining his papers, and her first day on the job, some six years ago, Maeve had scolded him so sharply for his disorderliness that he instantly abdicated all administrative details to her, thereby freeing himself to spend the whole day on the phone stroking artistic egos and seducing potential buyers. She hated his promiscuity and hard living and he barely tolerated her elitist contempt for his blatant commercialism, and yet it wasn't unusual for the two of them to take in a comfortably desultory dinner-and-movie together at the end of the day. When Maeve needed work done on her apartment or sank wordlessly into the abyss as her seventeenth relationship fell apart after six weeks, it was Grant who dropped everything, including his art babes, and set out for her place in Brooklyn Heights. And when Grant had a cocaine addiction back in 1985, it was Maeve who walked him stoically through recovery and single-handedly ran the gallery while he recuperated. Truth be told, theirs was the longest relationship that either of them had ever had, however flatly and immutably platonic.

'The smoke's airing out now,' he said optimistically. 'She'll never know.'

'Let's hope so.'

'So *hey*,' he said in his familiar old gravelly stoner's drawl. 'What about Saturday night, hey? It looks like a certain Hey-Zoos Mitchell is arriving. I've sold eight more paintings for that bastard since the show.'

'Seriously?'

'Dead. Word gets around fast. Especially when you get a nice little review in the *Times* on Monday morning.'

'Yeah. Jess was pretty happy about that.' We all were, in

fact. Flip had clipped it and magneted it to the refrigerator, but
Jess took it down the moment he saw it in a flush of happy
embarrassment.

'And I think it's pretty cool your brother's gonna do the artwork for Flip's club—of course I want a cut when someone
decides to buy the walls.'

'Flip's really glad, too,' I laughed, truthfully enough.
Whether Jess felt the same way about this unsought commis-
sion I really couldn't say.

Grant nodded knowingly, eyes squinting. 'That Palladium
was pretty scorching, hey? Some great ceiling in that place.
Too bad the artist himself couldn't come along.'

'Well, the artist must get his sleep, I suppose.'

'Looked more to me like the woman must get her artist.' I
laughed along with him, conceding the point. 'He's on a pretty
short rope with that Haitian chick, hey?'

'Damienne. To tell you the truth,' I said, surprising myself,
'I'm surprised she hasn't made it shorter. She puts up with
more than you think.'

He shook his head slowly, considering, then looked up at
me abruptly. 'Hey buddy—if I show you something, can you
keep it on the down-low, including to Jess? I mean, *especially*
to Jess.'

'Of course,' I said, instantly and guiltily intrigued.

'Come here,' he said, groaning out of his chair and padding
barefoot into the sunny gallery, me just behind him. He took
me around to an obscure, empty alcove where a canvas was
propped against the wall. 'Check this out,' he nearly giggled.

I stared at it: there, in the midst of what seemed to be a particularly overrun tropical garden, stood a white frame house
that I instantly recognized as our summer place up in Rye. On
the front porch, a parade of crabs escaped from an overturned
pail, and standing on the porch, quite apart from this exodus,
was a woman, faceless, her skin an indeterminate shade of
beigy-brown, hair long and wild, wearing a pink and black

striped minidress. I recognized the dress instantly; it had been one of Flip's favorites when she was about fifteen or sixteen. The image was basically figurative, but the paint was harshly applied, in colors that screamed as loudly as those on the other canvases in the gallery.

I said nothing, and Grant obviously took my silence for rapt admiration. 'Pretty haunting, huh? You know what he calls it? "La Muerte de mi Corazon". The Death of my Heart.'

'Jesus,' was all I could manage. It was so literal—he must have known that if Flip or I had ever seen it, we'd recognize the setting and the subject immediately.

He laughed, vindicated. 'You're trippin', right buddy? Right before the opening, your brother decides he doesn't want this to be part of the show. I told him it would fly out the door, but, you know—' He stooped down to scratch a bit of schmutz off his feet. 'You gotta respect the artist's wishes.'

'Of course,' I muttered, absorbed in the image.

'You know my hunch?' Grant continued, delighted. 'I think Jess wants to save it and give it to his main girl—what's her name?'

'Damienne.'

'Yeah. Damienne. I think he's saving it for her birthday or something. Or,' and he raised a mischievous eyebrow, 'maybe when they tie the knot? Huh?'

'Possibly,' I said absently, my eyes still on the empty oval of the girl's face. 'Possibly.'

'I know this particular buyer that would have been ga-ga over it, but,' and he sighed, 'far be it for me to make a buck off art made in the name of love.' The phone rang in the back room. 'Now where the *hell* is Maeve?' he spewed. 'Hang here for a second, Tiger. I'll be right back.' And he shambled off toward the phone.

I couldn't pull my eyes away from the image; a memory was hurtling back toward me now, that time that Lippy and I had rushed out on the porch to find Jess and Flip emerging from beneath it, Flip breathless with giggles, Jess mute with discomfort. *Pedro got away*, Jess had said by way of explanation. *So where's the goddamned crab*? I had thought to myself. Suddenly I very much wished that Grant hadn't been so enthusiastic to show me the painting.

Someone was coming up the steps behind me and into the gallery—stern Maeve, back with something unhealthy for Grant, reluctantly, and the same austere salad she ate herself every day, I figured—but I was still so transfixed by the painting that I didn't turn around until someone spoke directly behind my back—a man's voice, nasal and unpleasantly familiar.

'That's quite an image, isn't it?'

I turned. It was Goolsbee, all got up in his Wall Street armor, sporting a new pair of terribly expensive-looking Armani glasses. I didn't think I had seen him in person since he had appeared that long-ago night of my birthday party, drunk and saying absolutely wretched things to both Flip and myself—and now here he was, right beside me, smiling amiably as though we were old friends colliding at the intermission of a play.

'Hello, Tigger. You're looking well. I read about Jess's show and I thought I'd come on up and see what's for the taking before he becomes so expensive I can't afford him.'

'This isn't for sale,' I said dumbly, gesturing awkwardly before me.

He looked at the canvas again over the frame of his glasses. 'That's a shame. I remember that crazy dress of Flip's from St. Pete's. Don't you? I thought Jess's art was supposed to be a little more mysterious than this.'

'I didn't know you were such a connoisseur of art in the first place.'

He laughed and his face bundled itself into that sinister old squinting smile. 'There's a lot you don't know about me, Tigger. I know you think I've always been this boring philistine, but the truth is I've actually learned a lot about art and music, living in New York all these years. They enrich the quality of one's life.'

I smiled back, equally tight. Wouldn't Grant *please* emerge from the back room and save me from this scenario? 'I'm glad you're enriched.'

He laughed his thin, reedy laugh again. God, I really did hate him; how could Flip even bear to talk on the phone with him? Then, as though reading my mind, he said, 'So how's Felipika? I guess she's pretty busy with her opening night coming up. The Breeders Box, isn't that what I read?'

'That's what you read.'

'Hmmm. That's interesting. It's quite an investment your sister's making, and especially in such a risky market. I hope she's got some pretty good backers.'

'So do I,' I answered tersely. I refused to divulge what little I knew of Flip's finances, and if Goolsbee was contributing to them—if, indeed, that was the nature and purpose of their occasional furtive phone calls—I certainly wasn't letting on that I suspected as much.

We stood side by side, staring dumbly at the picture. Presently, Goolsbee took off his delicately wrought glasses, rubbed his eyes—for the first time I noticed just how blood-shot and lusterless they were, for all their frosty blueness—and said, 'Tell me, Tigger—'

'My name's Thomas.' I loathed the sound of this bastard using my family nickname just because he had heard Flip, Jess and Kira call me that at St. Pete's.

He laughed shortly. 'All right, then. Tell me, Thomas. It seems as though exciting things are happening for the Mitchells these days, so—do you think now that you're all finding your separate measures of fame, you'll finally go your own ways?'

'I don't know what you mean,' I said coldly. 'We do go our own ways.'

'It doesn't look that way,' he continued genially. 'All of you living in that big, dark loft together. It's kind of *Flowers in the Attic*-ish, don't you think?'

I don't know what I felt more: offense at his remark or mild shock that he had alluded to a work of literature, even one as low-grade as a V.C. Andrews novel. 'I'm visiting a friend here, Goolsbee. Why don't you leave me the fuck alone? Why don't you leave all of us the fuck alone? We'd all be happier.'

He raised a bemused eyebrow. 'Oh, really? Would *all* of you be happier? I'm not so sure about that. Maybe some of the Mitchells need me.'

'You think what you like,' I said, walking across the gallery floor to stare at another canvas. He was silent behind me, and for a moment I thought he might leave quietly . . . and then I had the great misfortune to hear him speak again.

'Tell me one more thing, Tigger—I'm sorry, *Thomas*. Do you think your sister will ever realize that she can't spend the rest of her life in conjugal bliss with her own older brother? That maybe her older brother doesn't want her *around* anymore?'

I shivered; it was horrid hearing speculation of such matters from a virtual stranger, especially one as contemptible as Goolsbee. I stared intently at the canvas—Jess had named this one *Nunca*, whatever the hell that meant (I had never taken Spanish)—and refused to speak.

'And do you think she'll ever realize,' he continued, 'that I'm not necessarily the monster you all seem to think I am, just because I'm a WASP and I work on Wall Street and I don't live in a hovel in Alphabet City? Because I'm not a monster, Thomas. I had a sister, too, you know.'

I caught myself before turning around. *This* was the dead sister of Goolsbee's Jess had referred to a long time ago—the one who drowned, the one whom Goolsbee had allowed to drown, according to the rumors that had damned him to iso-lation, and had sealed his early friendship with Jess.

'You've probably heard the story,' he said, as though reading my mind again. 'Her name was Libby. She died right before I started up at St. Pete's. She drowned that summer on the Cape. She was going to be thirteen years old.'

I turned, guardedly, and stared at him across the room, standing in a shaft of sunlight. *Dammit*, I hated to admit to myself, *but he was handsome. A miserable human being, but handsome.* 'Yeah, I had heard that,' I fessed up. 'I'm sorry.' I said it more out of politeness than anything else.

'I don't tell many people. She was my only sibling. And Thomas—' he surprised me by laughing quietly, 'she was *such* a brilliant, officious, bossy little shit. She could beat me at tennis when she was only eleven years old. *Eleven*, can you believe that? And she was going to be an amazing ballet dancer, too—unstoppable. I mean, I did *everything* this girl told me to do—half the time, I didn't even know why. She was going to follow me to St. Pete's, if she didn't end up some-where better, which she probably would have.'

He paused again, refitting his glasses over his squinting eyes. 'I mean, she was smarter than me. Anyone could see that.'

I felt an odd mix of contempt and pity. I remembered the summer our father died—the women screaming in the house, the gorgeous coastal afternoon, standing alone in the low tide and staring out at the vast oblivion of the ocean to which a member of our family had been hastily dispatched. It was a horrible thing to lose somebody at that age, when all the good, safe things in the world seemed as though they could only grow and grow, but never simply vanish.

He sighed, seeming almost spectral to me now in the strong light of the gallery, dust motes whirling around his blond head like a chaos of atoms. 'So then I went off to St. Pete's,' he said. 'And Thomas: the first time I ever saw your sister—she reminded me of mine. I mean, Flip was such a crass, loud-mouthed little *brat*. I loved it. She wasn't like those other uptight simpering little St. Pete's girls at all.'

'Well, then why were you such an asshole to her, Goolsbee?
You *tortured* her.'

'I didn't mean to be. That first year with her, before you
came, I tried so hard to get her to like me. I gave her little presents all the time. But she hated me. She hated everyone at St.
Pete's. And I couldn't get her away from your goddamned
brother.'

'They're really close, Goolsbee, I'm sorry. Jess took a lot of
shit when we were little and Flip was always there to stick up
for him.'

'But it's not natural anymore, Thomas. Flip should be with
me.' He said this with such quiet certainty that it seemed his
summary statement of years of consideration.

'Goolsbee! You can't *have* somebody just because you like
them. It doesn't work that way.'

'It can,' he said, still the image of calm. 'You have money.
You know that it can go a long way.'

'Yeah, it can go a long way, but not with emotions. You can't
buy somebody with money.'

'I know. You buy them with love. But you can use money to
show that you love them.'

'Oh God, Goolsbee, you are a *mess*,' I exclaimed in spite of
myself. It was all I could think to say before Grant came
bounding back into the gallery. 'Whoa Tiggerman, why is it
that women on Beekman Place have nothing better to do
than—' he stopped short, regarding Goolsbee. 'Oh. Hey.
What's up?'

'Hello.' Goolsbee offered Grant his hand, then was for a
moment startled when Grant accepted it in his customary
Black Power grip.

I stepped forward. 'Grant, this is Amos Goolsbee. We went
to high school together, and he came up to see the show.'

'That's cool,' Grant shrugged, nodding slowly.

'Actually,' Goolsbee said, 'I'm interested in acquiring. Can
you show me what you haven't already sold? And Tigger tells

me that this'—and he pointed to *La Muerte de mi Corazon*—'is not for sale.'

'Yeah, no bids on that one, unfortunately,' Grant said, winking slyly at me. 'But look, that's just one piece. Check out these small pieces on this wall over here.'

'Oh, I want a great *big* piece.' Goolsbee smiled.

'You do, huh?' Grant smiled broadly. 'Okay. That's cool. Come check out this series around the corner here. Tigger, sorry to have to ask you to hang tight again. '

'Actually,' I interrupted, 'I should be getting back, Grant. Our lunch order is probably ready and I haven't even picked it up yet.'

'All right, then, baby.' Grant gripped my hand and kissed me on the cheek; I saw Goolsbee wince and delighted that he might mistake Grant, a professional womanizer, for gay. 'It's pretty cool, you just dropping in like this. Do it more and protect me from my fucking conscience.' He was referring to Maeve, whose heavy, unforgiving footsteps we now heard on the stairway. 'I'd say we make plans to party again, but I guess next time we do, it'll be on home turf, huh?'

'This is true.'

'And remember, man.' He leaned in, *sotto voce*, fancying himself quite cryptic in front of Goolsbee. 'Not a word to Jess or to anyone about *you know what*, all right?'

'Of course.' I turned to Goolsbee, standing by with a smug little smile on his face. 'Take care, Goolsbee,' I muttered, hardly stopping to look at him.

'Good-bye, Tigger,' he said, grasping my arm and forcing my hand into a soul-shake, a cruel mimicry to which Grant was thankfully oblivious. His hand in mine was startlingly cold and chalky, like a stone. 'Be well. And give my best to Jess and Felipika.'

Enraged, I barely managed a nod and turned away, hurrying down the stairs, where I passed an indignant Maeve carrying a bag from Dean & Deluca. 'Has he been goofing off with *you* the whole time I've been gone?' she demanded, passing over my nervous salutation. I fumbled for an answer, but she cut me off. 'And don't think I can't smell the pot from the bottom of the stairwell. Not to mention that your eyes are as red as rust, Tigger.'

There was no use in protesting my innocence. 'You need help with that bag?' I asked, a final gesture.

'Two hands, one bag,' she declared, barrelling past me on the stairway. 'Does it look like I need help? If Grant falls asleep at his desk this afternoon, I'm going to blame it on you,' she barked back before disappearing, to my great relief, around the bend in the stairwell.

I stood mid-stairway for a moment, amused and slightly stunned, silently barking back to Maeve that she needed a good lay, when voices from the gallery floated down to me, accompanied by the creak of expensive shoes on polished hardwood floors.

'Felipika,' I heard Grant say, drawing out and savoring each syllable, as he was wont to do. 'That's some fine name, isn't it?'

'Mm, very fine,' Goolsbee responded, his tone equal parts faint sarcasm and dark concurrence. I hurried down the stairs, shaking off a shiver, and escaped back out into the cold, bright afternoon.

After Dark

Fifteen

'They're playing *Yahtzee*?' Seb misheard me, eyes wide, walking out of my bedroom—impressively, self-consciously stylish in the black Armani knock-off we had found for him the week before on Orchard Street—unruly hair pomaded into place, eyes free this evening of his signature owlish glasses. We were at the loft, preparing; it was December 31st, 1989, ten-thirty in the evening.

'No,' I laughed, putting down the phone and retrieving the gin and tonic I had fixed hastily in the kitchen—my third thus far, to be candid. 'Papa*razzi*. That was Jess, calling from the back office. He says the place is a madhouse. He says the front of the club is swarming with paparazzi shooting all the *names* coming in.'

Seth raised a skeptical eyebrow. 'Like what names?'

'Like Lauren Hutton. Like Sandra *Bern*hardt,' I enunciated haughtily. 'Like Luther Vandross. Like Diane Brill, and David Barton and Susanne *Bartsch*?'

'Who?'

'Susanne Bartsch? Nightlife queen? Haven't you ever read about her in Michael Musto's column?'

He walked toward me, fastening a coat button. 'You know I don't read that trash.'

I took another sip of my drink; I was so excited I felt like any minute I'd start flying around the room in my *own* Armani suit (authentic, and perhaps the most extravagant purchase I had ever made). Deee-Lite was on the stereo and I couldn't stop dancing. The whole week had been a prelude to this: our hurried overnight trip home for Christmas, the inability to run out for milk or cigarettes without bumping into at least three people begging for guest list privileges, the round of holiday parties that had seemed little more than promotional opportunities for our own place. Flip was absolutely radioactive, and whatever our misgivings had been at the start, it would be a lie to say that Jess and I weren't equally alive with anticipation. It was impossible not to be—these days, The Breeders Box had been all that anybody talked about.

Seb flurried a hand over his hair, succeeding in releasing the tendril I had just latched back behind his ear for him. 'I'm nervous, Thomas. This isn't my scene.'

'What do you mean it's not your scene? You know all these people, the core group, anyway—Flip and Jess and Cedric and the rest. And besides, you're my date. And besides, it's New Year's Eve. What *else* would you rather be doing?'

'Going to bed,' he sulked.

'Well,' I declared imperiously, shutting off the stereo. 'There's no bedtime for Sebastian tonight. Sebastian is going to ring in the new year with the rest of Manhattan, whether he likes it or not. So try to like it. *Embrace* your fabulosity.'

Outside, amidst a clear and cold New Year's Eve, revelers were strutting, stumbling, laughing through the streets of SoHo, brandishing bottles of wine and champagne, jamming the entrances to restaurants and bars, shrieking into the buzzers of apartment buildings and lofts where loud parties raged. And still, none of this prepared me for what I saw upon turning onto Spring Street and approaching the club.

The first thing you heard was the rhythm, heard it from at least a block away—this steady, insistent tattoo as though the throbbing heart of the earth itself had risen to the surface of the plane. And then the throng: noisy, restive, winding all the way down the block and halfway around the corner, alongside streets that ceaselessly disgorged cab- and limofuls of beautiful people, in shining white, shimmering silver, luminous gold, all offset by what seemed like acres of stolid New York black. And for all Flip's heady promises, I couldn't get over the extraordinary mix of creatures—packs of fashionable queens with their fashionable female friends in tow, a sea of familiar faces from the downtown worlds of music, theater and art (in fact, there was Grant, looking impossibly hip in a tight suit of all white, babbling on in Italian to three dark, furred, rail-thin contessa types while the love troika of Janine, Sasha and Toshiko stood by in their usual chummy huddle). There were the most gorgeous men I had ever seen congregated in one place, a few young uptown society types, competing against their will with the drag queens in all their soignee finery. Plenty of clubland icons, who possessed a hermetic celebrity of their own—in a space of five minutes, I spotted Carmen D'Alessio, who had brought the first wave of glam-trash into Studio in 1978 or so, and the McNally brothers of Odeon, and Anita Sarko, the old Mudd Club DJ, and Sally Randall, who had gladly ceded to Flip her former status as the 'It' girl of clubland, earned back when she worked the door at the spanking-new Palladium. And then there were the models— heaps and heaps of models, a forest of hair and boobs and legs and high heels, as though they had all been cooked up that very afternoon in some gigantic industrial kitchen and shipped here like pies, still hot, and unloaded off trucks, tray by tray by tray.

Seb and I stopped dead in our tracks. 'Holy God,' he whispered.

'I can't believe it,' I couldn't stop chanting. And suddenly I felt a wave of pride in Flip that I had never felt before. This was it, it occurred to me—she had been completely right— this was her grand achievement. 'Let's get up to the door,' I said to Seb, and I nearly reeled at the chorus of people that called out to me as I passed ('Tigger! Darling! *Please* tell Flip we're here!'), or who simply glared at us for walking past so blithely.

Jess, Ty and Miko were at the door behind the velvet ropes, clipboards in their hands, ski jackets on over their suits, harried and tense. Jess looked up, saw Seb and me, and bugged out his eyes.

'Thank God you're here,' he said, unlatching the rope. ('He's my goddamned *brother*,' he shouted to the protesting crush of supplicants.) 'Get in there and find Flip and tell her there's a major crisis out here. She way overbooked the guest list and I'm afraid that we're violating the fire codes or something. We passed our capacity max, like, an hour ago.'

'That's *not* a comp, it's an ad,' Miko was virtually barking at some slightly Long Island-looking couple who were waving about an ad Flip had taken out in *Seven Days*. 'All the comps for tonight were given out privately. *Privately*. It's fifty dollars. I'm sorry, it's fifty dollars or please stop holding up the line.'

My God, I thought to myself. *Fifty dollars a head? We must be making a fortune!*

'Don't get so excited,' Miko said, catching my hung jaw and reading my mind. 'Two out of three people in so far Flip put on the guest list.'

'Tig!' Jess shouted at me. 'Get in there! Tell Flip to stop being a diva and get out here.'

'Okay, okay. Come on,' I said to Seb, who was so overwhelmed that I had to grab his arm and yank him through the ropes. Just before I passed inside, some pancake-white, deeply eye-shadowed, insanely bosomy girl with a Day-Glo red French twist grabbed my arm. 'Hi, Tigger!'

I stared blankly. 'Do I know you?'

'I'm Opal from Palladium, remember? Parker's friend?'

'Oh, yeah.'

'Can we just slip in here with you?'

'Um—'

'Tigger, get *in there!*' from Jess, and Ty hastily pulled back the rope in front of Opal and company. 'Nobody be gettin' in unless all you people chill,' he boomed.

'Sorry.' I shrugged to Opal—she looked as though I had just refused to make room for her on my lifeboat as the *Titanic* went down—and stepped inside, instantly swallowed up in Sammy Fingers' booming house version of Blondie's 'Rapture'.

'Oh—my—God,' I managed, as Seb and I stood side-by-side, taking it all in. Of course, I had seen The Box in various stages of evolution, but always during the day, and never going at full kilowatts. Anthea and Miko had promised something celestial—a veritable altered state of consciousness—and they hadn't failed. You entered upon a kind of antechamber: the floors were a particularly iridiscent form of faux white marble, and the entire passageway was swathed in sheaths and sheaths of diaphanous white tulle that rose up some twenty feet like the trains of angels, up into thousands of tiny white lights that glowed from behind the tulle—like a tent in the middle of the sky. Then a kidney-shaped room—equally bejewelled in white lights but this time lacquered completely in a glossy black fitted everywhere with bands and bands of dull silver, a soundstage from a Fred Astaire dream sequence—where you paid your way in and checked your coat. Off to either side, I could see black passageways lit faintly blue with flickering candlelights that led to restrooms. And from there, in a field of black broken only by the tiny lights, you ascended a wide, spare staircase that curved like a boomerang to the heavens— the music growing louder with every step—until, with a breathtaking suddenness, you found yourself spilled into the main room.

I had never seen a dance space of such proportions or beauty in my life—even today, it lingers in my dreams, smoky and blurred at the edges. It was an arena of sorts, but so fluid in its lines that it felt more like a luxurious black hole, at the bottom of which was a throng of revelers in perpetual thrall to St. Vitus. Everywhere: levels and levels of gently sloping spaces to sit, to congregate, to hide away, to take a nap—one exquisite little brothel after another, each one fitted with enormous couches of the richest velvets, scattered with spindly gold and silver ballroom chairs, sheets of mirrors suspended by thick gold ropes from high above—all of this facing down, vortex-style, toward the dance floor at thrillingly vertiginous angles, until you reached the floor itself, which, in a brilliant inversion, had been paved with the kaleidoscopic prisms of a thousand mirror balls, perhaps all the mirror balls of all the clubs that had ever graced Manhattan—creating an effect, as the first throng of the night stormed the floor, of a dance party reflected back upon itself a thousand, a million, times.

And then, what delivered the entire space into the realm of the ridiculously, splendidly sublime: when you looked up fifty feet to the ceiling, there it was, Jess's work, a heavenly diorama of the richest whites and yellow and blues, a vivid, hyperreal landscape of sky and clouds and stars, and in the center, emerging like a goddess from the heights of Mount Olympus, the colossal shadow of a woman—faceless, nameless, head thrown back and exultant—extending her vast, feathery angel's wings down on the entire room like a benediction from the patron saint of pleasure. And all of this alternately bathed and obscured in a rich, semi-opaque play of lights (controlled from a booth high above, adjacent to the booth where Sammy Fingers reigned), so layered, so moody and evocative that it transformed the space from a mere club into an otherwordly haven, a ballroom for the gods.

Seb and I stood at the top of the vortex, looking up, looking down. Finally Seb turned to me and laughed with astonishment. 'I don't believe it. This is unreal.'

I just slowly shook my head, grinning. 'When my sister does something,' I said, still dizzy with shock, 'she does it big.'

'I just—I just—' And Seb finally just shrugged, incapable of saying more.

'I'd better go find her,' I said, coming to.

'I just—' Seb was still gaping.

I laughed. 'Sit here. I'll bring you back a drink as soon as I find Flip.'

Sammy Fingers was fading into some old Chaka Khan now as I wended my way down the arena toward the back office. It was eleven o'clock; the place was getting more and more crowded as parties of two, ten or twenty were let inside and spilled into this central space, their eyes large with drugs and wonder. Not two levels down, I bumped into Kira. Clubs certainly weren't her scene anymore, but she was here, of course, as a special friend of Flip. She was clinging with one hand to her drink, and with the other to Jeffrey, her fiancé now, who looked as dazed and disoriented as she.

'Hi! Long time no see,' I shouted over the music as we kissed.

Her mouth dropped open. 'Tigger, this—I mean, I don't know what to say. I mean, I thought Flip was opening up, like, a *little* place.'

'Not quite. Haven't you been reading the papers?'

'I'm so busy with work. I haven't been out like this since I don't know how long. We rushed here from a New Year's party at Jeffrey's parents' place on Long Island.'

'Oh.' I looked up at the previously unacknowledged Jeffrey and we shook hands. I seldom knew what to say to him, and moreover, he knew about my past history with Kira, as well as my present history, so conversation with him was always awkward. 'So what do you think?'

He shrugged. 'It's— it's amazing. What do you think the kilowattage is on that light system?'

'I couldn't even guess.' I smiled a little; it seemed like such a typically straight question to ask in the midst of such glamor. Kira blushed, looked uncomfortably away. She knew what I was thinking, and there was a time when she would have smiled the same smile. 'But I want to get married, Tigger,' she had told me last winter, just before meeting Jeffrey at a friend's holiday office party. 'And I can't spend my whole life hanging around with gay guys if I do, as much as I love them.' Of course we were still friends, old friends, but since then we hadn't had much to say to each other; around her now, I felt oddly irrelevant.

'I better go find Flip,' I said by way of leave. 'Have a great time. Stay all night—*we* are.'

Jeffrey laughed the same tight little laugh. 'Well—' Kira said, but I was already hurrying away.

I had to get to Flip now—Jess was surely cursing me—but it seemed impossible to take three steps without having to make the requisite small talk with someone or other. At length I came to the back office door, down a discreet hall from the glittering fray. I heard music piped in from within, knocked once. No answer. Knocked again harder.

Flip, tense, from inside: 'Who is it?'

'It's Tigger.'

'Come in, Tig.'

She sat at the brightly lit vanity she had installed for herself in one corner of the office, spotted me in the mirror and turned. She looked absolutely ravishing in a dress that one of Raoul's friends at Calvin Klein had designed for her expressly for this evening (in exchange for a lifetime's comp to The Box): black watered silk, cut on the bias, that revealed a fair degree of her breasts and clung to every inch of her body all the way down to her glittering white heels. Her hair had been styled that day by a friend of Miko's at his salon on West Broadway: massed up high in an enormous mountain, streaked with white, descending from behind in a frenzy of richly coiled tendrils. Her face was gloriously in place—eyes bewitching with shadow—and she sat royally, surrounded with congratulatory flowers. Two lines of untouched coke lay on the table in front of her, and she was sniffling and crying at the same time, her blackened eyes on the verge of smearing beyond repair.

'Tigger!' she sobbed. And she ran to me and threw her arms around me, trembling and smelling of something musky and disconcertingly unplaceable.

'Flip! What's wrong? Are you doing lines?'

'Oh, Tigger,' and she seemed to be holding onto me for dear life. 'Kristal Kleer gave some to me, and I didn't want to, but I had to. Tig, I'm overwhelmed. I just can't believe—' she sniffled, composed herself—'after all the hard work, this is it! This is *mine*. It's not a dream anymore. This is it.'

'No kidding. That's why you have to get out there and run your club. Jess is screaming for you to get up to the door. Come on,' I said, mending her eyes with a tissue. 'I'll escort you so nobody holds you up.'

'Tig, I can't! Didn't you hear the plan? Anthea's plan?'

'What plan?'

'The midnight plan,' she said, brightening and runwaying cokeishly across the room. 'I'm not supposed to come out until midnight, to greet everyone Happy New Year and welcome them to The Box.'

'Until midnight? Who're you coming out with? Anthea?'

'No,' she said simply. 'Just me. You want a line?'

I didn't want to want one, but I did, and snorted it up in Flip's rolled dollar without further ado. 'You mean you're just gonna *appear* before the masses at midnight like Venus de Milo or something?' I brushed away possible traces of coke from my nostrils and laughed—suddenly, it seemed like a particularly funny image, and perhaps all too appropriate.

'Yeah,' she said, lighting a cigarette and handing me a drag. 'Isn't that a great idea?'

I laughed, exasperated and affectionate. 'Girl, you are really too much. Well, you may as well go for it—it's your moment. I'll go help Jess. But listen—he says the guest list is overbooked.'

She frowned. 'Oh, shit. I was afraid of that.'

'What do you want me to tell him?' I hurried over to the vanity and helped myself to another line.

'Well, there's nothing we can do about it now. Just tell him to let in everyone that's on it. Anthea told me that Guillermo'—that was the cashier, a dwarfish, part-time accountant from Rome whom Miko introduced us to with absolute assurances that we could trust him with the money— 'Guillermo said we've already taken in something like twenty thousand dollars on all the noncomps. Can you *believe* that?'

'What about the fire code?'

'The F.D. has better things to do on New Year's Eve than do a head count at some little club.'

I laughed, sparkling now from the coke. 'Flip, it's hardly a *little* club.'

'Well,' she preened, proud. 'You know what I mean.'

'Are you just gonna stay in here all alone?'

'Kristal's coming back with some more blow.'

I sighed. 'Jeez, Flip. What are you doing with that piece of trash Kristal Kleer? I thought you were over this stuff.'

'I am. It's just for tonight, okay? And who are you to talk, Mr. Mooch?'

'Well,' I frowned. 'Don't do *too* much or you'll come out flying. Just like that picture of you that Jess painted on the ceiling.'

'That's not me!' she protested, although I was sure that upon seeing it, she had had exactly the same thought I had.

'Think what you like, girl.' We kissed.

'Oh, Tigger, I'm *so* happy. Thank you for everything. And you look fabulous.'

'So do you,' I answered. And from the way she smiled at me before blowing a kiss and sitting back down at her vanity, I knew that she already knew as much.

I was hardly out the door and back down the dark hallway before I knew that the coke had kicked in hard—suddenly, the music didn't seem to be this pounding external thing but an inner rhythm, perfectly in sync with my own heartbeat, and when I walked back into the space I marvelled anew at the glittering expanse. It had filled out considerably since I had gone; now I had to weave my way giddily through a thickening crush of people, nodding here and there, reprimanding myself not to gawk when I caught amongst a knot of raucous BPs the likes of Kate Pierson from the B-52s or Monica Lynch from Tommy Boy Records, accompanied by two of the guys from De La Soul. And sure enough, there was Michael Musto looking characteristically frumpy as he steadied a glass of champagne in Sylvia Miles' peripatetic hands, the Baroness Sherry hovering greedily just behind them. *All these people*, I thought, my brain humming and my hands bongoing a beat at my sides, *all these people at my own sister's club.* And I remembered that I had to get back to Seb . . . but . . . but . . . boom, boom, boom . . . but I had to get to Jess, too, had to help him mind the door. And I had to see who else was here, had to see . . . boom, boom, boom . . .

'Tigger!'

I turned, face to face with Lippy, all in rhinestones and organza, accompanied by Langley, looking very stiff in black tie.

'Lippy!' We embraced. 'You look amazing. Hi, Langley.' Langley nodded at me regally.

'Thank you, darling.' Lippy's painted face was aglow with overexcitement. 'Barbara Cook gave me these rhinestones, you know.' She was pensive a moment, then looked back up at me, gaping. 'Tigger! This is—I'm floored! This is bigger than Studio 54! We're too *old* for this!'

'No, you're not.'

'Thank you, Tigger,' Langley bristled.

'I mean,' Lippy went on, 'thank God Langley and I polished off a bottle of champagne at dinner, or—I mean, you've got to be *prepared* for something like this. Darling'—and she clutched my arm—'you're not going to believe who I met in the powder room, just standing in there unassumingly doing her lips, looking like a million bucks!'

'Who?'

'Eartha Kitt! And guess what?'

'What?'

'She *recognized* me!' Lippy shrieked. 'And she said she's coming to Julia's Room next week. And she wants us to sing together! She had all these gorgeous men waiting outside to escort her around.' Langley rolled his eyes extravagantly behind her back.

'Lippy, that's wonderful,' I said, perhaps too loudly. The coke felt like a car engine inside me now, and I didn't want Lippy to suspect. But she didn't seem to notice a thing, so preoccupied was she with talk of Eartha.

'How does Flip *know* all these people?' she went on. 'She's not even thirty yet.'

'I don't think she knows Eartha Kitt personally. I think word just went around. I'm sure Eartha's people called up and got her on the guest list.'

'Oh my Lord,' Lippy said, fingering Barbara Cook's old rhinestones and scooching in toward me to make way for a passing knot of disdainful, ravishing Brazilians. 'Where is that Flip anyway? I have to congratulate her. Tigger, didn't we always know she'd end up doing something marvelous, just like you and Jess?'

'Of course we did,' I said for niceness' sake; there was a time when I hadn't necessarily been assured of such a thing at all. 'But Lippy . . . Miss Mitchell is *not* making her appearance until the stroke of midnight.'

Lippy gasped dramatically. 'How sensational! I wonder who she gets her wonderful sense of theater from.'

'I'm sure you do,' I teased her—just what she wanted—before we kissed good-bye (Langley and I exchanged a grave nod) and parted ways in the crowd.

I began the long, winding ascent back toward the front of the club; everywhere now, people were gathering in raucous groups in the plush alcoves—popping open champagne that the preposterously good-looking fleet of Box waiters were serving for seventy-five dollars a bottle, or huddled furtively over the glass-topped tables, or already paired off in various gender configurations in their own dark corners. And it wasn't even midnight.

'Girl, girl! Tigger!' I turned again. Damienne, Sammy Fingers, Grant and his harem, Cedric and Joey—the latter two in the most extraordinary Scaasi knock-offs I had ever seen, complete with discreet pearls and little bags—had commandeered one of the settees and were calling to me.

We shared a hyperactive round of happy new years, and Joey offered me yet another line of blow (which I accepted somewhat guiltily in front of Damienne, who didn't go in for such things and who, I also strongly sensed, was the least merry occupant of the sofa. She had a certain grudging fondness for Cedric and Joey, despite what she called their 'inherent misogyny,' but Grant and his ceaseless parade of 'babecessories,' as she called them, irritated her no end).

'What are you doing down here?' I asked Sammy, looking very formidable in something resembling a turban. 'Are you on remote control or something?'

'Pepe's spinning for fifteen minutes while I chill.' (Pepe was Sammy's 'apprentice' of sorts, a short, tough, wiry little queen from the Bronx who aspired to be the next Li'l Louis Vega.) 'Girl, I've gotta go up there in a bit and heat everyone up for your big sister's unveiling.'

'It's so over the top,' I laughed.

'It's so Flip Mitchell,' Joey said, and we all laughed except Damienne, who managed to crack a tight little smile.

'Tigger,' she asked now, leaning forward in the din, 'Speaking of Mitchells, have you seen the eldest?'

'He's working the door. I'm going to find him right now. You

look smashing, Damienne.' I didn't think she looked smashing
at all; her batiky wrap dress would have been much more
appropriate for a mountainside wedding in Oregon than a
New York club opening—but by now I was overcome by a
wave of breathless expansiveness that didn't stop for anyone.

'Thank you.' She didn't sound particularly flattered. 'Would
you tell him that I wouldn't mind reuniting with him before
midnight?'

'Of course. Good-bye, babies.' A flurry of narcotic kisses all
around, and I plunged headlong back into the throng.

Finally I emerged into the black and silver anteroom,
choked with people queued at the cashier, at the coat-check,
elaborately lighting their first cigarettes as they waited for
friends. *My God*, I thought to myself as I virtually floated
across the carpet, all the tiny lights around me dancing and
converging before my eyes like drunken fireflies, *I'm* really
high. And then, before I could take another step, there was
Jess—ski jacket doffed, all slender and lithe in black and
white—cha-cha-ing his way toward me, face luminous with
bliss.

'*Mi hermano*.' He took me into his arms and waltzed us
toward the candlelit corridor of the men's room. '*Mi hermano*,
shall we dance?'

'Listen!' I laughed, fumbling over his feet. 'Flip isn't coming
out. She said to just let anyone in off the list that's already
there. She's making this special midnight appearance before
the crowd that Anthea thought up.'

'As befits a princess,' he said, dipping me now in his arms.

'Jess! What about the door?'

'The honorable Miko Ishizuka and Tyrone Packer have
relieved me of my duties. I am now free to walk among the
good people.'

'Jess, what happened to *you*?'

He threw himself up against the wall, breathing hard, the
candles lighting his face a glamorously spectral blue. 'Let's

just say that the honorable Miko Ishizuka helped me find my ecstasy.'

'No!' I gasped. 'Why didn't you get some for me?'

'You didn't ask,' he giggled. 'And besides, you seem to be doing just fine to me. Your pupils are the size of half dollars.'

'Well—I ran into Cedric and Joey.'

'And Flip, no doubt?'

'And Flip,' I conceded.

'Ah, Tigger,' he drawled. I had never seen him quite so loopy before. 'Ah, the ever impressionable, ever malleable Tigger.'

'Don't patronize me! You're one to talk,' I protested happily, bracing myself against his approaching noogie, or amiable half-nelson.

'Why isn't Tigger with his boyfriend on this of all nights?' He backed me solidly against the wall, pinning my elbows under his hands. 'Why isn't Tigger *ever* with his boyfriend?'

'That's not true,' I squirmed, feeling suddenly rather peculiar. 'I'm going to find him right now. God, you're fucked up tonight, Jess. Damienne's gonna love you like this.'

He leaned in, settling comfortably against me in the empty hallway, rumpling both our suits. '*Damienne*,' he whispered with silly drama. 'Come here, Tigger,' and he was drawing my face toward him by the chin.

'Jess, what the fuck?' I felt queasily as though the cocaine and the dim blue lights were perpetrating a complicated trick on me—surely what seemed to be happening wasn't about to happen. But what if it was? Every childhood blush and tremor that I had ever felt in his presence came rushing back to me now with headspinning intensity.

'Just a little closer, Tig.' He was scrutinizing my face with excruciating concentration, eyebrows knitted together, brown eyes focused.

'What the fuck?' I whispered again, closing my eyes and arching my head forward. I floated there, his hand on my chin, breathlessly waiting for the scandalous, unearthly impression of his lips on my own. It seemed like ages passed while I waited, his breath against my face. And then—then I felt his pinky finger flick against the inner lip of my right nostril, once, then twice.

'There,' he said. 'Got it.'

I finally opened my eyes. 'Got what?'

'This,' he laughed, showing me traces of cocaine dust on the tip of his pinky. 'You wanna go around looking like fuckin' Liza Minelli? You know if Seb saw that shit, he'd get all pissy.'

I crumpled a bit against the wall. 'I'm so embarrassed,' I groaned. 'I'm so fucking embarrassed.'

'Chill, baby.' He straightened himself out, adjusting the collar on his jacket. 'You don't look like a blow fiend anymore.'

'No, no,' I sped forth on a restless coke high. 'I'm embarrassed because—you know, I—'

Some shadow seemed to pass over the ecstasy glow of his face, and he raised a finger to my lips. 'Shhh, baby. It's okay. Why don't you go find your man Sebastian? He's waiting for you, probably.'

'Jess—'

'Go find Seb, Tigger.' He leaned in and kissed me drily on the cheek, as everyone in my family was wont to do to mark casual hellos, good-byes and thank yous. '*Prospero Año Nuevo*, Tigger. I'll see you after midnight, okay?' One last flashing smile, and in a moment, he had disappeared into the hallway.

Two guffawing A&R swells bounded around the corner toward the men's room. ('Dude. *Dude*. She said she'd be in the *second* stall.') I stood there against the wall, unlit cigarette in hand, vibrating with confoundedness. *You're straying*, I finally told myself, checking my watch. It was twenty-five minutes to midnight. I hurried back up the stairs, darting my way between whooping guests, until I arrived again at the top of the arena, dizzy.

The air now felt particularly thick with bodies and fragrance, smoke and anticipation; what seemed miles below, a frenzied crowd danced under the lights to Sammy's outrageous deconstruction of 'Lady Marmalade'. I wove my way down level after level until out of the moody dim, and something sharp in me pricked up defiantly when I made out Seb, slumped disconsolately where I had left him, playing absently with his hair. I hadn't brought us drinks as promised, it suddenly occurred to me. Oh, well—surely we could cadge somebody's champagne for the midnight toast, and of course the rest of the night lay stretched out before us like a marvelous gold-paved thoroughfare of opportunity.

'Hey, you,' I said, cuffing his lapel.

He looked up, his whole face swollen with irritation. 'Oh. It's you. I thought you weren't coming back.'

'Why'd you think that?'

''Cause you've been gone an hour, maybe?'

'The place is *packed*!'

'That's good. Look Thomas, I'm cutting out of here. I want to get out before midnight and head back to Brooklyn before the trains are too mobbed.'

I looked down at him—he was so frail, really, so profoundly unauthoritative despite his veneer of hauteur—just the kind of unsuspecting snot who ended up getting justifiably violated in all the best porn movies—and it suddenly occurred to me just how long we had conducted ourselves with a kind of carnal temperance and common sense that I certainly hadn't ever lobbied for. It had simply happened that way; I had simply let him let it happen.

'Fuck you, you're going home,' I laughed, pulling him up by the arm. 'You don't walk out on me just because I had to take care of some business for my sister. Come here,' and I dragged him behind one of the enormous mirrors that hung behind the sofa.

'You're on coke again, Thomas,' he said, startled. 'I can see it in your eyes.'

'I am, Sebastian,' I said, mimicking his voice, grabbing him by the lapels and mounting him against the wall. Briefly and intensely, I hated him—hated him for being such an agent of eventlessness, hated myself for needing him so, hated him for letting me use him as I saw fit despite his tiresome and ineffectual demands for exhibitions of unconditional love. He had nothing to do with the center of my heart—he had no place there—he had never excited in me any overwhelming spasms of passion or jealousy or exuberance, or anything that made life worth living, however long it lasted. And yet, and yet—he was the bulwark between me and chaos, and oh, how I suddenly wanted to eviscerate him until he choked and sobbed with an explosive understanding of all that he had fancied himself too good to discover.

'I am, Sebastian,' I said again, pushing his back up to the wall, and unzipping his pants. 'But you're not. All your senses right now are perfectly intact, as usual.' And I pinned his shoulder against the wall and pressed my lips to his own, thrusting my tongue roughly into his constricted throat while I reached for his trousers with my free hand.

He gasped. 'Thomas, what the fuck! Here?'

'Just—just shut up for a second. Just be a fucking whore for a second, okay?'

He relented after one last muffled protest. I couldn't quite remember the last time we had sucked face or humped with such rigor, our hands greedily clutching up whole chunks of each other—had it happened only once, that first night in the woods at St. Pete's, scored to the strains of a distant organ? Had it even happened *then*, or ever at all? *He met Marmalade down in old New Orleans,* Patti's voice boomed over the sound system, mixed down to a near baritone, *struttin' her stuff . . .*

struttin' her stuff . . .

struttin' . . . boom boom . . .

struttin' . . . boom boom . . .

struttin' . . . boom BOOM . . .

Sammy had stripped the verse down to this single word, repeated over a single rhythm track of drum and bass, and I suddenly felt that old sleazy pleasure of getting off with someone in a dark club, wildly high and driven on by one insistently coital hook from the DJ—but this time I was with my own boyfriend, robbed of his usual brittle rectitude, and it wasn't long before I sealed him up harder against the wall, and reached inside his boxer shorts, suffocating him with oily kisses throughout.

All of Patti's vocals dropped out then, opening up a stretch of bass line that twisted on and on underneath a high-hat. 'Oh, shit,' Seb finally whispered, at once ecstatic and full of rue, and I felt his ass and thighs shudder against me. 'Oh—oh—shit, shit, *shit*,' he gnashed, marvelously angry with himself. And that was that: I brought him off shamelessly all over the wall of my sister's spanking new nightclub. 'Oh, shit,' he whispered again, leaning into the wall in what seemed a paralyzing state of humiliation, his face lost to me inside his balled-up fists.

I put my arms around him and drew his trembling head into my shoulders. 'Why don't you ever do things like that to me if you're so in love with me?' I whispered in his ear—plaintively, not cruelly, because all my loathing of a few minutes before had evaporated in the vengeful pleasure of making him unleash himself.

The question only seemed to agitate him more, and his head trembled harder now, all his carefully groomed curls sliding out of place. 'I do love you, Thomas,' he said hoarsely. It sounded like he was crying, and yet I couldn't be quite sure. I had cried in front of him many times, me so generous with my histrionics, but I couldn't remember ever seeing the same from him. 'I love you, but I can't be that kind of person. I can't do that stuff.'

'But you just did,' I said, pushing back his tendrils.

'But I can't, though. It's wrong. It's not me. I'm not *this*—'

and he released one arm to indicate the general realm of the club. 'I'm not one of the Mitchells.'

No kidding, I thought ruefully, but I answered dutifully: 'You don't have to be. Just be Sebastian Hurwitz for me—but maybe with a little more *oomph*, you know? Like Lady Marmalade?'

'Like Lady Marmalade,' he repeated wearily, shaking his head.

'Now come on,' I said, cleaning off his recompressed cock with a hankie and drawing up his trousers. 'Let's pull ourselves together. It's almost midnight.'

He tucked and zipped himself into place, then turned toward me with a characteristic sober smile. 'I *do* love you, Tigger.'

'I love you, too,' I said, and whether I meant it or not, I didn't find it particularly hard to say. And then we were kissing companionably, and, though still racing with cocaine and personally unspent, I felt free of the tremendous wad of unhappy desire that had balled up my stomach in the hallway just a few minutes before.

And then Sammy's bass track faded out, but nothing faded back in, and thousands of voices were absurdly loud until people realized they no longer had to talk against the music. Seb and I hurried out from behind the mirror. And then there was a dull roar, which subsided yet more when Sammy Fingers, on high from his booth, spoke sonorously through the sound system:

'Ladies and gentlemen . . .

Party people, party people . . .

Ladies and gentlemen . . .

Only thirty seconds now until midnight—'

A great, surprised gasping now, then stiller silence.

'And the start of a new decade, the fabulous, gay nineties—'

Various whoops and hollers.

'And the remarkable young legend responsible for the very

roof under which we celebrate tonight—Ten . . . nine . . . eight . . . seven . . .'

Everyone was joining in now; I cast my eyes round at the folks on the upper levels, drunk and lovely and fists tight with confetti.

'Six . . . five . . . four . . .'

'Thomas, there you are!' A new voice suddenly, just at my shoulder.

I turned and convulsed swiftly with distaste. It was Goolsbee, high and beaming, natty and toxic, a bottle of Mumm's in one hand and a great white shark of some up-and-coming Elite model in the other.

'Three . . . two . . .'

'Here she comes!' Goolsbee shouted to the model, who smiled dimly, then to me: 'Here comes my girl!'

'One . . . *Happy New Year!!!*'

Sammy Fingers tore into a turbocharged remix of 'We Are Family'. The entire arena sprang back to life in a sprawling sea of hugs, kisses and dance. What seemed like a hundred lights trained themselves on the protruding performance stage just feet above the dance floor, and from behind swathes and swathes of white tulle, to the roar of a frenzied ovation, Flip emerged, walked slowly down center until she stopped, a thousand hands clapping and grasping at her feet. Confetti fell around her from above like a Las Vegas squall. She stood quietly in her liquid jet gown, immobile and erect—but as the applause crested and crested, only to reach a dizzying new pitch of adulation, and as the lights fixed on her so whitely it seemed as though she might be a figure descended from the heavens, I could see it, all too clearly: her extraordinary face, etched and ruined with luminous, inky tears.

Sixteen

I had had some vague idea that after the fanfare of opening night (and the uniformly gushing notices it received), once The Box was up and running, Jess and I would be able to step back from the nightly goings-on and retreat responsibly back into our respective personal and professional lives. Of course, there would be certain special projects from time to time, and of course, there would be certain special nights—like Flip's forthcoming Caligulan Valentine's Day Ball, which she promised would make Susanne Bartsch's annual gig look like a tea party—that demanded our presence. But Flip was fully staffed now, and, by and large, we expected that credit and responsibillty for the club would be rightly hers.

But as that harsh winter of 1990 slogged forward Jess and I found out that we were both right, and wrong. Flip *did* take credit for The Box—the clubworld invariably referred to it as 'Flip's place,' and she fondly took to calling it 'my little party.' But at the same time, she had no problems sharing responsibility with the two of us. There was no formal agreement—we weren't on her payroll—but virtually every day, in the most offhand and familial of ways, as though she were asking us to pick up milk on the way home, she found ways to keep us busy, calling Jess at his studio or in between classes at the New School: 'Honey? Hi, it's Flip. Will you be an absolute angel tonight and just drop by the club around eleven for a second? Anthea wanted to go over plans for a fresco in the bathroom with you . . . Oh, you do? . . . well, bring Damienne too, then—we'll all have a drink.' Or paging me at Mannes or tracking me down in the middle of a piano lesson: 'Tigger darling, sorry to interrupt, but would you stop by tonight around midnight? Sammy rewired the booth and I need a second pair of ears to check the mix on the dance floor . . . Well, it's just for a second . . . Well, don't *go* out to Brooklyn tonight. Just stay at the loft with Seb . . . Tigger, look, a photographer's here and I don't have time to fight about this, I'll see you at midnight. Oh, and would you bring my black boots down, too? The ones that zip up the side to the thigh? Thanks, honey.'

And then, once Jess or I showed up for our 'brief' assignation, it was hard to leave—inevitably, there were people there to linger with over a drink, either old faces or even more fabulous new ones. All the women were funny and glamorous and beautiful, quick with a bitchy remark or some mordant observation on somebody's latest artistic venture. And then the boys—so many of them, all young and stylish and handsome, nearly half of them gay or toying with it, all witty and flirtatious, plying me with drinks because I was Flip's little brother, the musician. And then, presiding over the whole scene, always, there was Flip, looking terrific in something she might never wear again, or return to the shop—reeking of cigarette smoke and occasionally stained with a drink—the next day, complaining of 'too loose a fit.' There was Flip, making connections, buzzing around, calling over waiters, night by night knitting together a vital new nocturnal world, which is exactly what she had intended to do.

She loved the press—the magazine people, the tabloid people, the MTV people—and made a point of treating them more like special guests than press when they showed up at The Box, calculatedly ignoring the fact that the next day they could write a squib which could seriously help or hinder her business. For these reasons they loved her back, and accordingly never wrote less than glowing words, even in those first few months when the club was the subject of almost absurd media scrutiny and expectation. Over time, Jess and I met them all, which led to a funny kind of refracted fame for the two of us, a portion of the light that emanated from Flip's media glow. The press just loved the idea of a 'family-run' nightclub, and it wasn't long before they were referring to Jess as a 'hot, up-and-coming Latino artist', and to me as a 'hot young gay pianist and composer.' Jess had already been on his way, but for me, still in school, and after years of quiet struggle and relatively slow progress, I finally found myself recognized for my work to an extent that far exceeded my output. Suddenly it seemed like a million small-time R&B and dance producers were asking me to record piano tracks for their albums, which I found particularly funny since I had begun my now-burgeoning pop music career laying down tracks for Sammy as a brief diversion from my more 'serious' studies in jazz and classical at Mannes.

But of course—and again, perhaps inevitably—all this face time at The Box garnering professional exposure left relatively little time for either Jess or me to do our actual work. Like I said, a quick stop-in at The Box had a way of stretching until closing time, whereupon the three of us would help the staff shut down for the night, then stumble the few blocks home, usually drunk, to the loft. And the scene the next morning— no, make that afternoon—when Jess and I encountered each other in the kitchen, guilty and hungover, started taking on an ominously repetitive quality.

'I'm fucked, Tigger. I told myself yesterday that I'd get to the studio by ten in the morning to finish that piece for Grant's open house, and now I've gotta teach a class in a half hour. Why did I stay so late last night?'

"Cause you were talking to that woman who used to own a gallery with that guy that just got promoted at the Whitney, remember?'

'Oh, yeah.' He rubbed his eyes, then winced. 'What was her name? Gita?'

'Amrita.'

'Oh, yeah. I've got her card somewhere. How you doin'?'

'Not so good. I slept through theory. And I've got composition at three.'

'Why don't you move your butt?'

'No point. I'll never make it. And I've got to get over this hangover if I'm gonna give lessons at Dalton at five o'clock.'

'Man,' Jess laughed ruefully. 'How did we end up staying so late last night?'

''Cause it got around closing, and we couldn't just leave Flip there to close by herself.'

'Yeah, I guess so. Anyway, I can't go tonight. I told Damienne I'd go visit her mother with her in Flatbush.'

'Yeah, me too. I'm in the practice room all night. I've gotta finish this piece.'

And then Flip emerged from the bathroom in her kimono, hair wrapped in a towel, glowing red from her shower and smelling of expensive shampoo. 'Hello! Wasn't last night the bomb?' she exclaimed, fumbling with the coffeemaker. 'Tig, that hot guy from RCA Los Angeles *adored* you. He asked me for your number—'

'He *did*?' I asked, flattered.

'Mm-hmm. But I told him you were taken. Sorry.' She shrugged and smiled. 'Jess darling, can you do cash register for an hour tonight until Guillermo gets there? His sister's in town from Rome and he promised to take her to dinner. And you know how late those Europeans eat.'

'Flip.' Jess frowned. 'I told you I had to go to Flatbush tonight with Damienne.'

She spooned coffee sloppily into the filter. 'You did?' she asked innocently.

'I did. Yesterday.'

'Oh. Well, what about you, Tig? Can you do it?'

I squirmed. 'Flip, I've gotta work on this piece. It's due in three days.'

'Oh.' She turned her back to us, then threw down the measuring spoon on the counter. 'Well, then *who*, may I ask, is going to help me entertain Lou Reed tonight when he comes?'

Jess and I started, glanced at each other; Lou Reed was one of our childhood idols. 'You didn't tell us Lou Reed was coming tonight,' Jess said suspiciously.

'I didn't have a chance,' Flip said. 'I only found out yesterday, when his PA called. And Tig, his PA asked if there were going to be any other music people there, 'cause Lou's looking for new projects, and I said, "Of course, my brother for one, who's working with Sammy Fingers." And now you're not even gonna be there.'

She was wearing me down, as usual. 'What time's he gonna be there?'

'Around midnight, I guess, after his gig. But I need someone on register at eleven.'

'All right,' I said. 'I'll be there.' I had planned to stay in the practice room all night—or at least until I had worked out the first passage of the piece—but a few hours would certainly be enough time to get started, I figured. And I didn't have to stay at The Box *late*, after all.

Flip smiled smugly. 'And it's too bad you're not gonna be there, Jess, 'cause I heard Lou was looking to do a big book of his poetry and he's seeking out illustrators.'

Jess squinted down into his coffee. 'I guess I could be back in the city by around midnight,' he finally offered.

Flip shrugged. 'Whatever you want to do.' She turned abruptly and stuck her head inside the refrigerator, sorting through the half-dozen cartons of milk to find the one that hadn't yet reached its expiration date. Jess and I just looked at each other and shrugged ourselves, broken once more.

And as it happened, Lou Reed wasn't there that night after

all. ('I guess his gig ran late,' Flip said.) But Debbie Harry was, and three o'clock found the three of us knocking back margaritas with her and her entourage, she and Jess drunkenly singing an expansive Spanish-language version of 'The Tide Is High'—a scene which, we later heard through her hangers-on, chagrined Debbie deeply when she woke up, heavy-headed, the next morning and recalled it all.

It wasn't just work we were neglecting; The Box seduced us into a nocturnal existence, wherein all things we used to do during the day—like calling home to our mother (who had greeted news of the club none too enthusiastically), or visiting Lippy—took a back seat to the need for sleep or for long afternoon hours spent in mute recovery in front of the TV set. And then, I'm rather sorry to say, there was the matter of drugs. Before the opening of The Box, the three of us had by and large stopped using them, rather unceremoniously, a cessation prompted in part by Flip's medical emergency. Even Jess had relegated his pot use to an occasional shared joint after dinner. But the age of Ecstasy was upon us—it seemed to be everywhere, and delivered such a euphoric high that weekends at The Box without it just wouldn't have felt right at all. We hardly had to seek it out, as people bestowed it upon us like other people bring tchotchkes and coffee cakes to a housewarming. And the relentless frenetic pace of The Box— the hyperactive crowds, the pounding music—seemed to demand it as a coping mechanism, a necessary buffer.

Our world suddenly seemed divided between people who 'got' the allure of The Box—Cedric and Joey, Anthea, Miko, Grant and a host of other committed *demi-mondains*—and those who didn't—Damienne, Seb, Kira, my nerdy schoolmates at Mannes, and, perhaps most unhappily, Lippy, as she made clear to me one gun-metal gray afternoon in late February.

I was walking around the Village with Cedric, helping him find a birthday present for his mother in the Bronx, whose recent forgetful behavior and semi-delusional ramblings had begun worrying him.

'Tigger, I don't know what's up with her,' he said as we browsed through a too-precious gift shop. 'We'll be talkin' about something regular, like family down in Georgia, and suddenly she's tellin' me crazy shit, like how the woman next door is always tryin' to break into the apartment. Or she won't be able to tell me what she had for breakfast. I'll ask her, and she'll get all defensive and say, "You know, just some stuff."' He shook his head, picking up a package of children's refrigerator alphabet magnets. 'Maybe I should get her these. Then I could spell out things so she couldn't forget them, you know? Like MY NAME IS VERA WILLIAMS AND I WILL HAVE EGGS FOR BREAKFAST, or MY NEIGHBOR MRS. BIGGS IS MY FRIEND. SHE IS NOT A THIEF.'

We laughed, which made my heavy head pound. Then, from behind: 'Tigger? Cedric?'

We turned. It was Lippy, standing before us in her great black cape, lips pursed, unsmiling.

'Lippy, hi!' I exclaimed, embracing her too vigorously and planting a kiss on her cold cheek. 'It's so good to see you!'

'It is,' she said tightly. 'I haven't seen any of you since New Year's Eve. I was wondering if you were all dead.'

A horrible pause ensued. 'I was gonna call you this week,' I continued. 'To get together.'

'I'm sure you were.'

Another horrible pause. 'Tigger?' Cedric nearly whispered. 'I just wanna check out that little jewelry store across the street. Meet me over there?'

I nodded. 'Good seein' you, Lippy,' Cedric added, and it seemed that Lippy received his kiss a little more graciously than she had mine.

'Good seeing you, Cedric.'

She and I were alone now. 'How's Langley?' I asked, quite unnerved.

'He's fine. Very busy, like everyone seems to be these days.'

'Lippy, I'm sorry. Honestly. I really meant to call soon.'

She seemed unimpressed. 'Your mother called me last night.'

I quivered a bit. 'She did?'

'She did. She wanted to know why none of you had called her in so long. She thought maybe something was wrong.'

I said nothing. 'So?' she asked.

'So what?'

'Is anything wrong?'

'No!' I virtually shouted. 'Of course not. I guess we're all just busy—with the club, and all.'

'I can't pick up the paper or a magazine without reading something about the club,' she said, with a faint note of irony.

I shrugged. 'The publicity is out of control. It's just what Flip wanted.'

'Tigger?'

'Yeah?'

'Do you have any idea how bloodshot your eyes are? You look like you haven't slept in weeks.'

I blinked, profoundly embarrassed. 'Oh, yeah. I've been running a little sleep deficit. With classes and all.'

'Right,' Lippy virtually snorted. 'Let me tell you something,' she said with frightful sternness, just as some impeccable middle-aged queen with a goatee and a long greatcoat swooped down and took her arm.

'Lippy?' he intoned dramatically.

She turned, blooming into her exuberant public face. 'Maury? Darling, hello! Oh my goodness, it's been so long. Maury, this is my nephew Tig—Thomas. Thomas Mitchell. Thomas, Maury used to manage Julia's Room back when it was The Ivory.'

'Hi,' I said, distracted, offering my hand, and he accepted it, with a kind but rather shrewd smile, I thought.

In a moment, the two of them were prattling on about old times and old faces, Lippy as animated and charming as if she hadn't been incensed at me at all. I only half-listened—I was preoccupied with guilt at having neglected both Lippy and my mother—but when I did, it seemed as though they were mainly shaking their heads over all the people they knew who were either sick or had died. Maury didn't look so great himself, I noticed; he had those too-large eye sockets and sunken cheekbones which had become all too familiar to me in the faces of queens of a certain age.

Lippy and Maury finally finished their chat amidst a great flurry of hugs, cluckings, exhortations to take care of oneself, and promises to convene soon at Julia's Room.

'It was nice meeting you, Thomas,' Maury finally said to me. 'You have a lovely auntie, you know.'

Shortly after he had swept away, his greatcoat billowing out behind him, Lippy turned back to me. 'He's a sweet man,' she said absently.

'He seems so.'

She was a bit lost now, hazy and remote. 'What were we talking about?'

'You said you had something to tell me.'

She snapped to. 'That's right. Tigger, I don't know everything that goes on with you and Jess and Flip, but I do know more than your mother, God bless her, even if these days it's only by merit of reading about the three of you in the paper. Or running into you when you look like death warmed over.'

I stared down at my feet, deeply embarrassed.

'And Tigger, I don't like being put in the position of having to keep what I suspect is not wholesome news from my only sister. It's one thing to keep her from worrying, but it's another to shield her from the truth.'

I looked up, slightly piqued. 'What do you mean by that?'

'What I mean is, whenever the three of you don't want me to know what you're up to, you don't call me.'

'Lippy,' I protested, 'we've just been busy and—'

'You don't call me,' she continued imperiously. 'Now Tigger,

I'm sure the club is very exciting. I was young once, too, and I spent my share of evenings at all the hotspots.' I held my tongue; Lippy's condescending jadedness was beginning to annoy me, as it did on very rare occasions. 'But I think you all have to remember the difference between fabulous—' and she paused dramatically—'and *fabulous*.'

'And what would that be?'

'Remembering your gifts, working on your craft, making art that reaches out to other people—now that is *truly* fabulous. But staying out night after night just to be seen with all the quote-unquote right people, always going for the immediate thrill, the cheap high—that kind of fabulous backfires on itself very quickly. And you're left with'—she prestoed her fingertips before me in a little *poof!* gesture—'nothing.'

'But Lippy, Flip owns a club now. Hanging out with the right people is her *job*. And she's good at it.'

'Which brings me to my second point,' she went on unruffled. 'I'm not so worried about you, because you've got your music, which you'll always come back to, and because you've got a good head on your shoulders. And I'm not worried about Jess, because deep down Jess knows that soon enough he's got to sever his ties and go his own way—'

'What does *that* mean?' I asked, somewhat offended.

'It means just what I said,' she added briskly, dismissing my protest with what seemed like a pointed abruptness. 'But Tigger—your *sister*. Flip is a bright, bright light. But if she doesn't watch it, Tigger, she's gonna burn out. I know it, because it almost happened to me.'

I wanted to ask Lippy what the hell *that* meant, but I didn't. As it was, she wasn't saying anything about Flip that I didn't already know, but I didn't particularly like to hear it voiced, especially when Flip was riding so high these days. And on top of it all, I felt a certain allegiance to Flip, if only because I had participated in her 'little party' so much in the past two months, despite the same reservations.

'Lippy,' I finally said, possessing myself. 'I think you might be wrong about Flip. I think you'd be impressed to see what a tight ship she's running. It's a business venture to her.'

'Good, then,' she said, playing my game. 'I hope it is. I was there New Year's Eve; *I* know what an extraordinary place it is. Like I said, I just don't want your mother coming to me down the line and saying, "How could you have known all along and not told me?" Isn't that understandable?'

'Of course it is,' I said shortly, indulging her.

A long, tense moment seemed to pass between us before she finally said, 'Good. Now I have to find a birthday gift for one of the waitresses at Julia's Room. She's a *mime* artist, what the hell am I supposed to get her? Anyway, will the three of you come to dinner next week? Before the club opens?'

'I'll set it up with Jess and Flip.'

'Good. You can bring Seb and Damienne, too, if you want. How are they, anyway?'

'Pretty well, I guess.'

'You and Jess are lucky to have them. Far be it for me to say that all a woman needs is a good man, but sometimes I wish that your sister—Isn't there *someone* in that crowd who's straight and something besides a bouncer or a model-to-be?'

I laughed. 'If there is, we haven't found him yet.'

Lippy shook her head. 'All right, darling. I'm glad we talked. I miss you.' She leaned in to peck me good-bye. 'And you *will* call your mother, won't you? She's a wreck.'

'I will. Tonight.'

I was more relieved to part with her than I liked to admit to myself; she left me feeling both indignant that I had been chastised and creepishly as though I deserved it. Moreover, the matter of Flip: was she *really* burning too brightly, and if so, was *I* responsible for her? Wasn't she a grown woman, after all? And finally, Lippy—what had been her private near-ruin, and what had saved her from herself . . . if she was to be believed at all, or merely credited with a pedantic hyperbole.

Pondering all this, I wandered wordlessly back out into the darkening afternoon to rejoin Cedric.

And then, my just desert—the envelope I knew I was pushing, couldn't help but push, always with the smug assumption that I'd never have to pay the piper. On a Saturday night in late winter, I finally paid.

It was a banner night at The Box. We were housing a benefit called Divas Diss AIDS, and the evening's roster glittered: 1970s warhorses like Jocelyn Brown and Loleatta Holloway, and fly young faces like Jody Watley and Salt 'n' Pepa (who had been flirting in Nuyorican with Jess from the moment they saw him backstage; fortunately, Damienne was in Detroit working on a discrimination case). The crowd was especially black and gay tonight, which always gave Flip a warm feeling of authenticity, and I was feeling particularly swank in my new black cowboy boots and suede jacket, drinking tequila with Jess, Cedric and Miko (Joey was home sick with a cold) in the back lounge. Seb was waiting for me in Brooklyn; I had promised to be at his place no later than two that morning so that he might give me a 'special gift' for our third anniversary (I hadn't yet found something for him)—this left me with enough time to catch the first few acts and hop a late F train. I was quite determined to make it—of course, the relationship had been more strained than usual since the opening of The Box, even though Seb had resigned himself to my temporary infatuation with the place. His outbursts, though still unsettling when they occurred, were increasingly rare.

If only Miko hadn't kept pouring the goddamned tequila!

'You have to have another, Tigger,' he insisted, pouring from bottles he had snatched from the bar. 'You're the only one here who's been married for three years. You have to toast yourself.'

Cedric laughed; he was drinking more heavily than usual tonight because Flip had arranged for him to meet Jocelyn

Brown, one of his idols, backstage, and he was a nervous wreck. 'Honey, he *is* toasted already.'

'I have to sleep alone tonight,' Jess slurred, drunk already.

Miko swooped over to him and fell into his lap. 'No, you don't.'

'No, you don't,' Cedric echoed, squeezing Jess's cheeks in his enormous hand.

Jess giggled. 'Tigger, should we all have a sleepover? No girls allowed?'

'I can't, I can't!' I mock-sobbed. 'I've got to leave by one-thirty or I turn into a pumpkin.'

'You turn into a *kumqua*,' Miko declared cryptically. 'A giant—'

'Shhhhhhh!' Cedric suddenly hissed, head cocked toward the door, index finger aloft. 'Listen.'

We all strained to listen, until the pounding bass from without made itself known.

'Oh my God, it's her! It's Jody!'

Miko and I shrieked, and Jess shook his head, laughing. We all ran out onto the dance floor, commandeered by Jody Watley singing her big hit.

'She looks a little tired,' Cedric shouted to me, hands in the air.

'But she still sounds fierce,' I shouted back.

And indeed she did. And so did Rozalla, who followed. And so did Jocelyn Brown, for whom the entire club silenced itself when she lumbered out onto the stage and, a capella, belted out the first exhilarating lines from 'Somebody Else's Guy'.

I can't get off my high horse.

And I can't . . . let you go.

You were the one . . . you were the one . . .

Who made me feel . . .

'*So reeeeeeeeeeeeeeeeeeeeellllllllllll!*' Cedric and I lipsynced, ecstatic.

And on and on it went, one sublime diva after another,

each one seemingly fiercer than the next, until all cognizance of the world beyond the dance floor slipped away, time froze inside this warp of ceaseless grooves—was it night or day, spring or summer, the seventies, eighties or nineties?—and soon we were shirtless, glistening with sweat, hemmed in on all sides by twitching bodies, slaves to the rhythm, like our girl Grace Jones, all snarling and angular, who had just seized the stage.

When I first recognized Seb untangling his way through the crush, some ridiculous wrapped package under his arm, my heart leapt—he was finally coming around to the seductions of The Box, he had heard the jungle call all the way from Brooklyn and had hastened to join us in this happy fraternity. I grabbed him by the arm, pulled him into our own private knot of space.

'You came!' I shouted, throwing my arms around him and planting a kiss on his lips. 'Ty comped you, right?'

He flinched away from me, grimacing from contact with my sweaty arms and chest. 'Do you know what time it is, Thomas?' he shouted over Grace Jones. He stood stone still in a sea of dancers, throwing dagger looks at them when freestyle arms and elbows jabbed his back and sides. I kept on dancing, knee-jerk, until his sobriety brought me to a nervous, foot-tapping stop.

'One-ish?' I wasn't wearing a watch, and hadn't taken note of the time since somewhere just after eleven.

'It's three-thirty.'

'Three-thirty!' I exclaimed. Where had the time gone? It felt as though we had come out to hear Jody Watley just twenty minutes ago. Of course, she *had* performed about seventeen divas back.

'Yes. Three-thirty.'

'Shit. Well, now that you're here, let's stay awhile and dance. I don't have to take the train out to Brooklyn alone now.'

'I didn't come to fucking dance, Thomas!' he shouted, so

loudly that he briefly overwhelmed the music; a dozen pairs of eyes, including those of Jess, Cedric and Miko, turned to stare. 'I came to give you your anniversary present. And to say good-bye.' He thrust the large, flat wrapped package into my hand.

My jaw dropped. '*What?*'

'It's over, Thomas. I can't compete with this anymore,' he said, gesturing. 'It isn't me. You're not me, anymore.'

'What are you talking about?' I snapped. Wasn't it just like Seb to show up in the middle of a good time and demand to be mollified? 'I'm just a little late.'

'You're not late for anything. You're exactly where you belong.' And he turned a poisonous look on Cedric, Miko and my brother.

Jess pushed his hair out of his face and stepped over to us. 'Seb, take it easy. Come and dance with us. It's my fault—I should have reminded Tig of the time.'

'It's nobody's fault, Jess,' Seb managed before his voice broke and he seemed to waver on tears for a moment before swallowing them back. 'It's nobody's fault.' He looked back at me. 'Good-bye, Thomas. Take care.'

He turned to go, but I grabbed his arm. 'Wait a minute! You can't leave, Seb. I love you.'

He bestowed upon me the most patronizing of smiles. 'I'm sure that in your own way you do, Thomas.' Then he turned again abruptly and slipped into the throng.

I stood there, package in hand, the subject now of a live mini-drama for about twenty-five people. I was absolutely stunned; Seb had never walked away from me before—somehow I had always been able to calm him into a reconciliation. But this time he had simply decamped—right here, on my very own territory. I didn't know whether to be furious or devastated, whereas in fact I was both.

Miko tapped me on the shoulder and started to sing, 'Don't leave me this way.'

'Shut the fuck up,' I spat at him before shoving my way off

the dance floor to catch Seb—I was so shocked and mortified that when someone in the throng pinched my behind I didn't even turn to see who it was—but by the time I emerged, he was nowhere to be seen. I flung myself into an empty loveseat and tore open the package. It was a painting, obviously rendered by Jess, mounted behind glass in a gorgeous antique gilt frame. I recognized the image instantly; Jess had painted it from a Polaroid Kira had snapped of Seb and me, lounging on the dock at St. Pete's in the late spring of our final year there. We were sprawled out in swim trunks, me mugging into Seb's face, Seb staring off abstractedly behind his horn-rimmed glasses out toward the water. It had been one of our favorite photos, and since there had been no negative, I had always grudged Seb his possession of it, propped in a cheap plastic frame on his bedside table.

I don't know how long I sat there crying, ruminating over all the times I had nearly blown it with Seb but had been given a second chance—then a third, a fourth, a God-knows-how-many-more—when I felt a presence settle in close beside me on the loveseat. I turned: it was Jess, who had thrown his sweaty shirt back on and pulled his wet hair into a ponytail with a rubber band. He threw his arm loosely over my shoulder and gave me something that I can only call a smile-frown.

'You're gonna catch a cold,' he said, pulling my shirt out from my back pocket. 'Put this on.'

'Thanks.' I climbed back into the damp, crumpled jersey.

'You want one?' he asked, pulling out a pack of cigarettes.

'Yeah, thanks.' He handed me one, lit it for me, then lit his own. For a few moments, the two of us just sat there silently, smoking. Grace Jones had finished her set; now some enormous white woman whom I didn't recognize but whose song sounded faintly familiar from childhood radio had taken the stage.

'You like it?' Jess finally nodded toward the painting that still lay face up on my lap, a lovely rebuke.

'It's beautiful,' I said. 'When did he ask you to do it?'

'He gave me the picture about four months ago. He doesn't know that I didn't start it until last week.' He grinned.

'He's better off not knowing,' I said, overcome suddenly by a fresh wave of dismay. 'Oh fuck, Jess, why did I do it? He's such a great guy. He's the only normal person in my life.'

Jess laughed, offended. 'Hello?'

'Well, I'm sorry, it's true!' I said, laughing in spite of myself. 'Why did I treat him like such shit?'

''Cause he let you. Up 'til now, that is. Sometimes I ask myself the same question about Damienne. Why don't I spend more time with her? Why don't I move in with her? Why don't I ask her to get *married*, for Chrissakes?'

'Well? Why don't you?'

''Cause she doesn't make me.'

'But Jess, she's almost thirty. You can't keep her hanging on forever. Don't you think she might want to have kids?'

He shrugged, examining the orange tip of his cigarette. 'I know. I know it's selfish, 'cause I *do* love her— I *do*, Tig, don't laugh, you little shit!—but I guess I'm just not ready. I'm having too much fun. I love my work these days. And I love the club. I mean, I was dreading it, but—but look around. It's pretty dope, isn't it? I love dressing up and coming here after a long, lonely day in the studio. And I guess I'm pretty proud of Flip for making it happen.'

'I know,' I conceded. 'I am, too. It's kind of like a family business, isn't it?'

'Kinda. Your father would be proud of her, I think. This is his kind of place, don't you think? Booze, babes, decadence, shadiness. Kind of Prohibitiony, hunh?'

'He's your father, too, you know.'

He stubbed out his cigarette in one of the marble ashtrays. 'Get real, Tig.'

'Whatever,' I said. This was a typical exchange between us; Jess never referred to our father as anything but 'your father,' or, more pointedly, 'Mr. Tommy.'

'Anyway,' he said, throwing his arm back around me. 'About Seb. Don't sweat it, Tig. He'll probably call you tomorrow.'

'I don't think so. Not this time.'

'Wait and see. He's crazy about you, kid. Can't live without you. That's how we Mitchells are. Irresistible.'

'The irony of "we Mitchells" coming from you isn't lost on me,' I said augustly, and we both laughed.

'What's this about "we Mitchells"?' a voice from on high asked. Jess and I looked up. It was Flip, martini glass in hand.

'The youngest of we Mitchells is unhappy tonight,' Jess said, taking Flip's hand and pulling her down onto the loveseat between us.

Flip turned to me, her mouth in a moue. 'What's wrong, baby?' she asked, stroking my head. 'How can you be unhappy tonight with all your favorite divas?'

'Seb showed up to give him that—' Jess said, pointing to the painting.

'Isn't it fantastic?' Flip asked. 'Tig, I think Jess totally captures the two of you there.'

'—and then told him off for not coming out to Brooklyn and stormed on out,' Jess continued.

'Oh.' Flip sipped thoughtfully at her martini. 'So *that's* why he seemed so grim when I saw him up front. Oh, Tig, for God's sake, you know how Seb is. He's a crabby little old man. I'm surprised he even got up the oomph to get on the train and come *in* to the city so late at night.'

'I think he was pretty upset,' I said.

'So maybe he was. But he'll get over it. He wouldn't have much of a life if it wasn't for you.' Jess and I exchanged fleeting glances; it was still hard not to wince at the severity of Flip's pronouncements. 'And did he really expect you to walk out in the middle of these divas?'

'Well—'

'And, oh my God!' Flip continued before I had a chance to answer. 'Have I told you yet how much Guillermo thinks we raised tonight for charity? *Eighteen-thousand dollars!*'

'What percentage are you taking for the club?' Jess asked.

'Well, none tonight. I told the beneficiaries it would all go to them. Besides, Absolut sponsored the liquor and the divas only worked pro bono.'

'But what about staff and the utility bills and all the non-volunteered liquor?' Jess pressed.

'Jess, who runs this club?' Flip asked tersely.

He sighed. 'Fine. Fine. I'm sorry I asked.'

Flip sank back into the loveseat, nursing her drink. 'I love doing good deeds. And as for Seb, Tig—don't worry about it. He'll come around. And you always have us.'

I turned to her, eyebrow raised.

'You do, Tig,' Jess said, that trace of irony back in his voice.

Flip popped up in her seat again. 'Oh God, darlings, we've got to go backstage and see Cedric meet Jocelyn Brown. The woman is *enormous* and it'll be so funny to see Cedric all buggin' out! Coming?'

But before we could answer, up stepped Manny Landau, one of the young Page Six photographers for the *New York Post*. 'Flip honey, mind if I get a family shot?' he asked, even as he was already kneeling down to snap us.

'Of course, Manny. Tigger, think about your smile this time.'

'Don't burn out the flashbulb with yours,' I shot back at her.

'Dude, could you make sure your editor gets my name right this time?' Jess asked. 'I know I look more like a José, but it's plain old boring Jess, no i.'

'Will do, my man. Okay, hang on.'

'*Fromage!!!!*' Flip burst out extravagantly, head back.

And the picture appeared on page six the next day, with Jess misnamed yet again we later heard—this time it was 'Jeesie'—but the morning it appeared, the three of us were too preoccupied with other, more personal news to care.

Seventeen

The phone in the loft rang at ten the next morning, only two hours after Flip and I had gone to bed—me unhappily alone, and she in a haze of druggy horniness with Ty (who had muttered the whole way back to the loft over what kind of excuse he could hand over to his girl Shereen *this* time). Hung over and half-asleep in my room, I listened to the bleep and whir of the answering machine from outside, nursing a shard of hope that I would hear Seb's voice: gentle, hesitant, contrite. But the voice wasn't his; it was the muffled pitch of a woman, distressed. I stumbled out of bed, dashed across the loft floor to the phone only to hear the last phrase—

—*just as soon as you can, I'll be right here*— and the final click. The voice was Lippy's, undeniably. I rang her place and she answered on the first ring, crying.

'Lippy?'

'Tigger, darling. Oh, Tigger—I've got bad news, honey.'

'Lippy, what is it?' I had a horrible vision of Langley having walked off with her life savings, or having told her that he was in love with a chorus boy and running away with him to Mexico, or some such thing.

'Darling, are you comfortable?'

'Yeah,' I lied, desperate to take my morning piss. 'What is it?'

'Tigger, I had a call from Sherry this morning.'

'Sherry? Ma's Sherry?' My stomach fluttered a moment.

'Yes, darling. She called from the hospital in Lowell. There's been a terrible accident. A car accident. It was raining hard up there last night, and—'

'Is Ma okay?'

'I guess the old station wagon—'

'Lippy, is Ma *all right*?'

'Honey, let me come over right now. Are Flip and Jess home?'

'Flip is, Jess is at Damienne's place. Lippy!'

'You should call him home, Tigger. I'm on my way.'

'Lippy!' I finally shouted. 'What the hell happened?'

'Oh, Tigger, my angel. Your mother—she didn't make it.'

'*What?*'

'She didn't—honey, I'll be right over.' And she hung up.

I stood there with the receiver in my hand, my whole mind a blank.

'What's that about Ma?' a cold, small voice asked behind me. I turned; Flip stood in the doorway of her room, shivering in one of my old T-shirts. Behind her, Ty loomed enormously in his jeans.

'That was Lippy. Sherry called her to say there had been a car accident. Ma—' There suddenly seemed no need to say more.

Flip stood in place, shivering, brows furrowed, looking puzzled.

'Was she driving that old station wagon?' she finally asked.

'Yeah.'

Ty wrapped her in his big arms from behind. 'I'm so sorry, baby,' he whispered with a tenderness I had never heard from him before, but Flip unlaced him numbly.

'No, Ty, it's all right, thank you. Would you—would you mind getting dressed and leaving?'

We both stood there silently while Ty hastily threw on his

clothes and slipped out with nary a word to Flip and no more than a gloomy exchange of nods with me. Flip disappeared briefly into her room, re-emerged wearing her favorite kimono, walked across the loft, lit a cigarette and sat down on the sofa. I came and sat by her, lit my own cigarette. Outside, the garbage trucks were making a racket. We kept looking at each other, then looking away. Eventually she stubbed out her cigarette and pushed her hair back behind her ear.

'We should call Jess now,' she asked, turning to me, 'shouldn't we?'

I nodded. But a full five minutes passed before either of us so much as moved.

Jess, Flip, Lippy and I rode up to Massachusetts with Damienne, partially because she was the only one of us that had a car, partially because Jess had asked her to come. We made the trip mostly in silence, broken occasionally by brief discussions of technical matters like funeral arrangements, the notification of relatives and friends, the need to contact Mr. Kittredge in Boston. Damienne speculated in her arid lawyerly way on what Mr. Kittredge might have to say about the estate. Flip bitched mutedly about the impossibility of finding a good radio station once we were well into Connecticut.

But on the whole, we were a silent crew, and it was a silence imposed in part by a collective unspoken guilt. None of us had seen our mother since Christmas (a tense affair on account of her disapproval over Flip's entreprenurial plans), and had hardly been in contact with her since the opening of The Box. I myself had only spoken to her twice since the beginning of the year, once on a Sunday morning during a call that I cut short due to a tremendous hangover (I claimed a cold), another time on a weeknight for five minutes before I rushed out to dinner. There were the strings of messages we hadn't responded to until she finally caught us at home at an odd hour, the clippings about The Box she had found in the Boston papers

('Leave it to three can-do siblings from Greater Beantown to open up glamorous New York City's swankest new hotspot,' *Boston* magazine had declared unctuously) that we hadn't acknowledged receiving, and our never having invited her to the club's opening night, let alone any of the nights since. *She just wouldn't enjoy it,* we had said to each other by way of justification. *The people would make her uncomfortable.* But of course we all knew that was only half the truth; conversely if not more so, her timid, clueless presence would have discomfited us. *Besides,* we had said, *she's so busy with her charity work. And she has Sherry. And two houses to maintain.* And having said all that, it had been rather easy to forget her.

We drove into Topsfield late that night; as always on the rare occasions when we visited from the city, the large, profoundly private houses, set back among towering trees far from the street, took me by surprise.

But the old house itself didn't seem so alien when Sherry came to the door, smiling sadly, one arm in a sling and an ugly row of stitches on her upper left cheek, which made her look even older and more tired than she had seemed at Christmastime. We filed in rather quietly, hugging her and whispering endearments one by one.

'It's a tragedy, it's a tragedy,' she muttered over and over again, and the guilt shot through me with renewed vigor as it occurred to me that Sherry was probably grieving harder than us. Ever since our father had died and we had gone off to St. Pete's, she had been our mother's best friend, confidant, caretaker and surrogate sister in addition to her housekeeper and personal secretary—and in many respects our mother had been much the same to her, ever since this unmonied, unskilled Yankee woman had divorced and her only child gone off with the Merchant Marines, leaving her with no family closer than the upper reaches of Maine, and no home other than our mother's.

'I fixed my room up for you, Lippy,' Sherry said, hugging our aunt. 'I'm gonna sleep down here in the guest room.'

Lippy kissed her on the cheek. 'Thank you, Sherry.'

We wended our way up the stairs with our bags and every-one made off to their separate quarters. Alone in the hallway now, I turned and examined the pictures hung down the length of the corridor. There was my mother in her graduation photo from nursing school, smiling with tense competence in her starched uniform, her flipped hair stiff and severe under her ridiculous, ruffled nursing cap. There was our father, grad-uating from business school, handsome and cocky in his good suit, dimpling underneath his rakishly slicked-back hair. Jess as a baby, swarthy and poker-faced; Flip as a baby, big-headed and surly; me as a baby, tiny, pink and passive. All of us in Rye, tanned nearly black except for our fair father, who always burned lobster red; all of us in front of our late grandmother's old house in Lowell, Jess, at eleven, looking palpably alien-ated; graduations from St. Pete's, polished smiles in a sea of blue blazers and white dresses, Flip, at seventeen, with the same cocky smile as our father, ripe and come-hither in her strapless ivory sundress.

And the centerpiece: the beautiful, formal wedding photo of our parents, taken in the springtime garden outside a function hall in Tewksbury. Our mother, the awkward queen for a day, in her simple, stylish white dress with the Empire waist, her veil, perched high on her updone hair like a halo, and cascad-ing down far behind her; and then our father, the awkward escort, the more-or-less good-humored but unnatural second banana, standing at military attention with an ironic, slightly sauced grin, his short, compact frame half-obscured by her outsize vestments.

He was so nervy and ambitious, she so shy and uncertain. Could they ever have thought that in just over twenty-five years they'd both be gone, reunited in a speculative heaven? Could they ever have imagined the children they'd end up raising? And then it suddenly occurred to me—so sharply that I gasped—that I was an *orphan*. I was well of age, of course, but that's technically what I was. And I thought of how very antique the word sounded, how Dickensian—and that only depressed me more, because *Dickensian* had been one of Seb's favorite words. He had used it all the time, to describe everything, often taking such gross liberties as referring to Cedric's tales of adolescent shoplifting as 'Dickensian' along the lines of The Artful Dodger from *David Copperfield*— one of the few books I had remembered well enough to discuss with him.

Flip stepped out of her room, looking disarmingly adolescent in knee-sprung jeans and an old Duran Duran T-shirt she had obviously left behind in her bureau. She smiled at me and joined me by the photo.

'She looks so pretty there, don't you think?' she asked. 'Kind of like a young Marlo Thomas without that awful nose job.'

'Kind of,' I answered. It was impossible for Flip to comment on somebody's looks, even her own late mother's, without comparing them to a celebrity.

She *tsk*'d quietly. 'I was never very nice to her.'

I didn't say anything, just kept staring at the picture.

'I was jealous of her, you know,' she continued flatly. 'I didn't think she was good enough for Daddy.'

'She certainly got by for enough years without him. She even ran a company.'

'I know—and I didn't give her much credit for anything. I know.' She wrapped her arms around me from behind, stroked my hair. 'Oh, Tigger,' she whispered. 'My baby brother Tigger. They call me Tigger 'cause I *bounce!*' she said in a cartoon voice.

'I really did bounce, huh?' I asked.

She squeezed me in her arms. 'I remember. You did.'

Just over ten years after we had received mourners in the front parlor of the gloomy old funeral home in shabby old Lowell— adolescent, sober-faced and scared—we found ourselves there again, forming with Lippy a receiving line near the casket (thank God it had to be closed!), accepting condolences heavy with Athenian or Massachusetts accents from aging Greek people, distant family or former business associates of my parents, who all seemed to remember much more of us than we did of them, if we could recall them at all. ('Here's the fella that used to want a spotted pony!' one old man named Nicky Pappadopolous croaked upon spotting Jess, chucking him violently on the cheek. 'You've grown up into a handsome old devil!' Jess just smiled, bewildered—on his life, he later swore, he couldn't ever remember wanting a pony, and neither could we.) Flip later claimed that Spike Broadhurst, a boozy old fellow salesman of our late father who had occasionally taken our mother to the dog races at Rockingham Park in her widowhood, had made a pass at her when she stepped out to go to the bathroom, and I found, much to my dismay, that I couldn't take my eyes off my nineteen-year-old second cousin Matty, whose face suggested a darkly Byronic John Stamos; the last time I had seen him had been in Rye when I was five, when he spat Za-Rex up all over me.

It was an uncomfortable scene for all of us—for some reason, everyone seemed to presume that the three of us would be moving back to the area, and more than one old fogey volunteered to introduce me to their 'beautiful' daughter or granddaughter or niece, who inevitably was 'very active' in the Greek Orthodox church and pursuing an elementary education degree at the University of Lowell. I deflected most offers with the reply that I was 'involved with someone' in New York—sort of a lie on top of a lie, I thought ruefully to myself.

But the funeral, and the subsequent wake, must have been hardest of all on poor Lippy, who had turned her back on this entire world years ago, never to return, and who, I knew, would never have been here if it hadn't been for allegiance to her younger sister and the three of us. I don't know how many times that day I heard her say, through a tight smile, 'No, no children yet. No, no husband, either. Why, thank you, that's kind, but I'm doing just fine. Yes, I'm in the arts. Cabaret—it's like a nightclub, yes.' As soon as the line slackened a little, she grabbed me and pulled me outside for a cigarette.

'If someone asks me one more time about my marital status, I'm gonna tell them I'm a dyke and living happily with a biker named Veronica. Or that I'm actually a drag queen waiting for my final procedure.' She tapped a cigarette out of her pack and lit it with shaking hands.

'Now I can see—' I began.

'Why I got out?' she interrupted me, violently exhaling smoke. 'That's exactly why. I can't stand them. They're all so goddamned old world and provincial and bigoted. They don't have an idea of what's going on in the world outside their own little universe. What do they know about making art or people dying, or losing all your friends?'

Her voice quavered as she spoke, and it seemed as though she were on the brink of crying. 'They *don't* know,' I answered. 'That's not their world.'

'Well, I'll tell you one thing. They,' and she pointed her cigarette toward the front door of the funeral home, 'are not a part of my world. And I was *never* a part of theirs, even when I lived here.'

I stared at her, speechless. She crumpled in sad laughter and put a hand on my shoulder. 'I'm sorry, darling. It's just all the stress. Your mother, and coming back here, and—oh God, did you see Mr. Gulezian? That poor little man!'

I had seen Mr. Gulezian, the shy, balding, middle-aged salesman who had courted our mother so steadfastly these past years. He was inside now, lingering awkwardly by the casket, not quite a member of the family but not merely one of the vast circle of relatives and business associates that had made up our parents' world. Jess and I took pity on him, telling him how much his companionship had meant to our mother in the years past, how our father had always spoken of him as a sterling contribution to the liquor company's sales force, how if we kept the house in Rye we'd be sure to make it available to him in the summers—all of which seemed to brighten him for a moment until he turned to Flip, who had nothing for him but a withering glance and haughty silence. Then his voice would dwindle to a humiliated mumble, and he would begin shuffling in place, anxious to retreat to his semi-sequestered chair by the casket.

'Why does he have to sit so close to the coffin?' Flip scowled after he had skulked off. 'He looks ridiculous.'

'Would you give him a break, Flip?' I said. 'Maybe he loved her, did you ever think of that?'

'He wanted her money,' she snorted. 'Daddy would break his stumpy little legs if he were here today.'

'But he's not, Flip. He hasn't been here for a long time. But Mr. Gulezian has. He really looked after Ma. Who do you think did all of the fix-up stuff on the beach house?'

'Him, of course!' Flip went on, unthawed. 'He probably thought it was going to be his.'

'You're ridiculous.'

'You wait and see, Tigger. He's not getting one cent from us.'

I walked off, fed up, to have a private cigarette in the basement lounge. On the way there, I nearly crashed into the impressive frame of Matty, who played hockey at the University of Lowell.

'Hey,' he said to me, with the well-intentioned unease of distant cousins who haven't seen each other in over a decade. 'Sorry about your Ma. That sucks—she was a real nice lady.' His voice was deep and stupid, thick with a Massachusetts accent, and insufferably sexy.

'Thanks,' I said, trying to match his baritone. 'You wanna have a cigarette with me downstairs?'

'Can't, thanks. I had to quit for the team. Besides, my girl-friend hated it. She said I tasted like an ashtray.'

'Oh.' Such news shouldn't have surprised me, but I was still crestfallen.

'That's okay.'

'You like New York?'

'Yeah, it's okay.'

'Pretty exciting, hunh? The fast life. My Ma told me about your club down there. Maybe sometime me and my girlfriend will come down and check it out.'

'That'd be cool.'

We bade each other a curt good-bye—did he hold his swarthy parting glance just a fraction of a second longer than usual, I asked, or was it simply wish fulfillment on my part?—and I slipped downstairs. Outside the lounge, just before entering, I heard voices inside, low and tense—Damienne and Jess. Perversely, I flattened myself against the wall by the door and listened.

'—so much credit that you made it through your childhood at *all*!'

Damienne was saying.

'It wasn't that bad,' Jess answered. 'Most people were pretty cool.'

'You never had any trouble?'

'Not really. There were a few incidents, one at the beach that I remember, some kids calling me a spic and throwing rocks at us. Flip went after them, cussing like crazy,' Jess laughed, 'and took a rock on the head. She was only, like, nine!'

Damienne laughed shortly. 'To think that Flip was such a crusader for social justice.'

'She wasn't, really. She was a crusader for me. And Tigger.'

'Hmph,' from Damienne. The sound of matches flaring, then a long silence.

'You know what Lippy told me a few years ago?' Jess finally asked.

'What?'

'I think she was a little drunk when she told me. It was at

some celebration at Julia's Room, I forget for what, exactly. Oh yeah, for when she cut her own CD. The one that only her friends bought.'

'I don't remember that party,' Damienne said.

'Maybe you were out of town.'

'Maybe.'

'Anyway. She was in some kind of funny reminiscing mood, and she told me that when I was in the nursery and Nikki wanted to adopt me, all these people gave her shit about adopting a Puerto Rican baby. Latinos were just moving in around here, and people didn't take so kindly to them. Her friends criticized her, her own mother, even old Mr. Tommy, probably, though Lippy was too sweet to say so.'

'Probably, though.'

'All except Lippy, of course. She told Nikki to tell them all to fuck off.'

'Of course,' Damienne laughed with a trace of affection. She was fond of Lippy.

'Anyway, she told me that when this nurse friend of Nikki's said to her, "Nikki, don't you think he's kind of *dark*? People are going to know that he isn't yours," Nikki held out her arm and said to whoever this was, "Look at *me. I'm* dark."' Jess laughed. 'Don't you love that?'

'It sounds a little naive to me, to equate herself with Latinos like that,' Damienne said sensibly.

There was a brief pause. 'But I mean,' Jess went on, a little impatiently, 'that's the kind of person she was. She *was* naive, but she didn't have one bigoted bone in her body. Lippy says that all she cared about was giving me a good home, that she couldn't believe someone could just give away such a beautiful baby.'

'She obviously didn't understand the social and economic circumstances behind your birth mother's choice, then.'

'Well, no, *obviously*,' Jess said, 'but she— you know, just forget it.' A long, uneasy pause ensued.

'I think she was a wonderful woman to give you such a

good home and education,' Damienne finally said, as though to mollify Jess.

'She wasn't a bad lady. You know, it was awkward growing up. Nikki lavished attention on me, and Flip only seemed to get on her nerves. And Mr. Tommy and I had nothing to say to each other, but he worshipped Flip because she was a tough little mick like himself.'

'Hmm. What about Tigger?' I stiffened, fearful and excited, as eavesdroppers always are when the conversation turns to them.

'Tigger was lucky, in a way,' Jess said. 'He came along after Nikki and Tommy had already taken sides, so they both treated him fairly warmly. Or as warmly as Tommy could manage. I think it's better for Tig that Tommy died before he came out of the closet. He never told Nikki he was gay, you know. She must have known, but it never came up. Tig was also lucky he had Lippy. She was the fag-hag mother that he needed.' Jess laughed. I felt like I should be offended, but Jess was more or less correct. And did eavesdroppers really have the right to be offended?

'I worry about Tigger now,' Damienne said, as though I were one of her cases. 'He's so talented, but so impressionable, and I feel like Flip's sucking him into the vortex. And now without Seb—'

I wanted to step in and tell Damienne that I could do just fine by myself, thank you, but I didn't have to.

'Tigger will be okay,' Jess said. 'He's got a good head on his shoulders.'

Damienne made some sort of noncommittal noise. It had seemed to me increasingly that their public conversations ended this way, trailing off into a cul-de-sac of unspoken disagreement, or mild rancor; apparently, their private moments weren't any different.

'Anyway,' Jess finally said. 'No more mami for us. Now I really am a foundling.'

'Well, I don't know about that,' Damienne said. 'What about that phone call?'

Blood rushed into my ears, pricking them up fast. I furrowed my brow, listened more closely.

Jess was slow to answer. 'Yeah,' he finally said. 'That was pretty strange, hunh? Anyway, I haven't had another one.'

'You never know, though. How would you feel if you got one?'

'I don't know. Not freaked out. Not all full of hope. Just curious—like, "Hmmm, here's an interesting little mystery."'

'Well, maybe you'll get to do some sleuthing. It's all very Alex Haley, isn't it?'

Jess laughed. 'I guess so. Maybe we should get back up there, hunh? Flip and Tig and Lippy must be going loca.'

'Oh God,' Damienne groaned, and I heard them rising from the couch. 'If we must. Do you know someone came up to me and asked if I was running coat-check? If I had worn a maid's uniform and served drinks and coffee I probably would've felt much more comfortable here.'

'Just be glad we're going back to New York in two days, then.'

'This is true. The gorgeous mosaic, as our fine mayor calls it.'

They were about to walk out of the lounge. I ducked around the corner and into the bathroom, my head to the door until I heard their footsteps recede at the top of the stairway. Then I slipped back out, lit a cigarette and sank down into the couch they had just left, tinged with guilt and consumed with a dark curiosity. *What phone call?* I kept asking myself. Why was I *always* the one in the family from whom secrets were kept? I sank deeper into the couch, sulkily nursing my cigarette, somewhat drowsy now. And why hadn't I been nicer to my sweet mother before it was too late? And why was Flip so rude to Mr. Gulezian . . . and Lippy so bitter about her past . . . and Damienne so certain of what was right

for everyone . . . and Seb so hard to please . . . and me so very
tired all of a sudden . . . and why, and why, and why . . .

'Hey.'

I nodded awake, the cigarette smoldering away between
the loose grip of my two fingers. I looked up—it was Matty
looming over me, his tie undone, revealing the heavy muscles
of his neck and shoulders, and a faint plug of black hair creeping up from his protuberant chest. His enormous, hair-flecked,
olive-toned hands hung at his sides, the knuckles chafed and
ruddy, suspended just before my face.

'You got a cigarette after all, man? It's a fucking madhouse
up there.'

'Sure.' I fished one out for him, lit it, and he heaved himself
into the appending couch with a mighty *Ah, shhhhhit.*

'So, hey,' he grunted prefatorily, and I raised a roguish eyebrow in his direction. 'In New York, right, is it true you can
pick up a hooker and pay for her with your credit card?'

I smiled, took the last soggy drag of my cigarette, feeling
very solitary, abject and old. Why, and why, and why?

The day after the funeral—a morose affair in a wet Greek
Orthodox cemetery on the outskirts of Lowell—we called Mr.
Kittredge, hoping to speed estate matters, but he called us
back to say that the will wouldn't be prepared for reading for
another two weeks, and that he would call us then in New
York. Lippy returned to New York, so that she might not miss
doing the late show at Julia's Room, but Damienne, of all
people, felt she and the three of us should stay the night for
one final dinner with Sherry, who had been wandering about
like a lost soul ever since the accident. So after we drove Lippy
to the airport amidst a round of subdued farewells, we
returned to Topsfield, picked up food at the grocery store, and
informed Sherry—who sat watching *General Hospital* with
listless, glazed eyes—that she should relax while we prepared
supper.

'What good kids you are,' she said absently, before passing us a frighteningly wan smile and turning back to the TV. She couldn't possibly have known that her very name triggered the horrific incident that followed.

The three of us and Damienne were in the kitchen, chopping various vegetables for an enormous salad and a lasagna, the rain beating drearily against the windows and the radio turned quietly to Kiss 108, when Damienne put down her knife and looked up thoughtfully.

'I've been thinking about Sherry,' she said. 'It doesn't seem that she has independent assets.'

The three of us looked at her curiously.

'I wonder if your mother left her partial management of the estate, given that she was her longtime retainer.'

There was an uncomfortable silence. Flip shot me a sneer that Damienne may or may not have caught. 'I'm sure Ma provided for her,' Jess finally said evenly. 'Sherry was like family to her.'

'We'll soon see,' Damienne said, before calmly picking up her knife and resuming with the peppers, head bent too low to notice Flip glowering at her. I knew something bad was coming, and I was right. Her face flushed with hot blood, Flip put down *her* knife.

'I'm sure if Sherry's not provided for, Damienne,' she said in the most acid of voices, 'you'll be happy to represent her pro bono when she takes us to court. Yet another social justice case for you.'

Damienne looked up and laughed, a horrible, incredulous laugh. 'What's that all about, Flip? I was just—'

'You were just suggesting,' Flip interrupted her, 'that my mother was a self-centered bitch who wouldn't have thought about her own best friend.'

'Flip, I was *not*,' Damienne protested. 'I was just speculating that if— if— Jess?' she finally pleaded, helpless.

'Flip,' Jess said low, ominously.

Flip shot around to him. 'Flip what? Does she really think we'd just *forget* about Sherry? Who does she think we are?' She shot back to Damienne. 'Do you really think the whole world is made up of evil oppressors and totally helpless oppressed people? Because this is America, Damienne, not some banana republic.'

Damienne gasped—a horrible, choked-off little 'Oh!'—and the silence that followed was excruciating. We all knew that Damienne's pro-democracy parents had been persecuted in Haiti under the Duvalier regime, that they had suffered terribly before they just barely managed to escape to America, fighting a long, tenuous battle before they were finally granted official status as political refugees, then citizenship. We knew how much they had sacrificed to move from Florida to New York and put Damienne through school. The topic was sacred, verboten; Damienne couldn't so much as hear a random allusion to Haiti without visibly tensing. And now Flip had delivered the lowest of low blows. Damienne sat there, stunned, her mouth wide open. Flip stared back at her, chalkily; it was obvious that she already knew she had gone too far, and in typical fashion, she was too horrified with herself to apologize.

If someone didn't break the silence, I was going to scream. 'I didn't know you were so patriotic, Flip,' I finally said.

'Shut up, Tig,' Jess said, rigid. 'Maybe you and Flip should get the hell out of here right now.'

'Maybe we should, Tigger,' Flip mumbled, staring down into her tomatoes.

'No, you needn't go anywhere,' Damienne said, drawing herself up with a terrible summoning of dignity. 'I'm the one who's leaving.'

'Damienne,' Jess said. 'Come on. Please. Let's talk.'

'There's nothing to talk about, Jess.' She formed her cut peppers into a neat square on the chopping block with her knife. 'You know this has been coming for a long time. I just—'

and she sighed, looking infinitely weary. 'I can't compete. I can't compete with her anymore.' She sounded more sad than angry. Where had I heard those dreadful words before? *I can't compete.* Was there really such a competition? Flip continued to stare down, saying nothing.

'I've tried and tried and tried not to be a bitch in the process, because I hate being a bitch.' Damienne went on. 'But I just can't. I'm going to pack my things and head back. I'm sure the three of you can catch a train tomorrow—or a plane.'

'Damienne, don't,' Jess said, stepping toward her.

'Don't go, Damienne,' I volunteered.

Damienne looked at me and gave me a curious smile, sympathetic or disdainful I couldn't quite tell. 'Thanks, Tigger, but no. It's the right thing to do. Excuse me.'

She walked out of the kitchen and up the stairs, her back unnervingly straight. Jess glanced wildly at Flip, then me. 'Shit!' he hissed, before following her up the stairs. In a moment, we heard the resolute click of a closing bedroom door.

Flip and I said nothing for several seconds. At length, she looked up at me. 'It's kind of like that scene on the balcony in *The Sound of Music* when the Baroness leaves, isn't it?'

I looked up at her, agog. 'Honey, don't even *compare* yourself to Maria von Trapp at a time like this.'

In a moment, she was crying, the knife trembling in her hand. 'Oh, Tigger. I hate myself. I didn't mean to say what I said.'

'You meant every word, Flip.' I knew it sounded mean, and I didn't even feel like being mean to her—just honest, for once.

'You're awful,' she choked. 'People are awful to me. They don't understand me at all.'

'I guess not,' I said, resuming my chopping. She kept on crying quietly for another five minutes, until finally she got up, wiped her face and blew her nose with a paper towel, poured herself a murky glass of water, and sat back down at the table, staring into her lap.

We heard the bedroom door again a few minutes later. In a moment, Jess and Damienne were coming down the stairs, Damienne's bag in her hand. At the front door, we heard the murmur of pinched good-byes. Then the door was open— the rain was clattering outside—then it was closed, and in another moment, we heard a car engine turning in the drive- way, gunning, then receding down the street. From my place at the kitchen table, I could see Jess staring out into the rain, his back to us. At length, he came back into the kitchen and continued shredding the lettuce without a word to either of us.

'Jess—' Flip finally said.

'Don't, Flip,' he stopped her. 'Please. Don't talk. Let's just finish the meal.'

We had a miserable dinner. I had burnt the lasagna, and its edges were hard and black, and worse (particularly for Flip, I knew), the house was bereft of wine or spirits. Sherry asked what had happened to Damienne, and Jess responded curtly, 'She had to get back,' and Sherry only nodded, respectfully saying no more. She told us that her brother had called from Augusta, and that she was probably going to visit him soon.

'You don't have to leave, Sherry,' Flip said. 'The will's not for two weeks, but I'm sure things are taken care of, and this is your home.'

To which Sherry just smiled politely and murmured, 'You kids are sweet.' Jess smiled back at her, but had nothing to say, and neither did I.

Silently we cleaned up the kitchen, then wandered our sep- arate ways—Sherry back to the TV, the three of us to our separate rooms. In mine, the rain continued to beat against the window. I felt peculiarly haunted, as though at any moment my thirty-something father was going to poke his head in the window, face red and tired from work, and ask indifferently after my day. In the bookcase, I found my old illustrated copy of *Twenty Thousand Leagues Under the Sea*, then lay down with it on the tiny twin bed that no longer accommodated my feet. But I hadn't turned three pages before the words started skidding across the page—the entire day seemed to weigh so heavily upon me—and I dropped it, spine cracking with age, onto my chest. Then I could hear the fight between them, Jess and Flip, muffled through the walls, just before I fell into a funky, fitful sleep.

When I woke up, sweaty and dislocated, it was near midnight. I padded out into the hall and down the stairs, but the house was dark, seemingly put to bed for the night. Trudging back up to my room, I caught a dim light from under the slightly ajar door of my parents' bedroom. I peeked inside—Flip and Jess had fallen asleep together under the covers of my parents' big bed, the light on the night table still burning. Her head was tucked in between his chest and shoulder, and he faced straight up at the ceiling. Most of their clothes were strewn over the chair at my mother's vanity.

My stomach seemed to bottom out in a particularly miserable way, and I was just about to skulk silently back to my room when my foot squeaked on the old wooden threshold. Jess started, leaned up a bit in bed. 'Tig,' he whispered sleepily. 'Tig, come here.'

'That's all right,' I whispered back hoarsely.

Flip started now, saw me, squinted and smiled. She extended a hand to me. 'Come here, Tigger.'

'It's okay,' I said again.

'Get in here, Tig,' Jess said. 'Take your shoes off.'

'I guess you two made up,' I said, relenting, closing the door softly behind me, doffing my sneakers and jeans, climbing under the duvet and lying rigidly apart from them, until Jess reached around and pulled me up against his side. Silently, we all twitched and twisted around until we found a fairly

comfortable approximation of the Chair. I pressed my face
into the small of Jess's back, wrapped my right arm around his
chest, took up a loose lock of Flip's hair and wrapped it
around the fingers of my free hand. The house felt drafty and
silent and enormously unpopulated. I pressed my face into
Jess's back harder and harder, and was surprised and
chagrined to find that my whole body was shaking rather
uncontrollably.

Flip turned a bit. 'Tigger, baby, what's wrong?'

'I'm scared, I guess.'

Jess pulled my arm around his chest tighter, and we all
hitched in closer to each other until my trembling subsided
and we were breathing as one imperfect organism, three
ribcages expanding and contracting in slow, arhythmic coun-
terpoint. Outside, the rain continued, numb to the passage of
years and indifferent to the parting of ways, all across
Massachusetts.

Eighteen

We were quiet on the train back to New York, passing back and forth a quart of orange juice and a couple of stale bagels we had picked up at Store 24 moments before boarding. Across the aisle, a young Korean mother held a sleeping baby. (Apparently she didn't speak English; when I asked her if she'd like a bit of bagel, she only flushed and smiled and murmured briskly, 'No, no, very sorry, no.') When the train stopped to change engines in New Haven, however, the sudden quiet and dark woke the child, who began crying at a pitch that set my teeth on edge. Jess looked as though he wanted to strangle the child, and I was terrified that Flip, staring dully at this loud pieta scenario, would turn to the poor, exasperated woman and say something nasty enough to transcend the language barrier.

But she didn't. Instead, much to my surprise, she turned to the woman and asked, 'Do you want me to hold him for a minute?', miming the offer in kind. The woman's entire face flushed again with relief, and she handed the child over to Flip, rather hastily, I thought.

'Shhh, little baby,' Flip cooed, smiling, cradling him in her arms with a facility I didn't know she possessed. 'That's it. Shhhh.' The child didn't stop crying immediately, but that didn't seem to deter Flip. And eventually, as the train car doors opened to allow for cigarette or soda breaks, the child's sobs subsided, then stopped altogether.

'What's his name?' Flip mouthed to the mother.

'Oh, yes, thank you!'

'No, no. What his *name*?'

'Oh,' and she smiled in recognition. 'Name him Christopher.'

'Christopher,' Flip repeated. 'Hello, Christopher. He's very pretty.'

The mother smiled obligingly before settling back in her seat and closing her eyes. Jess and I exchanged curious glances.

'You wanna go have a smoke with us, Flip?' Jess asked.

She looked up, a bit disoriented. 'Hunh? Oh, no, that's all right. We'll just sit here and rest.'

'Okay.'

Jess and I lit cigarettes on the platform outside, drab New Haven shrouded in rain for miles around us. Through the smoked window, we could see Flip with the baby, stroking his fuzzy head and staring off into space.

'Look at the new Flip,' I said. 'Madonna and child.'

'Hmph,' Jess laughed. 'She'll probably want to hire him to work the door at The Box in a few years.'

'No kidding.'

Back inside, Flip had handed the sleeping child back to his mother and was now leafing abstractedly through a British fashion magazine's spring preview ('Naughty in the Nineties').

'It's nasty outside,' I remarked to her.

She shrugged, indifferent. Then she turned to me and announced rather flatly, 'Tigger, I'm a horrible person.'

'What?'

'You heard me. I'm a horrible person.' She kept leafing through the magazine, at one point backtracking to further study a six-page spread for Gaultier.

'What makes you say that?'

'I'm like the anti-Midas. Everything I touch I kill.'

I wondered how much I should protest; she didn't seem to be joking, nor did she seem especially anxious to be talked out of her pronouncement. Instead, I put my palm before her.

'Hold my hand.'

She smiled, lopsided. 'Why?'

'Just go ahead. Hold it.' And she did, with a tentative, questioning half-grasp.

'See?' I said, squeezing it. 'I'm still here.'

She laughed quietly. 'Tigger, you queer.'

'I'm still here.' I settled our hands down onto the chair-arm between us. We fumbled a bit, getting comfortable, and we kept our hands together like that for a while, both of us settling back in our seats in a state of pretended ease, like dating kids at a movie.

Anthea had sat house for us while we were away, and we found her eating rice cakes, smoking and flipping through magazines in front of MTV when we arrived back at the loft that afternoon. I felt a happy little quiver upon entering the loft, all soothingly gloomy and permeated with the familiar old smell of cigarettes and dank wooden floors, and I was surprised to find just how much I had missed it.

'Darlings!' Anthea cried, scrambling up from the couch and showering us all with kisses. (Vodka hung heavily on her breath; in the past few months, her 'amateur' alcoholism had increased to a near-professional level that terrified Katja, and already we had begun talking nervously amongst ourselves about what we should do for her.) 'It's so good to have you all back! The Box wasn't the same—everybody heard you were out of town, Flip, and none of the really *nice* people came— and I've gotten so lonely in this big, drafty flat all by myself. Katja left me to go do a magazine shoot in South Beach. She'll be furious if she tans! They love that Transylvania undead look about her.'

'Your hair looks great, Anth,' I said.

'Thank you, love.' She had had it cut into that Jane Fonda *Klute* shag that was re-emerging among a handful of Manhattan's most outré women; in three years, it would be everywhere and the sight of it would still remind me of Anthea. 'Was home absolutely wretched?'

Flip moved to answer, but thought better of it, wandering toward the kitchen. 'Yes, on the whole,' Jess filled in good-naturedly, 'but it's over, so—'

'Who sent these?' Flip called from the kitchen, carrying out an overwhelming arrangement of tropical flowers.

'Aren't they brilliant?' Anthea gushed. 'They came yesterday. Wait on, I've got the card here.' She retrieved it by the mail table near the door. 'I respectfully acknowledged your privacy, Flip darling, and didn't open it, so you simply *must* tell me who from. Ty, d'ya think? He fancies you *tragically*, Flip.'

'Ty couldn't eat for a week if he bought those things, unless he stole them, and I don't think he's *that* shady.' Flip laughed as she opened the small card. She frowned, rolled her eyes. 'Oh, for God's sake,' she said.

'Who from?'

'Goolsbee. Listen to this: "Dearest Felipika (and Tigger and Jess). Heard of your sad news, and just wanted to express my sympathy. If there's anything I can do for you, please don't hesitate to call me after the 16th, whereupon I'll be back from Singapore. Reach me at the office—I virtually live there. Thinking of you, Amos." He's too much.' Flip laughed, dropping the card into her bag.

'Oh my,' Anthea murmured. Jess and I said nothing.

'How the hell did he find out so fast?' Flip asked.

'Well,' and Anthea blushed. 'He rang up Friday night looking for you, Flip. To see if you wanted to take in a concert he had tickets for before you hit The Box. And— and I told him you'd gone out of town, and he asked why, and I—'

'Told him everything,' Flip finished.

'Well, not *everything*. Just— you know, that there'd been a situation with your mum. He sounded quite dismayed, actually. He said he hated any sort of family tragedy. And then the flowers came around the next day.'

'Are they poisonous?' Jess finally asked drily, breaking the strange mood. I hadn't seen Goolsbee and had barely thought of him since having abided his unwelcome presence at The Box's opening night on New Year's Eve. All I knew was that he was now junk-bond trading on Wall Street, or some such bloated enterprise, and making more money than he knew what to do with.

'Hmmm.' Flip brightened. 'If they are, maybe I'll bake them up in a cake and send it to *him* as a token of gratitude.'

'Oh my,' Anthea peeped again.

'So Anth, anyway,' Flip went on. 'How's The Box? Did I miss anything?'

'Oh dear, where to begin?' Anthea paused dramatically to replace herself on the couch and light a new cigarette, and we all gathered around expectantly. 'Well, first off, good nights all despite the slight drop in quality, which can be directly attributed to your absence.'

'I'm there tonight,' Flip said, the old nocturnal glint returning to her eyes. 'Aren't you guys?' she asked, wheeling around toward Jess and me.

We looked at each other. 'Of course,' I said, after a pause. I certainly didn't have anywhere else to be. (Seb hadn't called, but a few days later I would receive a short, terse note of condolence from him—our mother had always liked him for his good manners—no 'Love' or 'xo' or any other valedictory, just his clipped initials.) And moreover, after a week in moribund Massachusetts and all its attendant stress, I found that my appetite for The Box, which had been just a touch waning before the news of our mother, had come back full force.

Jess smiled. 'Of course, Flip. Where else should someone go

the first Sunday night after a funeral?' His tone was jesting, but not mean. Flip knew as much and nodded, satisfied. 'What else, Anth?'

'Well, let's see?' Anthea continued coyly. 'Sammy's got to go away to London for a week next month to mix something for Martha Wash, but he said he thinks he might be able to get Cole and Clivillés to guest-spot Saturday night if you'll show them around the system, Tig.'

Flip, Jess and I turned to each other, agape. 'Are you *serious*?' I cried. 'Sammy got C+C Music Factory to spin for us?'

'He thinks so. He's just got to firm it up.'

'That's fabulous!' Flip exclaimed. 'How much do they want?'

'Sammy said they'd do it for free, as a favor for his promoting them so much.'

Flip clapped her hands together, elated. 'Anth, we should talk to Miko immediately and put together a fierce promo. At tomorrow's meeting, okay?'

'Of course, darling.'

'That's not half as traumatic as I thought it was going to be,' Flip sighed. 'Oh— Did you and Guillermo get a chance to do the books?'

'He did them yesterday afternoon. I couldn't join him. I had the nastiest little grippe. The bad weather, and all.' We nodded sympathetically, as blithely as she had spoken, but the stiff, brief pocket of silence allowed for what we all knew: she had either spent the afternoon drinking alone, or had been incapacitated with a hangover, or both. 'At any rate,' Anthea rushed on with forced brightness, 'Guillermo was a sweetheart about it. He's off from register tonight, so he said you should ring him first thing tomorrow, Flip.'

Flip raised a curious eyebrow. 'Why can't we just talk tomorrow evening at the club?'

'I couldn't guess,' Anthea shrugged. 'He said no more than that.'

Flip was silent for a moment, then she shook it off and proclaimed, 'Guess what we have in this house that we didn't have in Topsfield?'

'Roaches?' I ventured.

'British lesbians with shags?' Jess directed affectionately at Anthea, who gasped with mock indignance and threw a magazine at him.

'No,' Flip said, dancing toward the kitchen. 'Vodka! Who's having a screwdriver with me?'

'Me,' Jess called, as did I.

'Spare yourself and make a pitcher, darling,' Anthea called to her, heralding a happily drunk afternoon in which an increasingly loopy Anthea (she sank with frightening swiftness into what she called her 'Sally Bowles mode') regaled us with yet more stories from the first weekend at The Box any of us had missed since it opened. Sylvia Miles had come around again and gotten into a drunken row with three drag queens. Miko had stumbled on whom he was absolutely certain were David Geffen and Ross Bleckner tumbling out of a toilet stall with some beautiful kid who turned out to be a deserter from the Israeli army. An aging model, twenty-one, had taken too many hits of Ecstasy and was found near eight in the morning talking to herself in Swedish on top of one of the giant speakers.

And so on and so on, cozily, but as the afternoon wore into evening and the sky darkened outside over SoHo, I couldn't help feeling a bit unsettled that the answering machine never clicked in, as it often did on a Sunday, to reveal the faintly irritated, expectant voices of Seb, or Damienne, or our mother (*Hello? Guys? Could someone pick up the phone?*), and I wondered if Flip and Jess, beneath the obvious pleasure of our homecoming, weren't similarly, silently disconcerted. Those disembodied voices, crackling out of the old machine, had been a part of life at the loft for so long—a constant, sometimes less-than-welcome reminder of our lives outside of The Box—and I was surprised to find how eerily unmoored the afternoon felt without them.

Abruptly, I experienced a frightening moment of detach-
ment, slouching half-drunkenly on the couch, screwdriver in
hand, in which the laughing faces of Flip, Jess and Anthea
seemed curiously foreign. Here were the principals in my life
now, people I loved so dearly, still the center of my world, as
they had been long before Seb and would be forever after. Had
I been asking for this without even knowing it? And did I
want it? Sitting there, betraying none of this slightly unreal
episode behind my own cocked smile, I squirmed to concede
privately that I really didn't know the answer.

It felt good to be back at The Box that night—the crowd was
sizable but not insane, and I spent half my time up in the
sound booth drinking more screwdrivers and helping
Sammy's highly-strung sidekick Pepe pick out vinyl, until
Jess collected me and we finally left, exhausted, around three.
Flip stayed on until closing, undefeated despite an afternoon
soaked in vodka, exhilarated to be back at the helm of her
pleasure liner.

'Did you see Flip schmoozing with what's-her-face's agent's
boyfriend to get a booking for the Half-Year Party?' Jess asked
me as the two of us made our way home down a deserted
Spring Street. The Half-Year Party was to take place at the end
of June to celebrate the six-month anniversary of The Box, and
Flip vowed that it was to be a Box record-breaker.

'I did, from the sound booth,' I answered. 'It looked to me
like she was getting what she wanted.'

'She always does. It was good to see her back there tonight.'

I glanced rightward at him, looking for clues to the exact
thrust of his remark, but whatever might have been there was
cloaked in shadows. We walked on for a block in silence until
I finally found the courage to speak.

'What happened with Damienne, Jess?'

He glanced at me, glanced away, sent a stone tripping down
the sidewalk with the toe of his boot. 'What do you think?' he

finally asked, a touch defensively, I thought. 'We broke up. Wasn't it obvious?'

'Not necessarily,' I answered warily. 'So?'

'So what?'

'So . . . how do you feel about it?'

'I guess it wasn't meant to be.' He sounded heavy with irony. 'At least, that's what she thought.'

'*She?*'

He looked at me again, laughed derisively. '*She* meaning Damienne, Tig. Not every *she* refers to your sister.'

'I wasn't thinking that!' I lied in protest.

'Yeah, right.'

I swallowed my blush. 'Well, how do you feel about it?'

'How do you think I feel about it?'

'I don't know.'

'Sucky.' He lit a cigarette, briefly illuminating his frowning face. 'You want one?'

'No, thanks, my mouth's too dry from drinking. Did you love her, Jess?'

'Who are you?' he laughed. 'Baba Wawa?'

'Yeah, that's me. No, I just—'

'Yes, I loved her,' he cut me off impatiently. 'I still love her, obviously. We were together for two years, Tig. We were probably gonna get married.'

'When?' I asked, surprised. It was the first time he had mentioned such a thing.

'I don't know, exactly. Someday. It was more her idea than mine. We were gonna have the wedding in the Caribbean.'

'In *Haiti?*'

'Well, no, Tig, obviously not. Barbados or something like that.'

'So what happened last night?'

'You're working my nerves, Tigger.'

'I know. But tell me, anyway.'

He stopped underneath the street lamp at the corner of

Spring and Crosby, turned to face me. 'You heard what she said in the kitchen, right?'

'Yeah.'

'Well, that was about the long and short of it. She's not a fool, Damienne.'

'So what did you say?'

He stared at me hard, then looked down, kicked the toe of one boot with that of the other. 'What did I *say*?' he repeated, more to his boots than to me.

'Yeah.'

'I said . . . nothing.'

'Why?'

''Cause I was ashamed.'

I laughed, then suddenly wished I hadn't. 'Ashamed of what?'

'Ashamed 'cause . . . 'cause I had nothing to say.' He smiled at me sadly, put his open palms out before me as if to suggest he had little else to offer. 'Get it?'

I smiled back the same, sad smile. Suddenly, I felt an odd rush of vertigo, and steadied myself against the street lamp. It seemed that an awful lot had happened in only a week. 'Yeah, I get it.'

'Now, do you have something to say about *that*?' he asked me with what I thought was a certain hostility, dropping his cigarette and extinguishing it under his boot. My head rush hadn't quite faded. 'No,' I finally managed, picking studiously at a broadsheet peeling off the street lamp. 'I've got nothing to say.'

He regarded me keenly, I could feel it even as I looked away. Then he propped my chin up in his hand until I was staring directly into his frankly querying face. 'When did you get to be such a little man, Thomas?'

'Don't call me that,' I flushed. 'You-Know-Who used to call me that.'

He laughed and threw a long arm around me. 'You-Know-Who's a pussy. You know that, right?'

'Yeah, I do.' We started walking up the street toward the loft, stayed briefly by a rat that emerged out of trash bags and streaked across our path in an ovoid flash of black. 'It's just— well, he wasn't so bad. And he was there. You know?'

'Some kind of family we are, hunh?'

I yawned before I could answer, suddenly sleepy inside the crook of his coat. 'I'm so tired, man.'

'Look, Tigger.' He steered me across the street, to just in front of the enormous iron doors that led to our loft. I remained soporifically crumpled inside his arm while he fished out keys. 'Wake up, Tigger. We're home.'

It was Flip's voice that woke me in the morning, loud and indignant just outside my bedroom door. I threw on shorts and a T-shirt and wandered into the kitchen, where she held the telephone in one hand and a cigarette in the other. She looked haggard, as though she had had little sleep, and I put on a full pot of coffee.

'Since when?' she was barking into the phone. 'February? . . . Well, how the fuck did *that* happen, Guillermo? I thought you were balancing the books every week . . . every Friday night, right, like we said . . . uh huh . . . uh huh . . . but what about—' She exhaled a long, exasperated tunnel of smoke and motioned imperiously to me for coffee. 'I *never* said quarterly, I said weekly, *weekly* . . . well, when the fuck are you going to learn to understand English, Guillermo? You've been here for two years!'

I turned to her, shocked by her remark and her tone. *Don't you dare*, she mouthed at me viciously. 'What? What?' she continued into the phone. 'Okay, Guillermo, I'm sorry. Look, from the beginning. Electricity, right? . . . What else? . . . The *liquor*? . . . the *cleaning* service? Oh, shit . . . uh huh . . . uh huh . . . uh huh . . . All right, just tell me quick, just get it out,' she said in a small, tight voice. Then she fell back in her chair, her whole body slackening. A long, unattended roll of ash on the end of her cigarette broke away and fell on the front of her T-shirt. 'Are you absolutely sure, Guillermo?' she pleaded. 'Okay. Okay, I'll be there . . . Oh for God's sakes, don't cry, honey. There's a mistake somewhere. We'll iron it out . . . okay . . . ciao.'

She slammed down the phone with a mighty 'Fuck!' and dragged violently on the remains of her cigarette.

'What was that all about?' I asked, setting down her coffee.

'Yeah, what *was* that all about?' Jess echoed, emerging from the bathroom connected to Flip's room. His face twisted into an awkward grimace when he saw my slightly astonished reaction—I wondered if the two of them had had a talk very late in the night, or, more correctly, very early in the morning—but Flip hardly seemed to notice the weight of Jess's egress, so enraged was she by the phone call.

'It was that fucking Guillermo. I never should have hired him.'

'Why?' Jess and I chorused.

She sighed, bracing herself for a long, unpleasant explication. 'Well, you know he did the books this weekend, right?' We nodded. 'And you know how according to his book-keeping, we had this extraordinarily good month, and I couldn't believe how we had turned such an incredible profit, especially after accounting for all the expenses—the utilities, and the suppliers, the cleaning service, the lighting technicians, all of that?'

We nodded again, with deepening dismay.

'Well, it's all because Guillermo misread two months' worth of bills and invoices for *one*. We didn't turn a profit last month, we fell *way* below the line, especially with the AIDS benefit.'

'I thought you said the AIDS benefit wasn't taking a huge bite out of the budget,' I said.

'Well, it wasn't supposed to, according to the calculations Guillermo gave me.'

'Didn't they seem suspicious to you?' Jess asked. 'Didn't you check them?' Flip shook her head. 'Well, why not?'

'What do you mean, "why not"?' Flip bridled. 'He's a fuck-ing trained accountant. I thought he knew what he was doing. That's why I hired him.'

'And how did he mistake two months of expenses for one?' I asked.

'I made this deal with most of the suppliers and contractors that they could tack on thirteen percent interest if they let us pay them every other month instead of every month.'

'Why?' Jess looked utterly perplexed now. 'Why did you make a deal where you were going to get charged thirteen percent interest? That's astronomical.'

'Because someone told me that the interest our takings would collect in the bank in two months rather than one would—you know, like, would be bigger than the interest payments, and that we'd turn a profit on it. Doesn't that make sense?'

'Of course not,' Jess spluttered. 'Haven't you ever looked at your trust fund statements to see how it works? You *never* want to be owing interest to someone, especially on a scale as high as yours. Who the fuck told you to do that?'

'Just someone,' Flip answered flatly.

'Who?'

'Just someone in the finance world, all right?' she snapped, taking us both aback. I wanted to ask her at least why Guillermo hadn't accounted for this 'special deal' that Flip had cobbled—but I was too afraid it had something to do with more miscommunication, and I wisely said nothing.

'Anyway,' Flip resumed wearily, running her hands through her hair. 'According to Guillermo, what it means is this: we're very, *very* behind in bills to a lot of places. I usually have about a $30,000 cash flow every week to cover expenses, and as of the end of last week, I'm two whole cash flows behind. And they've been calling, and they want their money fast, or they'll cut off services.'

'How much behind?' Jess ventured. 'Like, ten thousand?'

Flip laughed grimly and shook her head.

'Well, how much?' I pressed anxiously.

'Forty seven thousand and change.' She spoke clearly and fearlessly, right into the depth of her coffee cup.

'Oh, holy Christ,' Jess whistled before a silence fell over us. Flip continued to stare defiantly into her coffee cup, as though she were auguring. Jess and I looked at each other, looked away. I ran my eyes over the kitchen counter, where Anthea had left behind her empty bottles of vodka and gin—six of them. Finally, after it seemed as though a dozen trucks and a few ambulances had passed outside on the street, Jess quietly addressed Flip.

'Hm?' She looked up reasonably, that look that said she was madly determined to possess herself and safeguard her pride.

'Just theoretically—if you had to pay it, you could, right?'

She laughed incredulously. 'Are you kidding? Of course not! I don't have that kind of money set aside.'

'But what about The Box account?'

'Jess, we're doing well, but not *that* well! When I get done with expenses and bills and staff checks, there's hardly enough for me to give myself a salary, let alone put away in savings.'

'Well, how much *do* you have in savings?' I asked. 'In The Box account?'

She sneered. 'Tigger, you know that the finances for the club are my business.'

'I know. But how much?'

'I don't know off the top of my head,' she blurted, frustrated. 'Something, I guess, like seven thousand.'

Jess and I looked at each other, astounded. 'That's *it*?' he asked.

'What do you mean, "that's it?" We've only been open two months. The lawyers told me that's a strong start for a start-up business. It's a hell of a lot more than I have left in my trust!'

I groaned inwardly. It was more than *I* had left in mine— Jess and I were coming to the end of ours—which meant that

Flip, who had blown through most of hers in her first two years in New York, probably didn't have enough left to buy a week's worth of groceries. Some of the potential gravity of the situation seemed to hit me suddenly, and I could tell from the look on Jess's face that he was thinking much the same.

Flip caught our wary, silent expressions. 'Oh for God's sakes, don't worry about it. I wish I hadn't even mentioned it. Guillermo's undercalculated before and he's probably overcalculated this time. It probably is something like ten thousand. And even if I had to pay the fucking forty-seven thousand, what's the problem? Kittredge is gonna open up Ma's will in a week or two. I'll just ask him to speed the whole process along.'

'Nice that even the worst things happen at convenient times.' Jess smirked.

'Fuck you!' Flip exploded. 'That's not what I meant at all.'

'All right, all right, I'm sorry,' Jess hastened. 'That was low.' He moved over to her and began rubbing her shoulders in comfort. For the first time, I had the odd feeling of being a stranger watching a lovers' quarrel, or, worse, a child witnessing a fight between his parents.

'I gotta get out of here and do some work today,' I announced, dropping my coffee cup in the sink. It was the truth—I was woefully behind on my work for Mannes, and I had remembered upon waking that I had forgotten to cancel my twelve-thirty lesson on East 92nd Street, and I certainly couldn't wiggle out of it now. 'I'm sure everything's gonna be fine, Flip.'

'Of course it is,' she said sharply.

I showered, dressed, assembled my backpack. When I emerged from my room, Flip and Jess were sitting at the kitchen table, smoking, rifling with furrowed brows through Flip's clumsily stuffed folders of Box-related material.

'You going to the studio today?' I asked Jess.

'Hm? Oh, yeah. Yeah. In a little bit. You?'

'Uptown to the practice rooms, then to a lesson, then back to the practice rooms.'

He nodded laboriously. 'Have a good day's work.'

'Have a good day, honey,' Flip cooed in a fashion that rattled my last nerve.

'You too,' I mumbled. 'See you tonight.'

'Of course.'

Outside, I gulped air, relieved to be out of the loft and alone. It was the serene interval now between morning rush and the lunchtime crush, and Houston Street was disconcertingly quiet as I walked to the train. On the platform, I waited and waited, and when the cranky old F train wormed its way around the dark curve in the tunnel and inched its way toward me, I could only wonder why everything seemed to be happening either too fast or too slow. It was like riding in the old station wagon when Flip drove— a nauseating procedure of fits and starts, giddy stretches of speed during a good song on the radio, or a highway crawl if she were in the midst of a personal narrative, heedless to what seemed like the whole world crowding upon us from behind.

More bad news when I arrived home that night. 'I went over the books with Guillermo this afternoon,' Flip announced, plainly overwrought. 'I was right, he miscalculated. It's not forty-seven and change, it's fifty-four and change.'

'Jesus Christ, Flip. What are you gonna do?'

'Just like I said, I'm gonna call Kittredge and get him to execute the will as soon as possible. There's got to be enough in there for me to pay off the debts, and then some. I know it's crass to talk about Ma's money that way, but what can I do?'

I shrugged.

'Now let's not talk about it anymore. I've been dealing with it all day, and I'll go crazy if I think about it for another second.'

I threw down my backpack and crashed onto the couch.

Jess wasn't home yet, and in his absence, even through the distractions of financial talk, I sensed an odd kind of tension between the two of us. She had been folding laundry when I came in, and I noticed among the pile of her own bras and panties a few of Jess's T-shirts and briefs. This, when the three of us had had a long tradition of doing our own laundry.

She saw me looking at the pile and laughed. 'Jess is so fucking lazy,' she said quickly, 'he asked if I'd do some of his stuff. Oh, wait, here!' and she fished through the pile until she found an old St. Pete's T-shirt of mine. 'I washed this for you. I found it in the bathroom, all smelly, so I threw it in.' She folded it meticulously and handed it to me like some kind of consolation prize.

'Thanks.' I laughed weakly, accepting it with an odd mixture of pity and contempt. *Why was she doing his laundry?* I asked myself. *When had my sister ever done* anyone's *laundry, including her own?*

'And anyway, Tigger, I don't think Jess meant what he said this morning,' she added nervously, breaking her own rule. 'He's just—you know how he is. It's probably just some old Spanish thing in his genes. You know: you shouldn't speak ill of the dead, or speak of their money until after the acceptable passage of time.'

'You don't have to defend Jess to me,' I answered with little grace.

'I *wasn't!*'

'Whatever. Go on.'

'Anyway,' she continued awkwardly. 'I mean, there's gotta be the money in the will to cover it, and then some, right? Either in cash or stocks or bonds, right?'

'I'd think so.'

'So, I mean, if can just get Kittredge to execute it a little earlier, we should be in the clear.'

'I guess so,' and it occurred to me a second after the fact that I hadn't even flinched when she said *we*. What if Jess and I had to hand over parts of our inheritance to bail her out? We'd do it, I knew—and I knew that Flip knew we'd do it too, to the point that the matter need hardly be mentioned.

We heard the heavy tread of Jess's boots on the stairs. 'Oh, shit, he's home,' Flip hissed, and turned furiously back to folding the laundry.

'Flip!' I said sharply.

'What?'

'*Take it easy.*'

She looked at me, laughed helplessly, and threw down two mismatched socks she clutched in her hand. 'You're right,' she said. 'God, I'm so uptight today.'

The door opened, and Jess struggled in with a covered canvas. 'Hey,' he called to us across the loft. 'Did you guys see the video shoot on Broome Street? Veronica Webb's over there.'

'Really?' Flip called back, her voice ascending to a hysterical pitch.

Really? I mimicked her, under my breath. I hoped this sudden demeanor of hers would pass, because I didn't like this new Flip at all.

I left early enough the next morning not to have to see who was coming out of whose bathroom, and on the way to the train I spotted Joey walking at a furious clip along the other side of Houston Street, head bent down and hands stuffed inelegantly in his coat pockets. I hadn't seen him in ages—he hadn't been going out much, and I assumed he was busy at the carpet showroom—and, stayed by the passage of cars, I called across the street to him, eager to play catch-up. He looked up, bewildered, like a fugitive who hears his name called out by the police, and stared back at me plainly (I'm quite sure), before abruptly turning the corner onto Broadway and disappearing into one of the stores in what seemed a redoubled panic.

I was so surprised by his behavior that I didn't even think to follow him. Instead, confounded, I continued on down Houston to the train, fighting a strange flash of paranoia: had everyone, including Cedric and Joey, heard about our freakish new living arrangement and were now avoiding us as though my two siblings and I wore scarlet letters visible to everyone but ourselves? And thus commenced another distracted, less-than-productive day; for the first time ever, I snapped at one of my students, a fish-lipped, flat-knuckled little girl on Beekman Place who refused to use her pinky finger when the sheet music called for it.

'No, Beatrice, your *pinky* on the D. Look,' and I clamped my own clammy fingers rather roughly over hers. 'Okay, see, "Old . . . Paint"—that's it— "Is . . . My . . . Po-NEE"—pinky on the *D*!'

'Ow!' she shouted, wrenching her hand out from under mine. 'You're *hurting* me.'

'I am?' I asked, rather startled.

'Yes!'

'Oh. Bea?'

'What?'

'I'm sorry.' I truly was—I was flushed with a strange surfeit of remorse. For a moment, I wondered if I should excuse myself to the LaFollette's lavish gilt bathroom.

She frowned at me. 'Well, you don't have to nearly cry about it, Tommy.'

'Hm?' I asked, distracted. All I could picture was that god-damned pile of laundry from the day before. 'No. You're right, Bea. I suppose I don't. So where were we?'

When I returned home early that evening, I found Flip lying on the couch, staring straight into space, oblivious to the raucous episode of *Oprah Winfrey* blaring on the TV set. I shrugged off my backpack and walked toward her, bracing myself for bad news.

'What is it?' I asked, nudging her legs aside and sitting down on the end of the couch.

She ran her hands through her dirty hair and blew out a long, defeated coil of breath. 'We're fucked, Tig. We're absolutely, totally fucked.'

'Why?'

'I talked to Kittredge today.' She seemed as if she could hardly go on.

'And?'

'And he told me he pulled out Ma's file today, and she left instructions that the will not be read for six months.'

'Why?'

'He explained it to me, but half of it went over my head, all his legal gobbledy-gook. Something to do with taxes.'

'Well—can't he just go ahead and open it now?'

'No. I begged him to. He said it would be violating his client's wishes, and that he could be debarred or something if anyone ever found out.'

'I can't believe it.'

'Believe it.'

'Didn't he tell you if you had any other options?'

She laughed darkly. 'He said I should take out a loan.'

'Did you tell him you couldn't?'

'Uh hunh. And he said he was very sorry, but there was nothing he could do. I don't think he ever liked me anyway. He just put up with me and all of my questions because of Ma.'

I pondered that one for a while. 'What are we gonna do?' I finally asked.

'I don't know,' she said blankly, then, with another bitter little laugh, 'I could sell myself, I guess.'

A moment later, Jess came home, bitching loudly that one of the custodians at the studio had dropped one of his canvases, and that he had had to spend two hours cleaning it of soot from the floor. Dully, Flip told him the news; he asked her all the same questions I had asked, and Flip and I flatly gave him the same dead-end responses.

'There's gotta be something we're missing here,' he finally said.

Flip snorted. 'Tell me what it is, and I'll act on it.'

'I don't know just yet. But there's gotta be something.'

Jess and I were hungry, and even though Flip didn't feel like getting off the couch, we dragged her out to the dingy little Chinese place around the corner. She snapped at the waitress when she brought fried spring rolls instead of steamed, dispatching the poor woman back to the kitchen virtually in tears. I waited for Jess to scold her for her imperiousness, but he said nothing, and we ate our miserable dinner in near silence, hurrying back to the loft so that Flip could change for work. We were hardly in the door when the phone rang. Jess picked it up.

'Hello?'

There was a long pause, during which Jess frowned and walked the phone into the far corner of the loft, his back to us.

'Wait a minute? When? When?' we heard him finally say, in something approaching a harsh whisper. 'Hold on . . . hold on . . . yeah, but wait . . . *shit!*' Then he hung up the phone.

'Who the hell was that?' Flip asked.

'Hm? Some fucking crank call, that's all.' He still had his back to us, busying himself with the day's mail.

'You certainly sounded interested.'

'I was trying to make out what the fuck they were saying.' He turned to us, and we stared at him, eyebrows raised. 'It was some kind of funky religious freak, I think. It was kind of funny, that's all.'

'Okay,' Flip said skeptically, and we all stood there for a moment in an almost comical triangle.

In a moment, the phone rang again. 'I'll get it,' Jess and I said simultaneously, and we ended up engaging in an odd little foot race for the phone, which I won.

'Hello?' I asked, glaring at him. He stood there, a nervous wreck, one arm outstretched, knee-jerk, for the receiver.

'Darling?' from the other end of the line. 'It's Lippy.'

'Hi, Lippy,' I responded, and Jess's whole body seemed to slacken with relief. He smiled at me strangely; I gave him a look as if to say *Honey, you're losing it*.

'How are you three? Are you hanging in?' Lippy asked breathlessly.

'We're hanging in. How about you?'

'Just the same, just the same.' Then, with a burst of exuberance, 'Oh, Tigger, darling, I'm so glad you're the first to know!'

'Know what?'

'Darling, I have some very peculiar news.'

'Lippy, what?'

'Oh, God! You're all going to think I'm awfully bourgeois and conventional.'

'Lippy, what *is* it?' By this point, Jess and Flip had crowded near me, keen with curiosity.

'Tigger—I hope you simply won't hate me, but—Langley proposed! We're getting married!'

'Married?' I echoed, astonished, and Flip brought both hands to her mouth to stifle a cry.

Nineteen

Despite the financial dilemma of the moment, Flip insisted that we throw some kind of engagement party for Lippy and Langley. And so, the following Sunday afternoon, with the matter of the fifty-four thousand dollars as unresolved as it had been a week before, we opened up one of the VIP rooms at The Box to host a brunch for Lippy and Langley and their longtime circle of friends—mostly gregarious middle-aged theater people, some who, like Lippy and Langley, had carved out a fair degree of success for themselves, others who were still struggling valiantly to find that niche, acting in industrials or working as legal proofreaders, seeming all the more nervously gregarious for their unfinished journeys. Of course Grant was there, his harem now whittled down merely to the ever-lovely Janine, and when I asked him privately how this had come about, he fumbled sheepishly around an answer, awkward for the first time I could ever remember, and I wondered if he had had his first experience with a romantic scenario where he hadn't come out unscathed. Anthea, Katja and Miko showed up as well, as did Cedric, who brought flowers for Lippy. Joey, however, was in absentia.

'She's not doing so hot, Tigger,' Cedric confided to me when the two of us settled into a corner with Bloody Marys and plates of catered omelettes and muffins. 'And she's not facing up to facts.' I hadn't really spent much time with Cedric in recent weeks, and I noticed now how tired he looked, especially around the eyes.

I stared down into my omelette. 'Is it that?' I began.

He nodded slowly. 'More or less. She says she's fine, that she's been checked out and all, but I know it's a lie. All the signs are there. She was sick all winter. She's lost, like, twenty-five pounds . . . not that she couldn't use it, 'cause she *was* a pudgy little belly dancer. She can hardly finish a sentence without breaking out into this cough that works my last nerve.'

'Is he going to the doctor?' I asked.

'On and off,' Cedric harrumphed. 'When she's really sick. The doctor told her what she's gotta do—you know, that she's gotta face facts and get on some serious medications, that nasty AZT and shit. But she's, like, in complete denial. She won't even tell her parents, and you know them—they think they're still back in glamorous Beirut before the war started. They can't deal with nothin'. She keeps saying that it's all just from the long winter, then she blames *me* 'cause I couldn't go to Miami with her this year to take the sun.'

'Why didn't you go?' For as long as I could remember, Cedric and Joey went to South Beach for three weeks in February, to 'take the sun' and to debut the drag apparel they had been collecting all winter.

'Child, I couldn't go because I've been on 24-7 call for my mother up in the Bronx all winter. She's going crazy on me, Tigger. She calls me in the middle of the night thinkin' she's back in Georgia as a little girl and people are trying to burn down the house. I got to pull myself out of bed and get on the goddam train at two in the morning and go up there to spend the night with her. Then I got to help her make her breakfast in the morning. Then I go to work and I'm buggin' the whole time that she's flippin' out, or wandering the streets.'

'Do they think it's—you know?'

'Old-timer's disease? You got it. I'm probably gonna have to move up there soon 'cause I can't afford a nursing home for her, and I don't wanna put her in one. Maybe I can hire one of the ladies in the neighborhood to look after her during the day.' He paused, shaking his head. 'So *now* you know why I couldn't go jetsetting off to Miami this winter with the ailing Miss Barbara Ghanoosh.'

'How about you?' I asked. 'Are you okay that way?'

'Yeah, I'm okay, last I checked. Not that it's much consolation.'

I put my hand over his beefy arm. He seemed so beaten down that I could hardly remember the blond-wigged, big-thighed Cedric-Urethra who used to run screaming around the loft on a Saturday night, lipsyncing to Gloria Gaynor.

'Tigger, between my girl Barbara and my moms, I'm just so low, baby. I can't *remember* the last time I really carried on.'

'Ced, I'm so sorry. You know I'm always here for you.'

'Thank you, baby,' he grumbled. 'It ain't like you haven't had your own little slice of the tragedy pie, lately.'

'I guess so.'

'You miss your man?'

'Kind of. Yeah, I do,' I amended myself, with more directness than I had intended. 'I guess I had it coming to me.'

'Well, you got your little kingdom to tend to,' Cedric said, gesturing around at The Box. 'And Miss Sebastiana never really featured being one of the subjects in Flip's royal court.'

'This is true,' I murmured absently. Across the room, over by the buffet table, Flip and Jess were listening to Langley and Lippy animatedly coauthor an anecdote. Cedric and I picked at our plates, watching them silently.

'Suddenly, all these happy twosomes,' he finally mused. I said nothing. 'It's a good thing Jess is adopted, isn't it?' he continued casually. 'Otherwise, that would be some freaky shit.'

I was startled by his candor. 'Does everybody know about that?'

'Everybody pretty much knows how he left his proud negress for his vivacious yet crazy sister-by-law, if that's what you mean.'

It was almost comforting to hear it put so casually, and I laughed. 'Do you think it's fucked up?' I asked him.

He sipped at his Bloody Mary, seeming to ponder this question. 'If I didn't know them so well, I'd think so. But watching them all these years—no. I'd say it was either bound to happen, or someone was gonna go crazy.'

'Maybe someone is.'

'Child! Are you not having it?'

'Well,' and I squirmed, confronted with all my confusion. 'I mean, it's not really relevant whether I have it or not—it's still there. The question is—I guess it's whether or not I should get out of the picture.'

Cedric looked at me shrewdly. 'It must be hard watching your brother and sister all shacked up together when you all hot for one of them.'

'Cedric!' He had made me upset some of my drink on my lap, leaving a bright crimson stain there. 'What makes you say a thing like that?'

'Child, please—I've watched you all for three years now. White folks are so easy to read.'

A spoon clinking on a champagne glass interrupted our conversation. It was Flip, striding to the middle of the room, already tanked on mimosas. 'People, people!' she declared in her favorite center-of-attention voice. 'Please gather around. I'd like to make some toast—I mean, make a toast.'

And so we all did, Lippy and Langley shyly holding hands just to Flip's right. Lippy was beaming, at once joyful and awkward. I wondered, too, if she had any idea about Jess and Flip. Probably not—very often, Lippy was capable of seeing only what she wanted to see and ignoring what she didn't,

especially with regard to those she loved, and even if she privately acknowledged what was going on, I knew, especially
with our mother now gone, that she'd resolutely never let on.
You had to do something really egregious to pierce Lippy's
fierce armor of *live and let live.*

'Now, I know it's barbaric to have called you all here so
early on a Sunday,' Flip began, and everybody laughed—it
was three in the afternoon—'but last week my brothers and I
received a phone call from our Auntie Lippy. At first, we were
scared. Very scared.'

More laughter. Flip was in rare form.

'I mean, with Lippy married, half the theater queens in New
York are going to lose their dinner date.'

Another burst of knowing laughter. Langley was smiling
stiffly, I noticed.

'But I don't think she'd ever do such a thing. After all, we all
know that Lippy's greatest love will always be Manhattan. We
all know that her door will remain open to all of us lost souls.
Only now, that door will lead into a bigger apartment.'

'With a river view, too!' Lippy interjected gaily, squeezing
Langley's arm.

'And a butler to receive her guests,' Flip added.

Langley, deferring to the general roast, bowed stiffly and
announced, 'You rang?', in his best Boris Karloff voice.

'And so,' Flip continued, 'fully assured in the knowledge
that she shall remain in the public domain, I'd like to propose
a toast.' Everyone quieted down respectfully, glasses in hand.
'To a woman who has been not only the best auntie that any
wide-eyed newcomer to New York could ever ask for, but also
a surrogate mother— and a friend— and a shopping compan-
ion. And to a man who knows not only how to take a woman
out on the town, but also how to get her home before breakfast. You have all our best wishes, and all our love. Lippy and
Langley— *Felicitations.*'

'*Felicitations!*' the crowd called back, breaking out into a round of 'For They're a Jolly Good Fellow,' rendered, as always at gatherings of Lippy and Langley's showbiz friends, in impromptu and startlingly polished three-part harmony.

There were hugs and kisses all around, and Flip sauntered over to Jess, Cedric and me and asked, 'Well?'

'You were brilliant, darling,' I responded, kissing her upraised hand.

'The girl with the golden tongue,' Cedric added.

Flip laughed, pleased with herself. 'Wouldn't you just like to find out, Cederica!'

'That's okay, baby,' Cedric snapped her back. 'I'm afraid to say I'm not in *that* little club.'

We all kept our smiles, but the effect of his remark was palpable. 'Don't feel bad, darling,' Flip finally salvaged with a vicious grin. 'You've got to be born into it.' And with that, she sauntered off to the bathroom, leaving the three of us standing there, at a total loss.

Jess looked like he wanted to crawl under the rug. 'Fierce mimosas,' he finally said, absurdly.

'Mmmm,' Cedric replied, dramatically sipping from his glass. '*Toxic.*'

In a moment Flip was back, having retouched her face and smoothed back her hair. 'I've got to slip out for a moment,' she said to Jess and me quietly. 'Can you pay the caterers?—the check's on my desk in the back. I'll be back in time to open up the club.'

'There's a party going on,' I said. 'Where are you going?'

'I just have to slip out for a minute,' she said impatiently. And it was then that I turned toward the far entryway to the room, first Jess, then Flip and Cedric following my line of sight.

'Oh, for God's sakes,' Flip hissed, annoyed. 'Why didn't he stay up front?'

It was Goolsbee, lounging expectantly in the doorway, staring at us with that old bemused squinty smile, impressively sleek in a fur-collared suede car coat, super high-tech ski goggles propped up on his head. When he saw that he had caught our attention, his smile broadened and he waved us a cheery hello.

None of us waved back. 'What the fuck is he doing here?' Jess asked, low, turning darkly on Flip.

Flip shrugged. 'I told him I'd have coffee with him.'

'Today of all days?' I asked.

'He's very busy,' she answered. 'It was the only day he could make it.'

'Why are you having coffee with him in the first place?'

'Because, Tigger, it was sweet of him to send us those flowers. And because he's not as bad a guy as you think he is. And because I think he's lonely.'

'Sweet Charity,' Cedric observed.

'So you're leaving the party that *you* organized to go have coffee with Goolsbee just because he sent you flowers?' Jess asked.

Flip sighed, irritated. 'It's not like I'm going to Cancun with him for the weekend.'

'Why the hell don't you?' Jess asked.

She stood there for a moment, lips pursed. 'Look, I'm not going to have a fight with you about this now. I've got to go. I won't be long.' And she insisted on giving us all a peck on the cheek before she fished her own sunglasses out of her pocket and strode away.

'Take your time,' Jess called back.

At the entryway, Flip loosely grabbed Goolsbee's sleeve to drag him along, leaving him just enough time to wave at us again and mouth a smug 'Bye-bye.'

'She is unbelievable,' Jess said quietly, watching her go.

Cedric looked at him, eyebrow raised once again. 'Isn't she allowed to have a coffee klatsch?'

Jess looked as though he were about to respond unkindly, but thankfully Lippy killed the moment when she descended on us, face flushed with champagne. 'Tigger, darling,' she said, wiping a bit of muffin away from my mouth. 'Can you play "Bosom Buddies" from *Mame* on the piano? Langley and his friend Clayton want to entertain us with song.'

'I can play that, yeah.' I swapped glances with Cedric, standing by with a smile tugging at his lips, eyebrow still held comically aloft.

By five, the engagement party had broken up and Flip hadn't yet returned, leaving a brooding Jess and me to help the caterers pack up and depart. By eight, when Anthea soddenly arrived, Flip still hadn't shown. Jess and I helped Anthea open up the club, then, tired from the afternoon's goings-on, retreated to the back office. I worked on music theory for the next day's class and Jess sulked over *ArtForum*, talking only to ask me for the occasional cigarette, or if I wanted to order in Thai food from the place around the corner.

It was nearly midnight when Flip came barging into the back office, rousing the two of us from our dozing.

'Hi,' she said casually, hanging up her coat and sitting down with a cigarette, as though she had stepped out for ten minutes.

'Where the hell have you been?' Jess mumbled, propping himself up on the couch.

'With Goolsbee,' she said, walking to her desk to pick up some book-keeping. 'He wanted to go to dinner in Chelsea, so I went with him.'

'How lovely for you,' Jess said, glaring.

'It was, thank you.' She didn't look up from the books. 'I had the biggest, bloodiest steak you've ever seen.'

Jess kept glaring at her until he turned to me. I said nothing, glanced back down into my book. When I glanced up again, he had retrained his eyes on her, ominously, but she gave every impression that she was absorbed in the books.

'We did well last weekend,' she finally commented neutrally. Neither of us answered. Outside, I could make out Pepe's warpy remix of Madonna's 'Justify My Love'. I glanced then at Flip, caught her looking warily at Jess.

'So guess what?' she said, before retraining her eyes blandly on the ledger. Again, neither of us answered. 'So guess what?' she repeated, more heavily.

'What?' I finally asked.

'The Box is saved. I got the money.'

Jess wouldn't take his head out of his magazine, but I saw him look at her out of the corner of his eye.

'From where?' I asked.

'From Goolsbee,' and I couldn't believe the maddening casualness with which she withdrew an envelope from her coat pocket and opened it. 'Look,' she said. 'It's a cashier's check for sixty-thousand dollars. He had it cut for me on Friday.'

'So you obviously went to him for help, then?' I asked. Jess refused to look up, acknowledge this transaction—he sat there fake-reading like a Rodin.

'Of course I did,' Flip answered lightly. 'Where else was I supposed to go?'

'So now Goolsbee's a partner in the club, I guess?'

'Of course not, Tigger. It's a loan. Interest free. I'll pay him back as soon as the will is executed.'

'And Goolsbee gets nothing in return for his generosity?' I asked.

'Nope. Just me, that's all.'

'So he basically owns you now.'

She laughed blithely. 'Let's just say he's leasing me.'

'I see.'

'At least I'm not out of a job.' She looked at Jess, daring him to say or do something, but he didn't.

'No,' I answered, feeling ill. 'It sounds like you found yourself a new one.'

Again, the blithe laugh. 'You could look at it that way. Isn't it all a relief, Jess? I saved the family business.'

Jess stood up, closed his magazine with a terrible control. He grabbed his coat. 'Good-night,' he said flatly, to no one in particular, and walked out the door. For a moment, Pepe's bass line and ululating synth blasted into the office, muffled a second later as Jess closed the door, firmly and gently behind him.

'Are you crazy?' I asked her.

She looked at me and shrugged. 'Lippy looked so beautiful today, didn't she? Did you like those caterers? I didn't. Didn't you think those omelettes were awfully runny?'

Jess wasn't at the loft when I returned there shortly afterwards, and he wasn't there the next morning when the phone rang only moments after I had emerged from the bathroom.

'Is Jess Ramirez there?' asked a man's voice, cool and measured.

Jess Ramirez? I thought to myself. 'Do you mean Jess Mitchell?'

'Um . . . yes. Jess Mitchell.'

'Well, no, he's not here. Can I take a message?'

'Um . . . yes. Would you tell him to call—' The voice stopped dead. I heard the steady rhythm of breathing on the other end. Then a click.

'Who was that?' Flip asked, wandering sleepy-eyed out of her room.

'For Jess. But then they hung up.'

'Who was it?'

'I don't know.'

'Hm,' she grunted, putting on coffee. 'Is Jess up?'

'He didn't come home last night.'

She turned. 'He didn't?'

'No.'

'Really?'

I frowned at her. 'Well, does it really surprise you that much?'

'I don't know what he's so upset about,' she protested. 'Does he really think I've signed myself over to that scumbag?'

'Well, that's certainly the impression you gave him.'

She lit a cigarette, exacerbating her morning rasp. 'So let him wonder a little bit. It's good for him. Nobody owns me, Tigger.'

'But you own everybody, right, Flip?' I snapped back, retreating into the bathroom to take a shower before she could respond. Under the hot water, I wondered where Jess had gone off to—Damienne's? Unlikely, I thought. I myself wished I had some other place to go—the situation between the three of us was becoming unbearable—but I wasn't going to impose on Lippy at the beginning of her engagement (besides, she'd desperately want to know why I couldn't deal with the loft), and I'd be damned if I was going to go crawling back to Seb, much as I'd have liked to. After my shower, I hastily dressed and assembled my backpack, including a few changes of underwear and some toiletries just in case.

'I'm planning a special little something at The Box on Thursday night to celebrate paying off the debt,' she announced as I was on my way out. 'You'll be there, right?'

I turned. 'Is Goolsbee gonna be there as your benefactor?'

She shrugged. 'Well, that would only be appropriate, wouldn't it?'

'Then I'm afraid I'll have to decline,' I said coldly, before closing the door behind me.

Dully, I sat through classes all afternoon, then decided to pay Joey a surprise visit, whether he liked it or not. I trained down to 23rd Street, then buzzed his apartment at London Terrace. There was a brief pause after I announced myself, and I wondered if he was going to beg off, but in a moment he buzzed me in and the elevator man was taking me up to his apartment on the fifth floor overlooking the courtyard.

'It's open,' he called from within when I rang his bell. Inside, the apartment was gloomy and a bit unkempt. It was well-appointed (all the fine Middle Eastern carpets certainly helped), but I hadn't been there in ages and I couldn't remember what was old or new except for the enormous framed travel poster from the late 1950s that showed a glamorous, sophisticated Beirut with the inscription 'Découvrez les trésors de Liban!' Apparently, Joey's father had been a prosperous merchant in this thriving, cosmopolitan Beirut, and Joey well on his way to studying political philosophy at the American University of Beirut, until the worsening civil wars forced much of the Christian ruling class out of the country in the late 1970s. They moved to a comfortable house in Forest Hills, in Queens, but Joey's memories of this city on the Mediterranean had stayed so vivid that he still spoke with ease of streets and neighborhoods, intricately linked families and social ties, plush Franco-Arab restaurants and chic late-night cafés full of the latest music from America, often to the point that people assumed he had only arrived in New York a month ago.

He was sitting in an armchair by the window in a bathrobe and sunglasses, sipping tea, watching a talk show, his fat old Siamese Maria balled up in his lap, purring loudly. Approaching him and finally discerning his face in the half-light, I was shocked to see how much weight he had lost, how sunken his cheeks looked underneath the ridiculously over-sized aviator glasses.

'Hey, *habibi*,' I said, bending down to kiss him hello, then settling on an ottoman nearby. 'I was in Chelsea and thought I'd come by and say hello.'

He smiled thinly and stroked Maria, who arched her old back contentedly. 'Long time no see,' he said, before coughing so harshly I could understand why Cedric had said that it worked his last nerve.

'Honey, you don't look so hot,' I laughed, hoping to cut to the chase in an agreeably light-hearted fashion.

'I know,' he wheezed dramatically. 'Can you believe it's the beginning of spring and I still have this horrible winter cold?'

His words chilled me; Cedric was right—he was in complete denial. 'That's pretty strange. What's up with the sunglasses? I can't see your soulful brown Arabic eyes.'

'The TV was straining them,' he answered flatly, with no suggestion of removing them. He pointed a skinny finger at the talk show, some unintelligible, crosstalking nonsense. 'This fifteen-year-old girl from Ohio is president of the John Wayne Gacy Fan Club,' he announced neutrally. 'They write to each other every week. Isn't that brilliant?'

'That's some fucked-up shit.'

He shrugged. 'At least she's keeping busy.'

'That's true.' He had a studiedly indifferent affect that chilled me; it seemed he was trying to make it clear to me that he didn't care whether I was an old and best friend, or some clinically cheerful volunteer from a shut-in agency come to deliver his free hot meal. Maria pressed her flank sensuously against the fur-matted front of his bathrobe, and he leaned in to purr something to her in Arabic. I had an odd flash of paranoia—surely the cat understood Arabic (how could she not, after all these years with Joey?), and he was saying something nasty and conspiratorial to her about me right now: *Don't worry, my habibi, he shall be gone soon and it shall be just the two of us again.*

Then, as if to mollify my suspicions, he turned back to me and said with weary generosity, 'She needs a good brushing, but I just told her to be patient and I'd do it tonight after dinner.'

'Oh,' I laughed, relieved. 'So she's a diva kitty?'

He shrugged again, with elaborate indifference, as if to say *Why shouldn't she be?* I felt a growing sense of frustration in the face of his studiously bland ennui.

'So did you hear about Lippy and Langley?' I attempted.

'No. What about them?'

'They're getting married! You haven't heard?'

'No. Why should I have? I haven't talked to any of you in ages.'

I swallowed back the guilt—he was right, after all. We hadn't seen each other since some time in February, but we had simply thought that he was too busy with his father's business to be going out much. Cedric hadn't spoken a word of his condition to any of us until we sat alone together at yesterday's brunch.

'Cedric didn't tell you?' I continued.

He startled me by breaking out into a shrill, spiky laugh that ended in a fit of coughing. 'That blue-black cunt?' he rasped with new vigor when he had collected himself. 'Let me tell you something about *her*, habibi. Maybe if I hadn't spent all my time with *her* these past six years, I wouldn't be sitting here now with nobody but my fucking *cat*.' His sunglasses had started sliding down his nose, and as soon as he saw that I had a glimpse of his recessed eyes, he pushed them back up clumsily. 'I'm sorry, baby,' he said to the startled Maria, who had looked up at him querulously when he sputtered the word *cat*. 'Don't listen to me.' Then his face chalked over and he slumped back into his easy chair, spent.

'You know he's going through a hard time with his mother right now?' I ventured.

'Yes, I know that,' he drawled, waving his hand dismissively. 'Poor put-upon Cedric, she has to work those construction sites all day, then expend the rest of all her big, brawny good health on the ailing. She's an angel of mercy.'

'Would you take off those fucking glasses and look me in the face?' I finally exclaimed, reaching for the Ray-Bans, unable to tolerate another minute of his evasive irony. Gasping, he reached up to keep them in place, but he was too late. I had snatched them away, and now he stared at me, full of rage and humiliation, out of eyes that seemed to have shrunk far back into his skull. He lifted his hand to shield them in what he meant to be an elegant gesture, but he only looked awkward, like a marionette jerked into an ungainly posture, and suddenly I was overcome with a genuine, queasy fear for his life.

'Why don't you get some help for yourself before it's too late, Joey? You've got the money. You can't make excuses.'

'What do you think I am, an idiot?' he hissed back at me, and Maria, frightened, pounced off his lap and lumbered into the other room. 'Don't you think I looked into it? Because I did, Tigger. But I was too late. What do you think my T-cell count was by the time I finally had it checked?'

'What?' I murmured, chastened suddenly.

'Twenty-seven. *Twenty-seven!* And it's dropped since then. I'm past the point of any therapies. It's my own fucking fault, all right, because I waited so long to get help.'

'Well, *why?*'

'Because I was an idiot, Tigger, all right? I was like—why stop partying as long as you know someone's going to be there for you at the end of the party? You know? If someone's gonna be there, that means it all counted for something, right?'

I didn't quite understand his reasoning, but I didn't question it either. 'If you mean Cedric, he *is* there for you,' I said instead. 'She's just going out of her mind right now watching all the people she loves—' I didn't bother to finish the thought.

'I feel bad for her,' he said, free of sarcasm. 'I can sit here quietly watching *Geraldo* until my day comes—and it will, soon—and pretty soon his mama's gonna be completely in la-la land—but *she's* got to go on and on. And habibi, I can't imagine there's anything worse than having to go on and on. What . . . a . . . *drag.*'

His words had the ring of eternal damnation to them, spooking me. 'Cedric's tough,' I said.

He harrumphed, in a fair imitation of Cedric himself. 'How old are you now, Tigger?'

'Almost twenty-two.'

He was thoughtful a moment, then asked: 'Have you—no, forget it. You're probably too young.'

'Have I what?' Maria crept back in and climbed tentatively back onto his lap, staring at me shrewdly. The TV programming switched over to *Oprah*.

'Haven't you ever kept on doing stupid things because you basically felt like someone was watching out for you? Like, when your little party of life is over, when everybody has paired up and gone home, you're not gonna be there alone with the mess?'

His words rang a faint, irritatingly admonitory bell. I wondered if he knew about Seb. I wondered if he knew about Jess and Flip. And I wondered what he thought about me. 'I hope I've at least got a good cleaning crew,' I finally quipped, wanting to shrug off this chafing stab at existentialism on his part.

He looked at me, calmly retrieved his sunglasses from my lap and put them back on, then thought better of it, took them off, looked at me again, bemused. 'So do I, Thomas,' he said. 'So do I.'

I squirmed briefly in our uncomfortable silence. 'I guess I should get going,' I finally said, unable to sit here with him through another idiotic talk show. 'Look, Joey, is there anything I can do? Can I bring you anything? I can stop by most days after class, you know.'

'That's all right, habibi. She's cunty, but she does run most of my errands for me.'

'You want to come to the loft for dinner some night, if you feel up to it?'

'I'm sure Flip doesn't want some withered mess cramping her glamorous scene.'

Again, I was rather shocked at other people's perceptions of Flip—even the perceptions of those people, like Joey, who purportedly knew her well. 'Do you really think Flip is that shallow, Joey? You're one of her oldest friends—she *loves* you.'

'It's not Flip, per se,' he said. 'It's her whole world. It belongs to the beautiful.'

'Only if you let it.'

'Tigger,' he repeated, more sternly. 'It belongs to the beautiful.'

I remembered the night I stayed home from The Box because I had two enormous zits on my face that no amount of Flip's concealing lotion would efface, and thought best not to go on battling Joey on this uncomfortable point.

'Will you call me anytime?' I asked, bending down to kiss his concave cheek. 'I'll come to visit in a few days, okay? You want some porn videos or something?'

'No, thanks. I don't need to see what I'm missing. Maybe some incense, or candles, or something.'

'Definitely,' I said, taking up my backpack. 'Take care, habibi.'

'Take care.' He turned back to the TV as though I had already walked out the door, toward which I ventured awkwardly. My hand was nearly upon the knob when he called back to me.

'Uh hunh?'

'Are you in a hurry?'

'Not especially, no.'

'There is something you can do for me.'

'Of course.' I doffed my backpack.

'It's not the kind of thing I'd ask just anybody to do.'

'You wanna hand job?' I laughed.

'No. Decidedly not. It's just—my back aches from sitting all day. Do you know how to give a little backrub?'

'Sure. I'm not a Swedish masseur or anything, but I'm okay. You wanna lie down for it?'

'I guess that'd make sense, wouldn't it?'

I helped him out of the armchair and toward the bed. He

had never been muscular like Cedric, but he had his share of mass—they had both looked like full-figured gals in dresses. But his heft was gone now, and when I laid him gently on his bed and he creakily raised his arms over his head so that I could take off his T-shirt, I couldn't believe just how much his back and shoulders had narrowed, how the skin now hung slack over the places once voluptuous with flesh and muscle, how the spine protruded knobbily all the way down to the waist of his pajama bottoms.

'Press the tape deck,' he said, his lips against the pillow. I did—it was that sad old ballad 'I'm Wishing on a Star' sung by Rose Royce, who had sung all the music for the movie *Car Wash*.

'There's baby oil in the drawer,' he said now, already groggy. I found it, rolled up my sleeves, poured a small amount in the center of his back and spread it around in a rolling motion with my fingertips, into the exaggerated clefts of his shoulder blades, up to the bony nape of his neck.

He purred happily. 'Thank you, Tigger. Sometimes I wonder if this was ever all I really needed.'

'What?' I asked.

'To be touched.'

He spoke to me a few moments later, half-asleep.

'Uh hunh?' I whispered back.

'I'm sorry about your mother. That must have been hard.'

'Oh. That's okay. I mean, thank you.'

'Ced told me. Mmmmm. Feels so nice.'

Five minutes later, he was fast asleep, dark lids closed thickly and mercifully over those stricken eyes. I turned off the tape, wiped off my hands, nearly stumbled on the cat. I thought to brush her, and much to my surprise, she complied when I approached her with the bristles, resuming her uncannily loud purring by the touch of the third stroke. I cleaned up Joey's place a bit, stacking magazines and rinsing out dirty things in the sink. It was seven o'clock by then—time for me to go home, I supposed. But acutely, I didn't want to. And it wouldn't be pleasant for Joey to wake up in an empty house, I reasoned, when I had been here last.

So I didn't make much ado about it. I kicked off my shoes, turned out the lights, and compressed myself onto Joey's couch under a batikish quilt. In a moment I felt the warm buzz of Maria scooching into the crook behind my knees, and in another thick, distended moment, I was quite thoroughly asleep.

Twenty

Through a kind of sullen, stubborn inertia, I ended up staying at Joey's all week, which turned out to be not such a bad thing. In the morning, I'd fix us both breakfast, before leaving him in front of the morning shows and heading off to classes (I was to graduate in the middle of June) or to lessons, and in the evening I'd come home to him with groceries to make us dinner. We got on well—he wouldn't admit it, but I knew he had been lonely, and the cool hostility he demonstrated upon my initial visit soon enough fell away to the comfortable fabric of our old friendship. He didn't ask me why I was avoiding my own home, and if he had his suspicions, he was gracious enough not to voice them. More than once that week, I implored him to go to the doctor yet again and see what could still be done before he had to be rushed to the hospital. Blandly, he said he would 'look into it,' and, not in the least satisfied but essentially stymied, I left it at that.

Thursday night passed—I thought fleetingly of Flip's 'salvage' party in honor of Goolsbee, asserted for the umpteenth time that I wouldn't attend so heinous an event, and put it solidly out of mind.

Cedric stopped by the next day after work in overalls, flannel shirt and work boots—what he referred to thickly as his 'construction drag.'

'It's my little cous-cous and my little runaway urchin,' he announced, kissing us both before unloading groceries for Joey. 'Habibi,' he called to Joey from the kitchen doorway, brandishing a box of Product 19. 'I brought you your favorite fitness food.'

'I don't like that kind anymore,' Joey sulked. He talked about Cedric virtually all day long, but when Cedric finally showed, he made a special point of treating him as icily as possible.

But Cedric was in high spirits and wouldn't be fazed. 'Oh, you'll like them, baby. And you'll eat them. Child!' he bellowed at me, coming out of the kitchen. 'You weren't Chez Box last night for the salvage party.'

'No, I wasn't, obviously,' I prickled.

'And neither was Miss Jessica.'

'Oh, he wasn't? Well, that doesn't surprise me.'

'Well, that's too bad,' he said, sitting down and reaching for a Newport before thinking better of it (that cough of Joey's, after all), 'because you missed the *scariest, nastiest, fiercest* drama of the century.'

'And what would that be?' I asked indifferently. 'Did some child model go in a K-Hole and fall down the stairs to her death?'

'Hardly that mundane.'

'So? What happened?'

'If I'm gonna tell you a good story, you better perk up and appreciate it.'

'Okay. I'm appreciating it.'

He frowned at me reprovingly before beginning. 'Well. You know how last night was a little party so Miss Flip could thank that Amos Ghoulish for the money to help pay the taxes on Tara?'

'Of course I do. Why do you think Jess and I didn't go?'

'Oh, children, you wish you had!'

'*Why?*'

'I'm coming around! Don't rush a juicy story. Anyway, so that's just what it was—you know, some of the usual crowd, but that Ghoulish, too—what's her name, anyway?'

'Goolsbee,' I said sourly.

'That's it, Girlsbee. Anyway, so this Girlsbee shows up—he *is* a good-looking motherfucker, ain't he?'

'I guess so,' I conceded. Cedric nodded, satisfied, settled into a lumpy old chair, and proceeded to tell us the story.

It had been a heavy crowd that night, not unusual for a Thursday, and among this crowd were Goolsbee and a pack of his Wall Street friends. Goolsbee was taking great relish in telling everyone that would listen how it had been *he* who had saved the club, and how Flip was now his own 'Pretty Woman.' His whole posse had arrived drunk, and they proceeded to get drunker, until they had their paws all over the women, and were saying rude things to the gayboys, and were feeling up some of the better-looking drag queens. ('Girl, you could smell "closet case" on some of them Wall Street dudes from a mile away,' Cedric insisted.) Every time a black woman passed them, they started shouting 'Yo, yo, hootchie, yo baby, you got back!', and other things that they had apparently picked up off of MTV, according to Cedric.

'Gross,' I interjected.

'I know, right? Child, I was *not* having it an' I was just about to smack their skinny little motherfuckin' heads, when Flip comes over, all sweet and sexy, and she says to me, "Now, Cedric, these guys ain't so bad, you just gotta give 'em a chance an' you'll find out they're real nice guys." And I whisper to her, "Flip, you gone crazy?", but she just laughs at me and starts drinkin' round after round of God-knows-what with them, and they're sayin' all sorts of nasty things to her about her body and shit, and things like, "Flip, why you hang around with all these faggots and drag queens when you could be hangin' out with us?" And she just says,

"Oh, I don't know, I guess they entertain me," and by then she's sittin' in this Girlsbee's lap and he's got his hands up and down her leg, and that's when I just had to get away from there and go off and find Miss Pepe and Miss Kristal Kleer and say, "What is up with that girl? I am not *having* her behavior tonight."'

'Ced,' I cried, dismayed. 'Why are you telling me all this shit?'

'Yes, Cedric, why *are* you?' Joey asked from his armchair.

''Cause *listen*, queens, a'ight?' And he proceeded.

People started dancing, including Goolsbee and his friends ('lookin' like fools out there, all actin' like monkeys and shit and thinkin' they're so funny'). Flip went out to join them until she was doing the lambada like some rent-a-girl for an office party. 'And just when I'm about to get my walk on and cut outta there,' Cedric said, Flip called for the music to settle down and climbed up on the stage. Goolsbee and his Wall Street posse started applauding and wolf whistling—and Flip, 'though I know she's *really* tanked by this time,' affirmed Cedric, seemed to be utterly in control.

She waited for the crowd to quiet, then cast a blessed smile upon the assembly. 'People, people. *Please*. Tonight—' and she stopped, waiting for her drunken ovation to subside. 'Thank you. Tonight, I'm happy to inform you that today I cashed a check that helped me save our Breeders Box from extinction. That means we're all going to keep on partying into the '90s!'

The shouts and hollers rose up again.

'Thank you,' she continued. 'Now—this all wouldn't have been possible if it wasn't for the extreme generosity of someone who's very special to me. Amos Goolsbee, please come up here and join me.'

Goolsbee clambered up onto the stage until he was arm-in-arm with Flip, squint-smiling into the bright lights, 'in his little motorcycle boots that *I* was sportin' two years ago, hello,' Cedric added. His friends down below were laughing, but no

one else was, "cause they're just, like, "What's our Flip doin'
up there humpin' with that asshole?"'

Finally, Flip spoke down to the crowd: 'There's something
very special I'd like to share with you. You see, I promised Mr.
Amos Goolsbee here that if he wrote me the check that saved
our little den of misfits and freaks, he could do whatever he
damn well pleased with me for as long as he liked until I paid
him back. That's how much The Breeders Box means to me
and my two brothers.'

I turned to Cedric. 'She really said that?'

'Oh yes she did, honey.'

Then Flip just stood up there, smiling serenely. Goolsbee
started looking a little nervous, but all his friends were laughing and hooting, and he was forced to stand there, dumb, and
smile along.

Flip put her arm through Goolsbee's as though she didn't
want him to get away. 'So last night at his sumptuous coop, we
got down to business. First, Mr. Goolsbee poured me some
very fancy champagne, Veuve Cliquot seventy-something, I
think it was. Then Mr. Goolsbee put on some fine, *smooth*
music, Kenny G I think it was'—a wave of knowing laughter
from the crowd—'and then Mr. Goolsbee came out wearing
some *fine* European-cut bikini briefs, in a canary yellow, I
think it was.'

By now, Flip was having a fine time sharing this story, and
everybody in the crowd was hooting and laughing—except, of
course, Goolsbee.

'Come on, Flip,' he whispered to her through a frigid smile.
'That's enough, sweetheart. Put the music back on.'

Flip turned back to the crowd with a look of vaudeville
sympathy. 'Awwww, he wants me to put the music back on,
but I've got to tell the rest of the story, right?' ('And girl,'
Cedric added now, 'there be some *scary* glow in her eyes right
then. Like I never seen before.') The whole crowd, Goolsbee's
Wall Street friends especially, started chanting: *Finish! Finish!*

'So we get down to business,' Flip forged on, quieting the ruckus. 'And Mr. Goolsbee stands before me and pushes me down on my *knees*, in a very gentlemanly way, of course, and says, "Bitch, I've been waiting all these years for you to suck my dick, and now you're gonna do it."'

The crowd gasped, to Flip's delight. Goolsbee stood there, mortified, his legs crossed awkwardly. 'So I say, "All right, Amos, if you so desire,"' Flip continued. 'But the problem was'—and she stopped here to laugh her own frightening private laugh—'the *problem* was, his— uh, his *member* was so *little*, even fully erect, that I can't get it to stay in my *mouth*— it just keeps slipping out like a little hard candy!'

Flip cackled along with her audience, fully assured of her skills as a masterful raconteur. 'So then Mr. Goolsbee got all angry and shouted, "That's it, you smart-ass bitch—I'm going to fuck you 60,000 times for every dollar I gave you." Which would have been very thrilling, don't get me wrong—and he tried, but we had the same problem *again*—He just couldn't keep it in! In fact, half the time we couldn't even *find* the motherfucker, because it kept getting lost in his little pube-jungle!'

Waves of mirth. Flip and Goolsbee stood there, her hand clutched firmly around his arm, he powerless to strike back in front of all these people.

'Okay, now I know you all think that a bitter girl can go around telling nasty lies about a guy she hates . . . so just so you all know I'm not lying about this I'm going to prove it.'

She called offstage for Ty as well as the two enormous new bouncers, Miguel and Dino ('that Russian motherfucker, right?' from Cedric). In a second, the three of them bounded onto the stage and grabbed a shocked Goolsbee by the arms and legs. Flip bent over and unbuckled his belt, then pulled down his trousers and his underpants—Flip was right, he *did* wear microbriefs, this time in a vivid cobalt.

Flip stood back from the writhing, cursing Goolsbee and

gestured dramatically at his private parts. 'Now, look, people, what did I tell you? Am I correct?'

YEEEEEEEEEEEEESSSSSSS! One long roar from the crowd, Goolsbee's friends shouting loudest of all, laughing so hard they were spilling their beers all over each other. Flip hadn't lied—even up close, it was hard to discern anything in Goolsbee's private realm except for the tiniest, palest nib of an instrument.

Cedric stopped for a moment, and lowered his voice, sober. 'But then, Tigger, it gets worse. Kinda sad actually—even I had a little sympathy for the motherfucker.'

'What?' I demanded.

And he told me how the laughter and applause thundered on, Ty and Miggy and Dino still holding Goolsbee up, and Flip just standing there, triumphant, pointing to Goolsbee's over-whelming lack as though she were Vanna White showcasing a consolation prize. Then Pepe put down some vinyl—a thoroughly evil dance mix of 'It's A Small World After All' that Flip had asked him to whip up.

For Goolsbee, that was the breaking point. 'Let go of me, you motherfuckers!' he screamed through tears. 'Let go of me, you fuckin' faggot niggers and spics!'

'An' then, right there, guess what he did?' Cedric broached gravely.

'Oh no,' Joey groaned, predicting, and he was correct. Amidst the tussle, Goolsbee's beer-filled bladder gave way and he began urinating on himself before thousands of people—a miserable clear stream that fell unbidden from his privates and started to form a shining pool at his feet—provoking a new round of horrified jeers and laughter. Suddenly, I thought of Goolsbee at thirteen, hardly a teenager and rumored to have let his beloved little sister drown. I thought of him a year later, instructing Jess, St. Pete's other misfit and his only friend, in the game of tennis. And I thought of him that strange afternoon in Grant's gallery, looking eerie and beautiful in the sunlight that flooded the place where he stood. I remembered the flat, nervous mention of his dead sister; his insinuations about me and my brother and sister; his casual assertion that if money couldn't buy love directly, it at least could buy access to the channels of love. For a moment I was nauseous with pity, disgust and fear—and I knew, decidedly, that if I had been there on the night that Cedric was now recounting, I would have done everything in my power to stop Flip from doing the ghastly thing she had done.

'An' all of a sudden, Flip ain't smilin' anymore,' Cedric went on after the weight of this moment had settled, 'an' . . .'

Flip turned to Ty and Miggy and Dino. 'Let him go,' she commanded, low. They did, dropping him into the puddle of his own piss.

Flip stood over him and stared hard for a moment before she drew her booted leg back as far as she could and kicked him viciously in the ass. 'Get the *fuck* out of my club, you motherfucking piece of shit.' She was screaming now, and once again the entire club had fallen silent, including the music. 'Get the fuck out and don't you *ever*, *ever* come back or I'll kill you—I swear I will.'

Goolsbee slipped and slid his way up, drawing his soaked trousers high up around his stomach. 'You're going to pay, you cunt,' he said, as cool as if he were ordering a scotch. 'You're going to pay.'

He staggered off the stage then—the entire house could hear him running up the endless gyre of ramps and stairs, through the lobby and out the door. There was dead quiet in the house—no one said a word, even Goolsbee's friends who stood immobile in their blue-suited pack in an attitude of collective astonishment. For a moment it seemed as though anything could happen—good, bad or utterly alien.

And what happened was this. Flip, still onstage, turned and looked out across the entire shell-shocked crowd as though it was a legion of demons sent to vanquish her alone. Her whole face cracked open with one blood-chilling sob, followed convulsively by more.

'Nobody fucks with me—*ever!*' she screamed, her voice flying up stories and stories, all the way up to the fresco of Jess's nocturnal angel, wings outspread. 'Look at all I give to you,' she continued, trembling, gesturing wildly about her, indicating all the recesses of the grand room reverberating with her pronouncements.

'You stand by me. You *stand—by—me*. But you don't fuck with me, do you understand me? *Nobody!* Because I'll cut you—I swear to God, I will.'

She stood there shaking and glaring, both feet clamped to the stage floor, for what seemed like forever. Then she turned to a trembling Ty, Miggy and Dino and pointed to the pool of urine. 'Clean it up. You hear me, *clean it up.*' Her eyes shot up to the sound booth, where Pepe cowered in his seat, watching the scene from above. 'Play some fucking music goddamit! This is a motherfucking club!'

She waited, staring up at Pepe as though to curse him as an unyielding god, but the music came on immediately, loud and fierce and absurdly joyous. Finally, she stalked off the stage. The crowd should have exploded in a frenzy of gasps, screams and gags, and it did—but not until after a few unreal seconds when everyone remained frozen in place, mouths wide open, agape at what they had just witnessed.

Cedric sat there, with the self-satisfied look of having delivered a story well-told. Joey muttered something in Arabic.

'An' that's why you shoulda been there last night, Tigger,' Cedric concluded, then laughed. 'Or maybe you're glad you weren't there after all.'

I looked at Cedric, unable to speak, my face too seized-up with the absorption of all his breathless narrative. Out of all the random fragments and strands of the story, one in particular seemed to emerge again and again. People had called my sister all sorts of things: High-spirited, full of life, unstoppable, willful, charismatic, difficult, stubborn, electrifying . . . so many things, all of them more or less complimentary, more or less either evading or blunting in euphemism what I now knew, with absolute, unequivocal clarity to be true—she was crazy. She was ill. It was simply that.

Joey seemed to read my thoughts. 'She's not happy, habibi,' he said plainly. 'She needs help.'

'I know.' I could hardly hear myself saying the words. 'It's like— she's snapping, or something. Don't you think so?' I asked Cedric.

Cedric turned to me, still aglow with his narrative feats. 'Do I think what? That Miss Flip's crazy just because she showed up that motherfucker? Damn, no! You know our girl, Tigger. She gives as good as she gets. And that's what that goddamned fool deserved for thinkin' he put one over on her.'

'But the way she—' I began, but it was Cedric's frown, cautionary against my overreaction that stopped me. She wasn't crazy, I about-faced uneasily. Or, if she were, then who the hell *wasn't* in this unreal world we lived in?

'Does Jess know about this?' I finally asked Cedric.

'Uh hunh. He's been stayin' with Grant, 'cause obviously the three of you are havin' one of your little family dramas, but Miss Miko told me today that Anthea told him all about it in front of the Puck Building this morning.'

'And?'

'An' Jess told her that he was comin' back to the loft tonight. He ain't got no reason to be jealous now, Tigger. Mad-buggin', maybe, but not jealous.'

'Did Jess tell Anthea when he'd be back?'

'Honey, he didn't hand her a schedule, no.'

I considered a moment. 'I'm gonna get back there myself.'

'Habibi, you're not gonna stay for dinner?' Joey asked. 'I won't pee on you or anything, I promise.'

'I can't, but—' and I took hold of an idea. 'But can I look at your new *Village Voice* for a minute and make a few quick phone calls in your room?'

'Of course.'

'Tigger?' Cedric looked up at me worriedly. 'You ain't mad that I told you all this, are you?'

'No,' I answered, with more truth than they could ever imagine. 'I've always hated Goolsbee,' I added, aiming for levity. 'But I don't know if even I would have driven him to incontinence.'

'What's the moral of the story?' Cedric trilled. 'For those trying social occasions, wear a catheter.'

I grabbed the *Voice* and slipped into Joey's bedroom. From without, just before I closed the door, I heard the two of them.

The smacking of lips, then from Cedric: 'How you doin' today, my kibbee?'

'Lemme have one of your cigarettes, please?'

'No, baby.'

'A little cocktail, then?'

'No, baby. You know what I told you. I'm about to lose my moms, an' I'm gonna hold onto you for as long as I mother-fuckin' can, even if that means feeding you leafy greens and protein drinks for the rest of your life.'

Joey spat in Arabic at Cedric, something epithetic and gut-tural.

'That's right, baby.' Cedric laughed gently. 'That's right. Now get on up, Miss Beirut 1990—it's time for your little rub-down.'

Flip was chattering on the telephone when I got home. She turned, smiled brightly at me, blew me a kiss, gestured to indicate 'one second,' and turned back to the conversation. Finally, she hung up and sighed happily. 'That was Ricardo, my old copromoter from Limelight. He just wanted to make *absolutely sure* that he and Nils were on the guest list for the Half-Year Party.'

'That's nice,' I said blandly.

'They're angels,' she said, her blithe coda for practically everyone. She ran over to me, hugged and kissed me. 'Hello, darling. I'm *sooo* glad you're back. Cedric told me you were staying at Joey's, helping out. That's sweet of you. How is he?'

'Not so good.'

'That poor thing,' she said, picking at a hangnail. 'He's just got to be strong and pull through this.'

Her ignorant naiveté infuriated me, but I said nothing of it. 'Cedric told me all about last night,' I said instead, neutrally.

'Oh, God, you've heard then,' she laughed. 'Tig, it's like I was just saying to Ricardo—I *never* expected it would go that far. But what's done is done, right? I'm good for the money, that's what counts. And I guess Goolsbee won't be bothering us anymore, right?'

'What if he tries to sue you for—for assault or something?'

She laughed, still preoccupied with her hangnail. 'He wouldn't dare. I'll sue him for—for being a public nuisance, or something.'

She suddenly looked up and caught my angry glare. Startled, she averted her eyes. At length, she turned to me again, eyes wide and hopeful, and broke forth in a sudden unsettling gust of earnestness. 'Tigger, honey, I'm glad you got home before Jess, because there's something I want to talk to you about.'

'Same here,' I said.

She giggled nervously. 'Oh, really?'

'Yeah.'

'Well . . . do you mind if I go first?'

'That's fine.'

'Okay,' she said, nodding her head. 'Okay.' She moved over to the couch, lit a cigarette. *How many cigarettes did she smoke in a day?* I asked myself for what felt like the first time. *At the rate she's going, she's gonna have lung cancer by the time she's thirty.* 'Won't you come here and sit down by me?' she asked, settling onto the couch. I sat in the opposite armchair instead. She said nothing, just smiled at me with some dreamy, condescending affection.

'Well?' I finally asked.

She exhaled long, stubbed out her cigarette, then folded her hands primly in her lap. 'All right, Tigger. I won't beat around the bush.'

'Good.'

'Um . . . um . . .' She suddenly seemed to have lost her self-possession. 'Um . . . this thing with Jess and me.'

'What thing?' I asked perversely. Just that she would try to bring the subject up in some civil fashion infuriated me.

'Well, this . . . oh, Tigger, please, don't make this any harder than it is.'

'I genuinely don't know what you're talking about,' I said again, as cool and hateful as could be.

'Why are you doing this to me?'

'Doing *what*?'

'Tigger,' and I suddenly noticed that her hands were shaking uncontrollably. She clamped one on top of the other, then tucked them both under her thighs. 'I know you know that Jess and I are . . . that we've *been* . . . romantically involved.'

'You're kidding me,' I said, deadpan.

'Oh, Tigger, *stop!*' she pleaded.

'Well, what the fuck do you want me to say, Flip? You tell me that you, my sister, and Jess, my brother, are fucking right here under my nose in this very house, and you expect me to give you some kind of blessing?'

'No, I don't expect that!' she said, flustered. 'I mean— I mean— Tig, we never expected it to happen, ever!'

'No, I guess most people engaging in incest never planned it that way, either. It just . . . *happens*.'

'Tigger, how can you dare say that?' She was starting to cry now. 'You know it's not incest, because—'

'Because Jess was adopted? Flip, we all grew up together. We shared the same fucking crib! It's sibling incest!'

'Okay, fine, damn you, Tig! Call it what you want, then! But we never meant for it to happen. It's just—always been there, all right? For as long as I can remember. He fought it longer than I did, but it was always there for him, too. And then when Ma died— we just—'

'I guess that made it a hell of a lot easier to justify, didn't it?'

'That's a terrible way of putting it!'

'Well, it's true, isn't it?'

She didn't answer.

'And Daddy's dead. And God knows where Jess's real family is. And you know Lippy'll never say a word for as long as she lives, even if she knows. So, in effect, there's no one left in the way except me, right?'

'Well, this is about you, Tig. But not in the way you think.'

'What the fuck is that supposed to mean?'

She fumbled to light another cigarette, but couldn't hold it steady enough to do so, and threw it down on the coffee table instead. Another first, as far as I could remember, Flip refusing a cigarette.

'It means—well, as long as you're being so brutally honest—'

'Oh, would you call this *brutal*, you fucking bitch?' I almost stopped short from shock—I had never called Flip a bitch to her face in my entire life—but suddenly my hatred for both her and Jess seemed to be cresting out of nowhere, invulnerable to temperance. 'You invented the *fucking word*!'

Her head was in her hands now; she was sobbing, huge racking sobs that scared as much as they satisfied me. 'Would you just give me a goddamned chance and listen to me?' she begged.

'Go ahead and talk, then!'

'Tigger— oh, Tigger— Jess knows how you feel about him. I do, too. We've always known.'

'Oh, Jesus Christ,' I said, my whole face burning red with a humiliation the likes of which I had never suffered before. Suddenly, I wanted to run out the door of the loft and never come back, never see either of them again, light out toward a vast and dry frontier of blissful anonymity, where I was nobody's brother, nobody's lover, nobody to anybody at all, just a single, transient cipher, free of old ties or crushing memories or wrenching ambivalences. I just wanted to be nobody.

'You're both just so fucking perceptive,' I finally said.

'We know your feelings for him. We've talked about it,' she sobbed.

I was about to protest vehemently, call them both wildly presumptuous egotists for even thinking as much just because I had stood by them both in the natural, clean way that brothers and sisters should. Wouldn't most people, in such a situation, do just that? Deny the evil, sordid thing, just to salvage some shard of their dignity in the face of such a ghastly accusation? It was clearly the right thing for me to say.

But I didn't—it would all be irrelevant in virtually no time, I knew, and so I spoke the stupid truth, for whatever it was worth.

'So what if I have? So what if I do? What does it matter?'

'Tigger, it matters so much!'

'WHY?'

'Because I—' and she gasped, then quieted. 'Because I love him, too. And how could I ever be jealous of someone who loves the person I love, when we love him for all the same reasons? And how could I be jealous of that person when I love him just as much as the person in question?'

I said nothing, suddenly stunned.

'And Tigger, baby, he loves you so much, you can't even guess. I mean, maybe not— maybe not *that way*, but— he loves you fiercely. He'd stop time before he ever let you go.'

I was completely bewildered now, so much so that the room

had taken on an unpleasantly vertiginous feel. 'So what the fuck are you trying to say?'

She looked up at me and smiled, so sadly I could sense a rent in one of the seams of my heart. 'I'm saying that we have a—' and she laughed, at a loss. 'A situation, I guess.'

Wrecked, I looked at her. How had I ever ended up having this insane, monstrous, wonderful woman as a sister? How could I love and hate someone so wholly at the same time? With every fiber of my being, every ounce of my soul that wished never to leave either of them, I wanted to respond to them in kind. But I swallowed my heart and all my happiness, for grief will out over love, and I knew it was not to be.

'That is what we have, Flip,' I said. 'But— but it's not a good situation. Especially for me, because there's nothing I can contribute. So listen to me. I love you, Flip. And you know I love Jess. And I don't doubt the love that either of you have for me. But I've got to get out of this situation, if it's going to work out for the two of you, or if my life is ever going to work for me.'

I held up the *Village Voice*, where I had circled several entries in the real estate section. 'And so I am, Flip. I am. I'm going to see a few places tonight.'

There seemed so little else to say, and just to sit there seemed beyond the pale of cruelty to either of us. I stood up and began walking to my room.

'Tig, wait!' she called back, and in a moment she was upon me, her face white and trembling. 'Don't do that just yet.'

'I have to, Flip.'

'No, not just yet,' she pleaded, holding my arm. ''Cause there's something else to tell you—the most important thing. Jess and I were going to wait until he got home, but I want to tell you now. There's a bigger reason why you've got to stay.'

'You can't bait me this time, Flip. You're both gonna be fine. I'm sure you'll find somebody else to help out at The Box.'

She laughed out loud, startling me. 'You think *that's* the

reason we want you to stay? Oh, God, Tig, don't you think you mean more than that to me?'

'Honestly? Sometimes, no. Anyway, Flip, listen—'

'No, Tigger, listen to me!'

'I'm not going to stand here and go over—'

'Would you listen to me? I'm going to—'

'And go over for the fortieth time—'

'Tigger! *I'm going to have a baby.*'

So boom . . . time stopped. Flip had spoken, words borne out on air, absorbed by me, processed now, and it was my turn to speak. But I couldn't say a word. Not a word, but, well, why not? What was a baby? It was a dark-skinned orphan in a crib in the nursery at Lowell General Hospital, 1964. It was a little girl that screamed with Olympian lungs when you raised her up, 1967. It was an agreeable pink thing that bounced in his crib to Dionne Warwick, 1968. Or it was something lost on sweaty sheets, announced long gone in the chaotic waiting room of St. Vincent's Hospital, long after midnight, while an almost-not-quite mother slept, exhausted, in a back-room bed, 1989.

'What?' I finally managed.

'Like I said. I'm going to have a baby. I mean—*we're* going to have a baby. The three of us. And I'm not going to lose it this time, I know that much.'

'Since when?'

'I'm four weeks pregnant. I knew last week, but had it confirmed on Wednesday. I caught up with Jess and told him this morning, even before Anthea could tell him about last night. That's it. That's the latest.'

'What do you mean, "the three of us"?'

'I mean, we want the three of us to raise it together—right here.'

'Flip, it's yours and Jess's baby. It's not mine.'

'Tigger, listen to me. I don't want the three of us to break up—not after all the people we've lost, and everything we've been through. Neither does Jess. We want to stay a family. We couldn't live without you here.' She wiped her face, composing herself somewhat. 'Maybe it could've been different, a few years back, say, if you'd moved in with Seb, or if Jess had married Damienne. But not now— with all we know. It's too late to pretend it can be any other way.'

I regarded her, woefully confused. 'So what do you want me to be? Like, an uncle? An auntie?'

'No,' she laughed. 'A parent. The baby will have three parents.'

'Isn't that kid going to be awfully messed up?'

She laughed windily. 'Look at the world we live in! Stranger things have happened. And just think of the big, crazy family that kid is going to have.' Knee-jerk, she placed her hand over her stomach—she didn't show at all yet—and rubbed it in a circular motion.

'What would you tell Lippy?'

'The truth—not right now, but soon. You know she'll understand in time. And besides, Jess is going to officially delegalize his adoption, or whatever you call it.'

Here was another surprise for me. 'So what will the three of us be, Flip? I mean, you two will be lovers—but what will I be?'

'Well, for one thing, you'll be my brother, forever and always.'

'So what the hell will *we* be then?'

'Well—' She smiled at me and shrugged. 'I guess most of all we'll be a family. A household.'

'I—' but the sound of Jess trudging up the stairway stopped me.

'Oh, God. Hold on a second, Tigger.' Flip ran to the door, caught Jess at it— 'Hey, what the . . .' and pushed him out into the hall, leaving the door just ajar behind them. I sat down on the couch, dazed and confounded. I was moved, and offended, intrigued and utterly afraid. People older than I had always told me that at some point my life would come to a juncture where I'd have to make a decision that would shape the rest of my days. Was this it? If it was, I thought, I certainly could have waited a few more years for it.

Jess stepped in, with Flip smiling shyly behind him. 'Hey, amigo,' he said to me.

'Hey,' I answered, then erupted into nervous laughter. We all did. The situation was simply too absurd.

'You shacked up with Joey for a while, hunh?' he asked me.

'Yeah.'

'And Cedric told you about this one's'—he gestured at Flip—'little piece of performance art last night?'

'Yeah, he told me. In excruciating detail.'

'I can't believe either of you honestly thought I was going to give myself over to that monster,' Flip said.

'A girl's gotta do what a girl's gotta do,' I quipped tightly, before silence descended upon us. Jess lit a cigarette. Flip shuffled through the mail again and again.

'So Tig,' Jess finally said. 'Flip told you what's the story, huh?'

'Yep.' I was feeling perverse again.

'Did she tell you how badly we want you to be a part of this deal?'

'Yep.'

'I thought—' he began, before looking back at Flip. 'We thought that—you know, if you were going to maybe stay here, well,' and he laughed, 'we thought we could maybe blackmail you. So here goes.'

He handed me a slip of paper. I looked at it—it was a purchase order from the piano store on 20th Street in Chelsea. For a Yamaha baby grand piano. The very piano I had always vowed I'd buy someday when I moved into a bigger space, my own space, my gift to myself after years of working on the tinny consoles in the airless practice rooms at Mannes, or diddling around on the clinker-fraught old upright I had bought at the flea market and had had hauled up into the loft when I moved in. In a word, the very piano I had counted on to someday make my domestic life, wherever it would be, real—complete.

'It's our graduation present to you. I took all the measurements of the loft's doorway, the stairwell,' Jess said now. 'We can fit it—'

'Right over there,' Flip chimed in, pointing to the far corner of the wall where we had long-ago banked a group of dusty ficus and palm trees.

'We put money down on it for a week,' Jess continued, 'to give you time to think. But we figured if you were going to stay with us, it was only fair that you have a legitimate grand piano. Where you can compose the great works of the twenty-first century.'

'And play lullabies for the baby,' Flip added impetuously.

I finally looked up from the purchase order. 'That's sweet,' I said. 'But you're wrong. You *can't* blackmail me.'

'We know,' Jess said. 'I was just kidding.'

'I don't know if you have any idea how weird this whole proposal is to me,' I said. 'Especially when I came home today to tell you both I was moving out.'

Jess laughed. 'Oh, it's definitely weird. But we've already accepted the weirdness, because—'

'Because we want to stay together,' Flip finished. She still hadn't joined us by the couch, and I wondered if, after her own weepy plea, she was deferring to Jess now.

Jess turned to her, then back to me. 'Right,' he said.

'I just don't know how much you guys realize I feel like the third wheel here, as much as you're trying to include me.'

'We're not trying to include you, Tig,' Jess said. 'You've always been included. We're trying to get you to stay included.'

I shrugged; to me, his amendment seemed little more than semantics.

'Look at us,' he laughed ruefully. 'I let Damienne go. You let

Seb go. But the three of us are still here, together. Doesn't that tell you something?'

'Yeah,' I snorted. 'It tells me we're all a bunch of fucked-up messes.'

'But we're *fabulously* fucked-up messes, aren't we?' Flip asked. 'And at least we stick together. Don't you think that's what Ma and Daddy would have wanted?'

Not quite like this, I thought to myself, but I had to concede her the main point—we had been through some catastrophic times ever since leaving St. Pete's, and here the three of us were, still bound to each other inside this ridiculous loft. I still brought home three copies of the *Village Voice* every week so we wouldn't fight over it, or so no one would leave the house with the only copy. Jess still remembered to pick up orange juice at the deli next door every night, no matter how late it was. And even when the rest of the loft was in a complete state of disarray, even when we had to scream to each other from inside the bathroom because someone had forgotten to buy toilet-paper, Flip still made sure that there were always cigarettes inside the scarred silver porringer she had snatched from the house in Rye. Jess and I still made a point of checking on Flip after we had put her to bed drunk to make sure she hadn't fallen asleep on her back so that she wouldn't die in the night by choking on her own vomit. And there had never been a time when I was sick that Jess (and even Flip, though a touch less reliably) hadn't brought me chicken soup, Saltines and ginger ale, even stayed home whole afternoons just to watch sitcoms with me while I blew my nose and hacked up a lung under blankets on the couch.

'You're pensive,' Jess said, a smile pulling at the corners of his lips.

'Can you blame me?'

'Of course not.

I rose from the couch. 'Listen, guys. I'm going out for a while—by myself. I need to think about this. I'll catch up to you later tonight at The Box.'

Flip darted toward me. 'With an answer?'

'Not necessarily.'

'Give him some time, Flip,' Jess said. 'Tig, you don't have to tell us tonight. Christ!'

I grabbed my coat, straightened my hair, nodded a cordial good-bye to both of them—they did the same, with studied casualness—and stepped out the door. I yearned to know what they were saying now—I could simply put my ear to the door—and I was deeply afraid to know as well. So I yielded to the latter instinct and made my way down the stairs, into the street.

I walked, because it was a lovely evening and because I didn't know where I wanted to go anyway—walked up to Houston Street, to Bedford, all the way up through the noisy Village, where people were having their first outdoor meals of the season at the cordoned-off tables set up on sidewalks, across 14th Street and into Chelsea. For no good reason—and because I much wanted a drink, or two, or three—I walked to the gay bar near Barneys, which was still a relatively popular spot a year after it opened, no small phenomenon in that fickle, restless world.

It was loud with an afterwork crowd, a conservative and mostly white assemblage for all the slickness of its myriad video screens and buffed, shirtless bartenders. They were playing Mariah Carey—no trancey remix the likes of which Sammy Fingers might have mastered, but the same pure pop version you could hear on any hit radio station. I ordered a beer from the woodenly amiable, freshly waxed and bronzed bartender, lit a cigarette, and zoned. Dimly, I heard some queens—marketing assistants at HBO or MTV, I speculated lazily—talking about the video montage of movie musical clips that the bar would show in only a half-hour, and I vowed to be out of there, just pleasantly cocked, long before the show began.

At length, I exchanged glances with the man sitting across the bar from me; he smiled in a shruggy, what's-up sort of way, and I smiled back as unsuggestively as possible. He was older than I, mid-forties maybe, with an obviously balding head of hair that he had had the good sense to shave down into a military cut. Behind his small, round glasses he offered a nice-enough looking face—Irish, maybe, or a little Italian, easily the better-manicured face of some regular guy from a town like Topsfield. I could picture him walking his springer spaniel up and down the tree-lined cross streets of Eighth Avenue every evening after work, all veiled glances and expectant nods of the head—then returning to his catalogue-perfect apartment and making the motions toward an empty bed.

And I lost myself in the composition of this speculative life so thoroughly that I was doubly startled when someone spoke at my shoulder and I turned to see that it was the man himself, who had alighted from his seat and walked round without my having noticed at all.

'Hey, guy.' I was startled again—his voice was perhaps two notches lower than I had imagined, and it sounded more midwestern than New Jersey, which I had expected.

'Hey, what's up.'

'You were really lost in your own world there for a while.'

I braced myself to be cold, but there was nothing even faintly predatory about his stance or his tone; much as I imagined, he already seemed a model of decent, well-meaning congeniality.

'I did,' I said, loosening. 'I guess Mariah Carey just doesn't do it for me.'

'Yeah, she's all right,' he said, as though this throwaway of mine was actually worthy of a thoughtful reply. 'I like Paula Abdul a lot better.'

'Yeah, she's pretty good,' I managed. I hated Paula Abdul, even though I took caution never to say so around Joey, who called her a 'fellow sister of Lebanon.'

'You want another beer?' he asked.

I looked at my first. In my reverie, I had drunk it to the last. 'Yeah, sure,' I said. 'Thanks.'

He ordered us each another. 'To spring,' he said, smiling, and we toasted. 'So,' he said, after he had taken his first long draught. 'You just hanging out after work?'

'No. I mean, I didn't work today.'

'Lucky you. Where do you work?'

'Well, I teach piano. I mean, I'm in school for piano.'

'Oh, yeah? What kind of stuff do you play?'

'A little of everything, I guess. Classical, jazz. I'm in school for composition.'

'Oh, yeah?' His interest seemed constant and sincere. 'You're gonna be a composer, hunh?'

'I hope so,' I said, then, to turn the conversation away from me, 'what do you do?'

'I work at Chemical,' he said, then, after a pause, 'in investments.'

I nodded. 'Hm.' I never knew what to say when people told me they worked in finance. I knew nothing of it—ignorance combined with indifference. 'So, I guess you're just hanging out after work, hunh?'

'Yeah, just until my husband finishes making dinner. He doesn't like to be bothered when he's cooking.'

'Oh,' I said, quick to hide my surprise. 'You guys live around here?'

'Right over on Eighteenth,' he said. I nodded, and we were both quiet for a moment before he picked up the thread: 'I needed a drink, anyway. Today was a fucking strange day at work.'

'Oh yeah?'

'Yeah. I go into the copy room and I find one of the secretaries making Xeroxes of her face, crying.'

I laughed. 'Are you serious?'

'Dead. She said her boyfriend had just dumped her after,

like, six years and she was making all these copies to send to him. You ever notice how when people copy their face and hair on a Xerox machine, it comes out looking like a Wyeth?'

I laughed again. 'That's true,' I said, because, come to think of it, it was. He was funnier than I had given him credit for, and, it occurred to me, sexier, too. 'So what'd you do?'

'I said, "Jeanni, you can't be carrying on like this. What if the office manager walks in?" And she just kept on crying and telling me the whole tragic tale. So I told her to go to the bathroom and wash her face, then I took her out for lunch and she told me the whole story from the start.'

'And?'

'And it turned out that the guy hadn't really dumped her after all. He just wanted to go up to the Finger Lakes with his buddies to do some fly-fishing and he had left without telling her. He just left her a note.'

'That's fucked,' I said.

'Yeah, well, straight people are fucked.'

'This is true,' I nodded, thinking with an unwelcome little pang of Flip and Jess.

'Yeah,' he said, taking another sip of his beer. I did the same, and more silence ensued. He lit a cigarette, asked me if I wanted one. I accepted, and he lit a second for me.

'So,' he said, 'when you compose, do you, like, plan it out ahead of time, in your head? Or do you just sit down at the piano and let it come to you.'

'Kind of both. I guess it depends on the situation.'

'Hm. You know, my husband would be really interested to talk to you. He's an agent at CAMI.'

'Really?' CAMI represented some of the best musicians in New York, and at Mannes it was spoken of with a kind of awe.

'Oh yeah,' he said. 'He's pretty big there. Hey,' he said.

'Yeah?'

'You should come over for dinner.'

'Well—'

'It's cool. He's making some kind of pasta tonight, and he always overcooks. We end up giving half of it to the dog.'

'Oh, thanks!' I laughed.

'You interested? You got plans?'

'Well—' I was torn; I had an odd weakness for seeing other people's apartments. They always seemed more evolved, more real, than our own cave-like dwelling.

He reached up and scruffed my head. 'You ever been with two guys before?'

He caught me mid-puff. 'Um,' I choked, laughing. 'Yeah. It's been a while, though.' It was a lie—I had never been in a three-way, a sorry lacuna on my sexual résumé.

'You think you could take two guys?' he asked, his hand on my knee now. His voice hadn't lost its congenial tone—if anything, he sounded even more agreeably fraternal than before.

'Well,' I answered, laughing, 'it's not whether or not I could *take* two guys, it's just—'

'We could party, if that'd make it easier on you.'

'That's cool. It's just—'

'Would you be cool with maybe my boyfriend fucking you while I jerked off and watched? He likes skinny young guys. I like big Latin guys, but you're pretty cute. What's your background, anyway?'

'Um . . .Greek. And Irish.'

'That's a pretty hot combination. I have a feeling you're gonna be pretty big in the compositional world.'

'Thanks.' *The compositional world?* No one said *the compositional world*, I thought wretchedly.

'So what do you say? We'll feed you well first. Or later.'

They were starting the musicals: Jane Russell in a swimsuit cavorting around a gymful of indifferent musclemen. The musical theater queens started screaming and singing along.

'You know what?' I said to the guy, removing his hand from

my knee and sliding off the stool. 'I gotta get home. I hate movie musicals.'

He laughed. 'So do I. So what about it?'

'That's okay. Thanks, though. It sounds really hot, but my head's just not in that place tonight.'

He laughed gently, took my arm. 'What's wrong? You've never been fucked before?'

'No, it's not that,' I answered—true enough, though it had been so long now that it certainly felt that way. 'It's just—I told my brother and my sister I'd be home soon.'

'Your brother and sister? Where you from? Long Island?'

'No. SoHo.'

'Really?'

'Yeah, and I told them I'd get home. For supper. But thanks—and thanks for the beer, too.'

'No problem,' he shrugged, bewildered now. 'Maybe some other time, huh? Me and my husband hang out here a lot. We'll look for you.'

'Cool.'

'You should really meet him. He's pretty big at CAMI.'

'Okay. Definitely. Thanks. Definitely.'

I was pulling away now, but he pulled me back and kissed me roughly on the cheek. 'Hey, guy. Take care, okay? Take care of yourself.'

'I will. You too. See you later.' My cheek burned where he had kissed it, not unpleasantly, but I still wiped it off thoroughly with the sleeve of my jacket first thing upon leaving the bar.

I don't know why I walked home so fast, but I did. The streets and sidewalk cafés were even more crowded now, and I had a strange, slightly dizzy feeling that if I slowed down, some stranger, or some group of strangers, was going to collar me, and scruff me on the head, and invite me into their group, or their home, or their infinitely bizarre, highly coded private lives, and that I'd be unable to resist, because it suddenly seemed the entire city was a vast complex of thinly perforated worlds, one grafted virtually on top of another, and you could spend your entire life phantom-walking from one to the next. I started to have some kind of weird, unreal, dizzy feeling, especially when crossing streets, and the panic of that only propelled me back to the loft faster.

They were in the kitchen when I got home, dressed handsomely for The Box, hunched over a take-out box of pizza. The kitchen was warm, and there was some old Gladys Knight on the stereo, 'Midnight Train to Georgia'. *I'd rather live in his world/Than live without him/In mine.*

They looked up when I entered, flushed and breathless. 'Hi!' Flip said. 'You want some pizza?'

'Yeah,' I managed, doffing my coat. 'I mean, no. I mean— I've got something to tell you guys.'

They both put down their pizza slices respectfully, said nothing.

'I'm gonna stay,' I said, and suddenly I was in their arms, feeling like I was going to cry. 'I mean— I mean, I want to stay.'

Flip combed my hair back from my face, her palm on my wet cheek. 'Shhh, Tigger. It's okay, baby. And I'm so glad. *We're* so glad—aren't we, Jess?'

'Yep,' he answered, beaming. He kissed me full on either cheek. 'Welcome home, my brother. Welcome home.'

Twenty-One

All of a sudden, it was late spring—as though God had taken the winter lid off Manhattan, filling it with light and warmth— and all of a sudden, all our days were rich with a sort of anticipation I hadn't experienced since the months before the opening of The Box. Many anticipations, really, each of them marvelous in their own way, and all of them pointing toward a new kind of calm, something that promised not so much heady excitement as a sturdy platform to see us through the decade ahead, in which we would all enter our thirties, the balance of our lives.

For starters, there was the marriage of Lippy and Langley, to be conducted by a justice of the peace in the Japanese rock garden behind a friend's brownstone in early September. I had so little patience for young brides; it seemed, the past year, that the marriage pages of *The New York Times* were full of familiar faces, the remade, professionalized faces of girls we had known at St. Pete's, due to marry men my age or slightly older of similar schooling or professions, then take up residence in Bronxville or New Canaan or Westport, after marriages at an Episcopal church on Martha's Vineyard. Even Kira—our frazzle-haired, sack-dressed Kira, our sole conspirator in all matters of social defiance at St. Pete's—had abandoned the academic track, become a lawyer, and married her long-time boyfriend Jeffrey, a fellow lawyer. The two of them were holed up somewhere in a coop on the Upper West Side, lost to us except for the occasional polite phone invitation to a dinner party we'd never go to, or the stray Broadway encounter on a weekend afternoon.

But where Lippy was concerned, we couldn't have been happier for her, or more grateful to Langley, for all his affectations. They were partners in good living, after all, bonded by music and theater, cocktails and friends, so many years now of shared memories. They were like Cole and Linda Porter, I pointed out to Jess and Flip, who couldn't have lived apart, for all their various complications.

'Now I'll have my accompanist and my publicist and my best friend and my lover all under one roof, twenty-four hours a day,' she gushed to us one evening over an early dinner at her place, squeezing Langley's hand while he blushed.

'Honestly, Lippy,' he muttered.

'Well, it's true!' Lippy exclaimed. 'And I'll have my friends, and my fans—and my children,' and she encompassed the three of us with one sweeping, dramatic gesture. 'I swear to you all, I'm the happiest girl in the world.'

My children. At the word, Flip blushed, and the three of us exchanged a round of fleeting, giddy glances. Of course, we hadn't told a soul our news—wouldn't, we decided, until it became wonderfully, astonishingly obvious on Flip's part—but of course, here was our other great anticipation, our treasured secret, this latest project that really felt as though it belonged to all of us, curiously enough, and it tied us up together in a new, inviolable intimacy that, to me, had about it the whiff of our old, innocent childhood subterfuges.

It (He? She?) changed everything—the way we interacted, how we lived our lives, the tone with which we talked about our days, our near and distant future. Suddenly, we didn't stay at The Box until the wee hours anymore; instead, Flip appointed Anthea the unofficial hostess after two o'clock (by which time we were usually gone) and hired two more people to stay until closing and do the work we were no longer there to do. Suddenly, we all gave up recreational drugs, and, excepting the rare, guiltily cadged cigarette or half-glass of wine, Flip stopped drinking and smoking. Suddenly, she wasn't scrambling all night over the floor, making glib, disjointed conversation with a dozen people at once; instead, she'd summon old favorites and honored guests to a couch in one of the quieter corners of the club, limed mineral water in hand, charming and startling them with long conversations they could actually follow. Suddenly, she didn't seem a chronic, often overwhelming discharge of endless energy—she radiated an almost Zen-like calm. Her voice was lower, her speech less breakneck, her smile slower and broader, no longer a quicksilver spasm of generalized response to anything from an air-kiss to a backhanded remark on her hair, her shoes, or her dress.

Needless to say, all this bewildered everyone, especially after her public 'breakdown' the night of Goolsbee's chastening—an event so ripe for gossip that it made it into all the rags for two succeeding weeks and became an instant part of the long annals of clubworld lore. Word went around about this new Flip—was she strung out? Depressed? Ready to bail out of the business? But no—she seemed healthy, self-possessed, *happy* in fact, talking with quiet confidence about her marvelous plans for the upcoming Half-Year Party. And yet—she seemed different, changed.

No one was more confounded than the newly elevated Anthea, who had learned months before, the hard way, not to step on Flip's toes, regardless of her assistant manager's position at The Box. Grateful for a livelihood in addition to designing lampshades, and for her own generous share of Flip's refracted glow of celebrity, Anthea had made peace with her lot. And now, just like that, all tables had turned.

'Flip, darling,' she cooed one night, signature martini glass in hand, approaching the distant sofa where Flip lounged, legs up inelegantly on the back of a chair, chatting with Sammy and his old neighborhood friend Rochelle, and me. 'Guess who's showing up in five minutes? His driver just called from the carphone to let you know.'

'Hmm?' Flip looked up, politely interested.

'Are you quite sure you're ready to know?'

'I'm fine,' Flip said. 'Who?'

'*George Michael!*' Anthea shrieked. 'Our Georgie, Flip! He's finally coming round!'

We all thought the name would elicit a bigger response from Flip. We had always ribbed her and Anthea about their longtime schoolgirl crushes on the singer; Flip had harbored an inexplicable 'thing' for him ever since she saw the 'Wham! Rap' video for the first time at the age of fifteen, and Anthea often claimed he was the only man she fancied enough to leave the world of Sapphic pleasures—too bad, she'd add with exaggerated rue, that he was such an obvious poofter himself.

But Flip hardly flinched. She just gave Anthea her new, mysterious smile, slow and broad. 'That's marvelous, Anthie. When he gets here, why don't you ask him if he wants to come up and join us?'

Anthea snapped her mouth shut in puzzlement. 'But darling, don't you want to come 'round and greet him with me?'

'Anth,' Flip said, reaching knee-jerk for a cigarette on the table, then jerking her arm away, as though she had been scalded. 'I can't now. I've got guests here already.'

'You're quite sure, Flip?' she asked once more.

'Quite. I think I've outgrown George Michael.'

'Well, what shall I tell him?'

'Tell him I'm having a business meeting with my DJ, the legendary Sammy Fingers, and if he'd like he can come up and meet us both. Comp him plus however many he wants, of course.'

'Of course,' Anthea mouthed before shooting me a look of irritated confusion and darting off.

Flip looked around at the three of us and shrugged. 'Well?' she asked. 'It's only George Michael.'

Meantime, Jess experienced his own, infinitely subtler, transformation. If anything, I guess, he became a bit less flaky, and, to my great amusement, terribly, unprecedentedly, concerned about the quality of life at the loft. Atmospheric deficits we had lived with for years, such as the lack of natural daylight, the unconquerable griminess of the floors and walls, the leaky ceiling and rusty pipes overhead, now became topics of great import to him. Was the loft a healthy place to live? he now wondered. Was it *safe*? Was it cheerful? Maybe as soon as our will money came in, we should look for a finished loft . . . or a brownstone in Brooklyn . . . or a place just outside the city, like Hoboken or Nyack? Why was everyone so down on living outside of New York? he suddenly asked, contradicting years of his own urban snobbery. There were *plenty* of artists outside of the city—why, Grant had three clients in Nyack alone—

And of course, Flip would always stop him right there. She had no problem with looking for a better, brighter place, but it would *always* be in Manhattan, preferably below 23rd Street, and we would *always* be city people. And when she said that, we knew what she really meant was that she was determined to have city children. The life that she knew was going to be the life that *they* knew, and all the people in that life were going to constitute an enormous, kaleidoscopic extended family of uncles, aunts and uncle-aunts. And that's when Jess would shrug deferentially, and that was the end of the conversation.

He was always deferential to Flip now, but not in the old brooding, conflicted way. She seemed to have taken on for him a sacred quality, wherein not even the most casual comment on her part—she was tired, or a little hungry, or she had a headache—failed to command his complete attention and solicitude. If she was tired, why didn't she take a nap before going to The Box? Jess would surely go pick up her laundry, or return her phone calls, and Tigger would surely pick up something for dinner, right Tig? If she had a headache, was that *all* it was, and how long had she had it, and how frequently did they occur, and shouldn't she call the doctor and ask her about it?

'It's just a headache, Jess,' Flip would say, weary of and touched by his attentions. And Jess would put one palm on her forehead and another on her as-yet untelling stomach—'You don't think you have a fever, do you? Anthea's sick this week, and you were with her in the office all day.'

'Anthea wasn't sick this week, she was hungover. I'm fine, Jess, honestly.' She'd roll her eyes at me and I'd roll them back before looking away, or wandering out of the room, leaving Jess to his ministrations and Flip to her half-felt protests.

It seemed that I was always walking out of these situations now—never obviously unwanted, and not necessarily *feeling* unwanted, but moved to leave by a faint, nagging sense of temporary dislocation and irrelevance. It was odd—when I was alone with either Jess or Flip, all I felt was a keen, warm sense of anticipation. Jess and I talked about all the places we'd take the baby—to museums and galleries, concerts and recitals, Central Park and the Bronx Zoo—almost as though we were two prepubescent brothers, quite mature by our own standards, awaiting the arrival of a third sibling upon which we could shower wisdom and affection. Alone, Flip and I would discuss the endless implications of having a boy or a girl, and the possibilities of a thousand different names, and who the baby would look most like ('I want it—him—her—to have Jess's eyes and my skin tone and your mouth, Tigger, and all our talent and style, and Lippy's craziness, and Daddy's gutsiness, and—' Flip would go on and on, as though she were assembling the child out of a mix-and-match kit), and how we'd introduce it to the world of The Box without scarring the child for life—almost to the point where I felt as though the two of *us* had conceived the child, and Jess had remained, as he always had, linked to us in every way but blood.

I didn't like that thought when I had it—in fact, I didn't like *any* thought that smacked in any way of jealousy or resentment or insecurity—and yet for all my better, stronger, wiser feelings of excitement and pride, I couldn't quite shake them. Dimly at first, then with an almost frightening intensity, I wished to tell someone the news, and, with it, all my attendant anxieties, but we had a compact of secrecy until we mutually ('mutually' meaning, I knew, when Flip decided in a panic of wounded vanity that she could no longer keep from showing) 'came out,' probably first to Lippy, then to Cedric, Joey, Anthea and the rest. If only Lippy knew *now*, I often thought, surely I wouldn't even *have* to articulate my icky, nagging feelings to her, surely she'd suss them out and privately, tenderly ask me all the right questions, furnish all the right answers. Or, I thought, if only Seb and I were still together, I could tell him— for in the months since our abrupt separation, I had come to realize, with a dull, indeterminate pang of loss (much to my annoyance, it sharpened as time went by), that what I most missed of us were our shared confidences, the things we could tell each other, about anyone, that we couldn't divulge to anybody else. But then again, I reasoned glumly, even if we *were* still together, even if I *could* share with him our new family secret, he'd probably announce severely that my staying with Jess and Flip in the loft was the stupidest, most self-destructive, ill-fated choice I could ever possibly make.

Was it? That was something else I ruminated over about a million times a day, despite all my best intentions not to do so. I couldn't answer the question—didn't want to, in fact. All I knew was that I didn't want to go out again into those scary, vertiginous streets hemmed in on either side by candlelit faces staring up at you, predatory and seductive, from their suppers *al fresco*. I didn't want to lead my life the way some people, too ravenous with hunger and conflicted with appetites, go crazy at a buffet table and end up simply sick to their stomachs, having consumed all and really savored nothing. What I wanted was just this—a family, and a home, and a child. And if my path to those three things weren't without their incertitudes, I thought defiantly, well then whose on earth were?

Lastly, we marshalled all our anticipatory energies around the Half-Year Party, just two weeks away. In only six months, in the turning of one New York season, The Breeder's Box had become all that Flip had ever meant it to be—and as the first sweet weeks of summer broke over the city, The Box's popularity showed no sign of waning.

The Half-Year Party was the talk of the rags—the guest list boasted a dizzying scroll of boldface names, remaining tickets had sold out weeks ago, Sammy Fingers promised he was preparing the ultimate mix list, we had booked three of the hottest new house divas with the possibility of a fourth, and, in what she promised to Jess and me would be her last grand-scale appearance before 'you-know-what' came along, Flip would appear at midnight, reprising her opening night stunt—but this time, she insisted, giggling along with Miko who was 'producing' the moment (whatever that meant), her entrance would be truly 'supernatural.'

'What's that supposed to mean?' I asked her. 'Are you gonna fly in on a broom?'

'Honey, please,' Cedric said. 'She does that every night. She just parks it in the back.'

'You're just bitter because I'm Elizabeth Montgomery to your Agnes Moorehead,' Flip read Cedric back.

Cedric sucked his teeth, yanking his head back dramatically. 'In that case, you should learn to respect your momma.'

'Seriously, Flip,' I persisted. 'What are you going to do?'

Flip frowned. 'Would Mizrahi show his collection before the actual show? I don't think so.'

'Oh, so you gonna come out carried by Isaac Mizrahi?' Cedric asked. 'I'm glad I'll know to look the other way.'

Flip took offense. 'Isaac's so *sweet*! He hates clubs, and he spent a whole hour on the couch with me last week. He said he wants to design a headdress for me.'

'Oh, Lord help us,' Cedric exclaimed, hands in the air.

'The point being,' Flip continued, 'that my midnight appearance remains for the time being Miko's private concept. And shall remain so until it is revealed in all its splendor.'

Cedric and I exchanged glances. 'Self-love is a many splendored thing,' he shrugged innocently, before ducking the pillow she hurled his way.

My piano came—a gleaming black beauty that five workmen had to carry up the wide stairwell, then remount on its legs in the far corner of the loft by the dusty plants. As soon as the tuner had come and gone, I polished it lovingly, ascribing to the Art Deco metronome Lippy had given me years ago a place of honor on its lid. The tinny, beat-up old upright by the kitchen became a shelf for old magazines and dirty plates now; it seemed that the new piano was the first thing I gravitated to in the morning, if only to wander drowsily over the luminescent keyboard while I drank my coffee. At first it felt strange to play and compose in the middle of my own home—I had always done it at Mannes, in the hermetically sealed confines of a practice room—but once I got used to it, realized that there was something comforting about scoring music while Flip or Jess lounged nearby, I found myself dashing home from classes in the afternoon to sit down to it, something I also loved to do in the quiet hour before bedtime. Jess and Flip respected my province—that whole far corner of the loft had become implicitly mine—encouraged it, even, as the territory they had gladly ceded to keep me in the loft.

The day before the Half-Year Party, a pleasantly, prematurely steamy Friday afternoon, I hurried home to my piano, only to find slung wide open the kitchen window leading out onto the fire escape. I poked my head outside; there was Jess, sitting up against the grate, the old twin mattress beneath him, a cigarette in his mouth and a beer at his side, with his sketchbook propped up before him on his knees.

'Yo, Jess.'

He looked up, startled and squinting, a random bar of sunlight striping his face across the eyes. He moved to close his notebook, then, encumbered, pressed whatever he was working on up against his bare chest.

'Tig. Hey. I didn't expect you home so early.'

'Class cancelled,' I said, ducking into the kitchen to pull a beer out of the refrigerator, then emerging full out onto the fire escape. 'What about you?' I shuffled a cigarette out of the pack he had left on the windowsill and lit it.

'It was too nice outside to stay in the studio. I felt lazy. Couldn't concentrate.'

'Well, you're working now.'

He shrugged. 'Sort of.' He seemed a bit wary around me, and quite determined not to show me what he had been sketching.

'What is it?' I tried him, pointing to the sketchbook.

'Nothing much.' He finished off the last of his beer. 'Just some crazy doodle.'

'A concept?'

'Not really.'

'Well, what is it? Let me see.'

He laughed out of the corner of his mouth. 'Tig, *why*? What's the big deal?'

'I'm just curious, that's all.'

'It's just a portrait idea.'

'That sounds cool,' I said encouragingly.

He deliberated a moment, then, in what seemed a rather violent fit of acquiescence, turned the sketchbook around to face me.

'There,' he said. 'Are you happy now?'

It was just the most rudimentary lineaments of a dual portrait—a man and woman, middle-aged and sad-eyed, sitting
on the same bench, at a respectable distance from each other,
in front of a cottage or house. The woman was overweight,
with sagging jowls but a soft mouth; the man was thin and
austere-looking, a cigar burning idly in one upraised hand.

'That's cool. Who are they?'

'I don't know,' he said, almost defiantly. 'Just a couple.'

'It's not Daddy and Ma, is it? Daddy was never that skinny
and Ma was never that fat.'

'No kidding,' he nearly snapped, 'because it's not supposed
to be them.'

'Well, who is it supposed to be?'

'How the fuck should I know? I made them up, okay?'

'Okay!' I insisted, dismayed. 'Take it easy, Jess.'

'Well, why are you so goddamned nosey?'

'I just—'

'Look,' he said, suddenly conciliatory, closing the sketchbook. 'Let's just forget it. Would you jump inside and get me
another beer? Let's get drunk, okay? Before Flip gets home, so
she doesn't see us drinking and get jealous. But it's definitely
the kind of afternoon to get drunk.'

I shrugged. 'Okay. I don't have anything else to do.'

Inside, I turned on the stereo and faced the speakers out,
then stepped back outside with two more beers in my hand.
And for the rest of the hazy afternoon, we proceeded to get
drunk—in an indolent, unhurried sort of way, borne along by
the music floating around inside, and the odd muffled noises
coming from the apartments across the way, and the creeping
slant of the sun as the hours passed. We talked, but in a disjointed fashion, about everything and nothing, recalling
fragments of old moments from St. Pete's, fragments of half-
forgotten songs from local Boston bands we used to hear on
WFNX, shards of memories from our first years in New
York—the time Flip and I, en route to a thrift warehouse, got

off at the wrong stop in Brooklyn and ended up in the middle of a Lubavitcher funeral, or how Jess thought Cedric was Isabel Sanford from *The Jeffersons* the first time he saw him in drag, or the weekend the three of us got so drunk at someone's party in Montauk that we all passed out in their kitchen and skulked away in shame the next morning, hitching a ride to the Southampton train in the back of a pick-up truck driven by three surfers on acid.

And so we talked on like this until all the beer was gone and all the cigarettes smoked, until Jess had lain his head down in my lap and fallen asleep, and I dozed in and out of consciousness, happily drunk, my head against the brick wall and my fingers caught up in Jess's hair. At some point, half-asleep, I bent down to kiss him on the cheek. He murmured something and turned his head away, and our lips grazed each other's for the briefest moment. I felt some warm, sharp stirring in my shorts—and an admonitory thump of my heart—and so I slithered down beside him on the mattress and tucked my head chastely into his chest, my breath fluttering the curly hairs around his right nipple, his dead-weight arm slung over my waist, and then we were both asleep.

I don't know how much time passed, but when I woke, it was dark, and the stereo had been considerably lowered, and I could hear the muted din of a Friday night coming to life in SoHo far on the other side of the building. I looked up toward the kitchen window, and there was Flip, hair damp and face lustrous with humidity, stepping out onto the fire escape in a T-shirt and cut-offs, something showing ever so faintly around her middle, lying down beside us and scooching us both over until we were all comfortably compressed.

'He's asleep, isn't he?' she whispered to me, smiling dreamily.

'Yeah. We drank all afternoon.'

'Honestly.' She rolled her eyes with mock approbation. She laced her fingers through my own, then pressed our entwined hands up to her lips. 'Guess what, Tig? I went to the doctor today. I know what the baby's going to be.'

'Don't tell me,' I hastened. 'I want to be surprised.'

'Should I wake Jess and tell him? I think he'll be happy.'

'I wouldn't. Why don't you keep it for yourself? You deserve something that only belongs to you, Flip.'

She was silent. 'You mean no one knows but me until the baby is born?'

'Yeah.'

'I like that idea,' she finally whispered. And she kissed me again, this time on the forehead. 'Thank you, Tigger.'

'It's okay.' I was falling asleep again.

'You know I couldn't live without you, right?'

'Mm-hmmmm.' What was she saying to me?

'I wouldn't want to, you know. You or Jess. You're all I have—and the baby, of course. But I don't really feel like I'd exist without the two of you.'

'Mmm-hmmmm. Let's take a nap, Flip.'

'Okay, darling.' Then she pressed in closer to me—I could feel her warm boobs and stomach and knees against my backside, and she smelled the same dense, gummy, satisfying smell she had smelled since she was twelve. A lock of her long hair fell over my shoulder and onto my chest, pressed up sweatily now inside the steady rise-and-fall of Jess's shoulderblades. We were all lost to this world in a moment, off that precipice where drowsiness plummets into sleep, and how was I to know that it was the last time that we would Make the Chair, be like that, ever again?

Twenty-Two

These days, I don't live for nighttime as I once did, and you might think that I look back on that nocturnal era of my life with a kind of startled rue, as in, What the hell did I think I was looking for? But the fact that I am usually asleep now by the time my *real* world was once just beginning has more to do with my present domesticity, and the desire not to court certain memories of my brother and sister, than it has to do with the newfound Augustinian wisdom of a reformed hedonist. So what, then, drove this compulsive attraction to dark spaces that opened their doors only after most of the restaurants and movie theaters closed, spaces that disgorged their inhabitants and lowered their sound systems when other New Yorkers were just rising, afresh, on Sunday mornings, to collect their *New York Times*, or walk their dogs, or get their religion?

It was partly just that, I guess—if you felt in any way a freak, if the daytime streets of the city never seemed completely yours, you could always own them at night. But once inside those spaces, the broad black anonymity of the streets melted away and suddenly, emerging from the heart of each pounding beat, familiar faces distinguished themselves out of the muggy gloom—old friends and new prospects, discarded lovers, conspirators by association, those that you swapped kisses with because of shared memories of previous nights, or those that you assiduously avoided for memories of ugly things that had happened, or of reckless things that ought not to have happened. It must have been what other people felt when going to weddings, or high school reunions, or other events when all the faces of your life descend upon you in a giddy, disorienting confusion of recollection—for others, the kind of event that jarred you into pondering the entire sweep of your life for the whole week to follow.

But for night people like us, these were events of such regularity that you took for granted the idea of belonging to a sprawling and intricately connected personal universe. Not that it was all this rarefied, not that each night out carried with it the promise that you would be forever and deeply transformed. Just the opposite, in fact—so much of the allure deriving from the *illusion* of monumentality itself, as though you were bracing yourself for a great moment you knew ultimately, happily, you'd be spared. And still you prepared yourself like a bride, and everything leading up to the moment you passed through the velvet ropes, right up to the final ride to Eleventh Avenue or Twenty-Eighth Street in a crowded, drunken cab, had about it the ritual decorum of preparations for the public unveiling of a singular body—a bride, a baby boy, or a well-preserved corpse.

I guess that's partly why I so loved those nights, especially the ones that took on the weight of high holidays, as did Flip's Half-Year Party for The Box, which took place on a giddily lovely Saturday night in mid-July, just six months and two weeks after The Box had opened. Now, I wish I could break down the hours of that night into each of their requisite minutes, then seconds—frame by frame as they climbed toward midnight, then slid down into the morning. I can't, of course, but if I could—to be as precise and photographic as possible—it would have started like so:

Flip left for The Box late that afternoon, to supervise the

minutiae of 'absolutely everything,' and to be fitted by Miko into the trappings of her midnight appearance—not to be seen by any one of us again, like a bride, until she emerged, vested victoriously, before her loving populace. Jess and I took it upon ourselves to throw a cocktail party at the loft for the inner circle. By eight, the loft was presentable, glowing with candles, stocked with liquor, filled with acid jazz, and Jess and I sat across from each other, drinks before us and cigarettes in hand.

'Did you ever think we'd make it this far?' he asked me. 'Did you ever think she'd really do it?'

'I've never put anything past Flip.' That wasn't true, but happiness and success have a way of gentling over the memory of old ambivalences.

Did the buzzer sound five seconds later or five minutes? See, right there—so many moments lost to me now!

I left him there, eyes closed, and opened the door. 'You came!' I cried, and Joey *had* come, cane in hand, weak and ironic smile, sallowness effaced under make-up and blunt-cut blond wig, in a simple flowered A-line dress and white patent-leather chunk-heeled strap sandals, all of it conspiring to give him the look of a knock-kneed, peroxided Greek girl named Rosemary Karamatopolous whom my mother had gone to high school with.

'She came all right,' brayed Cedric from underneath a frosted black shag, self-possessed atop tiny silver heels, in a complicated Halston-style cream silk tunic that robed or wrapped every inch of his flesh except for six inches of breath-takingly wrought abdomen. He helped Joey inside, one enormous, silver-nailed hand under Joey's knobby blue elbow. Flash-like, Joey jabbed him away.

'Don't walk me like I'm Brooke Astor,' he snapped, indicating for Jess to pull out a chair for him, into which he descended stiffly, straightening his skirt. 'I hope you're all fucking happy,' he said, reaching for the scotch bottle and pouring himself a sloppy glass, 'because tonight is Barbara's last stand.'

'Fuck that, it is,' Jess said sternly.

Joey twisted around awkwardly in his chair, shaking his cane at him. 'Don't you contradict me, you arrogant *puta*. If I say it is, it is. I just suggest you tell the rags to snap plenty of pictures of me tonight, because this is their last photo op.'

'Listen to her go *on*!' Cedric boomed, descending on Joey to adjust his blunt cut and water down his drink, dismissing Joey's vituperative protests. 'She likes to think she can get away with rudeness 'cause she's in dementia, but she ain't yet.'

'How dare you, Cuntessa!' Joey shot out, and for a moment I was afraid he was going to spit lipsticked spit right into Cedric's face.

Cedric towered over Joey, hands on hips, setting the tunic's floor-length cape aflutter. 'I *dare*, bitch, 'cause I dressed you tonight, that's why I *dare*. An' when you're truly demented enough to be carrying on the way you are tonight, *I'll* let you know.'

Joey submitted blackly to the wig-fitting. 'I should read you good,' he said, low, to Cedric, who laughed and turned to us.

'Ooh, she can talk tonight.' Then to Joey: 'Come on, habibi. Be a princess for me tonight, because you know we love you like one.' He bent down to kiss Joey on the cheek, and Joey, murmuring something we couldn't hear, rubbed away any possible imprint of lipstick and smirked.

The buzzer again. Anthea sailed in, champagne bottles in hand, wrapped up in a gauzy black leopard-print coatdress, dragging her sullen, lovely Katja behind her by one hand.

'Darlings, you should have seen what Miko fashioned up in the front lobby of the club—' She stopped dead in her tracks, staring at Joey, who raised a trembling, bellicose eyebrow at her as if to say *Well?*

Jaw low, Anthea loosened Katja's nervous grip and

approached him. 'You—look—*fantastic*, Joey! Miss Barbara
Ganesh!' (Anthea had always mispronounced Joey's drag surname, provoking him to ask her if she thought he looked like
an elephant.) 'Fan-fucking-*tas*tic!' She bent down and kissed
him on both cheeks.

'Thank you, Anthie,' he murmured.

'I mean,' she gushed on, taking his hands in hers. 'I mean, so
do you, Urethra, but I see *your* tired ass all the time, and—'

Cedric extended his flattened hand, Supremes-style.

'—and I haven't seen *this* one in so *very* long, and I truly
wondered if I would ever see Miss Ganesh again, and—I
mean, *look* at her, Katja, isn't she sublime?'

'Sublimated.' Katja smiled agreeably.

'Sublimated, *yes!*' Anthea continued. 'Oh, God—look at me!
Now I'm starting to cry!'

'Don't ruin your eyeshadow for my sake,' Joey said burrily,
but he refused to let go of her hand, and I knew he was
pleased.

Anthea gathered herself together. 'All right, very well. I
shan't cry. But *look* at us—' and she gestured half a circumfer-
ence around the room. 'All of us children. We're all together
tonight. Tigger!' she gasped. 'Your auntie! Is she coming with
her Brit?'

I turned to Jess. 'Lippy said she and Langley were coming
when you talked to her yesterday, didn't she?'

'She said it would be like missing Flip's bat mitzvah, if she
ever had had one.'

'Thank goodness,' Anthea exhaled, throwing her beaded
antique purse down on the table and reaching for the
corkscrew and champagne. 'But still no reason that we
shouldn't start toasting now!'

'Honey, has anything *ever* kept you from toasting?' Cedric
clucked.

'Don't be wicked, Cedric,' Anthea tossed off, unbothered.

Suddenly Katja raised herself up, caught all our attention

with her anguished gasping. 'May I say? May I say?' she pleaded.

There was a short, bemused silence. 'Go ahead and say, honey,' Cedric finally responded.

'I read some books—' she began, trembling, and I was shocked to see tears mount in her enormous brown eyes. 'And— and—'

More awkward silence. 'Go on, darling,' Anthea murmured very quietly.

'And I know now. Ant-ie is al-col—, al-col—' she struggled.

Cedric tittered, but Joey hissed at him to shut up. 'What are you trying to say, darling?' Anthea persisted, leveling her gaze at Katja over her champagne glass. 'That I'm an alcoholic? That I'm a lush?'

Katja tried to speak, but only succeeded in dissolving into tears, head in hands, her sobs sounding curiously, and heartbreakingly, like the yelps of a distressed puppy. Jess and I caught each other's glance, alarmed.

'Oh dear,' Anthea said, businesslike, putting down her champagne glass and taking up Katja efficiently in her arms. 'Katja? Katja, my darling?'

Katja yelped in response, tears unabated.

'Katja, precious, you needn't cry. Anthea knows she's an alcoholic.' She took all of us into her amused, shaken glance. 'Everybody's known that Anthea's an alcoholic for a long time. It's just a simple fact of life, darling.'

'No!' Katja wailed, drawing back angrily from Anthea. Her muddled eyeshadow, and her increasingly violent tremor, only contributed to the effect of her as a small, distressed animal. 'No, Ant-ie, not *o-kay*. You have disease—not a weak heart, this is what I read in pamphlets—'

'What, have you been sneaking off to AA meetings and picking up literature for me?' Anthea snapped at her.

Katja nodded her head miserably, and Anthea could only

gasp in astonishment. 'I read the— the pamphlets— and leader, group leader, tells me that loved ones have to lead al-col— al-hol—'

'The alcoholic,' Anthea supplied sourly.

'Yes. Have to lead alco-holic to help. Otherwise, loved ones stand by and watch alco-holic kill herself. And if I lose you, Ant-ie, I kill myself too. Because I love you so, Ant-ie!' It was all too much to be borne by Katja, who broke down sobbing again, her trembling frame seeming slighter than ever.

We all just stood there, stunned, while Anthea faced the sobbing Katja, dumbstruck. For a moment, I wondered if Anthea was going to slap her into quiescence—she had been known to do this to a few of her former girlfriends when she was truly moved to fury (by drunkenness, of course)—and the entire room was taut with silent expectation. Then, suddenly, first to my surprise then to all our relief, Anthea laughed: one brief terse report that quickly escalated into self-knowing hilarity.

'You're absolutely right, Katja darling,' she said before turning to all of us. 'I *am* killing myself. We've all known it for years, so why shouldn't we talk about it? I'm thirty-four next month. I'm an expat who hates England as much as I hate the States, with the exception, I suppose, of this filthy little island. I failed as an actress—I'll never be the next Julie Christie like I wanted to be when I was your age—' And she stroked Katja absently on the head.

'Let's see, what else? I haven't made much of a go of my shop, and I'll never command the kind of attention that Flip does, and my girlfriend is so many times lovelier than me—' Anthea stopped briefly, and I noticed Katja peek up from her muted sobs to eye her expectantly. Anthea caught her glance and turned to her.

'Lovelier than me that I watch her when she sleeps. And I ask the heavens how is it that I've failed at virtually everything, and yet I've somehow managed to keep this beautiful—' she stopped suddenly and gently withdrew Katja's head from her hands by the chin. 'To keep this beautiful, kind creature in my life. Because—' I heard the cleft in Anthea's voice, suddenly husky with tears. 'Because I love you *immensely*, darling. So much so you couldn't even know.'

One final, quiet gulping yelp from Katja before the two of them were in each other's arms, each slimly shaking, clinging to each other for dear life, oblivious to the little group of men in suits and heels who stood around watching them in mixed states of amusement, teariness and surprise. Cedric and I held each other's stare until he could bear it no longer. He started singing that 'Sister' song from the movie *The Color Purple* under his breath, the one that Shug sings to Celie. He got louder, and it wasn't long before Joey broke in, too. Soon, all four of us started laughing; Anthea extricated herself from Katja and turned on us, grinning wetly.

'All right, slag off, you poofters and wankers,' she bellowed, one arm slung loosely around a bedraggled, weakly smiling Katja (no small feat, this—Katja stood a good foot taller than the compact Anthea). 'I'm going to make a declaration, and you're all here to witness it, and hold me to it in the months ahead . . . and that means you, too, Miss Ganesh, so you'd better stick around.'

Joey arched back in his chair. 'I'll see what I can do.'

'And the pronouncement is this,' Anthea continued, taking a deep breath and turning to Katja: 'Darling, I'll do this—this bloody *thing* with you. Meetings, twelve steps, the wretched little tracts and aphorisms—'

'I'll show to you the pamphlets,' Katja interjected.

'I'm sure you will. The whole bloody affair. But you make me one promise, darling. You *stand* by me. You don't elope with Paulina Poriskova, and you don't run back to Slovenia. If I've got to choose between you and the bottle, I'll take you anyday. But without you—' Anthea eyed her as-yet-unfilled champagne glass lovingly.

'Shhhh,' hissed Katja, surprising us all by holding an authoritative finger to Anthea's lips. 'A good woman you've got behind you,' she said confidently. Cedric burst out laughing and swallowed Katja up in his enormous arms until you could hardly see her underneath the batwinged sleeves of his tunic.

'And as for tonight,' Anthea said, holding the bottles of champagne aloft, 'I'll just pace myself. Jess darling, get those glasses there.'

So we descended upon the champagne, passing glasses around and coming up with all sorts of inane toasts until the buzzer rang yet again. I let Lippy and Langley into a generally raucous party of six, catching Langley's customary initial look of genteel dismay whenever he came upon Cedric and Joey in drag.

'I can't believe you've begun toasting without me!' Lippy exclaimed after kissing me and letting her sparkling summer wrap fall from her shoulders and into Langley's waiting hands.

'It's a work in progress.'

'Thank goodness, because I have such news for you.' She looked as though she might pop out of her skin. 'Oh, Tigger, I should tell everyone at once, but I really want you to be the first to know. Langley, should I?'

'Darling,' he responded with elaborate patience. 'He is your nephew to tell.'

'Okay, then. Tigger—' and now she put her hand on my arm. 'My dream's come true. I'm going to sing at the Algonquin!'

'*What?*' I clapped my hand over hers.

'Yes!' and she virtually hopped in place. 'Thursdays and Sundays for two whole months right after the wedding. Isn't it marvelous?'

'How did you swing that?'

'Well,' and Lippy preened theatrically. 'You know I'm friends with Barbara Cook, right?'

'Of course.' Everyone knew as much; dropping this fact had

taken on a talismanic power for Lippy, like inadvertently rubbing a special stone in one's pocket for good luck.

'Well, she was slotted for that month, but had to pull out to
do an Asia tour, and I guess they were going to try to bring in
Rosemary Clooney, but Barbara said, "Well, for God's sakes,
why don't you bring in this gal Lippy Pappas that's been pack-
ing the house at Julia's Room in the Village for fifteen years?"
And the next thing you know, Ira my publicist calls me and
says, "Darling, you're booked at the Algonquin."'

Langley touched my arm authoritatively. 'It should have
happened *years* ago, Thomas.'

Lippy blushed appreciatively. 'Come on,' I said, directing
them toward the crowd. 'I've got a new toast to make. Look
who's here,' I said, folding them into the loud sextet. A round
of effusive hellos followed, of hugs, kisses and baroque decla-
rations of awe and envy over each other's ensembles.

'People, people,' I intoned, mimicking Lippy when she
wanted a group's attention. 'Raise your glasses because I've
got another toast to make.'

They hushed. 'Very well,' Anthea shrugged, refilling her
glass and holding it aloft.

'To the imminent Algonquin debut of the premier voice of
downtown cabaret, the inimitable song stylist, Lippy Pappas.'

'Girl!' Cedric cried, sparking the latest round of clinking
glasses and congratulatory proclamations. It was Cedric, at
length, who brayed that the clock was nearing eleven, and
within a remarkably efficient twenty-five minutes, during
which Lippy, Anthea, Katja, Cedric and Joey hastily retouched
their make-up and Langley, Jess and I polished off the last
bottle of champagne, we were nearly out the door when the
buzzer rang again.

'Who's left?' Anthea asked. We soon knew—it was Grant,
unflappably tardy, with Maeve sturdily on his heels.

'My apologies all around,' he proffered, as we handed the
two of them a quick glass of champagne each. Grant took his

back, neat, with one swallow, but Maeve limited herself to a handful of prudent sips before setting down her glass.

'He forgot to set the gallery alarm at the last minute,' she said, dourly indicating Grant.

'One little oversight, give me a break.'

Maeve sighed. 'You do it every night. One day we're going to come in and we're not going to have any art to sell.'

Grant shrugged in the face of her implacable frown, and in moments, the ten of us were out the door, down the noisy stairwell and into the street. Maeve briskly led the procession in her flowing black plus-size pantsuit like an army general, but Grant skulked along in the back sullenly, and when I noticed, I slowed down to join him.

'Where's your babe Janine tonight?'

He laughed hiccupingly, lighting a cigarette. 'She's out of the picture, Tiggerman. I got a new girl now. For real, this time.'

'Are you serious? Who is she? Why isn't she here tonight?'

'She is.' He exhaled smoke, looked at me challengingly. 'She's right up front, leading the jamboree.'

I looked up ahead where Maeve was striding capably ahead like a downtown den mother.

I turned to Grant. 'You mean—' but shock overwhelmed my question.

'Yes, baby, I mean.' He absently smoothed down his left sideburn. 'It's been going on for about a month now. And believe me,' he laughed, 'it's not gonna stop as long as I want her managing the gallery.'

'Jesus, Grant. So you guys are— like—'

'Shacked up? Not yet. She says she needs her space for the time being. But getting down to business? Yeah.' He shrugged. 'I like a big girl, Tigger,' he added, as though reading my thoughts. 'When she's there, you *really* know she's there, you know what I mean?'

'So, that talk we had about settling down? I mean, are you—'

He laughed again, cynical and happy. 'I wouldn't dare

fucking try to get out of this. And besides—' He stopped again, stroking the other sideburn for symmetry.

'Besides what?'

'Besides. I don't want to get out.'

'You're really serious, aren't you, Grant?'

He nodded, reflecting my own surprise. 'She's a winner, Tiggerman. I probably should have accepted the fact a long time ago. But better late than never, right?'

'Of course,' I said, knee-jerk, too astonished to elaborate. I looked ahead at Maeve, who had stopped at the corner to let her small army pass. Eventually, we reached her.

'Why do you always have to lollygag, Grant?' She frowned, taking his arm efficiently.

'I was *talking*,' he protested weakly, but no matter. The two of them passed on in front of me, and I stayed there for a moment, watching them, the way she at once dwarfed and sheltered him with her formidable girth. It was always like this—just when it seemed that the order of the world had been made clear and banal to me, something came along to remind me there was no order, to ends both joyous and grave. I shook my head slowly, then walked on.

It could have been New Year's Eve again, but for the exquisite summer night and the fact that the crowd this time seemed twice as thick, winding around the corner and spilling out into the street like an open-air bacchant. At the door, Ty and the others had set the velvet ropes perpendicular to the sidewalk, runway style, and I was shocked to see the banks of gossip columnists and photographers that crushed in on them from either side, snapping and yapping toward the celebrities as they passed through the entrance into the booming depths of the club. The ten of us stood by, catching a sample of the glitterati that emerged from limos and cabs and rushed between the ropes with all the self-importance of visiting dignitaries arriving at a presidential inauguration.

'Yo, Ty!' Jess shouted over people's heads, and everyone turned to stare, some with a mild start of semi-recognition that was like an ironic little grace note after the fanfare provoked by the previous lights. 'Can some no-names like us slip in now?'

'You can try your luck right now,' Ty boomed back wryly, stepping forward and unlinking the ropes for us, pushing back attempted coattail-riders as easily as a goliath might have blotted out ordinary mortals with his thumb. He was the only doorman on duty at the moment and I could read the wariness behind his professional, unsmiling poker face.

'I'll try to get someone to come out and help you—or I'll come out myself,' I said to him, low.

'I'm a'ight, Tigger.' He nodded tautly.

Cedric ran a teasing hand over Ty's thigh. 'Honey, I hope you're packin' your gat, tonight,' he purred absurdly, ''cause this crowd is too much for one man to handle—even you, baby.'

'Now don't you worry, Miss Urethra, I'm packin',' Ty responded with a low rumble of chuckles.

'I know, baby.' Cedric ran an enormous, lacquer-nailed hand over Ty's face, forcing from him a sheepish, exasperated smile, before he swept toward Joey to help him over the threshold.

My adrenaline was running high, and it was just as we were filing inside, joining the crush toward the coat-check, that I looked back behind me and caught my breath in a jolt of unhappy surprise. Just behind the velvet ropes, his face almost lost in the impatient sea of non-luminary ticketholders, stood Amos Goolsbee, hands thrust in the pockets of his pants, that galling, squinting smile on his face. Our eyes met, and he waved at me with his characteristic mocking hail-fellow-well-met cheer. I glared at him, no time to rid my face of its sudden shock and dismay, before I was pressured to pass through the door.

I grabbed Jess by the shoulder and he turned to me. 'Guess

who I just saw waiting to get in?' I whispered. He raised an
eyebrow inquiringly. 'Goolsbee,' I said.

His eyebrow dropped darkly. 'No fucking way.'

'Yes fucking way! I just saw him, with that evil smile all
over his face.'

'Man, he's got no shame.'

'Should we tell Ty not to let him in?'

'I guess—' Jess began, at a loss, before he collected himself.
'No. Why should we? He's only gonna alienate himself, 'cause
everybody here hates him. And he's not gonna do anything to
Flip with all of us here.'

'I guess so,' I said warily.

'Let him have his fun—or what he thinks is his fun. Jesus,
the guy really doesn't have a life, does he?'

I shrugged, troubled.

Jess put a hand on my shoulder. 'Don't let him sweat you,
Tigger. If he comes up to you, just cut him. That's what I'm
gonna do. I'd take care of him, but Flip already did, obviously.'

'I guess you're right,' I mumbled.

He smiled broadly. 'Of course I am. Now let's grab some
drinks and get up to Sammy's booth for Flip's spectacle.' I felt
like I should say something else to him, but in a moment, Liz
Smith and Cindy Adams had stolen upon us, raving about
Miko's design theme, and Goolsbee fell away behind the old
velvet ropes of my mind that I had always employed to separate the unwelcome from the bidden, the unpleasant from the
divine.

Sammy was spinning a madly accelerated Soul II Soul remix
as we negotiated our way through the glittering throng,
accepting greetings, congratulations and kisses all the way.
Cedric was screaming hellos left and right, Joey looked happily overwhelmed at the legions of old friends, in all sorts of
drag, that descended upon him with virtual tears of reunion,
Lippy's wide-eyed face read dazzled confusion, and Langley

surveyed the scene with such a look of dignified duress that I laughed aloud upon spotting him. Indeed, Miko's design work was remarkable—he had decorated the entire space as though it were a twisted, Alice-in-Wonderland birthday party for a six-month-old infant, an explosion of little-girl pink and baby-boy blue set against The Box's sleek black and silver surfaces. Glossy pink and blue bunting hung everywhere, pink and blue helium balloons in wildly distorted shapes and sizes floated and bobbed from ceilings to floors and everywhere in between, and all around there were the most lascivious pictures of evil-faced pink and blue toddlers. I noticed that the drag queens and models seemed to have gotten the monopoly of party favors, pink and blue rattles, pacifiers, and liquor-filled formula bottles scaled with comic grotesqueness to the size of Amazonian babies.

Eventually we made it up to Sammy's kingdom-on-high, where he saluted us jauntily as he continued to spin. Pepe threw his hands in the air by way of greeting before turning his wiry fingers back to Sammy's enormous catalogue of vinyl to pick out the coming tracks. Sammy's booth was spacious and plush, and we all took seats on the velvet banquettes that lined the booth, pouring bottles of champagne that had been fitted for us there in iced vessels by the staff, bracing for Flip's midnight moment. I looked down through the glass at the writhing, flashing congregation below and felt my heart race; I had been up here dozens of times in the past six months, and this lordly aerial view of the club on a good night never ceased to thrill me.

Sammy faded out of Soul II Soul into a long, hypnotic Latin house cut that sampled the opening piano riff of 'Don't You Worry 'Bout a Thing' again and again. Then he slipped his earphones off his head and turned to us, forehead gleaming with sweat, poured himself a glass of champagne and sat down in the banquettes with a great heave of relief.

'That should eat up the ten minutes left until midnight. Dag!' and he mopped his brow with his sleeve. 'This crowd's got a three a.m. tweak goin' already. I haven't stopped spinning since ten o'clock.'

'Sammy darling,' Anthea slurred, curled up comfortably with Katja. 'Do you have any idea what Miss Mitchell has planned for us?'

He *hmph*'d emphatically. 'Any *idea*? Child, I am an integral part of the plan.'

'Aieee!' Anthea shrieked. 'Hurry! Tell, tell!'

He shrugged apologetically. 'I can't. Her and Miko swore me to secrecy. Miss Mitchell said she'd take away my booth and give it to Pepe if I said anything. An' then everyone'd stop coming, 'cause nobody wants to listen to Gloria Estefan all night.'

Pepe reeled off something in Spanish, of which I got the general toxic drift.

'I'm just clownin' you, baby,' Sammy said to Pepe, who retreated into surly silence. 'And anyway,' Sammy went on, 'she's gonna show soon enough.'

'Say what?' Jess blurted, voicing my own alarm. The word *show* had taken on a heavily singular meaning in the past few weeks.

'Chill, baby,' Sammy said to Jess. 'She's gonna appear any second now. Which reminds me—' And he put his earphones back on and wheeled around to his turntables.

Jess and I exchanged nervous, aren't-we-silly smiles. 'What drama has the girl got planned?' Joey enunciated, speaking for us all. I looked around. It seemed everyone was holding hands or huddled close in tight pairs of anticipation—Anthea and Katja, Lippy and Langley, Grant and Maeve . . . even Cedric had his huge arm around Joey as though he were protecting his shrunken frame from the cold. Instinctively, I looked to Jess—but he had already positioned himself alone at the sound booth window, looking down on the crowd with rapt, solitary attention, and I glumly stopped myself from joining him as Sammy started fading out the long house cut, until it was fainter, fainter still, now nothing but the dimmest recollection of a high-hat, and by the time it had faded completely, all the lights in the house had faded, except for the red glow of the exit signs. Everywhere, we heard the dull roar of the confused, disoriented crowd, until Sammy snapped on his microphone and dispatched through the space in his deepest, most sonorous voice:

'Ladies and gentlemen, please relax. Please . . . *relax*.'

The buzz subsided somewhat.

'Thank you. The hour is midnight, ladies and gentlemen. And the event is the six-month birthday of The Breeders Box, the place where dreams come true when you wish on a star. So tonight, we ask you to wish on *this* star to make all your dreams come true, as they have for this very special young lady whom we all know and love.'

I didn't know whether to laugh or expire over what happened next. Suddenly, the guys up in the light booth cast an enormous spotlight onto the stage—and who should descend into it from on high, sitting in the cut-out middle of an enormous pink-and-blue lighted star, but, of course, Flip: barefoot, wearing the simplest white silk dress, her generally teased or updone hair parted in the middle to frame her glowing face, then flowing with pre-Raphaelite artlessness over her bare shoulders and down her back. She didn't outright smile so much as radiate a kind of illuminated Maxfield Parrish, nymph-like serenity, seeming not at all unnerved by the matter of hovering so very high above a sea of thousands of people, isolated in a spotlight. Her bare feet swung from her perch as though she were an eight-year-old idling on a swing, lost in her thoughts.

'Oh . . . Miss . . . *Thing*,' Cedric uttered in the midst of our silence with a funny mixture of hilarity and awe that seemed to capture the general buzz floating through the entire club, a buzz that accelerated and mounted the longer Flip sat there, staring down upon everyone, saying not a word.

Finally, she spoke, with an odd kind of throaty vibrato, into the microphone Miko must have fitted her with. 'Good morning,' she intoned. A chorus of *good mornings* raced up to her from all corners of the club, and her face broke into a slow, dreamy, expansive smile that brought a surge of applause and hollers from the crowd. Was she high? I wondered to myself. It didn't seem so—she seemed far too self-possessed to be coked out, and since receiving the happy news, her reformation had been absolute.

'She looks like Lillian Gish,' Lippy said, shell-shocked.

'I hope she's not about to pull some crazy Patty Duke-or-Sally Field-at-the-Oscars, or Bette Midler-at-the-end-of-*The Rose* drama,' Joey nearly yawned. 'Not up on that crazy star.'

'No, she ain't.' Sammy laughed, turning to his keyboard and striking the first maudlin notes. 'You just hear her now.'

'I have nothing to say,' Flip continued over Sammy's bluesy chords. 'Nothing to say except . . . thank you . . . for everything . . . and I love you . . . and bless you. Because'—she laughed here, quietly, almost to herself—'because . . . you are . . . *all* . . . my children.'

And then, much to our acute surprise, and followed by a club-wide holler of encouragement, Flip took a deep breath and sang—yes, *sang*—the opening line to 'God Bless The Child'.

Them that's got shall get . . .

Cedric touched me on the shoulder. 'This is not happening,' he intoned.

Sammy laughed delightedly while he riffed out his next phrase. 'Oh yes it is, honey! Introducing the next white blues mama.'

And on and on Flip sang, as the raucous house subsided, then quieted itself so thoroughly that Flip's voice reigned supreme, her face heart-breaking and serene.

Them that's not shall lose . . .

So the Bible says . . .

And it still is news.

Slowly, my alarm gave way to amazement. Flip had always had a decent voice, and wasn't shy about letting it go around the loft or in the shower, but she had never sung publicly before, never expressed any desire to. And what I couldn't get over now was just how good she sounded—throatily sexy, as usual, but with a simple purity of timbre and phrasing I had never noticed before. She didn't seem to be trying to imitate Billie Holliday, or Dinah Washington, or any of the other old divas she had always loved; she just seemed to be singing from her own place—indeed, her own star—with a total lack of affect, as though she had been born for this moment, plain and simple.

The strong seem to get more,
While the weak ones fade.
An' empty pockets don't ever seem to make the grade.

My observation wasn't lost on the others. 'Lippy!' Anthea hissed. 'Did you have something to do with this?'

'I wish I could say I did,' Lippy answered. 'But this is as much a surprise to me as it is to you.'

Rich relations give crusts of bread
And such.
You can help yourself, but don't take too much . . .

On Flip sang, her voice stronger and fuller as the old song crested.

Mama may have,
And Papa may have

I glanced over at Jess, who was rapt with attention, and held my stare until he caught it. He shrugged and gave me a look as if to say *Go figure*, then turned his attention back to Flip, who was coming to her finish, not showily but softly, as though she had succeeded in putting a child to sleep. No dramatic vocal tricks or hand gestures—throughout, her hands hadn't strayed from her lap.

But God bless the child that's got his own . . .

And then, after one final, beatific breath,

That's got . . . his . . . own.

The house exploded in frenzied applause that seemed to build and build and build, until a rhythm emerged—the steady clapping of hands and stomping of feet, accompanied suddenly by the chanting of 'Encore!', a chant which built in intensity, while Flip sat there on the star in the spotlight, merely smiling, giving no indication that she'd sing again. I felt a frisson of dread, suddenly—Why wasn't Flip responding, and why wouldn't they put out the white-hot spotlight on her?—and out of nowhere, I had a flash of associations: Flip's high-altitude vulnerability, my passing recognition of Goolsbee's face in the crowd, the .45 that Ty kept in his pants. That odd, premonitory panic, what self-declared psychics say they've felt seconds before an assassination or some sort of catastrophe, came over me—it was palpable, a wave of despairing nausea that passed from my head to my stomach and up to my chest, where my heart started pounding intently.

'When are they gonna put out the fucking spotlight and let her up?' I exclaimed, earning everyone's startled glance.

And just then, when I thought I couldn't stand another minute of it, Flip finally announced 'Thank you,' and her image snapped into blackness, and I could make out the illuminated star floating its way back up to the catwalk, far beyond the sight or the reach of her thousands of frantic supplicants. My heart stopped pounding but I was sweaty and enervated, and I sat down leadenly on one of the banquettes and poured myself a full glass of champagne.

Twenty-Three

Sammy quickly darted back to the turntable and laid down some hyperactive salsa track, then turned to us as everyone joined me on the banquettes in recovery. 'Well?' he asked. 'What did you think? Was she not fierce for a white girl?'

'Is this the start of a new career for her, or something?' Jess asked.

Sammy shook his head. 'I don't think so. She just said that she really felt like singing something tonight and asked if I'd help her put it together. And when I asked her what she wanted to sing, she said "God Bless The Child"—right off, like that, like she'd wanted to sing it all her life.'

'Should we go find the girl?' Anthea asked.

'No, you stay put,' Sammy said. 'She told me to tell you she's coming up here with Miko after the appearance 'cause she don't want to go down on the floor alone.'

'I don't blame her,' I said, my moment of unbidden anxiety having passed. 'Someone might mistake her for Ma Rainey.'

Cedric swatted me, delighted. 'Don't be shady, honey.'

In a moment we heard the clatter of heels on the stairway up to the booth, and Miko's excited chatter, and in another moment, they had entered, inspiring a mad tangle of shrieks and hugs. Why was it, I suddenly asked myself, that we never simply greeted each other with dry little kisses like other groups of friends did, but instead with war whoops and embraces that might have been mistaken for assaults? It was as though every time we gathered, we were a talk-show reunion of relations that had been torn apart by an earthquake, tornado or some such other act of God twenty years ago.

Everyone was abuzz. 'Darling, why didn't you *tell* me you could sing like that?' Lippy was demanding, and from Anthea: 'You've just *got* to sing regularly here, they all fancied you so!', and from Cedric and Joey: 'Girl, where *are* the boys from A&R?', and from Langley: 'Perhaps you'll honor us by singing at our nuptials? Wouldn't that be lovely, sweetheart?', and from Katja, who was virtually hyperventilating from excitement: 'So *beautiful*, Fleep, so *beautiful*.' Throughout, Flip maintained her equanimity—'Well, you see, Miko and I wanted to do something special, and I've always loved that song, and I didn't want to *turn it out* so much as just *deliver* it—'

'But she *did* turn it out!' Miko interjected. 'Didn't you love the way the spotlight made her shoulders glow? Mm! Just like those old photos of Rita Hayworth.'

'Oh, Miko, please.' Flip blushed. 'And it just—I don't know, came *out*.' She *was* glowing tonight, I noticed, even up close—unburdened of her customary theatrical make-up and sculptural hair, she seemed to have reclaimed a certain milky girlishness that to me was both ravishing and unsettling in a way I couldn't define. And then, in one of those rare occasions when all the inchoate feelings you've ever had for someone suddenly consolidate themselves into one moment of terrible clarity, it became apparent to me how, ever since our childhood, I had loved and hated her at the same time—wanted to protect her, elevate her, *be* her even, with all her galvanic energy and fearlessness and charm, and simultaneously wanted to break her, humiliate her, obliterate her from the landscape of my life, this girl—no, this *woman*—who was the very image of me if I had been a girl, who shared my features

and colors and blood, who had vouchsafed my security as
much as she had robbed me of myself. It all came together for
me with such horrible totality in that moment, right there in
the noisy, lively sound booth, that I gave up my place in the
informal queue of Flip's well-wishers and stepped back—
nearly walking into Jess, who had been hanging back from the
crowd all along.

'Whoops!' I laughed, my face flushing plum. He looked at
me curiously—sharply, rather, I thought—and for a woozy
moment I was convinced that everything I had been just
thinking read clear as newsprint on my face.

But he hardly indicated as much. 'I'm giving Flip her space
right now,' he said, distracted, fumbling with a cigarette.

'Me too,' I responded, taking cover.

He turned to me and placed a cold hand on my shoulder.
'After all, we're her family, right?'

'Right,' I answered tentatively. 'What about it?'

He didn't answer. Instead, he smiled at me with what
seemed to be the ghastliest contempt and, before I had a
chance to stop him, slipped quickly out of the sound booth
and down the stairs, marooning me in my hurt and confusion.

Sammy called for peace and quiet, and, grabbing glasses
and bottles of champagne, everyone pulled themselves
together with rare speed and filed out of the sound booth.
Flip was the last out, and, still shaken by my thoughts of a
moment ago, I hung back, hoping she'd hurry off before she
took notice of me. Wouldn't it figure, then, that I heard her
heels stop clattering after the first few steps. 'Tigger?' she
called out, and clattered back into the booth.

'Yeah?' I looked at her quickly, then turned away. She was
too beautiful, too wonderful, too terrible for looks to bear.

She rushed over to me, miming an apology to Sammy (preoccupied again now alongside Pepe with choosing tracks),
and sat down beside me on the banquette, putting her hand
over my own, which felt exquisitely, unbearably soothing and

warm. 'Aren't you coming down with us? I'm terrified of going down there without you.'

'I'm coming . . . in a minute.'

'Tigger?' She laughed. 'Why don't you look at me?'

'Hm?' I turned, forced myself to look her in the face, felt my face turning a thousand colors. 'I'm sorry. I think I'm a little drunk.'

She laughed again. 'Already? God, I'm glad *you're* not the one having the kid.'

The remark hit me with such force that I'm amazed I was able to respond at all. 'No kidding, hunh?'

'Hunh,' she responded. I had turned away from her again and I felt her hand tighten on my own, as though to reach me. I felt horribly, miserably trapped inside myself—venal for not responding to her, yet paralyzed by my own choked-up, tangled-up feelings. At any minute, I expected her to bring up her performance to break the silence, to tell me all about how she and Miko had come up with 'the concept,' what it had felt like to swing on a star high above thousands of rapt acolytes, what I had thought of her hair, and dress, and voice, and did she even *dare* think she should pursue singing further?

But much to my surprise she didn't. 'Tigger, can I *please* tell you that thing about the baby?' she asked softly when she finally spoke.

Her own narcissistic monologue would have been better than this, I thought. At that moment, the very thought of the baby filled me with an inhuman sadness and dread. 'I thought you wanted to keep it to yourself,' I managed to say.

'I did,' she laughed. 'But you know I can't keep anything to myself. If I can't share it, it's like it doesn't exist.'

'I know,' I answered, struck by her insight. 'But I thought—'

'I know,' she interrupted. 'Okay. Can I tell you something else instead?'

'Sure,' I said, defeated.

'I won't tell you outright whether it's a boy or a girl. Just this: If it's a boy, I'm gonna call him T.J. Mitchell. For Thomas Jesús. And the "Thomas" isn't for Daddy. It's for you.'

I looked at her. Her eyes were wide and bright with expectation, her hand clutching mine as though for dear life. More than anything, I wanted to take hold of her and cry and cry against her bare, warm shoulder—even here, in front of Sammy and Pepe, I didn't care. But I didn't. With all my might, I swallowed the urge. Then, I made a cold, clear, unequivocal decision in my mind and tucked it neatly away for the rest of the night. And when I was done making this decision, I kissed her.

'Thank you,' I said.

'No.' She shook her head, kissed me back. 'Thank *you*. Now will you please escort your sister downstairs and promise not to leave my side for a minute?'

I smiled wirily. 'Of course.'

And that's just what I did—squired my famous sister around for the following hour, parting the way for her through crowds of unknowns, alerting her to faces she should greet, saying all the smart, witty, sassy things she loved me for saying because they enriched her aura of coming from some very special, glamorous place. I even said all the right things to Nile Rodgers and Quincy Jones, who were slugging tequila shots with a bunch of TV and music people in from L.A. Sandra Bernhardt was saying all sorts of lascivious things to Flip, who reacted with an endearing kind of straight-girl awkwardness that I knew was entirely contrived—she was too habituated to being an object of desire for even the most ribald remarks to faze her. Rosie Perez was there, and she insisted that I sit by her so she could run her hands through the recently buzzed back of my head while she kept asking Sandra of me, 'Do you think we should set him up with Lorenzo? Do you think we should set him up with Lorenzo?' Sandra was ambivalent about this idea, but neither of them would tell me who Lorenzo was, for all that I asked them a million times, which seemed to be just what they wanted me to do.

Eventually, we were on the dance floor with the inner circle (Langley and Joey sat just off to the side in two of the little gold ballroom chairs, shouting a conversation into each other's ears, and Cedric was lambadaing with Lippy, provoking her delighted laughter), and I was relieved when Jess's face, however serious, emerged from the crowd to join us. Flip cried out with happiness when she saw him, and he smiled sweetly and kissed her before turning to me and shouting tensely into my ear.

'What?' I frowned. Sammy had pumped up the volume to such deafening levels it seemed that the giant reverberating speakers would come crashing down on us at any minute.

'I said,' he shouted louder, 'can you step out with me for a second?'

'Why?'

'I just got a phone call. I have to run an errand.'

'Why can't you do it yourself?' I shouted back.

'Because—' he shouted, edgier. 'Because I'd rather not.'

He was annoying me. He was always asking me cryptically to come along with him on some 'very important' assignation, which usually turned out to be no more than keeping him company when he had to do something tedious like wash his paintbrushes. Moreover, he had cut me in the sound booth just a short while ago, leaving me alone in my distress.

'I can't,' I finally said. 'I told Flip I'd stay with her.'

'Flip'll be fine,' he shouted into my ear. 'Don't be a difficult prick.'

'Now you've really clinched it,' I laughed meanly. 'See you later.' And I turned back to dance, looking back only briefly to see him throw me the finger and storm off the dance floor.

Flip grabbed my arm, worried. 'What was that all about?' she shouted. 'Where's he going?'

'To get a drink,' I lied, rolling my eyes. It would only upset her to tell her he was leaving, however briefly.

'His fucking mood swings,' she shouted. I shrugged, and we continued dancing. The night was peaking, people screaming and dancing and making out everywhere, openly snorting bumps of cocaine off their fists with that drug-induced recklessness that always kicked in around this time. (Lippy and Langley were still here, remarkably, and I only hoped that Lippy wouldn't notice; the possibility of such goings-on also sent her into paroxysms of terror that we'd be busted for running a drug den.) I sloughed off the recent unpleasantness with Jess and gave myself over to the music and the crowd, made all the sweeter and more precious on account of the decision I had tucked away.

I guess I saw Goolsbee first, shouldering his way toward us through the crowd, but Flip didn't recognize him in time to stop him from grabbing her and kissing her full on the lips. She withdrew in shocked disgust.

'Your gall is amazing,' she shouted at him from a few feet away, shaking her head in coolly recomposed disbelief.

'What's so amazing about it?' he shouted back before turning to me. 'Hello, Tigger. You look pretty.' Then back to Flip: 'I've got sixty-thousand dollars invested in the place, after all.'

'Believe me, your money's coming to you anyday,' Flip answered.

'Don't worry about it. It's all a moot point now.' He reached out to touch her behind the ear, but she slapped his hand away.

'I can't stop you from being here,' she shouted, 'but could you at least go be a nuisance to somebody else? Winona Ryder, maybe?'

He opened his mouth wide, mock-impressed. 'Winona's here?'

'Yeah,' Flip said. 'Just to see you.'

'Poor thing.'

'No kidding. Bye-bye now,' Flip shouted with mock-sweetness before she turned away from him, rejoining the group with a great show of forced merriment. I caught the look he gave her as she turned away—some horrible mixture of desire, hatred, pity and glee—before he turned to me and brightened. 'Good luck, Tigger,' he lisped, extending a bur-lesquely limp wrist.

'You're a miserable person,' I declared flatly. Much to my chagrin, he exploded in delighted, psychotic laughter. 'God, I *love* the Mitchell family!' he exclaimed before striding off, laughing still.

Flip waited a safe interval before turning to see if he was gone. 'I think I'm going to have morning sickness right now,' she shouted to me.

'It's not worth it.'

'What do you think he meant about the money being a moot point? If he thinks he's got it all over me because I can't pay him back, he's wrong. That's the first check I write when the will comes in.'

'I think he was just being his customary psycho self.'

Flip grimaced theatrically. '*Such* an unpleasant person!'

'In-*deed*,' I responded with similar dudgeon. I had always loved her habit of diminutizing evil situations—she had that Sally Bowles thing down even better than Anthea—and we shared a laugh, which stabbed me with a pang that I quietly and firmly dismissed. My decision, after all.

And then I don't know how much more time passed before it all started happening. I smelled it first, but didn't think much of it—someone's hair had probably caught on fire from a cigarette—but then I whiffed it stronger, and so did Flip.

'What the fuck is that?' she shouted at me. 'If someone's free-basing, I wish they'd do it in the bathroom stalls.'

But the smell of smoke only intensified—looking around the dance floor, I could see that other people were smelling it as well, grimacing suspiciously and shouting into each other's

ears with expressions of vague, puzzled concern. Then I heard
the screams and shouts from the entryway that led back down
the winding stairs toward the front of the club—from which
smoke billowed in ugly, acrid black waves.

The dancing had stopped—everyone stood frozen in
place—but the music pounded on with diabolical incongruity;
I'll never, ever forget what it was: Sammy's new house mix of
'Someday We'll Be Together', the perfect track to play at this
euphoric hour. Suddenly, I was thinking a million thoughts,
but two words seemed to keep ringing in my head amidst the
growing panic: *Moot point. Moot point. Moot. Point.*

'Oh shit,' I said aloud, and suddenly it was all clear.

Langley bounded out of his chair, roughed his way through
the crowd to us. 'Something's amiss,' he kept declaring ridiculously. 'Something's rather amiss.' Cedric burst off the floor
and picked up the frail, frightened Joey in his enormous arms.

Flip grabbed me. 'God help us,' she cried. 'Where's Jess?
Where's Ty? *Somebody stop the fucking music!*'

Mid-demand, the music stopped, and for an eerie moment,
her voice rang out over all others': *the fucking music!* Then all
you could hear was the music of pandemonium: screams,
shouts, a thousand entreaties, demands, suggestions. The air
was growing thicker with smoke—our eyes were beginning to
smart now—to the point where you could hardly see the front
entryway for the evil haze.

A voice came on over the sound system.

'Yo, people. People! Ladies and gentlemen.' It was Ty. 'This
is management. Now chill out and listen hard, you hear me?
There's a fire in the boiler room and it's blocked the way out
the front of the house. If you're not on the main dance room,
get your asses there now. Now, listen up. Divide this room in
half and go out the doors that say EXIT in red on the right or
the left. Then go down the stairwells that come out on the side
streets. There's gonna be firemen and shit there to escort you
out. And nobody be buggin' and pushin' or somebody's gonna

get hurt. Just be cool—we all gonna be fine if we act sensible and shit. Now Sammy's gonna play some chill music to set the pace. So get on widdit, and be cool. Over and out.'

The procession that followed had the surreal, stilted rhythm of a nightmare. Sammy put on 'And I'm Tellin' You I'm Not Going'—one of the few end-of-set ballads in his collection, usually a bittersweet send-off for the die-hards who were still on the dance floor or passed out on sofas at nine in the morning, but a ghastly pick right now—and to Jennifer Holliday's histrionic strains, the stunned-silent throng began throbbing and inching itself toward the emergency exits, punctuated by the occasional hysterical sob or angry exclamation. Our crowd moved along in a mute huddle like a shell-shocked herd of cows, Lippy clutching Langley, Anthea clutching Katja, Maeve holding up Grant, Cedric supporting Joey, my hand and Flip's in a death grip. Her face was chalked over with fear, her lower lip trembling, and I could think of nothing substantial to say to her as we shuffled forward, so I only held her hand tighter and murmured again and again: 'It's gonna be all right, Flip. It's gonna be all right.'

Just beneath the red EXIT sign, she turned to me, stricken. 'Where's Jess?' she hissed.

'He's fine. He left the club to go do an errand.'

'That's not what you told me,' she said, more panicked. 'You said he went to get a drink.'

'I lied,' I said, wishing desperately now that I hadn't.

'No you didn't!' she protested, loud, and faces turned to us. 'Why would you do that?'

'Because I didn't want you to worry, *all right*?'

'Where did he go, then?'

'I don't know. To do some errand. Probably to get cigarettes or something.'

'But he could get cigarettes right here—at the bar, or in the office.' Her voice was rising now to a near-hysterical pitch. 'Why would he leave to do that?'

'I don't know, Flip, but he left, all right? He's *fine*. Now would you just chill out and take care of yourself?'

'I don't—' *Believe you*, I knew she was going to say, but she silenced herself, redoubled her grip on my hand, and shuffled forward, her whole face taut with fear.

The long march down the stairwell was excruciating, so many party people, seen usually at their height of shadiness or merriment, now staring like deers in headlights up or down the cinderblack stairwell at each other, their fucked-up, sweaty faces jaundiced and grotesque under the hideous fluorescent lights—muscle boys climbing back into their sweat-soaked shirts, party girls holding fingertips up to sniffling nostrils and clomping their new, outsize platform heels on the warped old steel stairs, goaded into dark, incoherent laughter by the irrepressible drag queens, who thought the whole thing was glamorous, just like *Towering Inferno*, and they'd have to fight it out to see who'd get to play Faye Dunaway—but it was a laughter that came to an abrupt stop as soon as they were made aware of Flip's presence.

We heard the sirens of the fire trucks and caught a slice of their flashing lights playing in the street just before we reached the sidewalk exit at the bottom of the stairwell.

Flip turned to me again. 'Tigger, I really think he's in there.'

'He's *not*, Flip,' I answered sharply. 'Now let's just deal with this and try not to get to shaken up 'cause you gotta think of you-know-what.' She placed a hand knee-jerk over her stomach and murmured something incomprehensible.

We emerged out onto the warm, dark street to find something of a catastrophic carnival atmosphere—the clubgoers on the stairwell ahead of us, tweaks at a peak and safe with their lives, were already laughing about the incident and debating shrilly over where else to go while their highs lasted—Limelight? Sound Factory? Already, their genuine terror was mutating to titillation, to the makings of a personal memoir of a night that would surely go down in clubland history ('Honey, I was *there* the night of The Breeders Box fire!'), and Flip, huddled close to me and the rest of the group, had little to say to the occasional familiar faces that sought her out to offer comfort, or support, or the assurance that certainly the damage wouldn't be that bad and she'd be open for business again tomorrow night, or if she felt like it why didn't she join them at Bowery Bar later on that night for a much-deserved recovery cocktail?

She seemed shell-shocked, and I decided that I'd better take matters into my own hands. 'Come on, baby,' I said, putting my arm around her, 'let's go talk to a fireman or Ty or someone around front.'

Joey grabbed her arm before we departed. 'We're not going anywhere, girl. We'll be right here, okay?'

Everyone echoed his promise, to which she could only utter a hoarse, barely audible, 'Thanks.' Grimly, she and I walked down the side street, me shielding her from people's various shout-outs of dismay and encouragement. Then she suddenly looked up, gasped, broke away from me with a terrible cry and ran around the corner. I followed where her eyes had gone— 'Oh, shit! *Shit!*'—and ran off after her.

Flames engulfed the entire front of the club—long, evil tongues of yellow and orange that were slowly eating away at the ancient converted structure that had first been a warehouse of sorts in 1914. Firemen aiming wide blasts of water from truckhouses seemed to be doing little to stop the conflagration. They had roped off the entrance, but you could look straight through the front door into an inferno raging within. Just beyond the fire ropes, an enormous crowd of people— evacuated clubgoers and SoHo passersby—had gathered to watch the fire. I had never seen a fire of such ferocity except on TV or at the movies but this one was real, vividly real against the cloudless black New York sky, and I couldn't believe it was happening to us.

'Oh my God,' Flip uttered once, low, and then she was in

my arms, sobbing. '*Oh my God! Look at it! LOOK at it!*'

'It's gonna be okay, Flip,' I shouted, holding her, but I was none too confident of that myself. Still, I repeated myself.

'What if Jess is in there?' she asked me again, her face a frieze of terror.

'He's not, okay? Now just think about the baby—think about T.J., okay?'

This seemed to stay her for a moment.

'Now, come on,' I said, walking her over to the firetruck.

'Stay back, stay back,' a fireman barked at us through a megaphone as we approached, blasting out my ears.

'We're the owners!' I shouted at him.

'Don't matter,' he megaphoned back to me. 'Serious operation now. We'll talk later. Please get behind the ropes.'

'Is it going to be okay?' I shouted.

'It'll stay standing—brick always does—but it's gonna be gutted. Not a good scenario.'

'Oh God,' Flip moaned. 'Ask him if everyone's out.' So I did.

'Looks that way,' he sirened back with what struck me as damnable casualness. 'We checked out everywhere before it really got bad, seemed like a one-hundred percent evacuation unless some idiot really wanted to stay. Anyway, can't do anything about it now. There's no getting out at this point, and no going back in, unless you've got a death wish.'

The flames were illuminating Flip's tear-soaked face when I turned to her, giving her stricken expression an even more frightening, fantastic cast. 'See?' I said. 'There's nobody in there.'

'That's not what he said,' she responded hoarsely. 'He said it looks that way.'

'I'm sure he knows what he's talking about.'

'Then where the fuck is Jess?'

Where the fuck *had* Jess gone to? I wondered. But I didn't say that. 'Look at this crowd,' I said instead. 'It's thousands of people. How do you expect to just find him like that?'

'Tigger! Flip!' someone called, and we turned. It was Ty and Guillermo, calling to us from the crowd behind the fire ropes, one hundred feet straight back from the flaming main entrance, the tiny sign for which I could still discern alongside the doorway. Guiding Flip behind me, I shouldered our way through the crowd—'We can't talk now, we can't talk now,' I barked boilerplate-style at dozens of people, half of whom, I knew dimly, were downtown press vultures looking for some to-die-for quote from the proprietress as she watched her kingdom go up in smoke. Finally, we reached Ty and Guillermo, who was weeping openly. That didn't surprise me—Guillermo had always been weepy and demonstrative—but Ty was crying right along with him, and the sight of this six-foot-four-inch straight homeboy in tears almost pushed me to the limit myself.

'There ain't nothin' we can do,' Ty said, taking Flip in his arms. 'I asked the firemen if we could help, and he said there ain't nothin' we can do. Flip, baby, I'm so sorry.'

'At least your announcement worked,' I said. 'What the fuck happened, anyway?'

'I do not know!' Guillermo said, collecting himself a bit. 'Door was closed for the night, register closed for the night—filled beyond capacity, you know—'

'But the F.D. don't have to know that,' Ty added, still holding a numb Flip in his arms.

'—beyond capacity, and I just sitting in lobby having ciga-rette with Tyrone, when all a sudden, we smell smoke. Tyrone run down to basement, run back up screaming "Call fire-house! Call firehouse! Whole boiler room crazy on fire, can't put it out, can't even step inside! You call firehouse, I go make announcement!"'

'Guillermo, take a breath!' I demanded. 'Now, listen—did the F.D. go in when they got here and check to make sure everyone was out?'

'Tha's the first thing they did,' Ty said, 'with just enough time to do, like, this *stormtrooper* technique, or whatever, then they come out an' shout to me "All evacuated," and they start hosin'. Say they can't hose from inside, it's too saturated, or some such.'

'Ty,' Flip finally spoke. 'Jess was up front with you guys, right? You've seen him out here, right?'

'No, I ain't seen him, come to think.'

Flip looked at me accusingly. 'Ty, didn't you see Jess step out about a half an hour before the fire started, out to run an errand?' I asked.

Ty frowned in recollection—I glanced up, only to see a resurgence of flames attack the part of the façade that hung over the door's slightly recessed entrance. 'No, I don't remember seein' him step out.'

'Tigger, you fucking liar!' Flip screamed at me.

'But I gotta admit, I was countin' cash with Guillermo and coulda not noticed—'

'You would have noticed!' Flip screamed. 'You *would* have! Jess just wouldn't walk out like that without letting someone know.'

And then everything seemed to happen so fast.

I was just about to tell Flip the story of Jess's leaving the dance floor in its entirety—verbatim—in a final effort to quell her worst suspicions, when some B-list Click model from Texas, this towering girl named Loanna, stepped up to us.

'You're Flip, right?' she asked, unleashing the full force of her twang on us in the perceived drama of the moment. 'Jess's sister?'

Flip inadvertently grabbed her arm. 'Yes. Why?'

"Cause—I mean, I don't know this for a fact, but some fella, some buddy of your brother's jus' told me that he thinks he's still *inside*, sweetie. Says he and your brother were the last two down the stairwell and your brother tripped or somethin' and broke his leg—or arm, or somethin'—and his buddy tried to get him down the stairs, but couldn't, so he ran out to get help and the fireman wouldn't believe it 'cause they'd already checked the building and said it was completely evacuated, an'—'

I glanced at Flip—her trembling had only intensified during this half-cocked story. 'Wait a minute,' I said to Loanna. 'Who told you all this?'

'That guy right over—' she began to gesture, but it was too late. Flip had bounded over the fire rope and was running, knock-kneed and furious, straight toward the entrance to the club, gaping now even more lasciviously with flames. Ty, Guillermo and I scrambled madly after her; her dash had been fleet, but surely we would catch her at the entrance, since, like the fireman had said, no one would willingly plunge into flames unless they had a death wish. And that's why I could only cry her name out in horror when, upon reaching the door, she didn't stop, retreat in a sudden, instinctively human phobia of fire, but ran right through one sheet of flames after another, down the long corridor that led to the coat-check room, and beyond, to the fiery center of the club.

For one split second, I paused in the entryway, my whole body seared by indescribable heat—Ty and Guillermo had already fallen behind—and then, just as I had resolved to go after her, waves and waves of flames fell down around me, along with the two cheaply erected inner walls of the lobby; it was as though by stirring the flames, Flip had enraged them and doubled their intensity. For a moment, my arms up before my face to shield it from heat and sparks, I could see nothing but pure, dense fire, swirling with brilliant chemical colors and a confetti of black ashes. The flames seemed to part for a minute, and I caught one more fleeting, electric image of my sister, fallen to the floor and cowering from the light, just before the burning walls came tumbling down with such force that the very heat impelled me away from the entryway onto the sidewalk, as though I had been slapped back by the hand of God.

Three firemen grabbed me, wrapped me in wet blankets. 'What are you, man, a fucking fool?' one of them shouted at me.

'You gotta get in there!' I screamed. 'My sister's in there!'

'Yeah, we saw it,' the same fireman barked back at me. 'Your sister's fucking crazy, man. We can't go in there now. The whole interior front of the building just came down. Point of no return.'

You gotta, you assholes! You fucking assholes, you gotta save my sister! I don't know how long I screamed while they forced me back behind the police ropes. I was delirious; I remember seeing in flashes familiar faces—Ty, Guillermo, Lippy, Anthea, Cedric—and a squall of unfamiliar ones, too. But nothing came into focus until Jess appeared before me and I grabbed him with all my might.

'Where the fuck did you go?' I screamed at him.

'Never mind that!' he screamed back. 'Where's Flip?'

'She's in there!' I babbled, sobbing. 'She's in there, and they can't get her out—'

'What the fuck do you mean they can't get her out? I'm going in right now.'

He moved to jump the fire rope, but I pulled him back with all my might, even as he struggled and cursed against me.

'It's no fucking use, Jess. She's already gone; I know it.'

His whole body fell slack and he looked at me with what seemed to be an almost academic curiosity. 'Gone?' he asked blandly.

'Yeah,' I ran on. 'Gone, because she thought you were in there, and I told her you weren't, and she wouldn't believe me, and then somebody told her you were, and she ran in—'

'Wait a minute. Tigger!' and he shook me. 'Listen to me. Who the fuck told her I was in there?'

I looked around wildly until I saw Loanna nearby, witnessing this spectacle with mute horror. 'Her!' I yelled, pointing at her. 'I mean, she said some buddy of yours told

her he saw you in there with a broken leg—broken arm,
or—'

'What?' Jess exclaimed with a horrible incredulous laugh. In
an instant he had taken Loanna in his arms and was shaking
her the way Flip had liked to shake her old Barbies, to make
their hair stand out in all directions. 'Who the fuck told you
that?'

'Jess, you're *hurting* me!'

'*Who told you?*'

She tore away from him and looked around, bereft, then
pointed through the first few layers of crowd and shouted,
'Him! With the little glasses! He said he was your buddy.'

Jess and I both whipped around, the crowd's gaze following
our own. It was Goolsbee Loanna had pointed at—Goolsbee,
standing back away so as not to have been too conspicuous,
quietly savoring every moment of his payback.

Jess stared at him, unblinking. 'Goolsbee,' he finally said,
with as much emotion as a schoolmaster calling names off a
roll call.

Goolsbee smiled at us then—not smug and squinting as
ever before, but a placid, gentle, sympathetic smile, a smile of
impeccable condolence. A terrible, terrible silence fell over
the crowd. 'I'm sorry,' he murmured to us.

Jess said nothing, didn't move. No one moved. At length,
Goolsbee shrugged at the two of us, as though to suggest that
the matter was settled. Then, uttering a quiet, polite series of
'Excuse me's, he picked his way calmly out of the confused,
restive crowd.

Jess watched him extricate himself, his face a blank, but I
could sense the machinations that were whirring behind it.
Then, with infinite composure, Jess sidled up close to Ty and
whispered something in his ear. Ty nodded gravely, their
bodies pressed close together. Ty said something rather firmly,
and I just barely heard Jess respond, 'No way, Ty. Me. It's got to
be me.' Ty cursed and finally nodded in assent. Then, still

pressed close to each other, they engaged in the briefest of transactions. No one saw the actual pass-off, not even me— but I didn't have to.

'Jess, don't,' I whispered to him, trying to hold him back by the arm as he moved to follow Goolsbee, who had begun walking calmly down the middle of Spring Street in the direction of the river, his back to the murmuring crowd. 'You'll regret it all your life.'

But Jess pushed me aside, firmly but gently. 'No, I won't,' he said, picking his way out of the crowd. 'You might, but I won't.'

'Please!'

'Shhhh,' he laughed gently, passing a cool hand over my head. 'Just sit tight and be a good kid, Tigger, okay?'

'Jess—'

But he would have no more of me. He began walking faster, faster yet, in the direction of Goolsbee, both of them in the long, empty passage of Spring Street that stretched toward the highway. At some point, Goolsbee must have heard the sound of Jess's footsteps behind him, because he turned and waved back—dimly, I heard him laugh—before he kept on walking, maintaining his illusion of fearlessness until Jess, who seemed relaxed except for the ever-increasing pace of his stride, was a mere twenty feet behind him. Then, and only then, did Amos Goolsbee break out into a run.

But it was too late. Within seconds, Jess was upon him. He and Goolsbee were evenly matched in height and size, but Goolsbee hadn't accounted for Jess's rage, and after only a few faint attempts at self-defense on Goolsbee's part, Jess had struck him enough blows to the head and kicks to the stomach to land him writhing on the ground.

And the final scene played itself out too fast for anyone to stop it, simply this: Jess pulled out Ty's .45, shot Goolsbee twice in the face—I saw the body leap and buckle for a second before it fell back to the ground, broken—and kicked him twice to make sure he was dead. When he was assured of this, he looked back up the street at the scene—the burning building, the screeching fire trucks and their colored volleys of light soaring over the hundreds of faces that stared after him, gaping and silent.

For one second, he stood still and stared at all of us. Then he thrust the .45 in his pocket, stalked to the corner, and hailed a passing cab, which carried him off and away up the West Side Highway.

Loanna's histrionic scream broke the odd silence of the crowd, and several more followed, all of it converging with the screeching of the fire sirens and the roar of the fire and the rush of nearby traffic into open-air pandemonium. Still in my wet blankets, I made out Lippy, Anthea and Cedric rushing toward me, Lippy with her arms outstretched. With a curious rush of clear-headedness, it occurred to me that in the space of just minutes, Flip and Jess had taken my cold, unequivocal decision of that evening—which had been to leave New York, part with them, as I had resolved to do the very next day, once and for all—and carried it out for me. With fire and bullets and passion, they had beat me to the defining moment once again.

Afterglow

Twenty-Four

Given the baroque spectacles Flip had engineered in her short life, her funeral ceremony was a notably simple affair, held in the early evening at the end of one of the rotting empty Village piers jutting into the gray waters of the Hudson River. We invited few people beyond our inner circle, and a Unitarian minister, a long-time friend of Lippy's, recited some simple, gentle prayers for Flip's soul before Lippy sang a Greek lullaby, her hair billowing in the stiff breeze that came off the river. We all said a few words, some of which provoked the obligatory laughter (Cedric said he hoped that Flip wouldn't mind his taking her white leather Courreges minicoat, even though he'd have to take it out fourteen sizes), but on the whole, it was a somber affair—I don't even know if the various people that craned their necks in our direction as they strolled, ran or cycled by the pier knew what we were doing, let alone for whom, until perhaps they spotted me holding a small vessel over the water and releasing Flip's remains to the wind.

As nearest of kin, this was my honor and duty, but I didn't like it at all; the vessel's contents weren't finely powdered, as I'd expected, but somewhat gritty, only increasing my slightly queasy sense of hearing in the ashy wind the ghostly cries of my sister and her unborn child, both of them crying out for more life before their remains were completely borne away.

And throughout the entire ceremony, Jess's absence was so palpable I thought at any moment he'd emerge at the other end of the pier, tardy and harried, to take his proper place among the survivors. Which he didn't, of course.

If I had hallucinated him, though, I wouldn't have been surprised. In the past seventy-two hours, I had lost track of the usual daylight clock in the surreal urgency of addressing such concerns as Flip's cremation, and at night my sleep had the shallow, fits-and-starts quality of insomnia patched over clumsily with medication. Standing there on the pier early that evening, as the sun hung midway in the sky over New Jersey and Lippy's unadorned alto rang out clearly until the wind carried it away over the water, it occurred to me that ever since the night of the fire, I had been living this achy half-dream, a narrative so remote and so absurd that surely it would come to an end and reality would be restored. But, of course, nothing of the sort came to pass.

The first thing I remember the moment after Jess jumped into the taxi and went screeching away up the West Side Highway was Lippy, descending upon me and taking me up in her arms. Fumbling for words, I tried to tell her something.

'Shhh, baby,' she hushed me, squeezing tighter. 'It's all right. Auntie's here. We're going to be all right.'

'But Lippy—'

'Shhhh!'

'But you don't understand. I must have wanted this to happen, 'cause I was going to leave them both tomorrow—'

'Of course you weren't, darling. You're upset now, Tigger.'

'—leave them both tomorrow, because Flip was going to have Jess's baby, and they wanted me to raise the baby with them, and I really wanted to, but I knew I couldn't because Jess and Flip—'

'Shhh, Tigger, you're all garbled,' Lippy interrupted sharply, pulling back from me and shaking me into silence. 'I know

Flip was pregnant, but it was Tyrone's baby she was going to have. You're all befuddled in your head right now.'

'Tyrone's?' I repeated, bewildered. I looked over to where Ty was standing, weeping, holding a nearly hysterical Guillermo in a virtual full-nelson amidst the overexcited crowd.

'Yes, Tyrone's,' Lippy repeated. 'Flip told me last week. She said she was pregnant, and that she and Jess and you were going to raise the baby. She hadn't even told Tyrone yet.'

My mouth moved to say something to Lippy, but nothing came out. 'Come on, darling,' she said. 'I'm taking you to my place. We can deal with all of this in the morning.'

I pulled away. 'We can't go home! She's still in there!'

'Darling,' and it was here that previously stoic Lippy started to cry. 'It's over. I talked to the firemen. They say—they say it's a lost cause. We can't go in to see what happened until the fire's out tomorrow.'

'We've got to go in tonight!'

'Tigger, we *can't*!'

I submitted to her tone like an unhappy child. She guided me out of the crowd, past Cedric and Joey and Anthea, who reached out to touch me on the shoulder as we passed, past photographers who snapped us, past all the garishly rubber-necking voyeurs watching the club go up in flames and smoke while the F.D. hosed its façades in vain. Out of the corner of my eye, I noticed TV news trucks and police cars congregated around Goolsbee's dead body—a peripheral vision of wires and blue uniforms and flashing lights—and then Lippy and I were getting in a cab at the very same corner where Jess had fled, and the last thing I remember seeing before our cab sped away from the corner was an invitation to the Half-Year Party floating in a puddle by the curb, Miko's slyly humping tigers bleeding their colors off the card and into the dark water.

Lippy held my hand in the cab, but we said nothing to each other. Up in her apartment, she pulled out the sofabed for

me, then emerged from the bathroom in her robe, a medicine
bottle in hand.

'I'm taking a Halcion tonight,' she said, chasing the pill with
a glass of water from the kitchen sink. 'Why don't you take
one, too?'

I nodded mutely, and she handed me a pill and a glass of
water, which I swallowed with a small fit of choking. She
kissed me again and retreated into her bedroom, leaving the
door wide open behind her. At first I thought I'd never get to
sleep, but then the Halcion kicked in in the most unpleasantly
phantasmagorical way—it seemed that all these images in my
head began merging and churning together: there we were in
front of the burning club, and in another moment, there was
Flip burning in the waters of the old Cove in Rye, or there was
Jess standing not in the middle of Spring Street, but in the
street of our old house in Lowell, fully grown, pointing Ty's .45
at our own father. And then they weren't images at all, just a
murky condensation of dark shapes underneath my eyelids
that got darker and darker until they congealed completely to
black.

It all came back to me the next morning, a disgusting, hazy
morning, when I awoke groggily to hear Lippy making toast
and coffee in the kitchen, listening to the news on the radio. I
heard the name of the club, the full names of Jess, Flip and
me, followed by our nicknames, Goolsbee's name, the names
of various firemen and cops. In the first second, there was a
kind of surreal novelty to it—*Gee whiz, they're talking about
us!* I thought—before it all fell back into context with a sick
thud.

That was the first taste of the overwhelming press coverage
the whole affair was to receive in the weeks and months that
followed, much of which Lippy tried to shield me from, some
of which was unavoidable. It didn't surprise me at all when the
story made the cover of *New York* magazine a few weeks later,

complete with an opening night photo of Flip, Jess and me
and a headline that screamed DISCO INFERNO. The whole
story was filled with ridiculous quotes from all sorts of people
we had vaguely known who billed themselves as close associates or confidants. ('She was doomed to die,' a repugnant
Kristal Kleer intoned absurdly of Flip, 'like a beautiful, fragile
china doll with a time bomb ticking inside her.') Nowhere at
all, though, in *New York* magazine or elsewhere, did I find
evidence that Anthea, Miko, Cedric, Joey, Guillermo, Ty,
Grant, Sammy Fingers or even the publicity-hungry, motor-
mouthed Pepe had talked, something which filled me with a
grim appreciation, as I knew it would have done for Jess and
Flip.

But as for that first morning, Lippy approached me with
coffee and toast, lighting one of her rare cigarettes and sitting
down near me on the coffee table beside the sofabed. 'So,' she
finally said, 'I should probably tell you what's going on.' And
she did: how she had called the SoHo precinct of the F.D.
earlier that morning, only to learn that The Box had been
completely ruined, gutted, on the inside . . . how they thought
somebody had drenched the boiler room with gasoline or
some such chemical, then set the whole thing afire . . . how
the police were putting together an arson investigation, how
they suspected it was Goolsbee but that, given the circumstances, they'd probably never know for sure . . . how the
remains of Flip's body had been recovered, and how a cremation had been arranged for.

I nodded silently.

'Very good. Now listen, Tigger. The police are coming by
here later today to talk to us, to get our official statements on
what happened. You know what your brother is now?'

I didn't answer.

'They're calling him a fugitive suspect, but the investigator
said that if he were available right now, they'd arrest him for
murder.'

From the radio in the kitchen, I heard a middle-aged man's overexercised voice—

—cum laude from Princeton, a hard-working young man, a source of pride to us and his siblings, shot in cold blood by a—

Apparently, it was Goolsbee's father. 'Basta,' Lippy said, switching off the radio, and the apartment was silent.

'Now,' Lippy continued, sitting back down on the coffee table. 'There's this other matter. The investigator said that your brother might try to contact us, for money or one reason or another, and that if we hear from him, we're obligated to let the police know, because they want to put a tracer on the phone at the loft, and here as well.' She paused, narrowing her eyes. 'I said of course we'd cooperate. Because the law is the law, right?'

I met her keen, curious gaze. 'Right,' I whispered.

'Good,' she answered, nodding her head slowly. 'I'm glad that's understood between us.' And no more on the subject needed to be said.

Lippy resumed her phone calls—notifying this person, arranging that detail—and I stayed in bed, groggy and half-numb, until the investigator, a reedy, beagle-faced fellow named Spanks with a thick Long Island accent and his stocky, nearly mute partner, showed up at the apartment around three o'clock, overpowering the room with their clanking presences and the cheap, blunt odor of Brut 33. As plainly as possible, I gave them my account of the night before—there seemed little reason, and even less room, for bending my recollection at all in Jess's favor. I told them I suspected Goolsbee had started the fire, or paid someone to start it for him, then, whether he knew Jess was out of the building or not, provoked the dim-witted, hysterical Loarma to tell Flip that Jess was still inside.

'He murdered my sister, as far as I'm concerned,' I finally said, but Spanks made it clear that that was a supposition much too subjective and tenuous to pursue with any confidence. Clearly, they were focusing on Jess's murder of Goolsbee.

They asked me if I knew that my sister was pregnant at the time of her death, and I said yes. *By Goolsbee?* they asked.

'By Tyrone Packer, the doorman,' I answered.

Spanks narrowed his eyes at me. 'That's not what Mr. Packer told us, Mr. Mitchell.'

'Well, that's what my sister told me. I'm sorry—I wasn't there when she conceived.'

Spanks's assistant squirmed a bit. 'I wasn't saying you were,' Spanks said.

I shrugged. They asked if I knew where Jess had gone.

'No,' I answered. 'Absolutely not.'

'Thank you, Mr. Mitchell,' Spanks said, and they asked if I would mind leaving the apartment for a few minutes while they questioned Ms. Pappas, who had been holed up in her bedroom. I summoned Lippy and weaved my way dizzily down the stairwell, then sat out on the sunny front stoop and lit a cigarette, which only made me feel sicker. Shortly, Spanks and his partner came down and bade me a stiff good afternoon. I found Lippy upstairs, leafing through her battered old address book.

'Were they hard on you?' I asked her.

She stared up at me from the desk, looking profoundly fatigued. 'No,' she said hoarsely. 'No. It was very routine.'

'Really?'

'Quite. With you?'

'The same.'

'There you go,' she said shortly, looking back into her book. I stared off into the other room, lost in my own thoughts, until I turned back and noticed that Lippy was peering at me intently over her glasses. 'I want to ask you something,' she said. 'Did the police ask you whom you thought Flip was pregnant by?'

I nodded.

'And whom did you say?'

'I said Tyrone. Did they ask you?'

'They did. I said Tyrone, as well. And I didn't mention what you said to me last night, in front of the club.'

'What did I say?' I asked, and she stared at me harder, as though to say *think about it*, before I recollected. 'Oh,' I said with a start. 'Oh.'

'So I guess all parties-in-the-know are either out of the picture or keeping mum, right?'

'Right.'

'Good. Now let's drop this, okay? But I'll just say one thing: you three kept a goddamned lot more from me than I ever imagined, didn't you?'

I shrugged, conceding. She said no more—just closed her little black book, clutched it in her hands, and peered incuriously over her glasses out the window into the narrow courtyard.

It occurred to me that I should perhaps call Cedric, or Sherry, or the lawyers, or the insurance company, or any other number of people—that I should go home and check on the loft, or at least call Anthea and ask her to do so—and yet I felt incapable of doing anything but collapsing back onto the sofabed and staring at the intricate old patterns of Lippy's tin ceiling for the rest of the afternoon. I dozed in and out of a sweaty sleep, waking at one point to find the apartment empty. Lippy and Langley must have stepped out for food, I determined, and had almost fallen back to sleep when the phone rang nearby. I answered it mumblingly.

'Tigger?'

'Jess?' I sat up instantly, blood rushing out of my head. 'Where the fuck are you?'

'Never mind. Listen to me. Are you alone?'

'Yeah.'

'Good. I was going to hang up if Lippy answered.'

'Listen, Jess, you've got to get back here. You're in deep shit with the police.'

'Why the fuck do you think I'm not coming back? I'm calling you 'cause I need money.'

'What do you mean, you're not coming back? You *have* to
come back. You've got to have a trial! Flip's funeral is on
Tuesday. What about the loft, and Lippy, and all your artwork,
and—'

'Tigger, listen to me. What did the police tell you?'

'What do you think they told me? You're wanted, Jess! They
told me that if they even found out I was talking to you and
didn't let them know, they could consider me an accomplice.'

'Oh shit,' he said, low. 'They really said that?'

'Yeah! Jess, will you just tell me where you are? Just tell me,
and I'll come to you right away. Where? In Massachusetts?'

'Never mind about that. The cops really said that, huh?'

'Yes!' I shouted, exasperated.

There was a brief pause. 'Look, forget about the money,' he
finally said. 'I'll be okay. I'm sorry, Tigger. About everything.'

'Look, would you just tell me—'

And then the line went dead. I sat tense by the phone, waiting for him to call back, resolving that if I could only find out
where he was, I'd slip away immediately after Flip's service on
Tuesday to join him, to be a fugitive with him. But I never had
to think about the details or impracticalities of such a plan,
because I didn't hear from him again any time soon.

After I scattered the remains into the river, there wasn't much
more for any of us to do except exchange the obvious round of
tears and hugs. Everyone was so sweet to me—Anthea, Katja
and Miko, Ty and Guillermo, Grant and Maeve, Sammy and
Pepe, even the almost-forgotten Kira and Jeffrey—that I nearly
failed to consider how much their own lives had been overturned by Flip's death and the destruction of The Box, how Flip
had forged this erstwhile family, and how profoundly dispos-
sessed they must feel now, some of them without jobs or salaries
and all of us without a place to call home in the evenings.

We all turned away from the water, and it was then that I made out the figure of a woman staring at us through the chain-link fence at the other end of the pier. Was that actually Damienne? I waved tentatively in the woman's direction, and she waved back, one tight little gesture.

I ran toward the fence, calling out her name. It was definitely her, Damienne, in career drag as though she had come straight from work, and it occurred to me that I hadn't seen her since that miserable night when she walked out of our home in Topsfield. God, I thought—she was such a decent person, and we had been more or less rotten to her.

'Hi!' I finally panted when I reached the fence. 'It's good to see you.'

Even as I was clutching the fence she was backing stiffly away. 'Hi, Tigger. It's good to see you.'

'You could've come down to the ceremony, you know.'

She laughed, and I noticed her jaw tremble. 'That's okay. I wasn't really invited. It's just—well, I've been keeping up on everything through the papers, then I saw Langley this morning on my way to work, and he told me you'd all be here tonight. I thought I'd come by to pay my respects, and if I saw you, fine. If not—' she broke off.

'Well, I'm glad you did.'

She nodded briskly, as though she hadn't even heard the sentiment. 'Look, Tigger—' By this point she had backed nearly two yards away from the fence, and I noticed an odd quaver in her voice. 'Look, I just want you to know, I never hated her, honestly. Regardless of how she felt about me. I just—it got to a point where I just—'

'Couldn't compete,' I finished for her. 'Right?'

'Right,' she laughed, embarrassed. 'But I never hated her, Tigger. I swear to God. If I could have stopped what happened from happening—'

She had begun to cry now, in her own rather muted way. 'You don't need to tell me that, Damienne,' I said, venturing toward the tear in the fence to collect her. 'Come on around the other side of the fence and join us. We're going back to Anthea's for some food. I know Lippy and Ced and the rest would love to see you.'

'Oh, God, no!' Briskly, she swatted away her tears as though they were summer pests. I checked myself and stayed back behind the fence. 'No, that's all right. I have to go now. Just tell me—do you know anything about Jess? Is he all right?'

'Your guess is as good as mine.'

'You haven't heard from him?' she asked, low.

'No.' I didn't bat an eye.

'My God,' she said. 'Where on earth could he be? It's not as though he doesn't have rights. He's entitled to due process.'

'I don't think Jess feels as though he's ever been entitled to due process.'

'No,' she said after a pause. 'No, you're right about that.' She stepped toward me on the other side of the fence and seemed just about to say something else, something terribly painful and grave, when Lippy, walking toward us, called out for Damienne to join us. They were all staring after the two of us now—touched by her gesture, I knew, eager to welcome her.

'Everyone wants to see you,' I pleaded. 'Come and join us. Please.'

'No, no,' she stammered, and already she was hitching her briefcase up on her shoulder and walking backwards away from the fence. 'I can't. I'm— I'm seeing someone now, Tigger, and— well—' she trailed off, shrugging. 'So— so you give them all my best, okay? And if you need anything, you call me, okay, at work? Same old number.'

'Come back, Damienne.'

'Okay? Same number. Same old number.'

She kept repeating the ridiculous phrase until she finally turned and hurried across the pavement toward the crosswalk back to the Village. I glumly watched her go, receding in her no-nonsense civil service weeds into the fray of waxed muscle queens, tanned girls in sports bras, and homeboys of indeterminate leanings with their pants falling virtually around their knees. New York never made sense, ever, I thought. A formal feeling never came, even after death.

There were so many people I was supposed to call, or call back, but I couldn't. Talking on the phone, or just talking, seemed to be taking on the weight of pushing boulders around a field all day, and I became creepingly aware of an eerie, anxious, clumsy feeling during conversations in which I felt as though I were saying too much, or too little, or the absolutely wrong thing. I did what I had to do—met alongside Lippy with the insurance company and with The Box's crabby landlady, Mrs. Scalia, with Flip's New York lawyers, and with Mr. Kittredge, who came down from Boston to guide me through our mother's will (he had bent some rules to open it ahead of time) and to take care of Flip's finances. The will revealed that my mother had decided to sell the Topsfield house, a matter to be dealt with largely by Sherry, who had been left the Rye house and a considerable inheritance. My mother, whom Mr. Kittredge had pushed toward investing wisely, bequeathed a great sum of money to various local charities, and an even greater sum to Lippy. After that, the estate was divided between Jess, Flip and me. By law, Mr. Kittredge explained, Flip's portion reverted to Jess and me, as next of kin, and in Jess's absence, his portion was to be frozen for so many years before it became mine as well.

All told, I was a very comfortable twenty-two-year-old, but all I cared to do at the time was have Mr. Kittredge put the money in various accounts and funds, then forget about it. It was no joy to me and little comfort, all of it having come through various deaths, and it seemed like an awfully large amount of money to have to manage over the course of years, years that I suddenly foresaw with despair, if not downright terror.

There were other occasions I had to endure—my graduation from Mannes, the marriage of Lippy and Langley (abbreviated, given recent events, to a brief civil ceremony downtown), and the hasty end-of-month transferral of Lippy's life from the walk-up where she had lived almost since moving to New York, to Langley's plush, slightly tacky modern penthouse overlooking the Hudson. Throughout, over a course of weeks, my lethargy and constant funky-headed anxiety worsened until I found myself almost all the time in Langley's black leather recliner, blankly charting the progress of barges on the river. With little fuss, Langley and Lippy had made it clear that I would stay at Langley's for just as long as I fancied. Under normal circumstances, I would have seized back my independence immediately, but in fact I hardly voiced a protest. It wasn't just lassitude that brought me to Langley's, but also a sudden new terror of being alone.

This was just one of several new phobias, the worst of which was my dread of returning to the loft. Concerned but obliging, Anthea had been looking after it. My piano was well, she would report, and it certainly seemed to be calling out for a good playing, and neighbors were asking after me, and the landlord wanted to know if I'd be keeping the place or looking for smaller digs.

All of these proddings on Anthea's part finally drove me one Saturday morning to gather my bearings and visit the loft—she'd be there to meet me, she promised—but I hadn't walked more than a few blocks across town before I was overcome with the most ghastly sense of exhaustion and disorientation—for a moment, then another, I felt completely lost, as though I had never walked these familiar old streets before, with little if no sense of east or west, north or south. I sat down on a stoop and lit a cigarette to collect myself, but it only seemed to increase my dizziness and confusion, so I stubbed it out and shuffled onward.

And it was then, at the wide, vertiginous, bustling intersection of Houston Street and Seventh Avenue, that I simply gave out. Every bone and muscle in my body seemed to fall away inside me, turning my legs to gelatinated things that could scarcely hold me up. A woman scolded me for nearly stepping on her dachshund, and I mumbled an apology, turning to walk right into a street sign, then stumble off the sidewalk, all askew. I held out my hand for a passing cab and clutched the door handle as though for my life all the way back to Langley's penthouse. The twelve-flight ascension in the elevator seemed interminable, the presence of the chatty, sweet-faced old lady at my side a source of unaccountable dread.

Lippy was at Langley's piano with her morning coffee when I stepped in, and she hastened toward me, ashen-faced, when she saw me reeling inside and heading straight for Langley's leather recliner.

'Tigger! My God, what's wrong?'

'I don't know,' I gasped before embarking on a horrible, uncontrollable crying jag. 'I'm sick, I'm sick. I think I'm dying. I need help.'

'What is it?' she asked, frantically palming my forehead. 'Do you have a fever?'

'I don't know. I couldn't walk just now. Everything scares me.'

'Oh, my baby. You just sit tight, all right, darling, while I call a doctor. Play the piano if it makes you feel better, okay?'

'Okay.'

She dashed into the bedroom and closed the door. I looked over heavily at the piano. I didn't think I could have gotten myself over to it, let alone play it at that moment. As it was, the lifting of an arm from the leather cushion of the chair seemed a torturous ordeal. I stared out paralyzed at the river, wishing with all my might that I could will myself down into its tranquil, gray oblivion.

I was in this special hospital in rural Westchester for all of August and a little bit of September, for what the people there called a 'major unipolar depression,' amidst a dozen other comatose people who apparently had the same thing. Twice a day I met with my main shrink, a blandly agreeable man named Dr. Krinick. I had a million questions for him, and I asked them again and again, with an obsessiveness that his detailed answers could never satisfy. Why did I feel this way, and when would it ever stop, and why did they call it 'depression' when I felt more diseased than depressed, and how did I know that I wasn't a sinner in the hands of an angry God who was punishing me for surviving Flip and not having stopped Jess, not to mention for all those years of nocturnal decadence and filial neglect? And why couldn't I concentrate well enough to read a magazine arti-cle, or sustain a conversation, or even do the simple math necessary to add up change for a Coke at the vending machine?

'Thomas. Thomas,' Dr. Krinick would repeat, with an almost incantatory patience, 'you're not going crazy. You're not being punished. You're sick right now, that's all. You're just sick.' But sick had never felt like this before.

By mid-September I was back at Lippy and Langley's, armed with an impressive array of sedatives and antidepressants, still staring out at the river from Langley's recliner most of the day, coveting the quiet abyss of the water. I still felt weak and spooky, loathe to venture outside further than the corner deli or the little nearby café where I'd sometimes slog my way through the morning paper. I carried on like this through the fall and into the winter, into the new year, improving so glacially I didn't even notice it happening.

When I finally felt well enough to call people, it was Cedric I called first. For months, he had been calling regularly, keep-ing track of me through Lippy, and I didn't know quite how much I had missed him until I heard his honey-thick voice on the other end of the line.

'Miss Franklin?' I inquired.

He shrieked in delight. 'Miss M.I.A.? Miss Thing In Action? Are you finally sane, girl?'

'Half the way there. About where you've always been.'

'Ooh, she's reading me, she *must* be getting better! Honey, it's so good to hear your voice. Times this winter I wondered if I'd ever hear it again.'

'I wondered the same thing. What's this new number you're at? Did you move apartments?'

'Yes I did. Right back up to the glamorous Upper Bronx, to the apartment of Mrs. Vera Williams.'

'Oh, God, Ced. How's your mother?'

'Let's just say I finally moved up here because I got tired of being woken up at 3 a.m. by one of her downstairs neighbors calling to say she'd been walking around in her nightgown, ringing doorbells and asking if anyone could take her home to Marietta, Georgia.'

'She didn't.'

'She *did*. On *several* occasions. It ain't easy here—I never thought I'd say this, but I'm tryin' to get her into a good H-O-M-E. Especially since I'll be goin' back to school in the fall.'

'You are?'

'That's right—I'm goin' back for nursing. I'll be damned if I'm going to get old working construction sites in the middle of these frigid-ass winters like the one we just had. No, thank you. I'm gonna get myself one of those smart little uniforms, just like Diahann Carroll.'

'That's so great, Ced.'

'I know, right? I figured as long as I was playin' Florence Nightingale anyway, uptown and downtown, I may as well get paid for it.'

'No kidding. So how's Joey?'

I heard him suck his teeth through the phone. 'Honey. Do you really want to know?'

'Not really, but you'd better tell me.'

'Well—Miss Ghanoosh departed this world February 15,1991. The day after Valentine's Day, from pneumonia—you know, that PCP kind. I brought her red roses at least, but I don't think she really appreciated them.'

'I'm sure she did.'

He laughed raggedly. 'I'm pretty motherfuckin' sure she *didn't*, 'cause that ho' really wasn't all that *lucid*, Tigger. She didn't even know who I was a few times.' I could hear him choking up on the line now. 'I've hardly been out of my mom's apartment since it happened. Do you know you're the first friend I've even *talked* to in about two weeks?'

'Ced—' I ventured, at a loss.

'What the fuck *happened* to us all this year?'

'Look, do you wanna get together?'

He paused. 'You sure you're good enough?'

'Yeah,' I said, lying. 'Definitely.'

I met him down at the piers the next afternoon, the kind of day in early spring when swiftly moving clouds scuff a blue sky, stiff winds cut the sun's warmth, and last night's puddles lie in otherwise dry streets—the kind of edgily pleasant day that suggests but doesn't fully deliver a bright new season, and a day much in accordance with my own nascent, fragile good spirits. The piers were deserted save for the occasional early-season runner, and I was much alone with my thoughts until I spotted Cedric hurrying toward me across the West Side Highway, arms wrapped around his chest, his formerly clean-shaven head sprouting the first goofy nibs of dreadlocks.

'You can't have *those* when you're an R.N.,' I said as we embraced, nodding toward the top of his head. 'My mother was a nurse, and she had to cut her dreads off.'

'Hmph. Well, I'll just wrap them up under a do-rag.' He shivered. 'Girl, it's so good to see you, but it's *nasty* cold out here. Can't we go have high tea or something?'

'In a second, I just want a little more air. Don't you think it's nice out here this time of year?'

'I think you've been stuck in the house for too long.'

'I have,' I conceded, putting my arm around him. 'Let's walk out to the end.'

The wind cut harder the further out we ventured. We had the pocked old concrete pier to ourselves except for some adolescent street queens smoking a blunt and twirling to house music on a cheap boom box. At length, we stepped gingerly through a gap in the fence and emerged out on the lip of the pier, the gray water lapping noisily on the concrete just beneath our feet. A Circle Line cruiser passed, and tourists waved to us from its decks. We waved back courteously, as was the custom, even though nobody liked tourists, least of all pier-goers.

'They'll never stand where we're standing,' Cedric said gravely, waving them off up the river.

'And when do you expect to take a Circle Line cruise?' I asked him.

'I took one once,' he snapped back touchily. 'Two years ago. I had some cousins visiting from down south. So touché.'

'Hmph.' We were both silent again. There was a lot we weren't touching on, I knew, but I was loathe to plunge directly into a litany of loss, especially after a half-year so bereft of the pleasures of idle chat. 'Can you believe this'll be a body-packed beach in just a few months?' I asked, stamping my boot against the cold concrete.

'Yes, I can, child. Yes I can.' He turned to me, his baby-dreads immobile in the wind. 'How many summers have you been in New York for?'

I counted back in my head. 'I guess this one will be my fifth.'

'Well, it'll be *my* thirty-third,' he announced imperiously. 'And let me tell you something. No matter how god-awful every winter is in this city, with all the filthy snow in the street and dark skies by four o'clock and tiny little dingy apartments to hole up in, you wake up one day, and it's summer, girl. An' sud-denly everybody's feelin' freaky again, runnin' around in their little tank tops and short shorts, and the air conditioning breaks, or you don't have it to begin with, and black folks outnumber the white folks at the movie theaters on the weekends, and you're in line for the train to Jones Beach at Penn Station every Saturday morning with all the other low-rent queens who couldn't afford a share somewhere, and there's no need to check your coat at the clubs—an' suddenly it's Labor Day Weekend, the whole party's over, an' you're damn happy it is.'

'And your point?'

'My point?' He seemed mildly offended. 'My point is that this motherfuckin' city just goes on, and on, and on, an' it don't give a shit what happens to anybody, whether it's you or me or Miss David Dinkins. It's got a life of its own, like some big underground machine that never stops, for no one.'

'And?'

'And?' he repeated, as though his point spoke for itself. I nodded. 'And— well, I guess that's both a good and bad thing. It's always here when you are, and it don't change much anyway if you're not.'

'Hmph.'

He hmph'd in turn, and we were both silent for a moment, breaking the cold off our faces with raised arms. 'You wanna know something Miss Ghanoosh said to me shortly before she passed on?' he finally broached.

'What's that?'

'She said she wondered who'd be working the door at your sister's big new club in the sky. And that she better be on your sister's guest list, or there was going to be one angry queen making a scene at the door.'

I laughed. 'So what made Joey so certain he was going to heaven, anyway?'

'Oh, believe me, she didn't think she was for a long time— didn't think she *deserved* it, like the messed-up Catholic girl she was. Then on her last day, she told me that she had changed her mind—she *knew* she was going after all. She had gotten *word* or something.'

'Do you think he was just delirious, or do you believe him?'

He cocked his head. 'I believe—' he began slowly, then stopped. 'No, I can't say that. I'll just say that if we all *did* end up in the same place someday, that would be fine by me. Because I *do* miss my girl, Tigger. And I really wouldn't mind carrying on with her again.'

He pulled me by the sleeve away from the edge of the pier. 'Come on. You've had your airing, and I'm freezin' my ass off out here.' I relented, and we walked back toward the street as a squall of gulls exploded over our heads and spiraled up into the racing sky.

Langley snagged me a studio in his building that summer, two floors down from him and Lippy ('You'll still have to come up for your tea every afternoon,' he insisted, gravely), and I finally summoned the wherewithal to break the lease on the loft and move our things out of there. Lippy and Cedric marched me in there one Saturday afternoon, along with Anthea and Katja, who had kindly kept on looking after things even as they made plans to leave for Paris in the fall. (Katja had a new agent there, and Anthea thought the change might help her in her ongoing battle to give up the booze; Katja had been escorting her to AA meetings for some months now, but Anthea still couldn't kick the habit of stopping for a martini on her way home from yoga now and then.)

Stepping inside wasn't as traumatic as I thought; Anthea had already packed and organized much of the space into a bearable anonymity, and she had sold back the new piano months before for just slightly less than what Jess and Flip had paid for it. Little troubled me, except for a notebook of Flip's peeking out of one of the boxes in her room. I opened it—it was blank except for a single page where she had inserted a pen:

July 4, 1990
My darling,
There's something very important I have to tell you, but I can't

seem to get you alone for a second, so I'm writing you a letter instead. I think that when you're finally ready to make your travel plans, that's the point that we should tell T. I think he'd be very hurt if he found out—

Oh, shit. There's the buzzer. I'll finish this later. Love u!!!

But she hadn't finished the note, and I was left to wonder what it concerned, and for whom it had been meant. I tore it out of the notebook and folded it into the pocket of my jeans, where I forgot about it. It ended up going through the wash a week later, transformed into a damp sponge that shredded apart when I tried to unfold it.

We had moved my belongings and the necessary furnishings, including my trusty old upright piano, into my new studio by the end of the weekend. Early on a Sunday evening, after a hasty round of cleaning, spackling and painting, Anthea and I stood at the door to the empty loft and took one final look inside into its gloomy recesses.

'I'll drop the keys off for you to the landlord tomorrow, darling,' Anthea murmured.

'Thanks.' I noticed that we had left behind on one of the walls a calendar, somebody's Christmas gift to somebody else from the Met gift shop, still pinned to July of 1990, almost every one of its day-boxes up to the night of the Half-Year Party marked with dates and appointments scrawled with a red marker in Flip's nearly illegible hand. I thought about taking it down, to have as a keepsake of our final year together, then decided against it. Let it hang, I thought, to show whomever moved in here next what a marvelous, topsy-turvy life we had jointly lived.

Anthea put her arm around me. 'We had lovely times in this flat, didn't we?'

It wasn't the word that would have come to me first, I mused, but Anthea was right—they were lovely times, all told. 'Yeah,' I finally said. 'We did.'

There wasn't anything left to say. I closed the door behind us, locked the three locks, and we clattered down the echoing stairwell one last time.

I joined the AIDS group ACT UP that November, in part out of an embarrassed desire to make up for my political apathy back in the days of The Box. The ACT UP people knew who I was, and wanted to make me a benefit planner because of my familiarity with DJs and promoters, but I begged off, content to Xerox fliers and make mundane, necessary phone calls out of their dingy offices two nights a week. I liked the anonymity of it; I was perfectly happy engaging in mindless busywork, chatting with the two elfin, cheerfully overpoliticized lesbians from Boerum Hill whom I shared the office with. And then one night, to my utter shock, in walked two shaven-headed, combat-booted coordinators, earnestly looking over documents with a neatly coiffed young woman in corporate drag.

I laughed in spite of myself. 'Kira?'

She looked up, startled. 'Tigger?' She excused herself for a moment and hurried over to me. 'What are you doing here?'

'I'm volunteering,' I said, leaning forward for a kiss hello. 'What are you doing here?'

'I'm volunteering, too— doing legal counsel, along with Jeffrey. Don't you love that— two straight Upper West Side corporate lawyers working for ACT UP?'

'I think it's great,' I said. 'What made you decide?'

'Well, I was going to do something with GMHC, but they had so many volunteer counsels, and—' she paused for a moment, 'um, well, Seb signed me up.'

'Oh. Hmph. How is he?'

'He's okay. More to the point, how are you? Better, hunh?' she asked under her breath.

'Much, thanks.'

'I'm so relieved.' We stood there while the two elfin lesbians and the two clone coordinators looked on. 'Um, look,' she said. 'We've got to go over some pharmaceutical stuff in the next room, but—-do you wanna have coffee in a bit?'

'I'd love to.'

That was how I became friends with Kira again, and eventually with her husband Jeffrey, who turned out not to be a bad sort, and eventually with their circle of friends, which, if overwhelmingly straight and white compared to the crowd I had known in my club days, turned out not to be as horrifically boring as I expected, and liberal-minded in their own stolidly urban, post-Ivy League sort of way. There were a few gayboys in this crowd as well, all of them some girl's best friend from Columbia or Brown or Vassar, all of them white, well-groomed, lonely, hopeful creatures who looked as though the gayest thing they had ever done was venture down to Chelsea once a year to buy new ties at the Barneys warehouse sale.

'Don't even try,' I said to Kira and Jeffrey the first time they gingerly suggested setting me up with one of these boys. 'I'd rather date a convict.' And so they stopped, dispirited—they were always trying to find matches for these hapless boys, but in their world there were only so many homosexuals to go around.

I knew Kira was in touch with Seb, but she was careful not to discuss him around me and I knew she refrained from discussing me with him—she had made it very clear that she didn't want to be our go-between, which I assured her was fine by me: what did he and I have to say to each other, anyway? That's why I was so surprised when I arrived at Kira and Jeff's annual New Year's Eve party, only to see him across the room, deep in some serious-seeming conversation with two Asian girls, sipping rather forlornly at what seemed to be his customary glass of seltzer with lime. He had finally pulled a look together for himself, and had grown sideburns, I noticed, with an irritating little pang of nostalgia and attraction. I darted into the kitchen before he could see me.

'You didn't tell me Seb was going to be here,' I said to Kira, thrusting at her the bottle of champagne I had brought as a party favor.

She was preoccupied with assembling a crudité, and short with me. 'What did you expect? He's our friend, too.'

'I know that. I just assumed that if you invited me, he had other plans or something. I just can't believe—'

'Tigger,' she interrupted me, 'I never made you any promise that I was going to bend over backwards to keep the two of you apart. There are plenty of broken-up couples here tonight that know how to stand being in the same room together.'

'Maybe I should go,' I sulked.

'Maybe you should grow up and go over there and say hi to him. You guys have known each other since you were fourteen, for God's sakes. He's been worrying about you all year.'

'He has? You never told me that.'

'I didn't?'

'No.'

'Oh. Well, I guess it slipped my mind. Anyway, he has been.'

'Maybe I should say hello to him,' I said a bit, softening. I reached for a glass, and for the bottle of vodka on the kitchen counter. 'I'll make a drink first.'

The buzzer sounded. She thrust the platter of crudités at me. 'Take these out when you go, okay? I've got to get the door. And then go into the bedroom and put some good music on the stereo, okay? I refuse to listen to Jeffrey's Beastie Boys CDs all night.'

I downed half my screwdriver and refreshed it before I ventured out into the living room, setting down the crudités on the coffee table.

Then I turned to him and the two Asian girls. 'Hey there,' I said, smiling with all the good grace and maturity I could muster. 'Cool sideburns.'

He blanched completely when he saw me. 'Kira didn't tell me you were going to be here.'

'She didn't tell me you were going to be here, either.' I laughed. 'But here we both are.'

He didn't laugh back. 'I—' he choked, setting down his seltzer on the bookshelf. 'I think I've got to go. Nice meeting you,' he said to the two Asian girls, who were watching us, bewildered.

'Oh, for God's sakes, Seb, don't be such a baby!' I called after him as he shouldered his way through the room. But it was too late—in a moment, coat in hand, he was making a hasty, huffy little good-bye to Kira, then he was out the door.

'What happened?' one of the girls asked me.

'Oh, I slept with his wife once,' I cracked, certain they'd get the joke.

'He's *married*?' the same one said to me before turning to her friend. 'Oh my God, Jennifer, aren't you glad you didn't say anything?'

'He's a lousy lay, anyway—you're not missing anything,' I assured them, and they laughed nervously. The vodka had already made me a little drunk, and I resolved that rather than walk out myself and celebrate the turning of the year at some point on the subway, I'd stay on and get even drunker. Which I did, well into 1992, until I passed out on Kira and Jeffrey's bed sometime around three in the morning. Kira later told me that people had pulled their coats out from under me all night, and I had hardly stirred.

So I started the new year with a tremendous hangover and a heavy dose of remorse, having been advised by Dr. Krinick not to drink to excess, as it could precipitate another episode of you-know-what. Moreover, Kira and Jeffrey had kindly deferred to my takeover of their bedroom and gone to sleep on the sofabed in the living room, surrounded by the wreckage of the night before. Careful not to wake them, I left a loosely scrawled note of apology and slipped out the door, making it home just in time to shower and head upstairs to Lippy and Langley's new year's brunch. It was a comfortable affair—

gallons of coffee, bagels and nova lox, dim jazz and sleepy conversation among a dozen old faces—but the merest sniff of somebody's Bloody Mary filled me with nausea, and after several cups of coffee, I put on my coat and excused myself to take a head-clearing walk in the cold streets.

It was a frigid New Year's Day, and the sky was so dark that at two o'clock it already felt like twilight. Heading off down the sidewalk, my face ducked into my muffler, I nearly crashed into Seb, who was loitering outside the building, face similarly mummified.

'Oh, Jesus!' I exclaimed. 'What are *you* doing here?'

'What are *you* doing here? Are you stalking me or something?'

'Oh, dream on! I live here now.'

'You do?' He loosened his scarf from around his mouth slightly.

'Yes, I *do*,' I rejoined, doing the same. 'So there's my excuse. What's yours?'

'I'm coming from a brunch.'

'Isn't that a happy coincidence?'

'Isn't it?'

We both just stood there for a moment in the cold, frowning. At length, I fished a cigarette out of my coat pocket and lit it.

'You're *still* smoking?' he asked. 'After all you've been through?'

'What do you think got me through it?' I snapped, making a point of exhaling richly in his direction. He made a face and turned away. 'And how do you know what I've been through, anyway?'

'Of course I know!'

'Well, how was I supposed to know you knew? It's not like you sent me flowers or anything, or even a sympathy card.'

He stared down at his feet. 'I wanted to, but I didn't think it would be appropriate.'

'You always were a master of protocol.'

He shrugged, defeated, and I suddenly felt badly for being so harsh.

'It's okay,' I said. 'I'm much better now.'

'I'm glad.'

'How are you? Are you still an editor?'

'Associate editor now. I got promoted.'

'You must be busy.'

'I am. But it's okay, 'cause I don't have anything else to do anyway.'

'Except go to straight folks' parties on the Upper West Side?' I asked.

He shrugged. 'I guess so.'

He looked up, and we regarded each other steadily for the first time. I couldn't believe that sideburns alone had improved him so. Or had I just forgotten that he had a pleasant face, handsome in a dark, sad, sleepy way? Had I even ever noticed? So much time had passed that I couldn't remember. The only thing that seemed not to have changed at all was his voice—that low, serious voice with the faintest trace of a New York accent, something he had picked up from his Brooklyn-born father. That unexcited, unhurried voice that had always been such a comfort to hear first thing upon waking, or last thing upon going to sleep.

'You wanna get coffee?' I finally asked him.

'I don't drink coffee anymore.'

'Tea, then. Hot chocolate. Whatever.'

He shrugged. 'Tea would be good.'

'Okay. Let's walk to Hudson Street.'

Which we did, wordlessly, my cigarette putting necessary space between us on the sidewalk. The day was so cold that the street was nearly deserted—a vast, unpopulated expanse stretching all the way down to the financial district, an expanse as vast and formidable as the year to come.

'You must have pretty good views from the twelfth floor,' he finally said.

'Langley and Lippy do, but my studio faces the other way, so I have this view out on a billboard of a— of— Wait a minute. How do you know I'm on the twelfth floor?'

'Did I just say twelfth floor?' he asked, turning crimson.

'You did!'

'That's the strangest thing. I guess I just meant it generically, 'cause the building's so tall, as in, you know, "Jesus, you must live on the twelfth floor!", you know? God, it's cold!'

He hurried into the café well ahead of me, hardly looking back as he held open the door. I grabbed it and followed him inside, all my desire to tease him abruptly quelled by an immense, startling surge of gratitude and affection.

I moved in with him in Park Slope the following June, after a second courtship of a half-year. For the first two months, it was nothing more than the reunion of old friends, meeting for dinner or at the movies to make idle gossip or kvetch about their days; it wasn't until March, when too much wine over dinner tipped me toward cheeky and him toward sullen, that we jarred the lid on the box of demons—and even then, we extracted them with a certain consideration and civility, only one or two demons at a time. With due awkwardness, as well: so much of his hurt and bitterness fell back upon my having put him second to Flip, Jess and The Box, but now he could only lance so deeply with his grievances, tilted as they were at fallen windmills.

There was the matter of my future devotion, which I vouchsafed. I had always been fond of him, although my attention had been divided; now, bereft of distractions, I only felt an enormous relief at his restored presence in my life and a strangely feverish hope that we might bind up our future together before any more calamities befell either one of us. (It hadn't been an easy year for him, either; his father was ill with cancer, and Seb allotted his lunch hour twice a week to accompany him to chemotherapy at Mt. Sinai.) Of the irrevocable loss of Flip and my mother, the indefinite loss of Jess and the temporary loss of my mind, I told him much less than I might have. More than anything else, I was full of edgy, pragmatic foresight: plain out and flat, I wanted to be not alone, and I wanted to be not alone with him.

I kept from him terrible fears about living in Brooklyn, and I must concede that the first few weeks in his rapidly gentrifying neighborhood, I walked up and down Seventh Avenue, the main drag, in such a funk of skeptical indignation one might have thought I'd moved back to Boston, or, worse yet, the increasingly voguish Seattle. It all felt suspect, too marginal, Manhattan's big, drafty back warehouse.

But then, as spring came on, I started noticing certain things. The shafts of blue light that turned the wide, brownstone-lined side streets into cathedrals of repose at dusk. Or Seb talking over the fence to the neighbors about the Democratic convention on a Saturday afternoon while he tended his prized garden in the tiny backyard. And most of all, children—not the well-reared infants inside the elaborate strollers of the new Slope, but real children, city children—squalls of them, kicking around a soccer ball in Prospect Park, or girls turning out nasally harmonized renditions of Whitney Houston as they walked four abreast, or the terribly industrious and serious-minded Ahmet and Riga who worked in their father's grocery every day after school and confided to me with grave faces that they could read aloud the entire front page of the *Daily News* without my assistance. There was a novelty to children in Manhattan, especially downtown, but now their noisy daily presence became a reminder of the world that had long existed beyond 14th and Canal Streets, a world in which people didn't simply appear at eighteen and vanish at thirty-five, a world where people lived on, in youth and old age, in sickness and health, often fat and more often in all sorts of awful clothes.

Every weekday, I still boarded the creaky F train to

Manhattan, to the Upper East Side where I now had a full-time job as music teacher at one of the all-girl private schools, or downtown for plans with Lippy and Langley, or Kira, or Cedric. (With the exception of Grant and Maeve, whom I occasionally saw for dinner at Lippy's, they were all that remained of that old set: Miko had followed Anthea and Katja to Paris, and, after the night The Box burned down, Ty had finally caved in to Shereen's harping—they married legally, he found security work in Yonkers, and to this day I don't know what has become of him or his feelings for the deceased down-town white party girl he guiltily half-courted for two years.)

But on weekends, increasingly, Seb and I found ourselves shambling around inside the vastness of Prospect Park, or lying abed with various parts of the newspaper, or returning to the apartment early on a Saturday night with Chinese food and an armload of old movies from the video shop. We settled quickly into an unsurprising division of labor: I took care of daily domestic tasks, including dinner, and he attended to the hard, sober responsibilities of finances and large repairs. In the evenings, he pulled out his pencils and manuscripts while I sat down at my old upright, fitted cantankerously in a tight corner of the living room, the worse for its wear but assured of my devotion.

We procured a two-month-old springer spaniel and named her Bella, after Abzug, who had been Seb's late mother's friend. And it was such that one early evening this past summer I was sitting on the stoop with her, waiting for Seb to emerge out of the blue light as he trekked home from the subway stop—waiting with an excellent bottle of wine and some new Etta James recordings, in fact, because it was his twenty-fourth birthday—when I suddenly floated well above myself, hover-ing there just long enough to look down upon this dreamy goodwife and wonder who she was, and if she actually remem-bered where she had been. But I had settled back down into myself, languor intact, well before he approached the bottom of the stoop and Bella sprung filially down the steps and into his arms.

So that was that: he went to work and I went to work, we ate, slept and woke together, hours passed and months passed, and we were two people in an apartment with a dog living our lives. Some times were sticky and most were pleasant, but nothing particularly untoward ever happened.

Until today, when I heard from my outlaw brother for the first time in over two years.

Epilogue

So, like I said, I'm sitting here now with Jess, whom I haven't seen in two years, in this stinking diner near Wall Street on a Saturday morning. All the bums are gone now, and it's just the two of us, and the proprietor in his apron, preoccupied behind the counter, and the salsa music on the radio. I've handed back to him the book of matches, and I've been crying, but I'm pulling myself together now before the proprietor notices our upset.

'I'm sorry, Tigger,' Jess says again. 'I shouldn't have shown you that little keepsake.'

'No, no. It's all right,' I say. 'But maybe you should hold on to them.'

'All right.' He slips the matches back into his pocket, and for one minute, while he's in profile to me, I discern through his new face a glimpse of the old Jess—the Jess I came up with, through Topsfield and St. Pete's and then New York. He was more delicate then, certainly less threatening-looking, and I wonder how much of this new demeanor of his has been applied, and how much was simply bound to happen. We had been a good-looking family—people told us so all the time— but would the years have eroded our good looks even if things hadn't come to such a sudden end?

I look back at him across the table; he's staring at me, his chin cupped in one of his hands.

'What?' I ask.

'Nothing. You got a cigarette?'

I fish an old pack out of my coat pocket, lighting two and passing one to him. 'I hardly smoke anymore. Seb hates it.'

'He does, huh?'

'Yeah.'

'Well—I guess you're better off.'

'I guess so.' The time seems to be slipping away now; I can feel it, palpably. He's tapping his foot edgily, his eyes darting about the empty room nervously, toward the door whenever he sees someone pass on the sideway outside. Soon we'll part ways and he'll disappear again into that abyss of remembrance—but not yet, I tell myself fiercely—not yet. There are a million things I want to ask him, but they all seem to be caught up in a riot in my head, and I'm having a hard time sorting them out.

'Listen,' I finally say. 'When you— you know,' I say, lowering my voice, 'when you shot Goolsbee—'

He looks at me sharply. 'Yeah?' he asks on an intake of breath.

'Well—I mean, do you know for sure that he started that fire? Or paid someone to start it, or whatever?'

He considers, slowly exhaling smoke in a long, shuddering gray column. 'He probably set it up. I guess we'll never know for sure. But it doesn't matter—he set it up for Flip to run in there, and that was reason enough.'

'When you had the gun in your hand, right before you— well, you know what I mean—did you even *think* about the consequences? About what was going to happen next?'

He frowned, recollecting. 'It's hard to remember exactly what I was thinking. I think I was just planning to beat the shit out of him, like, maybe shoot him in the leg to fell him, you know? But then I remember standing over him and looking into his face. You think I would have felt some kind of pity then—but I didn't. It's like I finally saw the real face underneath every fucking smirk he ever gave me. And suddenly I hated him more than I ever had before, and I just went ballistic, and I— I mean, it felt like it was over before it ever happened, you know?'

'I guess so.' But the truth was, I couldn't ever recall feeling so much rage and hatred for someone that I might have done what he did.

'But after I shot him, when I saw him lying there on the ground like a sack of shit—then the whole thing kind of hit me. I turned around and looked back up the street and this whole crowd was watching me. And all of a sudden, it was so quiet.'

'I remember,' I say, and I do. The sound of the gun cracked the pandemonium in two. The entire crowd turned, and, for a few dreadful seconds, made no noise whatsoever.

'And I freaked,' Jess continues. 'I just— I know it was ridiculous, but the first thing I thought to do was jump in a cab. And my first thought in the cab was, there, I finally did the kind of thing that everyone had been waiting for me to do my whole life. I cracked. And it was strange—my first feeling was this incredible relief, like this huge weight was off my shoulders.'

'That doesn't make any sense to me,' I say.

He laughs quietly. 'A lot of things about me wouldn't have made any sense to you. Or to Flip. Or anyone else. That's why I kept them to myself.'

'I wish you hadn't.'

'Well—I did.'

'So then what happened?'

He sighs, remembering. 'So then—I showed the cabbie the gun, even though I later found out there weren't any more bullets in it. The poor cabbie—he was some Pakistani guy in a turban, listening to dance radio to stay awake. I'll never forget what song was on. "Pump up the volume, pump up the volume—" remember that one?'

'Oh yeah.' I laugh in spite of myself. '"M.A.R.R.S.", right?'

'Right. So anyway, I told the guy to drive as fast as he could up the West Side Highway, then over the George Washington bridge into New Jersey, where I made him pull off the highway and down a side street. Then I told him to get out of the cab without looking at me, and he did. And I got in the damn thing and drove away.'

'You stole the cab? Shit, Jess!'

'What else was I supposed to do? So I drove all the way up into the Palisades, where I ditched the cab in the woods—it was too fucking conspicuous. And I went into some town and used the gun to steal another car at a gas station, and I drove that car all the way to Pittsburgh—'

'Pittsburgh!'

'Yeah. And then I caught a bus to—well, it doesn't really matter.'

'To where?'

'I said it doesn't matter.'

My cigarette has made me dizzy, I haven't had one in such a long time, so I stub it out clumsily in my saucer. 'And this whole time, you didn't once think about turning yourself in?'

'That's just it, Tigger. I mean, I did. But then I was, like, why turn back now? You've already killed a man. And the difference between going to jail and going on the lam seemed like six of one, half-dozen the other. And I knew that it was—you know, that it was too late for Flip, so what was the point of coming back?'

My heart drops in my chest, and I'm sure he knows it. 'Tigger,' he says, 'wait a minute. I didn't mean that. I thought about you every second. But I knew you'd be all right.'

'Well, you were wrong,' I say, furious. 'I wasn't all right at all. You're glad you weren't here to see what happened to me.'

'But you're all right now, aren't you? You've got a nice life with Seb. And you've still got Lippy and Langley, right?'

'Yeah, right.' I feel so defeated—I don't even know why I've come here today, and at the same time I can't stand the thought of leaving. He's been my brother all my life, and now I feel like I've never known him at all, like there are a million things he's kept from me.

'Would you just explain one thing to me?' I finally ask.

'What?'

'Where the hell did you go that night when you left the club?'

'Didn't I ask you to come with me? I was scared of going alone.'

'And I didn't,' I say. 'And I'm sorry. But where did you go?'

'Oh shit, Tigger,' he says. 'It's a long story. Do you really want to hear it?'

I nod, resolute.

'All right,' he says, leaning forward. 'Well— I don't know if you ever really noticed, but when we were growing up, I always wondered about who my real parents were. Like, what did they look like, and what did they do, and why did they give me up, and how many brothers and sisters I had. And whether they were still in Lowell or if they had moved somewhere else, or gone back to Puerto Rico. That kind of stuff, you know?'

'Uh hunh. I'm not surprised so far. There was a part of you that was always not there with us. Maybe we should have talked about it more.'

He shrugs. 'Maybe. Well, anyway—it really bothered me at St. Pete's. I didn't feel like I belonged with those rich bastards, because even though we were rich, I couldn't help thinking that my *real* family—'

I flinch a little, unintended.

'I'm sorry, Tig. My biological family— I couldn't help thinking that they were poor somewhere, and— well, you know. I remember in a history class, I did this paper on Latino immigration to the United States, and the teacher liked it and read some of it aloud, and when he handed it back to me, Goolsbee turned to me and said, "Writing from experience, aren't you?"'

And Tigger, I just wanted to kick the shit out of him, 'cause he *knew*, you know? Somehow he knew my biggest shame.'

'He really had a talent that way,' I remark.

'Yeah. Well, anyway. Then it kind of faded when I got to New York. I didn't think about it as much, 'cause not everyone was white anymore, and I met Damienne, and she kind of—well, she brought me out a little that way.'

'She came to Flip's funeral service, by the way,' I interrupt.

'She did, hunh? That doesn't surprise me—she was a good person. How's she doing, anyway?'

'Well, I guess, but I haven't talked to her in a long time. She got married. A Jamaican guy. A pediatrician in Brooklyn.'

He nods his head, slowly and, it seems, sadly. 'Well, good. I'm happy for her. She deserves to be happy.'

'I hope she is.'

'Me too,' he says, distracted, looking at his watch. 'So anyway—where was I?'

'So you met Damienne—'

'Right. And she brought me out a little that way, and I didn't think about it much. But then Ma died, and I started thinking about it again, 'cause it wasn't like if she heard I was looking for them, she'd be hurt anymore. And then, just when I was gonna call Mr. Kittredge and ask him how to start a search, I get this call one day. From this guy with a Spanish accent that calls himself Mr. Colon.'

'Who the fuck was that?'

'I don't know. All he says is that he's in touch with my real parents, who have moved back to Puerto Rico, and they're living in Cataño, just across the bay from San Juan, with my three brothers and four sisters, and my father and my brothers work on a sugar cane plantation, and my mother and all my sisters work in the Bootstrap factories. And he asks me if I know anything about Puerto Rico, and I tell him that I've read a lot about it. And he asks me if I've learned Spanish, and I say, yeah, pretty good. And he asks me to confirm, was my biological parents' last name Ramirez, and I say, yeah, as far as I know. And he says, is your birth name Jesús, but you're now known as Jess, and your legal surname is Mitchell, and are you the adopted son of Thomas and Nikki Mitchell? And I say, yeah, yeah, and yeah.'

'Yeah?'

'And he says, how would you feel if I told you that your birth parents were interested in getting in touch with you? So I tell him that I'd be very interested as well.'

'Jess, who the hell was this guy?'

'That's what I wanted to know, but he said he couldn't tell me, because he was in the business of reuniting adopted kids with their birth parents—he said he did a lot of Vietnam bastards who ended up in the States, but lots of Latino kids, too—and that it's an illegal business unless you do it through the adoption agency. And for all those reasons, he had to keep his identity and his whereabouts private, just in case I freaked on him and decided to turn him in. And he also said I must promise absolutely not to try to get in touch with them myself, but that all communication must go through him.'

'So did you go along with him?'

'What else could I do? He didn't demand any private information from me—it seems like he already had it—and he didn't ask for any money up front. He said all I had to do was wait for his calls, that he'd tell me what to do.'

'You really wanted to meet them that bad, huh?'

He looks at me, eyes wide and plain, and I feel like I'm getting another glimpse of that guarded, vaguely disaffected Jess I once knew. 'Can you blame me, Tigger?'

'No. No, I can't.'

He shrugs, eyebrows raised.

'So what happened?'

'So basically, I just do a lot of waiting. And sometimes he calls and gives me some small piece of information, like that things are going well and that the family's very preoccupied right now because my older sister is getting married. And sometimes he calls and just before he can tell me anything, he says he's got to get off the phone, and he hangs up. I swear, it was the biggest cocktease.'

Now I'm beginning to remember all the strange phone calls we had that spring: someone asking for Jess, then hanging up—or Jess trying in a tense whisper to keep someone on the line, only to slam down the phone with a muted *shit*.

'So in the meantime,' he continues, 'I just read everything I could about Puerto Rico, about Cataño, which is a pretty small town, I guess. Not the smallest, but—you know, I guess it's in the lowlands, where everyone plants sugar cane, or something. I studied up on everything. I remember we were at The Box one night in April, and I freaked out Pepe because I bought him a drink and toasted to the birthday of José de Diego, this Puerto Rican patriot. And Pepe was like, "Papi, I didn't think you knew *anything* about Puerto Rico. I'm gonna have to take you to the Puerto Rican parade this summer—just don't tell any of my friends I'm a *maricon*, you understand me?"'

I smile at him, but say nothing.

'So anyway,' he continues, 'time goes by, and I find out about Flip and— you know, about the baby. And Tigger, I know I should've wigged, but I didn't because—' and his voice cracks a little. 'Because I was just so *happy*.'

'You were?' I ask softly.

'I *was*. For the first time, I felt like everything was coming together, like my life existed on some chain instead of just being this island. I mean, hopefully I was going to meet my birth parents, and it turned out I had *real* brothers and sisters—'

'God, Jess, could you watch your language please?'

'I'm sorry, Tig. I mean, you know, biological— and because of that, it suddenly didn't seem so wrong what I felt for Flip, or what she felt for me, or what, you know, what you might've felt for me from time to time, or even that what you felt didn't bother me so much—'

'Oh God.' I blush, turning away.

'I *know*,' he laughs, 'but suddenly it was all right, because I was going to meet my—uh, my birth family, and you and Flip and I were going to stay a family, but just a different kind. And then finally this Mr. Colon calls again, and he says my parents want to know if I can come down and meet them that fall, in October, and I say yes. And Tigger, I was so fucking excited, I had to tell someone, so I finally told Flip.'

'How'd she take it?'

'She was happy for me. Just that—plain and simple. Happy. She made *me* so happy. And you know what she said? She said, let's all go down—you and me and Tigger. She said, let's go down there to that beautiful island and see where you're from. I don't want to be walking around SoHo as big as a house by that time, anyway. Tigger and I won't get in your way—we'll stay in a hotel in San Juan if you want, and you can tell your family anything you want about us, or nothing at all. But let's the three of us take a trip together. We haven't done that since we were kids. And so we started to plan it.'

'Were you ever planning on telling *me*?'

'We were gonna tell you right after the Half-Year Party. Honestly.'

I suddenly remember that half-finished letter of Flip's I found when cleaning out the loft—*Darling, There's something very important I have to tell you, but I can't seem to get you alone for a second*—and now it all makes sense to me. 'I believe you,' I say to Jess. 'So what happened next?'

'You got another cigarette?'

'Sure,' I say, fishing out another pair. He lights his and drags deeply, nervously, before going on.

'Anyway,' he finally says. 'Wouldn't it figure that I don't hear from this Colon again until the day before the Half-Year Party. And he says to me, all systems go. You just have to meet me tomorrow night at *fucking two* in the morning in front of The Archive apartment on the corner of Greenwich and

Christopher to go over details. I'll give you pictures of your family and a letter from them. And I say to him, I can't wait but can't we make it another time—earlier in the day, or the following day—'cause there's somewhere I have to be at one in the morning that Saturday night. A party. And he says, no way, you gotta stick to the plan, you can't do this to me after I've worked so hard for you, don't you care about meeting your family— stuff like that.'

'So that's where you went that night?' I ask him weakly, my temples throbbing.

'Yeah. That's where I went. I was so fucking nervous, Tigger. I asked you to come, remember?'

'I do,' I say. 'I'm so sorry, Jess. If I had only known. If you had only told me.'

'Don't worry about it now. It was all a hoax, anyhow.'

'What do you mean?'

'I get to The Archive, right, exactly at two. And there's nobody there. And I wait, and I wait, and I wait—I must have smoked half a pack of cigarettes—and finally I go inside the lobby and ask the doorman if anyone's come around looking for a Jess Mitchell. And he says, you're Jess Mitchell? And I say yeah, and he says, somebody left this for you earlier this evening, and he hands me this little envelope with my name typed on the front. And I ask him, who's this from?, and he says, I don't know, just some guy, he didn't leave his name and he doesn't live here in the building. And I open this envelope, Tigger, and there's a little card inside.'

'Yeah?'

'And all it says, typed-up, is HA HA HA.'

I can feel the blood rushing from my face. 'Fuck. Are you serious?' I ask him, low.

'Yep. That's it. HA HA HA.'

'That's a fucking sick joke.'

'Yep.'

'Who do you think it was?'

'Buddy.' He laughs. 'Who do you *think* I think it was?'

'Goolsbee?'

He nods his head slowly. 'Yep. Like you said, he had a talent for getting you in the place where you live. So then I walked back down to The Box, furious, and I was going to confront him and beat the living shit out of him, anyway. And then—Tig, then I saw those flames as I was coming up Greenwich Street, and I just had this really sick *feeling*, you know? And sure enough— and then you told me how Flip had run inside, and then that model chick told us that Goolsbee had told her that I was still inside.'

He takes the last drag on the second cigarette and extinguishes it in my saucer. 'And then it all came together, Tigger. And then all I wanted to do was kill the motherfucker. So I did.'

My hands are shaking on the table in front of my uneaten toast. 'So you think he planned the entire thing, huh? From the phone calls to the fire to setting up Flip? He must have been planning it for months in advance.'

'We'll never know for sure, will we? But yeah—I think so. Don't you?'

'It looks that way. God, Jess—you know, I wish you didn't do what you did. But insofar as you did it—I'm glad.'

'So am I,' he answers, hard.

'What a sick fuck he was.' Suddenly I remember my conversation with Goolsbee, that long-ago afternoon in Grant's studio, just weeks before the opening of The Box, when he told me that he had a sister, too, and how she drowned one summer on the Cape, into the vast sea that swallows us all in time.

'You know something else, too?' Jess asks. 'I think Goolsbee knew that Flip was having a baby—the second time around, I mean? Remember what he said to me when I got back to The Box that night? When he looked me in the face and said "I'm so sorry"? I think that's what he meant—I think he definitely knew that Flip was pregnant, and thought the kid was mine.'

'Well?'

'Well, what?'

'*Was* it yours?'

'Of course it was,' he snaps, uneasy. 'I mean—I don't know about the first time, but the second time—yes. Definitely. I know it.'

'How did Goolsbee know about it, then?'

'Flip probably told him.'

'Why would she do that?'

'Why do you think? To spite him, probably. She hated him just as much as we did. But you know her rationale for doing things could be pretty warped.'

I don't answer, just nod my head, thinking. Neither of us say anything for a long time. We haven't even noticed this whole time that the proprietor has been cleaning up all around us.

'Anyway,' Jess finally says. 'I don't spend much time thinking about Goolsbee these days.'

'So what do you think about?'

'Getting out of the country, for one thing,' he laughs.

'With your new girlfriend?'

'Yeah,' he says after a pause. 'With my new— my new woman.'

'Hm.'

'You wanna know what else I think about?'

'What?'

'Well—I still think about my family, and if they really *are* in Cataño, and how I can't even go down there to find out, because Puerto Rico is part of the United States, and if they do exist, I don't want to get them in trouble. So I guess I'll never really know where I came from.'

'You don't know that for sure.'

He just smirks. 'And I think about the daughter, or son, that I was going to have.' (*Son*, I almost say, but then I stop myself.) 'And how beautiful that kid was going to be, and how it was never going to be abandoned, or unloved. And I think about the three of us. Not so much the three of us in New York, but when we were younger. And how we'd sneak down to that cove at the beach and horse around while the sun was going down.'

I just stare down into my toast. I want to tell him that I think about the same thing—dream about it, even—but I don't.

'I felt so protective toward you, Tigger. You were just this sweet, sensitive little guy, and I didn't want anyone to give you any shit.'

'You never let them,' I say. 'Neither did Flip.'

'And Flip,' he says, smiling. 'I probably was falling in love with her even then, even though it took years for me to realize it, never mind accept it. But Jesus, Tig— she was a fucking force of nature, wasn't she? She was unstoppable. Totally insane, mind you, but unstoppable.'

'I worshipped her. It wasn't smart to do, but I did.' I shrug. 'What more can I say? She was my hero.'

'You don't have to say anything more. She loved you like crazy, Tigger.'

'I know.' We're both quiet again until the proprietor barks something in Spanish at Jess. He responds, then says to me, 'He's closing up. We gotta get outta here.' He fishes a few dollars out of his pocket and throws them down on the table. 'And I've got to get going.'

'I've got to go to the bathroom first,' I announce abruptly, rising with a clatter. 'Wait for me right here, okay?'

He shrugs. 'Okay.'

'You promise, Jess? There's something else I have to tell you,' I say, lying.

'I promise.'

'Good.'

'Hey,' he says, rising. 'Come here.' I hesitate, and he laughs. 'Come here,' he says again, pulling me toward him with a funny, sad kind of look on his face.

'What is it, Jess?'

He draws me in, one hand behind my neck, and kisses me softly on both cheeks. 'I love you, *mi hermano*,' he whispers, holding me close. 'You're my main fucking man, you know that?'

'Yeah,' I say, my head on his chest. I kiss him back, just to the left of his scratchy goatee. 'I love you too, Jesús Ramirez.'

'Hey,' he laughs. 'That's Jesús Ramirez Mitchell.'

'Whatever.' We just stay like that for a second, under the suspicious gaze of the proprietor, until I head to the back of the restaurant.

Like so many New York dives, the toilet is in a tiny closet just adjacent to the filthy kitchen, where, as I had hoped, a telephone lies on the table with the proprietor's paperwork. My hands are shaking so badly now that I can hardly pick up the receiver, but I do. I dial a *nine*, then a *one,* then a *one. He'll hate me for this at first*, I think, *but he'll thank me later.*

'Precinct,' rasps a man's voice on the other end. My heart is pounding so hard now that I can hardly speak. 'Yeah,' I stutter. 'Um—'

'Come *on*,' the voice rasps again, harsher. 'This is an emergency line. What is it?'

'I wanna— I wanna—' And then I hang up, crashing the receiver back into the cradle. I can't do it. I can't betray his trust.

I slip into the bathroom, splashing cold water on my face, my heart pounding, devising a hasty plan. I'm going with him, I decide. It's that simple. First, we'll go to the bank and I'll take out all the money I possibly can, then we'll hit the road together. If he's going to live in exile for the rest of his life, then I will, too. As for Seb and Lippy and everybody else—well, they'll be fine without me. It's my brother I should be with. It's my brother who should be with me.

I rush back up front, exhilarated with my decision, but he's not at the table. I stop in my tracks, cursing aloud.

The proprietor says something to me in Spanish. I shake

my head furiously, and he says, 'No here. Leave just now.' Then he mimes Jess, looking about nervously and breaking for the door.

I rush out of the diner. 'Jess!' I call into the street, looking around everywhere. 'Get the fuck back here! *Get back!*' I rush to one corner, but he's nowhere to be seen, run to the next—ditto. In a sick wave of loss, I realize that he could be anywhere by now—catching his breath in one of a hundred alleys or doorways, down into the subway, making another clean getaway in a yellow cab. *I'll never find him*, I think to myself now. *I should have watched him closer. I should have watched him closer.* I keep cursing those lines to myself again and again, until they become a mantra of regret and self-reproach.

Finally, I slow down, catching my breath. This is turning into the loveliest, sweetest September Saturday I can remember in years. The blood still pounding in my head, I start walking uptown, dazed. I walk and walk, up to Sixth Avenue, through the rural cast-iron expanses of Tribeca, until I'm in our old neighborhood, SoHo, just two blocks below Spring Street, For a moment, I think I'll go to the old spot, that burned-out lot, just to see what's been left behind for me.

But I don't. I don't, and I know I never will. Instead, I start walking west on Broome Street, until I hear a steady thump—dimly at first, as dimly as you hear a heartbeat when you lay your head against another's chest. But it gets louder as I walk, until I can hear a high-hat just above it, and it happens that I've come upon a new club in a space that used to be a hardware supply store. It's nearly eleven o'clock in the morning, and it's still pounding inside, disgorging undead souls from its black front door—some of them in noisy groups, some of them encoupled shamelessly, and many of them alone. Dazed and offended by the sun, they're falling into cabs from the yellow queue that idles just outside, off to bedrooms all over the city where they'll blind themselves against the affront of daylight, awakening in the gathering dark with their old flames, or new lovers, or just their solitude and their own smoky memories.

One kid stumbles out, fair-skinned and slender, his hair slicked back in sweat, his eyes issuing a radiant narcotic blaze. A damp T-shirt swings from his belt buckle, and his bare chest is flushed and luminous in the sun. He takes a few steps to the right, a few to the left, sees me standing there seeing him, and stops, his mouth ajar in an O of happy surprise and good sportsmanship.

'Hey,' he says. I respond in kind—and I wonder if I ever could have fired up the heart of people with the kind of shameless and pure animal blush that this kid's lighting up mine with right now. He couldn't be a day over nineteen, and with all my might I wish I could just reach out and possess him again.

And Jesus Christ, this ceaseless beat that's just at my back now! I haven't heard it in a long time, but I can't believe how readily it seizes me, reminding me how there was once a time when, the moment I heard it, I knew I was alive. Walking to the place you were walking to as the night neared midnight, you picked it up in the air and it immediately marshalled every fiber of your senses, until it grew in volume and pulsed in concert with your footsteps and your heartbeat and all your hopes. It was leading you to black doors, behind which you would find the people you loved, and those you'd once loved, and those you had yet to love, and all night long you'd be borne along on that glorious, stubborn sonic pulse. It kept you on your feet long after your feet had failed you, and it carried your spirit long after your spirit laid down to rest. And in the morning, when you walked through those black doors again—with your posse, or your lover, or your lonesome—that beat receded behind you, but it didn't really leave you, not for a moment. It was what buoyed you through your daylit life, through all the tedious, lonely hours of cold commerce when everything is transparent and obtuse. But as soon as you were back behind those closed doors, where the half-light cloaked everything in the rich shades of swollen ardor and limitless possibility, when the lineaments of time and space fell away— that's when you knew that you hadn't lost the beat at all. It had been right there with you all along, as inevitable as joy itself could sometime seem, or at least as insistent as the promise of joy, which you never stopped believing was waiting for you just over the sinuous warp where one rhythm coiled itself into another.

So there's that crazy beat right now, and it's killing me. And I stand before this beautiful boy and think that I want to go home with him and make love as sloppily and hungrily as I did when I was eighteen. Or I want to walk through those black doors and plunge into that familiar old crucible of smoke and cologne and sweat, to take up on its dance floor as though I had never stepped away. Or I just want to keep on walking, all through Manhattan, until I pass through one of those invisible, perforated partitions between my life and someone else's, until I become as unknown to myself as everyone I've ever loved remains to me.

But I don't. I don't. The kid asks me where I'm going, and, passing my hand over his stomach, I tell him home, to take my dog to the vet. On the F train, I'm alone in the car except for one man, recumbent and unshod, who hardly stirs as we hurtle under water and earth back to Brooklyn. And when the train comes up from underground, there's that goddamned sign for KENTILE FLOORS, so plain and proud. All its fickle lights are dead now—every man-sized letter poised there for all the world to see, and each one of them as clear and cold as the sky over this vast, waking city.